MW01520507

FINDING TAYNA
Book Two

OATH KEEPER

Jefferson Smith

creativityhacker.ca

Oath Keeper

Copyright © Jefferson Smith 2014

Written by Jefferson Smith
Edited by Fleur Macqueen
Cover Art by Merridew Smith
Published by Creativity Hacker Press (creativityhacker.ca)

All rights reserved. Neither this book nor any portion thereof may be reproduced or used in any manner whatsoever without the express written permission of the publisher, except for the use of brief quotations in book reviews and commentary.

First Printing, 2014 (Rev. 2014-02-24)

Printed in the United States of America

Library and Archives Canada Cataloguing in Publication

Smith, Jefferson, 1964-, author
Oath keeper / written by Jefferson Smith; edited by Fleur Macqueen. – First edition.

(Finding Tayna ; 2)
Issued in print, electronic and audio formats.
ISBN 978-0-9919334-3-3 (pbk.).–ISBN 978-0-9919334-4-0 (epub).–ISBN 978-0-9919334-5-7 (mp3)

I. Macqueen, Fleur, 1965-, editor II. Title. III. Series: Smith, Jefferson, 1964- . Finding Tayna ; 2.

PS8637.M5635O25 2014 jC813'.6
C2014-900968-2 C2014-900969-0 C2014-901059-1

Acknowledgements

Often, the author thanks their collaborators, and then goes on to thank their families for putting up with them. Well I must have cured leprosy in a previous life or something, because for me, both of those groups are the same people.

The road to *Oath Keeper* was a convoluted one, with many twists along the way. Oddly, it was working on the cover that finally brought everything together for me, so for that, I owe a huge debt to my number one artist and number two daughter, Merridew.

While I'm off doing depraved things to nice characters, I have a staunch editor at my side, making sure I don't leave any tear-soaked commas lying around once the weeping is done. It's Fleur who keeps me on my grammatical and punctuarial toes, and that is only the least of the reasons for which I'm glad I married her.

There wouldn't even be a Methilien if not for my number one daughter, Brinna. As the original model for Tayna, she has seen it all—weird character arcs, implausible coincidences, abandoned story lines—and been a mountain of support throughout. More than just my right hand, if there is a keeper of Tayna's soul, it is she.

Daughter Rigel continues to put up with a mentally absent father without complaint, and youngest daughter Tayna (yes, really) keeps me young too. (I can't wait for her to read about her name-sake.)

There are other folks who have made the journey easier, too. Folks like Caroline, Helen, and the rest of the gang at McNally Robinson Booksellers in Saskatoon, whose support has been astounding; Suzanne Paschall, whose initial guidance helped *Strange Places* see the light of day; Agnitha, for that first, amazing review; and Will Carlson, whose infectious enthusiasm reminds me almost weekly why I do this, and who it's all for.

Lastly, I want to thank my readers. Whether you're a high schooler in Saskatoon, a librarian in Texas, or a bookseller in Kuala Lumpur, your emails and tweets have kept my imagination fed and watered since *Strange Places* first came out. Thank you for believing in Tayna. And thank you for coming on this latest journey, too. I really hope it melts your face.

Jefferson Smith
January 2014

chapter 1

Sadness. There was no other word for it. More than just a feeling, it was a throbbing, convulsing presence. Like a snake living in her guts and entwined around her heart, pressing outward against her lungs. It kept her from breathing. It kept her from thinking. All she wanted to do was curl up and hide, but how do you hide from something inside you? Something that was part of you? The blackness in front of her tightly clenched eyes began to sparkle. A tingling sound rattled inside her ears, and her head began to float away. Holding her breath seemed to keep these images at bay, but was it worth blacking out? Probably not. Tayna sucked in a ragged new breath.

And then she was five.

"Don't you know how to dress yourself?" The ugly Sister loomed over her with glaring, angry eyes. The woman's face shook and spittle flew from her mouth as she leaned in close, shouting and gesturing. Sister Critica. She was like that. Tayna looked down at the shirt and pants that Debbie had helped her put on. What was wrong with them? Her shirt was tucked in. Her socks were pulled up. Why was Sister Critica so mad?

"It's got flowers," Tayna said. All of Tayna's shirts had flowers, but this was her favorite. It was orange and cozy and it had three yellow flowers stitched on the chest.

"New rule!" Sister Critica barked. "No adornments! Now get back up there and put on a decent shirt, and be quick about it!"

"What does 'adorements' mean?" Tayna asked.

The nun rolled her eyes and leaned in closer, her nose almost touching Tayna's forehead. "Adorn-n-n-ments, you idiot girl! Adorn-n-n-ments! It means pretty things. Fifth floor girls may no longer wear frills on their clothing! And that includes flowers. Now march!"

All chatter in the busy dining hall had stopped and everyone turned to watch. Tayna felt her lip beginning to tremble. "But Sister, all my shirts got adcrements on them. They're just flowe—"

"Are you deaf as well as stupid, girl? No adorn-n-n-n-ments!" She dragged out the 'n' sound for a long time, making fun of Tayna's mistake. "No flowers! No ponies! No kittens! No puppies! No initials! No stripes! Plain, stupid garments, for plain, stupid girls! Just be glad you're still allowed to wear colors! Now go!"

No flowers? But... But... All her shirts had flowers. If she wasn't allowed to wear flower shirts, she might have to come back down in an undershirt. Everyone would see her in her underwear! "But—"

"I SAID GO!" Sister Critica shot out a hand that quivered with barely suppressed rage, pointing up the stairs.

Tayna bolted toward the staircase before the yelling turned into hitting, but her eyes were all blurry and she couldn't see. She tripped and fell hard on her knees. Behind her, all the nuns began to laugh, but Tayna ignored them. Stupid nuns were always shouting and laughing at her. She wiped her eyes quickly on her sleeve as she stood up, so that the nuns wouldn't see. They would only get meaner if they saw her cry. But what was she going to do about a shirt? This was so unfair!

She was all the way up to the second floor landing before the tears came.

The memory subsided as the air in her lungs went stale, and Tayna held her breath to prolong the quiet, but even that couldn't keep the remembered feelings from pressing in on her. The shame. Humiliation. Sister Critica had known full well that Tayna loved plants and flowers. As a little girl, she had drawn them every time she was allowed to hold a pencil. She'd made up songs and stories about them. She'd even snuck up to the roof to visit Sister Diaphana's garden once, and received a week of punishment when she'd been caught. She'd known the Goodies would be furious and that their punishment would be brutal, but she'd gone anyway. Such pretty flowers. And the smell of a hundred things growing. It had all been worth it. That's how much young Tayna had loved flowers and greenery.

So obviously, if any piece of clothing had ever come up to the fifth floor with even the slightest touch of floral decoration on it, Tayna had been drawn to it like a magnet. Debbie had been the

Senior Girl in those days—one of the good ones. In hindsight, Tayna realized that the older girl had probably felt sorry for the strange little dark-haired girl. The one the nuns all loved to pick on. For whatever reason, Debbie'd made sure that, as often as possible, little Tayna got first pick of any new flower clothes.

Everyone had known about Tayna and her flower shirts. How could they not? And looking back on it now, it was so obvious. Critica's new rule had been aimed specifically at her. Tayna. Sister Critica hadn't just *happened* to notice her shirt. She'd been standing there, *waiting* to notice it.

And she'd been waiting for what happened next too.

⎯⎯⎯⎯⎯⎯

As young Tayna stomped back down into the dining room, those children closest to the stairs began to titter. Their mirth spread like a crackling fire, as each girl nudged her neighbor and cocked a head toward the brazen little kid sauntering across the floor, heading back to her job scrubbing pots in the kitchen. Tayna had spent ten whole minutes going through every single shirt she owned, but each of them had boasted some kind of picture on it that was now against the rules. She'd tried turning them inside out too, but even at five years old, she'd known that the visible, flower-shaped stitching on the inside of the shirt would be enough to get her yelled at again. So she'd made the best of it, and now strode proudly across the dining hall floor wearing her new, legal, spring ensemble.

She made it three-quarters of the way to the kitchen door before she felt the grasping claw of a Goody bite down on her shoulder.

"What do you think you're wearing now, girl? That's not proper dress!"

Tayna twisted in Sister Critica's grasp and glared up at the woman defiantly, jutting out her little chin. "It is too! Lotsa girls are wearing the same as me right now! Look!" She waved her free arm at the crowd of onlookers, who just gawked back at her, but the old crone never broke eye contact.

"They are wearing them properly, you little sprat, and you know it! Now take that ridiculous skirt off your shoulders and go find something more appropriate to wear. This is a proper home for proper little ladies, and we'll not have you parading around with that tom-foolery draped about you like some street urchin. Now go!"

This time however, instead of crying, Tayna got mad, and she whirled to face the cruel old woman, stamping her foot and matching her, fury for fury, with her little arms crossed over her chest. "No!" Tayna shouted. "You do it! You know I don't got one! If you want me to wear an ugly shirt, then you go find one, 'cuz all my shirts are pretty, and you're the one who knows where ugly stuff comes from!"

The silence that filled the room was so complete that it radiated for several blocks in every direction.

And then Sister Critica grabbed her.

By the time the old woman was done, Tayna stood in the center of the dining area, on display for all to see. Her ingenious little skirt-shawl had been ripped from her and torn to pieces. Her jeans had been yanked down and pulled off, along with her socks and shoes, and it all now lay in tatters on the floor, leaving Tayna standing alone in the middle of the room, shivering in front of the entire orphanage—every girl and every nun—in nothing but her little pink underwear.

"Let that be your lesson, then!" Critica thundered. "If you cannot follow the dress code, then you will not be allowed to wear clothing! You will stay that way for the rest of the day, and for every day until you can find proper clothing!" Then she whirled to glare at Debbie and the other fifth floor girls who were now peeking out from the kitchen door. She raised a bony finger to single them out. "And don't let me catch any of you trying to help her either!"

Tayna tried to keep her lip from giving way, and she might have made it too, if the other nuns hadn't started to chuckle. First Sister Anthrax had snorted one of her vile choking cackles, but it seemed to catch on and soon all of them were doubled over with delight, laughing and pointing at the helpless girl in the middle of the room. It wasn't long before the fourth floor girls joined in, and even some of the older third-floors.

Which is when Tayna's lip finally surrendered and the flood-gates opened. She'd tried to be brave. She'd tried to stand up, but it had been no use, and now every person in the Old Shoe hated her and was laughing at her, and seeing her bare arms and legs and her skinny little tummy. It was total humiliation. So five year old Tayna did the only thing she could do. She stood there, in the center of the cold and laughing orphanage basement, and cried her heart into tears.

⁓——

Again the dream memories let go their ferocious grip and the images melted away, but it was getting harder to fight. The visions were lasting longer, and the gaps between them were getting shorter. Tayna tried to hold her breath, tried to keep the next scene from forming, but it was a losing battle. Eventually she would have to breathe, and as soon as she did, she would be plunged again into that tossing sea. Her own personal history of misery.

Obviously, something was wrong. These were not the normal twinges of half-remembered embarrassment or bitter recollections of past humiliations. She was actually *reliving* the moments, feeling them, as though she were experiencing them all over again. When she'd felt Sister Critica snatching her up to peel that skirt from her shoulders like a banana, Tayna had wailed in actual terror, as though she was still five years old and it was all happening for the first time. She was older now, and she knew that nothing drastic was going to happen, but even so, she was unable to escape the body-seizing terror that had gripped her as a child. Somebody was doing this to her. Somebody, somewhere had found a way to get inside her memories and was having a party with them. She tried to fight them off, tried to resist, tried to refuse to remember, but her resistance was toilet paper, and the memories kept coming. Every new breath brought a new recollection, from deeper in her past, from a more vulnerable and terrified version of herself. From her earliest memories, and her greatest fears.

Again her lungs began to burn, and once more, she drew a breath and tried to brace herself, but there was no bracing. There was only terror.

The man who held her had no face. The sky was dark, and the moon had not yet risen, but even in the faint light of pre-dawn, Tayna could see that his features were... missing. Like nothing–or no one–she had ever seen before. But if that was the case, then whose memory was this? The blackness of his silhouette blotted the sky-glow behind him and he seemed impossibly large. Or perhaps she was very small. Either way, he held her tightly across his chest, with his powerful arms entwined around her own limbs, making it impossible for her to even squirm. But it was not a fatherly embrace.

It was the iron grip of a captor.

Tayna craned her neck, trying to see around him, but could get no sense of just where they stood. There was loose gravel at his feet, and she could make out a jagged mass of darkness behind him, snuffing a great triangular wedge out of the sky, but there was nothing more, save for the winds that swirled around them.

"Well, that didn't work," a voice said, but it was not her captor speaking. The voice had come from behind her. And she recognized it.

Angiron.

Tayna redoubled her battle against the iron grip, but could not get herself turned around to see him. After a moment, her little body gave up trying even that much, and sagged to hang limp against Blackie's straightjacket of muscle and bone. Poor kid. Unlike the previous scenes, with the Goodies, Tayna didn't recognize this scene at all. Could her attackers be tormenting her now with somebody else's memories? Whoever she was, this body felt as though it had been crying for days, and not sleeping much either. The batteries were too low to put up a Tayna-style resistance, so Tayna hung limp, and focused instead on what Angiron was saying.

"... been so much simpler if it had worked today. Seems we will have to wait for her flower day after all, so we go to Plan B. She'll have to go missing. Sooner or later, she'd have come here, either with her parents or on her own, but that cannot happen until I'm ready. So we drop her in a hole. And I've got just the hole too. Nobody will ever find her. But before we get to that, there's a little ceremony I need to perform."

Suddenly Tayna knew where she was—when she was—and what was about to happen. A memory so deeply buried that she hadn't recognized it as her own. She kicked out—frantic—thrashing with sudden desperation against the man with no face.

"No! No! Please no! Not this! Don't make me be here!"

But the blackest man with the blackest skin held her in rigid stillness, shifting only slightly to place his smooth black hand over her mouth, forcing her to silence, and glaring down at her from his smooth, featureless face.

She didn't want to miss her own wedding, did she?

Abeni marveled at the unfamiliar world in which he had awakened. Marveled at its strangeness. He did not know how he and the Little Fish had come to this place, but it was an ominous land, where ice fell from the sky in tiny shards, driven by a furious wind. Yet that very strangeness tugged at his curiosity. Everywhere he looked was whiteness and cold. Truly, this was a place worthy of exploration.

But not now. He had managed to bandage the tattered wound of her wrist, but still the Little Fish lay shrouded in her dreams. When she did arise, his first duty would be to see to her safety. And upon the heels of that, he would then resume his sworn bond and return the Wagon of Tears to its rightful place in the house of his father, upon the Anvil. The time had nearly arrived for its next procession, and the dead would not wait kindly. So no, there would be no time to explore once she had awakened. Assuming she ever did.

Abeni reached up and placed a hand on the cold, firm stone of the Wagon's undercarriage. Upon his own waking, he had climbed under it to join the Little Fish in what scant shelter it provided from the raging storm, but he knew they could not remain here much longer. Already, he feared that his young friend's skin was turning chill and she had taken on a bluish tone. Surely that could not be a sign of vibrant health, although he was not well versed in Wasketchin lore. But try as he might to wake her, she had resisted every trick he knew.

The terrain around them seemed flat and clear. He had no doubt that he would be able to Ward the Wagon on his own, singing its great bulk up onto the air and driving it forward with the magic of his chant. He would need no assistance from any Way Maker until they reached more encumbered terrain. Yes, he could do this. But not while carrying the Little Fish upon his shoulders as well. Nor could he place her in one of the great cylindrical sky chambers atop the Wagon. She was not dead, and to place a living body within any of its silver shrines would be a desecration. Somehow, he must rouse her so that she could walk of her own accord. Perhaps later he would teach her to Make Way for the Wagon, but nothing could be done until she at least Made Way for herself.

Abeni looked down at the troubled face of his young friend. At times, she would lash out, resisting the firm grip with which he held her, but his body was the only warmth he could wrap her with, and if it truly was he with whom she struggled, she would just have to endure that fight. Someone had stripped the Wagon of its customary supplies and left him nothing. The great tailbox, which usually held the traveling tent, firewood, blankets, and food, was now empty. Another mystery that Abeni would consider when the current crisis had passed, but for now, he needed to awaken his companion. And until he could devise a way to do that, he would continue to hold her, lest she freeze to death before she woke.

For just a moment, the wind whistled down to a sigh, and the sigh blew down to a murmur, and the white dusting of ice settled from the air into an unexpected quiet. Abeni seized the slender opportunity to search the world around them with his eyes. To the east and the west and the south, there was nothing, save for flat, featureless fields of white. But to the north, he beheld a grove of stunted trees, near bent to the ground with the weight of whiteness upon their branches.

And it was that image–brought to him by a chance lulling of the storm–that sounded an echo of memory clearly in his mind. A memory of stories from his boyhood. And in that one, clear moment, he knew they had been more than just stories. He knew where he and the Little Fish now stood, and he knew at last what lay at the heart of her unceasing slumber.

"Weavers!" Abeni gasped. He lurched awkwardly to his feet and dragged the still-tormented form of his young friend up with him. "We must flee!" he shouted. Then he stumbled to the rear of the Wagon and flung open the tailbox.

And around them, the winds returned to fill the sky with blindness.

Something shifted in the world, and suddenly, Tayna was no longer three years old, struggling against her captor's grasp. She floated idly for a moment, as thoughts flickered through her mind. Memories again. But this time, like a slide show on fast forward. Images rippled in her mind, and then the disorienting recollections stopped and another world sprang into being around her. She was in someone else's arms now, though this time she was bound at ankles and wrists with what looked like skipping ropes. She craned her neck to see who was carrying her, and then hissed in recognition.

Sister Regalia.

But the Sister Superior was not carrying her back into the Old Shoe. Instead of the familiar orphanage that had been the only home she'd ever known, the evil old harpy was ducking through a door into an unfamiliar building. Low and squat, with dingy concrete walls and absolutely no charm. But the moment they were inside, Tayna recognized the smell. She'd never come in the back way before, but she'd know that putrid stink anywhere. Gruesome Harvest. Sister Regalia had brought her to the crematorium. The ropes around her arms and legs now filled her with dread.

With a cry, Tayna lashed out, kicking against her bonds, trying to free herself from the nun's grasp. If she fell to the floor, maybe she could get up and hop away. But Regalia wasn't about to drop her, and the old nun clamped down harder with her claw-like grip.

"You won't be robbing me of this satisfaction!" Regalia cackled. Then she kicked a pair of iron doors open and strode through. The furnace room.

"No!" Tayna shrieked. "You can't! This is murder! The cops'll be all over you and your stupid Sisters for this! You can't do it!"

"The police?" Regalia spat, her voice thick with scorn. "You think we've been running that pathetic dump on luck and lawyers all this time? We've had the police in our control for years now. And you are not the first problem girl I've ever had to deal with either."

That shut Tayna up. She'd always wondered why the police or Children's Services had never come through the doors of the Old Shoe with guns blazing. Or at least with warrants held high. But it had never occurred to her that the nuns might have been paying them off. Could they really have that much power?

"Not even the Health Department?" Tayna asked, still not willing to believe that all her little fantasies of rescue had been so pitifully pointless. "The Labor Board?"

"Hah!" Regalia chortled. Then the woman yanked the end off a plain wooden box and shoved Tayna feet-first inside. Her head bounced painfully off the floor of the box when the old woman let go.

"Hey! That hurt!"

"Good!" Regalia spat back, and then the lid came back up into view. "No!" Tayna screamed. "You can't!" She tried to kick against the end of the box, to push herself back out past the closing lid. If Regalia couldn't get the box to close, maybe she wouldn't do what came next either. But the box was too deep, and her kick met nothing to push against.

"Feeling comfy, are we?" Regalia sang in the distance. Her voice echoed thick and muddy within the box, falling away into the distance as the lid settled into position, the bright wedge of light around it narrowing in terrifyingly slow motion. "I can't tell you how much I enjoy this part," Regalia said. "And I don't believe I've ever enjoyed it as much as I am doing with you, dear."

Then the lid closed firmly into place with a thunk, and silent darkness enveloped her, pounding against her ears. The air in the box was close and heavy, and the sound of her own breathing grew a dozen times louder.

She was inside a coffin.

Tayna thrashed her entire body, trying to find anything she could bash *with any part of herself, but aside from striking her head against the wooden floor, there was nothing. The box was too big.*

"No! Let me out! Let me out!" she screamed.

The box shifted and Tayna slid to one side. A loud clunk and another bang against her head told her that she and her box had been dropped onto something metallic. The rollers.

"No!" she screamed again, her voice ragged, her breath coming in short, frightened gasps. The sounds echoed within the box, almost loudly enough to mask the thunk-thunk-thunk of the box as it slid over the rollers, but she heard it. All she could see in her mind's eye was the pair of scorched metal doors that awaited her, just beyond her feet. Any moment, there would be another thump and jolt, as the end of the coffin banged them open, and then there would be nothing left between her and the bright, white flames.

Sobbing out in loud inarticulate syllables of despair, Tayna thrashed herself against the walls of the coffin. Kicking with her legs, heaving with her hips. Anything to fight the inevitable. With a savage cry, she jerked one hand free of the ropes that bound her, and slapped her palm painfully against the lid above her head. It was cold to the touch and heavy. Unmovable. Soon, it would not be cold either.

Tayna pounded on the lid and screamed her rage. Her terror. Not like this. They did not get to win like this. And then she felt the final thump of the furnace doors, and a moment later the box dropped down onto the hot bricks of the inner chamber, and she knew in her heart that it was over.

"I'm sorry," she said, to everyone who had been depending on her.

And then a brilliant light flooded into the box.

Despite the cold and the wind, Abeni kept his watery chant splashing in his throat as he pushed on through the strange storm. The whiteness and cold had whipped itself into an impenetrable wall around him when he'd set forth, and now he could see nothing in any direction, except the dark silhouette of the Wagon hanging in the air in front of him, barely visible through the flying ice. But he did not need to see where he was going. The Wagon knew. All he had to do was keep it aloft and follow its unerring sense of direction.

The winds pulled at his vest and flung needles of ice against his flesh, but still he sang his charm song. Warding the Wagon entirely by himself was easy enough here, and he'd pushed on for a good long way. He wanted to be sure he had come far enough away from the reach of those trees before he stopped, but the sounds coming from within the tailbox shredded his heart, and in the end, it was pity that brought him to a halt. Abeni had no idea what torment the Weavers had placed into his young friend's dreams, but he could stand her cries no longer.

He sang his last syllables and stood aside, allowing the Wagon to settle firmly onto the icy plain. By then, the shrieking inside had stopped and Abeni feared that the Little Fish may have done herself some grave harm. As quickly as he could, he pulled the end gate down, and what he saw inside made his heart twist in his chest.

Her arm was bleeding freely again. Somehow, in her torment, she'd torn the simple bandage away. But worse, the entire hand was swollen and was already beginning to purple with hideous bruises. How had they done this to her? Abeni took her gently by the shoulders and pulled her toward him, sheltering her from the wind as best he could, as he dragged her out to lay on the open gate. Like her arm, her face was a mass of swellings and bruises. Her lip was split, her nose bled, and there was an angry looking welt above one eye.

"What evil have they done?" he whispered, but still she did not stir. Abeni leaned down low, placing his ear against her chest. He strained there for a moment, fearing the worst, and then finally, he heard the quiet, steady beating of her heart over the wind. Encouraged, but still worried, Abeni scooped up a handful of snow from the ground near his feet and pressed its coldness to the greatest of her wounds. It made no sense. He remembered the stories, but how could they be that strong? To reach past him and beat her unconscious within the tailbox, even as he walked behind it? What weapon had they used? How had they done it? Surely the charms of the Wagon itself would have blocked any of their evil, no matter how great it might have been. But the how of things was of no consequence. Clearly, even after many thousands of years, Wasketchin were still vulnerable to attacks of this kind, and there was no telling how much further harm she might have taken on the inside. In her mind. All Abeni could do was press coldness to her swelling injuries and hope for the best.

A little while later, as he applied his ices to the bruises on her feet, her eyes fluttered open at last.

"I'm not on fire!" she said, blinking in the bright afternoon light.

But Abeni did not hear what else she might have said.
His joy had momentarily deafened him.

———⌄———

"The Little Fish has come back."

It took Tayna a moment to realize that Abeni was talking to her. With effort, she shrugged the last tatters of dream from her mind and twisted around to face him, blinking against the gray light. They were under the Wagon. The big Djin was leaning back against the runner and had pulled her back against him, his arms wrapped around her shoulders. To keep her warm, she knew. Nothing weird. As soon as she turned, he released his grip, and cold air seeped between them, shivering the slightly damp skin where his arms had been pressed against her.

Abeni's face was full of concern. Had he been there the entire time? And where exactly was "here," anyway? Tayna looked around. They were in the middle of a field of snow. The air around them was crisp and cold and still. The sky was blue and the ground was white. No clouds. No trees. No rocks. No birds. It was like sitting at the center of beach ball. Well, a beach ball with a giant granite and silver hearse parked above your head.

"It was the Weavers?" Abeni asked, still not certain of her recovery.

"Weavers? What do you mean?"

Abeni reached out and tapped her forehead with a meaty finger. "They attacked the Little Fish, in here, did they not? In her dreams?"

"Well, yeah. I guess. Is that what it was? I thought I was just having nightmares."

"The Little Fish has been beaten bloody before? By a bad dream?" He looked at her suspiciously.

"Well, no," she said, thickly. Every inch of her was either swollen or sore, and some inches were both. "What did you call them? Weavers?"

"Yes, the Miseratu. Weavers of Misery. The Little Fish has done battle with the ancient enemy of her people."

"Looked like nuns to me," Tayna said, attempting a smile, but her face was too sore to cooperate. "Who won? Me?" She reached an arm up in a tentative victory salute, but she had to stop half way. The bandage around her wrist pulled tight over painful skin and her shoulder cried out in sympathy. "Call it a tie," she said, lowering her arm back down to her lap.

Abeni's face folded into a scowl. "It is strange," he said, as he pressed a handful of snow over her throbbing wrist. "Abeni has heard the stories. Tales of tree-women destroying entire villages of Wasketchin. But to see it. To see such hurts made with nothing but a dream..."

"No dream," Tayna said, shaking her head. She had to choose her words carefully, forcing them one by one through the battered meat of her face. "Was real." She shuddered at the memory of the fears that their "dream" had unleashed in her. "*Felt* real, anyway." She could still feel the heat of the flames licking at her feet.

"But even the most real dreams do not hurt the body," Abeni said, as his fingers probed a particularly nasty bruise on her upper arm. Tayna winced and pulled away.

"Nope. Had help. Showed something... scary. Did the rest m'self. Trying get away."

"And what was this scary thing that caused the Little Fish such fright?"

A cold shiver shook Tayna from head to ankles. "Furnace," she said, quietly. "Put me n'a box. Shoved me in. To burn."

Behind her, Abeni went rigid. "A box?" The tone of his voice told her everything.

"Yes," she said. "Like the tailbox. Used what was going on around me. Made dreams more real." Abeni's face darkened with self-loathing as she spoke. "But not your fault," she added quickly. She wanted to say more, to tell him that if she'd been sleeping in her bed, they'd have shown her a dream of strangling in the sheets, but it was too many words. All she could do was pat his hand to reassure him. And even that hurt.

Abeni was quiet for a while. Then he shuddered. "Abeni believed that the magic of the Wagon would protect the Little Fish from their evil..."

Tayna nodded, thinking back over the details of the dream. "Think it did. Mostly." After the box had closed, she couldn't remember hearing anything from dream-Regalia at all. Maybe that's why they had picked that burning-in-a-box dream. If they'd known Abeni was putting her into the Wagon, and that it would shut them out when it closed... All they'd had to do was paint a picture of what kind of box it was, and then they could just let her brain provide all the horrifying visuals from then on. "Rest was me."

Abeni shook his head. "Abeni should have known. He should have stopped sooner. He should have done more." Her big friend looked at her sadly. There was shame etched across his face. Tayna felt bad for him, but she hurt too much to frown. She wanted to tell him it was okay, that he'd done the only useful thing in the entire sorry misadventure, and that he'd probably saved her life along with it, but she was too sore for speeches, and that all sounded like so many words.

"No big," she said. Close enough.

Abeni nodded half-heartedly, but Tayna could tell by the haunted look in his eyes that, for him, it *was* big. Time to change the topic. "So. Misery, huh?"

The youngest son of Kijamon raised his eyes. "It is how they feed," he said, his tone still glum. "To create evil visions that terrify. It is said that they use the memories and fears of their victims against them, building great misery and sadness. Such feelings in others are power to them. As the Djin draw vim from the unliving stones and ores of the Anvil, and as the Wasketchin take magic from the living Forest, so the Miseratu draw their vim from misery."

"But didn't attack you?"

Abeni shrugged. "It is said in the old stories that the Weavers hunted only among the Wasketchin. Perhaps they must have life-vim."

So what, they got religion? They don't do that anymore? Now they just eat toast? But all she said was, "*Old* stories?"

"There have been no Weavers since before the Forging of the Oath," he said. "When the Dragon Methilien and the Great Kings met upon the Anvil to create the Dragon's Peace, the races that would not so swear were sent away, beyond the Forest. The Weavers were such a race."

That made sense. Who would swear to give up their only source of food or power or whatever it was? "But why not feeding now?"

"We have come far," Abeni said. "They must be nearby to feed."

Tayna tried to scoff, but the necessary movement of her stomach muscles made her ribs hurt. "Far? In two minutes?"

"Two minutes?" Abeni said. "The sun was low in the sky when the Little Fish began her battle." Tayna looked up. That sun now stood high above them. Noonish.

Great. They steal time too. Tayna sat then for a while, applying handfuls of snow to the places that hurt most, only to pull them away when the pain of cold began to outshriek the pain of the injuries themselves.

"Proves one thing," she said, as she withdrew a handful of slush from one elbow. Abeni raised his eyebrow in curiosity.

"Drove my brain like a rented car," she said. "Must really be Wasketchin."

"The Little Fish still has doubts about this?"

"Thought I was human," Tayna replied, with a ghost of a shrug. "S'a hard belief to change."

Then she struggled up to her feet. Abeni quickly jumped up beside her.

"It is too soon. The Little Fish must rest." But Tayna shook her head.

Everything hurt either way. "Can walk and throb same time," she said. Then she set out across the snow, walking in the direction the Wagon had been pointing before they stopped.

Abeni had no choice but to resume his chant and follow along.

They had been walking for over an hour when Tayna suddenly lifted her eyes from the flat, obstructionless snow spread out ahead of them, and turned to look back at Abeni. So far, her task as Way Maker had been effort-free.

"You know," she said, stepping aside to let the bulk of the Wagon glide past her. "Just realized something." The exercise and the steady cold wind had numbed her face, and though she was cold, it had at least made speaking a little easier. "Think the Miseratu made a mistake."

Abeni rarely broke his chant, but he was able to squeeze a few words in between the bubbling sounds of his music.

"What mistake?" he managed, before resuming the song.

"Been a long time. They must be out of practice." Abeni had said that the more real their attack was–the more connected to her real life they could make it–the more effective it would be. "Used real memories."

Abeni nodded.

"Most were about the Old Shoe–orphanage where I grew up." Before the whole cremation thing, the dreams had been getting worse and worse, like they'd been working their way through her memories, finding scarier and scarier things to make her see again. Misery Deluxe, with extra pickles. As the Wagon finished sliding by, Tayna fell into step beside Abeni.

"Well, one was earlier. A lot earlier." She glanced at her friend out of the corner of her eye to be sure he was paying attention. "Didn't even recognize it. Think it was guy who took me from my parents. Gave me to Angiron."

Abeni looked at her with curiosity. "And the mistake?" he asked, obviously torn between asking the million questions on his tongue and maintaining the flow of his splashing melody.

"Was on a mountain," she said. "The Anvil, I think." The more she thought about it, the more certain she became. That black thing had seemed totally at home there... And it hadn't felt as though he'd had her for very long either. Yes, this felt right. Tayna turned to look her big friend in the eye. "Think my family lives on the Anvil." Could it be true? Could those Misery hags have accidentally shown her a clue?

Abeni raised an eyebrow, but he didn't break the rhythm of his chant, and the Wagon continued its calm glide forward as he sang. Still, he hadn't said, "No," and that was something. Tayna turned her face back into the wind and resumed her trudge. Could she really be from the Anvil? How cool would that be?

In the distance behind them, the wind began to laugh.

chapter 2

Since the Forging of the Oath she had slumbered, waiting, a vouchsafe against the day when the Dragon's Peace might fall and she would be awakened to her ancient duty. Once, long ago, she had had a name, although so long ago now, and through such sleeping, and through the dreaming of so many lives, that her own name was now lost in the tangled weaves of memory.

She awoke in darkness. Whether due to the hour or to the place, she did not know. She did not know where she was. She did not know *when* she was. Her only knowledge was a hunger that gnawed at her belly, at her memory of a belly, but it was not food she craved. It was knowledge. Who yet lived? Who was dead? What stories had unfolded? What new ones were a'birthing throughout the world even now?

As she struggled upward from the depths of her non-being, the questions grew more urgent. More specific. What had befallen the Dragon's Peace? Clearly it had faltered, but how? Which duties had been forsworn? Whose carelessness or malice had betrayed the ancient pact? Like a vapor of thought, she rose from the chamber of her silent keeping and floated upward, toward the light. Toward life. Toward the Oath. Toward her duty.

The memory descended from out of the sky toward a ridge that ran north-east, protruding slightly above the flat and tangled expanse of forest on either side. A line of travelers wended their way in single file, up one flank of the ridge, along its spine for some goodly stretch, and then descending back down into the colored leaves on the other side. Some old, one quite young, most women, a few men. All Wasketchin. They appeared weary, but resolute. Not frail, but not accustomed to long travel either. Names hovered in the awarenesses of those upon the ridge. Arin. Lan'ia. Arkenol. M'Ateliana. But one was more than simply aware of her name. One with spirit and abandon. This one sang her name to the sky as she walked. "Winry, Winry, Whin An're, Annery..." The memory remembered the joy of smiling. There was a rightness to this procession. These people. Though it lay about them in tatters, still the Oath clung to them. The woman at the end scented most strongly of it. M'Ateliana. Queen of the Wasketchin. From her the Oath shone out with a radiant glow. Her thoughts showed that she herself had heard the words, had once stood upon the mountain and witnessed the renewal of the Pact. She had reveled in its magics, but too, she had also keened. Most lately, this queen had stood bereft upon the Bloodcap, when the words had been silenced and the Promise flayed into tatters. Now she strove to knit those tatters together once more. She was newly come to this troupe of wanderers, but somehow, her joining with them had been in service to the Oath. She would be useful. But not yet.

Satisfied with the story of this group, the memory folded itself into the air, and resumed its search.

She did not have far to travel though, unfolding herself out of the air scarcely a morning's brisk walk more easterly and north, ahead of the Queen and her hikers, to a shallow valley that lay between two higher fingers of escarpment. But whatever had drawn her here was not visible from so high a vantage point. She quested downward with her thoughts, sinking slowly down toward and then through the leafy canopy, until the subject of her visit was revealed. A small band of Gnomes parading noisily through the trees. Two ranged ahead, skulking through the undergrowth, while a third ambled along behind them, leading a taller figure through the trees by a length of rope. One Who Waits. The skulking Gnomes carried long, heavy sticks that glowed with soft emanations of vim. The third Gnome had no stick, and clutched a large chalice to his chest instead. Its metal sides vibrated uncomfortably in the thoughts of the memory, oscillating between here and there, between right and wrong, then and now. It sang a song of opposite, although what it opposed, she could not say. And while the chalice projected an air of too-muchness, the One Who Waits who accompanied them projected one of too-little. It was a he, yet he did not seem entirely present in his selfness. A faint echo of the song of opposites clung to him, matted into his very fur. He did not walk–he shambled. His mind was quiet. His face was blank. He simply... existed.

By comparison, the thoughts of the Hordsemen were focused and clear. They hunted Wasketchin. Alone or in groups. It did not matter. Even though the Dragon's Peace had only recently fallen, already they stalked the forest in search of their cousins. Already men had learned to hunt men. Their prey, approaching along the ridge to the south, had not yet learned caution, and the hunters were unafraid.

Sensing that things were unraveling more quickly than they should, the memory withdrew from the squad of Gnomes and reached out again.

———————

A cave. Dim flickers of yellow moss painted the walls with a damp, ghostly light. At the back of the cave, a great chair of gleaming white bone. Once the pelvis of some huge and forgotten beast, now it was Hordefist, the Gnomileshi throne. And upon that throne, there was a Gnome. Lord Angiron. First Prince Angiron. Contender Angiron. King Angiron. Newly crowned, judging by the jabber of names that still hovered, unsettled within his mind. The new king gestured to a throng of attendants gathered before him. One by one, each stepped forward to take from their king's hand a golden chalice and the end of a white rope. Tucking the chalice under an arm, each one saluted his king and then turned and strode from the room, with a rope trailing behind him. It pulled tight when he reached the doors at the end of the royal chamber, and only then would the Gnome stop and look back. At the other end of each rope, a large, disheveled creature, next in the line of such creatures arrayed beside the throne, shuffled forward, following the pull of their slender bond. Mindless. Matted. And more than twice the height of the tallest Gnome in the room. But completely obedient. Strangely vacant. Those Who Wait.

When the last of the attendants had led the last of the creatures from the room, she knew with a cold certainty. This king had spoken no oath. His reign, his attendants, the very land around him and the air upon it, all stank of Oathlessness.

Troubled, the memory of duty folded herself once more into the air.

———————

There followed a series of flashes. A series of images, names, and vague details. Moments frozen in time.

A Wasketchin youth. Elicand. Alone in total darkness, surrounded by thundering waters.

Zimu, a Djin adventurer and merchant. Haggard and weary, he emerged from the trees at the skirts of the Anvil and began the climb toward home.

The Wasketchin King, Malkior, sat in a dehn, conferring solemnly with his advisers, but there was worry on his brow. Worry for a missing wife.

A Gnome chaplain, alone and terrified, wandering the forest in search of someone. Some "her." A goddess? A corpse? A sorceress? Even he was not certain who or what she was. But his search had been ill-fated and he meandered now, lost in unfamiliar lands.

Another squad of Hordesmen, picking their way down the steep slope of the Throat of the Forest, trailing two behind them on ropes– One Who Waits, and a slender Djin. The names of the Gnomes ran together, but the name of the Djin was clear. Sarqi, son of Kijamon.

The memory sensed that her view of events was drawing to a close. The flashes became more numerous and short-lived. More players in the game of history, each one involved, but with every passing flicker, less deeply connected. Less important. And then it was over, and she knew what she had to do.

It was time to choose.

Yet even after the images had faded, and she knew that she was pressed to choose, she knew also that she had *not* seen all. She knew that, impossibly yet truly, there were others in this pageant. Other places. Other peoples. But for some reason, she could not reach these others. Could not touch their minds, nor witness the events of their present. It was a strangeness that boiled in her mind for a time. That there could be such others, beyond her reach, beyond her knowing, and yet that they might bear upon the crisis of here and of now. Distant yet present. Untouchable, yet active. It made no sense. It was a puzzle.

Still, it was time to choose.

The nexus of her existence floated there for a time, motionless, high above the forest, resplendent in its multi-colored song. And in that stillness, a calling tugged at her being. A silence. As she floated there in her stillness, that puzzle of silence caught at the tendrils of her thought. Somewhere below. Another Other. Once distant and untouchable, like the ones she could not reach, but no longer. Now here. Now present. Not yet acting, but capable of action. As her thinking focused on this enigma, her nexus followed, flashing invisibly across the morning sky, to the east, and down, through the treetops and the branches, until she settled upon the wing of a beetle, crawling along a single twig of a specific branch, overlooking a quiet ravine containing nothing of interest save an old, discarded blanket.

Below her, as the morning light pierced the leaves and burned rays of brilliant light down into the lower reaches of the trees, the blanket trembled, and a moment later, a head appeared, peeking cautiously from beneath its folds.

It was the Other. She could sense its thoughts. Fear. Loneliness. Strangeness. Confusion. But behind all that, there was... amusement? Impatience? What manner of creature was this? A female, clearly. Young. Wasketchin, in appearance. But not Wasketchin. Another impossibility. But this impossibility possessed a strength of spirit like none she had yet felt. This was a shell she could use. This was a host. An agent to channel the full will and power of the Flame of the Dragon that Was.

Satisfied with her choice, she released the focus of her nexus, and allowed it to expand. Then, with a shifting of her thought, she willed herself to the center of the Other and gathered the nexus to her once more.

But it would not close.

Again she tried, working by instinct, rather than foreknowledge or experience. She had not done this before. She knew only that it *could* be done, and the how of it. Instinctively. Relax the nexus. Let it swell. Clench the nexus. Occupy. Only the last step refused to cooperate. Stupid nexus. Pretty much a total possession fail! What's up with that? And why did her words now come so strangely?

Weary and frustrated, she expanded her being one last time, and returned to the beetle on the branch, to rest and to consider. There had been a touching. A linking. She had felt it. The shape of the mind. The wry twist of words. Strange words. Alien words. But though their shapes had been strange, their meanings had not. One more puzzle for her to consider.

But time for such pondering ended when a crow swooped down out of the sky and landed on the branch next to her. The last thing she saw was its enormous beak descending to claim its breakfast.

———————

The memory of an ancient duty relaxed her nexus, and then clenched it. There was a rippling in the now, and a moment later, she shook herself from head to tail.

"Scraw!" the crow said, resisting her presence, but she ignored him and stretched her new wings in the morning light, reveling in her ability to do so. To move. To feel.

"Scraw!" the crow said again, complaining bitterly about having its body moved about without its permission.

"Shut up, you!" A pebble thunked against the trunk of the tree below her, and the memory turned the crow's head to see where it had come from. The stranger under the blanket scowled back at her.

The girl's words had been strange, but the memory had understood the thoughts behind them easily enough. *Shut up? Shut up yourself,* she thought back. *Possessing a bird isn't as easy as it looks.*

The girl in the bush snickered. *Had she heard that?*

"Yes, I can hear you," came the girl's reply. "Why? It's normal to wake up dressed in a blanket while being attacked by freakish monkey men, and it's fine for the trees to look like a toxic Crayola spill, but a dead girl mind-melds with a crow and *that's* weird? I'm gonna need a rule book if you expect me to know when I should be freaking out."

I am not a crow, the memory thought to itself. *I am the Flame of the Dragon that Was. I am merely... borrowing the crow.*

"I was worried there for a moment," the girl said. "Here's me thinking I could suddenly read the minds of all creatures great and small, but it turns out I'm only jacked into the Ghost of Dragons Past. That's loads better."

The memory felt a forgotten lightness in her mind. Laughter.

"K-k-k-k-keh!" said the crow.

"Was that you?" asked the girl in the bush, pointing at the bird. "Or is your ride about to cough up a hairball?"

The crow shrugged.

I am not sure, thought the memory.

22

"Well, I guess this is pretty cool," the girl said. "I finally meet someone I can actually understand in this crazy dream, and it turns out to be a ghost haunting a duck. What are the odds?"

I am not a ghost, thought the memory. *And this is not a duck.*

"I know," the girl replied. "It's a crow. But 'duck' was funnier."

Then nobody said anything for a moment. They all needed a moment to think. Especially the crow.

"So do you have an actual name?" asked the girl in the bush. "Does your duck?'"

I am the... I was she who...

"I'll take that as a no. Maybe I should call you 'Flamey.'"

Patience! the memory thought back. *I have spent an eternity asleep, awaiting and dreading this day of my need. I cannot recall the name I once had. All I remember is that I have a duty.*

"Well, I'm not going to call you 'Duty.' If you don't know *who* you are, then *what* are you, exactly? Without all that 'Flame of a Guy I Used To Know,' stuff. All you've said so far is that you're not a ghost. That doesn't exactly narrow it down much."

I am the spirit that will renew the Oath, thought the memory. *I am the Flame of the Dragon That Was. I am... Mardu.* The word just popped into her mind. A name? Her name?

"Madoo!" said the crow.

The girl in the bush smiled. "Now that's a name I can use. Pleased to meet you, Mardu. My name is Eliza. Now could you tell me where the hell I am?"

chapter 3

Warding the Wagon of Tears was a job that usually required three people: one to lead the way around trees, rivers, boulders and the like, one to sing the Wagon up into the air and move it forward, and a third to keep the path clear of anything that might trip up the second guy. Unfortunately, all they had was Abeni, and one damaged idiot.

So while the field of hard-packed snow they now trudged across was not as taxing as a twisted mountain track or a gnarled game trail in the forest, it still required all of Abeni's focus to keep the Wagon up and moving. Tayna did what she could, staying out in front, protecting him from the most likely of all obstacles.

Herself.

They marched that way all day, slowly crossing the great white tundra known as the Cold Shoulder, the frozen domain to which the Dragon Methilien had long ago exiled the Miseratu, who were now, hopefully, behind them. Shivering in her kirfa, and leaning forward, squinting into the wind and the bright white snowscape in front of her, Tayna had nothing to do but stumble and think.

She did a lot of both.

Her body still ached from her stupid cremation hallucination. The cold continued to ease the worst of it, numbing her face and hands and feet, but it would be days before she would be able to move freely again, without her battered extremities throwing her off stride. Until then, that stride would remain a combination of lurching, stumbling, staggering, and other varieties of spasticness.

As for the thinking part, most of that centered on what she would do next. Part of her knew that things were heating up in Methilien. Everything seemed to be about Angiron lately. First Prince this, and Contender that. And let's not forget the whole dangly blue earlobes revelation either. Her own life had been sucked into a tight orbit around that creep. Tighter even than anyone who actually lived here. But marriage was the last thing she wanted to think about right now. She was still a kid, and a kid her age shouldn't be worried about abusive, ego-maniac villain husbands trying to take over the world. She should be acting out, refusing to do the dishes, and rebelling against her parents.

But first she had to find them. And so far, it had been non-stop husband issues that had been getting in the way. Even that word was a problem. "Husband." There was no way it applied to her life. Not even a little bit. But English can be so unimaginative sometimes. Where was the word for "delusional psycho-stalker with a magically signed marriage license" when you needed it?

Whatever word you called him though, he had been her biggest problem so far. But as she dragged her feet across the snow, with her shoulder lowered into the biting wind, it occurred to her that maybe things were changing. Angiron was a Contender for the Gnomileshi Crown now–maybe even King, for all she knew. So he was probably ten kinds of busy back there in Gnome Land, giving speeches and making up war slogans and stuff. Where was he going to find time to be chasing after a useless girl-wife like her? Especially one who worked so hard at being a pain in his everything? And from what he'd said on the Braggart's Arch, he really was planning some kind of war, so that would only make him five times less patient than usual. All she had to do was keep her distance and stay off his radar, and she probably wouldn't see him again for a year or more.

And where could she go that wouldn't be all tempty for Captain Creepy? Well, if he *did* start a war, that would happen in the Forest, against the Wasketchin, right? Certainly not up on the mountain against the Djin. Not even Angiron was stupid enough to pick two fights at once. So that meant the safest place for her to go, to keep out of Angiron's reach, was also the most likely place to find her parents: on the Anvil, with Abeni. It was almost too convenient to be true, but at this point, any good news was a welcome change of scenery.

Smiling, despite the twinge it wrung from her battered face, Tayna picked up her pace and stumbled on into the wind.

Late that evening, after the sky had dipped from gray, through soot, and had settled into the deep darkness of coal, Tayna heard a squeak of snow behind her and turned back to look. Abeni had given up his chant and allowed the Wagon to sink to the ground onto its runners. Sleepy time. Too tired to say anything, she nodded her agreement and trudged back across the snow to join him. There was no moon in the sky, nor any starlight to see by, and that totality of night made her feel oddly claustrophobic, even though she knew there was a vast, open plain stretching out in every direction around her. She found the edges of the Wagon as much with her fingers as with her eyes, and ducked down quickly beneath it to get out of the wind. Abeni was already there.

As she crawled under the Wagon's bulk, Tayna remembered another time and another place, when they had first set out from the Wayitam's village. On those evenings, before Elicand and Shondu had been lost in the pocket, and before Sarqi and Zimu had been left in the clutches of the water sprites, preparations for night had been almost fun to watch. Soothing. A sort of ballet of the familiar–each of the sons of Kijamon tending to his own duties, each brother working constantly, yet simply, as they went about the practiced ritual of their tasks. And in no time at all, that ballet had produced a tent, and a fire, and food.

But today there was no ballet. No food. No tent. There was nothing at all to organize. Today, preparing for sleep consisted of crawling under the Wagon and then trying to get comfortable. Sort of. That was all. Despite her half-hearted protests, Abeni insisted on wrapping his arms around her. Better that at least one of them be sheltered and warm, he said, but Tayna was too tired and sore to argue sincerely, so she slumped herself gratefully back into the warmth of his arms and closed her eyes.

"The land rises," Abeni said, as they waited for sleep to overtake them.

"Does it? Hadn't noticed."

"The wind rises, also."

"Noticed that part," Tayna said, reaching up to rub warmth into her strange new earlobes. Apparently her magic ear extensions hadn't come with the electric heating option. "What does it mean?"

"Who can say?" Abeni said, shrugging against her back. "Perhaps it is nothing."

They lapsed into silence then, and before she knew what happened, Tayna and her earlobes were asleep.

Morning broke with all the subtleness of a train wreck. The sun just seemed to hurtle itself above the horizon, right into Tayna's eyes. With nothing to eat and no camp to break, the pair of them were ready to get under way again in no time, pausing only long enough to stand and stretch a bit, and to pick up a few chips of ice to suck on. At least they wouldn't die of dehydration before they starved.

There was a moment though, when she stretched out her arms in the brilliant sunlight, and then froze. My knapsack! She glanced about quickly, but search as she might, it was nowhere to be found, and Abeni confessed that he had not seen it either. Not here, nor anywhere since he had awakened in this place. The last time she could remember seeing it had been on the Braggart's Arch, and that meant it had probably been swept away when she'd hit the river. A dull ache throbbed briefly in her stomach, but what could she do? It wasn't *that* big a deal, really. The only thing in it had been her journal. Her letters to Shammi. But as important as that had once seemed, she realized now that Shammi was just another one of those icons of childhood that fell away as you got older, like Santa Claus and sleepovers. Given everything that had happened to her recently, losing a powerless fantasy figure who never responded to your pleas for help was probably the least of her problems. Plus, the whole thing just felt a little silly now. She'd miss her journal, for a while, and the ritual of pouring her heart out into it, but that would pass. So when Abeni sang the Wagon back up into the air and they set out across the snow again, Tayna walked a little taller, realizing that an important milestone of her childhood had just been passed.

Quickly, her thoughts returned to the present, and the problems that hadn't gone missing. For one thing, she could see that Abeni had been right. As they continued to march, it became obvious that the land really was rising slowly ahead of them, although if that caused any problems for him or the Wagon, Tayna didn't notice. And by the time the sun had risen midway into the sky, they had reached the brow of the long, slow incline, so it didn't much matter, anyway. They'd been climbing steadily since sometime yesterday, and now from the top, she could see all the way to a new horizon, down a much steeper slope that dropped away in front of them.

Or. . . Wait a minute. What the freakity frack is *that*?

It had taken a moment, but Tayna now saw that there *was* no horizon. There was something in the way, spread out before them. Something *huge*–as perplexing as it was big. An enormous bubble of milky... sky-ness, stretching as far as they could see, to both left and right. But it wasn't just below them–it rose up in front of them too, and beyond, reaching high up into the sky. High enough to have clouds drifting across its upper reaches. The slope of dirty, wind-blown snow they now stood on ran down sharply, but it stopped when it met the bubble. The great dome was so high that it had surely been visible for days, but they hadn't noticed it because its whiteness was almost identical to that of the rest of the sky. It had only really become visible now that they could see the slight contrast along its base, where the shadows and ripples of the uneven snow halted abruptly. Even with that edge to start from, Tayna could only just barely follow its arc into the sky with her eyes. She looked back at Abeni, the question clear in her eyes.

"Abeni does not know this thing," he said quietly. He had ceased his chant and allowed the Wagon to settle once more into the snow beside them. "But he thinks it would take many, many, *many* days to travel around it. More days than any journey Abeni has ever made."

But there was little else to say, and so, with a hesitant shrug, Tayna stepped forward to begin the long descent that lay before them. Behind her, she could hear Abeni's renewed chant as he sang the Wagon back up into the air to follow.

By mid-afternoon, they had been walking downhill for half a day, with Tayna slipping and stumbling on the icier patches, and getting her foot caught in the wind-blown ruts and cracks that were too hard to see in the blank, gray light of the blustery sky. Abeni, meanwhile, plodded along behind her, as sure-footed as ever. Some-how it didn't seem fair.

Even after half a day of relentless down-sloping, it was hard to see any progress against the vast bubble of whateverness. Tayna had to keep turning to look back up the slope to reassure herself that they were actually moving, because the only thing in front of them that ever seemed to change was the apparent height of the bubble, which now loomed impossibly high above them. Like airplane high. Higher maybe. Well, that wasn't entirely true. There was one other thing that was growing too. Her sense of unease. Even with con-fident, competent Abeni at her side, walking down into this giant crevice between the hill and the bubble made her feel... trapped. What if somebody was following them? They hadn't seen any sign of skulking pursuit since they'd left the Miseratu things behind, but until now they'd been walking across huge, open expanses of whiteness. Now that they were descending into this giant ditch, her view was much more confined. And she didn't like that feeling at all.

The bubble now took up more than half the sky and Tayna found she couldn't look at it. Every time she tried, her vision refused to catch hold of it, and her head swirled with vertigo. That made her stumble even more frequently, and twice she actually fell. Abeni's chanting continued unabated though, and unlike her, he showed no signs of difficulty with his footing on the shifting slope.

Tayna's shins were now burning from the strain of all that walking—first uphill for days, and now downhill. Was there any such thing as a leg doctor? If so, she'd like one now, please. Or maybe two. Dr. Left and Dr. Right to O.R. please. To say that her calves and shins ached would be to misunderstand the meaning of the word "ache." And it was different from the battered throbbing that had been her companion since the tailbox. She needed a new word. Crambarking. Her legs were now totally crambarking, and it was only because gravity gave her no option that she continued to flop one numb and burning leg in front of the other, step after step after crambarking step. She seriously doubted her feet would ever function normally again, but still, onward and downward they trudged.

The swirling winds on this face of the slope drove the cold and the snow through the gaps in her kirfa, and even though her Wasketchin boots were warmer than they had any right to be, they still weren't much use on densely packed snow. Wasketchin, it seemed, had never heard of treads for the soles of their boots. Probably because there had never been a winter in the Forest before, but that seemed like a pretty lame excuse now.

Down and down they walked, steadily descending the slope, as the bubble wall grew higher and higher above them, with nothing to entertain or distract them other than the wind, which flung a continuing barrage of tiny ice darts into their faces. Still, despite the difficult conditions, there was no question of turning aside. The Wagon continued to point straight down the hill toward the place where the sky-bubble met the ground—a place that Tayna realized with a start had gotten noticeably closer.

"We're almost there," she said, as much to herself as to Abeni. "It's like, suddenly one parking lot away from us. Maybe two." Tayna knew about yards and feet and meters and inches, and she could use them to measure shoes or hallways, but those measurements meant nothing to her for judging distances outdoors. And how big does a mile look, anyway? Or a kilometer? She had no idea. The only thing she could actually visualize that was large enough to be useful was the parking lot at the grocery store where Sister Disgustia had sometimes sent her when the Goodies were planning one of their special parties. And right now, by her official estimation, the base of the sky bubble was exactly two point three parking lots away.

She paused to look back and check the ridge behind them again. Still clear. Still no tree-hags following them. No axe murderers or insurance salesmen either. It didn't make her feel any easier about being in this ditch really, but one problem at a time. And for now, the giant bubble dome in front of them was the biggie.

They reached the base of the slope more or less together. Abeni looked around with a puzzled expression as Tayna turned to look at him, but he did not stop his chant. It took a moment for her to realize the problem. The slope did not level out–it continued at a steady downward angle right up until it met the enormous bubble wall rising up out of the snow. So if he stopped chanting, the Wagon would settle to the snow and then slide downhill to strike the wall. He couldn't turn the Wagon either. Not alone. Not even with her help. It had taken both Zimu and Sarqi working together, sometimes even requiring Abeni's help, when they had needed to turn its great bulk in the forest. So here, on a slope? In the wind? This Wagon wasn't going to be turning aside any time soon. Not for nobody.

So it was Tayna who first went up and placed a hand tentatively against the bubble, while Abeni continued to sing. The surface was neither warm nor cold. Not rough, not smooth. Neither wet nor dry. It just *was*. Strange. Weird, even. Otherworldly. But it was strong, too. Tayna kicked it gently with a cold, snow-clumped boot. Nothing happened, so she kicked it again, harder this time. Still nothing, although she wasn't even sure what she'd been hoping for. She tried slapping it with her hand, but that was a mistake. Nothing changed about the wall, but the cold had numbed her hands. She'd forgotten how sore they still were, and the wall was happy to remind her, so now the bones in the middle of her palm throbbed at the top of their lungs. Angry at her stupidity, Tayna slumped against the wall and slid down its slippery face onto the snow. She was completely out of ideas.

In the end, Abeni just stopped chanting. The Wagon settled onto the slope with the usual sound effects of heavy things crunching on dry snow, and then it slid forward until it bumped rather loudly against the bubble, with a deep and heavy thud. But that was all. Abeni inspected the point of impact, satisfying himself that there was no damage to the Wagon, then he took several steps backward, up the hill, craning his neck way back, as though trying to see if he could see the top of the wall. But there was no top. The wall just curved away from them, impossibly high, yet still indistinct, as the colors of the wall and the sky faded into each other like milk into cream. After scanning the sky for some time, the big Djin smiled at her and shrugged.

"It is *very* big," he said.

"Thank you, Commander Obvious," Tayna replied, still rubbing at the sore fingers of her slap-hand. She had said little all day and was surprised now to find it somewhat easier to speak. Abeni grinned at her, ignoring her jibe, and came back down the slope to stand next to her. He placed his own large, dark hand against the whiteness of the wall.

"Very unusual," he said. "It is like nothing Abeni has ever touched before."

"Is there a door, do you think?" Tayna got to her feet and took a few steps off to the side, trying to follow the smoothness of the wall with her eyes, hoping to see if there might be a crack or maybe the tell-tale bulge of a secret entrance. But there was nothing to focus on. A huge looming white nothingness–nothing to see, nothing to catch the eye–set against a huge sky of white nothingness, and framed against a white hill of snowy nothingness. It was almost like being blind, but in shades of swirling white instead of the blackness she had always imagined blindness must be like. So it was a relief when she turned back to Abeni and her eyes could once again find purchase on real objects with discernible edges and differing colors–things she could actually focus on.

It wasn't anything she heard or saw that made her look back. It was just a feeling. The low sense of dread that had been plaguing her all day suddenly fluttered at her mind–on the right side–and she turned toward it, looking up the long, icy slope. There at the top, framed against the sky was a tiny, black dot that winked out as soon as it had registered. Tayna twisted angrily at her wrist. They *were* being followed! And then a sick wave of recognition swept over her and she knew exactly who it was. "Run!" she cried.

Angiron had found them.

Tayna had only just convinced her rubbery feet to get moving when the air beside her was split by a wild crackling sound and Angiron stepped out of a brilliant, yellow gleam. The tip of his long, white staff whistled through the air where her head had been. Then her husband stepped forward triumphantly, ignoring the fact that she had evaded his attack. He strode toward her with the white bone staff held high, and a gleam of metal under his other arm. It looked exactly like one of Regalia's urns. But there was no time to examine it. Angiron had found her, and she was trapped.

With nowhere to go and nowhere to hide, Tayna turned and bolted toward the protective bulk of the Wagon, where gravity still pressed its nose against the great wall. Between it and her, Abeni turned to confront the unwelcome Gnome, his eyes wide with rage.

"The First Prince has no honor," Abeni snarled. "To attack a child is a cowardly thing! Swing your dragon leg at Abeni, if you dare! Abeni will prove the cowardice of princes!" With those words, the big Djin launched himself across the snow, his great legs driving him forward with his shoulders lowered, braced for impact. But Angiron barked out a short laugh.

And then he began to sing.

The effect was instantaneous. In one blink, Abeni was charging across the snow, narrowing the gap between himself and the Angiron-shaped sack of Gnome-meat, ready to dismember it. In the next blink, every muscle in the Djin's body froze. No longer able to move his legs, momentum hurtled him face-first into the snow, where he rolled over onto his side, still locked in the pose of his murderous charge.

Angiron's song caught Tayna too, just as she had reached the front of the Wagon. She'd been intending to slip under its bulk, hoping to put more... anything between herself and her crazed husband. But whatever the song had done to Abeni it had done to her as well, and Tayna froze in mid-crouch, bracing herself with one hand on the bubble of nothingness and the other on the Wagon in front of her. She couldn't even see what was happening from this position. All she could do was listen to the scene playing out behind her.

Angiron paused his song, long enough to speak. "What made you think you could beat me *this* time?" he taunted. "You Djin are like salmon to my bear, with all your talk of honor and duty. Pah! I toss you aside. All of you. Any of you. Whenever I like, and as easily as I like. And like a salmon, my tossing does you injury each and every time." Tayna heard a Gnomish grunt of effort and a dull thud that told her he had landed a vicious blow of some kind, but Abeni made no sound. Abeni! Tayna boiled inside. She couldn't stand that he was being savaged by that monstrous little creep. It was all her fault and there was nothing she could do to stop it.

Her right hand slipped slowly down the cold stone face of the Wagon, and Tayna realized that she was regaining the ability to move.

"No, let's have none of that now," Angiron called out, and then he immediately resumed his whiny, grating song, immobilizing Tayna's arm once more.

Had he seen *her* move, or had Abeni moved? How could she do anything if everything happened behind her? Apparently the effect of his song didn't last for very long, and he'd have to keep singing to keep the charm powered. Like Abeni's Wagon chant. Could she use that information somehow?

"So my dear, we meet again." Icicles of dread slid down Tayna's back as that sickening voice came closer. Snow crunched under his feet as he approached. "I'm so sorry I couldn't take more time with you back on the Arch. I'm afraid I was a little busy at the time. Although I did send you here. To keep you... safe."

Tayna shuddered as she felt his hand touch lightly against her back. "But I have so much more time for you now," he added. The hand moved up from her kirfa to paw at her hair. She still couldn't see him, but he was close enough now that she could hear his breathing. She could even smell him–a revolting blend of coffee, cologne and decaying vegetables. He leaned in closer, and she could feel the hot dampness of his breath on the back of her ear. "I'm the King now. Have you heard? Everything is working out just as I planned," he whispered, "and with you at my side–"

It was his nose that changed everything.

The first time Tayna had seen him, weeks ago, back at the Old Shoe in Grimorl, Angiron's face had looked like that of a normal human man. Short, but normal. It was a trick, she'd later realized– a charm he worked whenever he traveled to Grimorl, to disguise his true Gnomileshi features. No Gnome could pass for human. They were just too... misshapen. Especially the almost comically large hotdog-bun of a nose they had, hanging in the middle of their face. But even though he must have some kind of charm to hide all that, Angiron didn't need it here, of course. So that left his bulbous schnoz just floating there, filling the air between them. She could see it in the corner of her eye as he leaned in beside her, and then the damp, fleshy tip of it brushed against Tayna's ear.

And time stopped.

She felt it then. A completeness. A wholeness. As though all of her life had been a dream, waiting for this one single moment of waking clarity. She could feel it. Or them. Three different magics, like three different currents, pulling at different parts of her body. The unliving Djin magic of the Wagon, cold and weighty, seeping from the stone beneath her hand. The oily death magic of her leering husband that slimed against her ear. And between both of those, herself, filled with Wasketchin life magic. The magic of her own people.

Terrified as much by the thought of using it as not using it, Tayna reached out from within herself and took hold of the power.

When time unfroze, everything changed. No doubt, Angiron had been expecting to continue his sick little tête-à-tête with his child bride, secure in his complete and total domination of the situation. So it was probably something of a surprise when the frightened girl cowering before him in the snow whirled suddenly and buried her elbow into the small of his throat, knocking him backward, gasping and choking into the snow, struggling for breath. At least, she hoped it was a surprise.

Tayna darted past Garbage-Breath and hurried over to Abeni's side. Now was the time to find out if her instincts were right. She knelt in the snow beside him and put a hand on his arm. Then she pulled, sort of. In her head. She could feel the knotted vim of Angiron's charm song coiled inside Abeni, like a snake of stone under his skin, locking his muscles tight. So she drew it out, pulling it into herself, and undoing the knots as she went. Abeni's rigor melted away and he rolled onto his hands and knees in the snow. There was a large red welt over his right eye, and he moved sluggishly, but he did make it to his feet.

"Come on, Big Whale. Get moving." Tayna took him by the arm in exactly the same way a toddler might do with a telephone pole, and urged him toward the Wagon. Angiron had recovered his breath, more surprised by her blow than injured by it, sadly, and was now hunting through the snow for his staff. Abeni stumbled over a golden gleam at his feet, and the lid of Angiron's fallen urn popped free as Abeni staggered forward. Whatever had been in it spilled out into the snow with a hiss, but Tayna paid it no mind, and hurried to catch up with her still-woozy friend.

Angiron cursed when he saw the empty container roll away from Tayna's feet, and he renewed his struggle to stand up on the snowy slope. But *he* had not just spent three days tramping through the treacherous stuff, and his feet skittered and slipped, sending him to his knees several times.

Tayna looked quickly from Abeni to the Wagon. When she'd first drawn power from it, she had felt a response from the milky bubble wall as well. A sort of ringing. Like when you run your finger around the rim of a water glass. She wasn't sure what it meant, but she was flying on instincts here, playing hunches like sure things. It's all she had time for. She'd wanted to save both Abeni *and* the Wagon, but with Angiron about to rally, she could only take time for the living. So she grabbed Abeni by the elbow and turned him straight toward the Wall. "Change of plans," she murmured. It took only three disoriented steps for him to reach the wall, and his nose was in imminent danger of being flattened by it, but instead of stopping him, Tayna took a deep breath and placed a hand firmly at the base of his back, where his bare skin peeked out from between his all-weather Djin vest and his belt. Then she shoved him forward.

And Abeni vanished.

"Water leeches and gormless fathers!" Angiron spat. "You will *stop* interfering in my plans, woman!"

"Bite me!" Tayna yelled, then she turned back to face him and dropped into a fighting crouch, bouncing on the balls of her feet, waiting to see what he would do next. She was taller than he was, but that didn't count for much. He was probably heavier, and very certainly meaner. Plus, she was pretty sure her brief moment of power was over. She'd felt it drain away when she'd pushed Abeni through the wall. Still, she was through with running. If she could find a way to hurt him, maybe he would back off for a while. Even if she managed to break his freaking arm, she didn't kid herself that it would keep him away forever. But she was tired of him popping in for these surprise visits like he owned her, and something had to be done.

Angiron looked at her and cackled with self-righteous delight as he advanced, raising the white bone staff above his head. He slipped sideways just a little on the slippery downward slope, but he didn't even blink. Tayna saw it, though. It wasn't much, but it was enough to remind her that she still had that one small advantage—she could move better on the snow than he could.

And that gave her options.

Tayna feinted toward him, making him pause, uncertain what she was doing. The moment he flinched, she turned and ran for the Wagon, dropping and sliding under its bulk just as a flash of heat burned past her hair and buried itself, sizzling and steaming in the snow beyond her. Fireballs? How was that fair?

But she was committed now, so she didn't hunker down to wait. As soon as she had cleared the Wagon, she was up again, moving uphill. She passed the end of the Wagon and kept going, heading in the one direction he could not easily follow—up the slope. Maybe if she got some distance on him...

"You think you can run away?" Angiron yelled, moving toward the end of the Wagon so he could line up an easy shot. "Should I pick you off like I did your little friend? What was her name? Eliza?" Another bolt of smoking hate bit into the snow at her feet, and she stopped, but that wasn't what stopped her. Tayna turned to glare down at him.

"What did you do to her?" she said. Her voice was quiet and low. Within herself, she reached out for power.

"Exactly what I plan to do to you if you keep running. Or if you keep defying me. Now come here!"

But there was no power there to grab. Tayna's shoulders slumped. Where had it all gone? What use was magic power if it wasn't there when you needed to brain your stalker husband? Defeat welled up from her stomach, and slowly, Tayna began to trudge back down the slope. Her head hung low and she loaded her glare with all the hate she could muster, blazing it out at his stupid, smirking face that waited below her.

Then she smiled.

It was an unexpected, happy smile, like the one that sneaks up on you when you find a book you thought you had lost. To line up his last energy bolt, Angiron had moved, and he now stood at the end of the Wagon, with his back almost up against it, glaring at her with all the superior smugness of a newly crowned king.

He was also directly downhill from her.

When she was still five good strides away, Tayna let out a yell and began her charge. Startled, Angiron backpedaled and slipped in the snow, falling to one knee and jabbing his staff down to try to keep himself from falling over.

But then Tayna hit him. With her arms crossed in front of herself, she slammed into the Gnome King with all the force she could muster, hurtling him backward to collide with the Wagon, then he bounced off it, twisting, and fell face-up on the snow.

Tayna dashed past him and grabbed hold of the Wagon with one hand. Then she stooped down low and grabbed at her dazed husband with the other hand, wrenching his nose savagely as she shoved the Wagon with everything she had.

Once again, she felt the circuit complete, recharging her. Her body hummed, stretched out between the power at each of her two hands, like the negative and positive poles of an enormous battery. She smiled. And once again, she reached out from within herself and gathered the power to her.

The moment she took hold of it, she flung it back, through the Wagon of Tears and up against the giant wall, which melted into nothing wherever the Wagon touched it, just as it had for Abeni. With no barrier in front to resist it, the Wagon lurched forward, sliding through the wall like a runaway freight train on skis, which is sort of what it was.

Tayna had thought she'd have time to climb aboard, but it all happened so quickly that she had only an instant to grab hold before it yanked her forward, as it began to disappear into the Wall.

"Consider this a divorce!" she yelled over her shoulder.

And then the milky whiteness of the wall sucked her in.

When Tayna and the Wagon had finished passing through the barrier, Angiron picked himself up and batted the snow from his knees, standing easily on the slippery slope. His gaze remained fixed on the point of her departure for a moment, deep in thought, then he nodded curtly and waved his arm in an arc, off to the side. A crackle of yellow light trailed his hand, and when he had closed the circle, the disk of air within it changed color and began to expand.

"You saw?" Angiron said, turning his head slightly, as though he were talking to the swelling disk of air.

"I saw." The voice emanating from the disk was muffled, as though being spoken through the flames of a camp fire. The disk continued to expand.

"Stupid cow!" Angiron spat, shaking his head in irritation. "I was beginning to doubt your word that she would ever find it."

The voice was silent.

"You're sure the rest will work?" The Gnome King yanked his gaze away from the milky white wall to face the disk that yawned open beside him. It was now almost as tall as he was.

"She has felt the completion," the voice said. "It will call to her. She will answer. It will grow."

"It had better," Angiron muttered. "But I don't want that kind of power running loose once she has ripened." Then he walked forward into the disk, where the other figure stepped aside to make way, coming into view as he did. It was the jet black shape of a man, slender, smooth and sleekly muscled, like a panther. The surface of his face was smooth and featureless, save for two stumpy black horns that protruded from the sides instead of ears.

"I will harvest her before that happens."

"Good," Angiron replied. "See that you do. I want you in position before she starts getting any ideas of her own. Leave now." The man of darkness nodded.

Then the disk snapped shut with a muffled clap of air, and nothing remained but the ominous howling of the wind.

chapter 4

"I'm going to die in this place," Sarqi said to the moss-covered rock that was supposed to be his bed. "Abeni has gone mad, Zimu is safely back at father's forge, and they've all decided to leave me here to rot."

The only reply was the sound of the cursed river racing past his quarters. Sarqi hated water in any quantity larger than a mouthful. He always had. He hated buckets of the stuff, and barrels. He hated dew on the rocks and fog in the air. Water was the all-destroyer. It wore even the greatest of mountains down into nothing but dust and then swept it away, never to be seen in the world again. If it hadn't been for his unfortunate need to actually drink the stuff, he might have wished it banned from all the world. Sarqi hated water. And most of all, he hated rivers.

So naturally, Angiron had placed him as close to one as possible.

"A place of honor," the Gnome King had said, but Sarqi knew the truth. Hard against the edge of the river, and just downstream of the Braggart's Arch, this "shelter" was a place where all of the Horde would see him easily, as they came across the bridge on their way to the harvest tables nearby. He was just another trophy on display, like the colossal pointing finger of stone that stood on the far bank, a remnant of the Wasketchin King's Mourning Dove statue that the Gnomes had destroyed during their Contest for the Crown. And here was Sarqi, a matching giant to complete the pair, also toppled for the glorification of the Horde. A proud son of Kijamon, enchained by his own word and set upon a public corner to be seen and mocked.

And to make it worse, the place was constantly covered in spray.

Sarqi grumbled to himself as he paced the narrow confines of his "cell." It had been three days since he had last seen the new king of the Gnomes. The strutting little skite had been prancing and preening ever since the coronation, and took no end of delight in shaming the "Official Emissary" representing the Djin Crown. Meaning him. Sarqi. Not that he'd been consulted about taking the position or anything. Angiron was not big on consultation. When the Gnome patrol had shown up to collect him from the sprites who had captured him, Sarqi had been prodded with the tip of a wooden spear until he'd finally agreed to become their "honored guest"–with his hands tied and his back leaking from a dozen little prod-holes. Honored guest? What choice had he had? His elevation to Ambassador had been equally voluntary.

Unfortunately, Angiron's court was a traditional Gnomileshi court, which meant it was underground, in some system of caves and tunnels barely high enough to admit a badger, let alone a full-grown Djin. So the wise and benevolent turd-Lord had assigned Sarqi to these luxurious guest quarters. Why, he had his own rock and everything. All the comforts of home. Abeni had always said that their little neighbors simply did not understand the ways of those who lived above ground, but Sarqi knew that they did. This wasn't ignorance. This was scum-minded spite. It really wasn't complicated or hard to understand. He was being punished for being a Warder of the Wagon, and for having respect and power in the world above the Throat. For being a Djin.

Sarqi stood up and went to the door of his embassy to summon his aide. Oh, crack it! They even had him doing it. He went to the *gap* between the walls of his *cell* and called out for his *jailer*. "Ishnee!"

A moment later, a Gnomish head popped out of a small hole in the ground, just beyond Sarqi's cell, and blinked in the morning light. "Ambassador?"

"Has your king returned yet?"

"No, Ambassador."

"Has a message arrived from my father, or from *my* king?"

"No, Ambassador."

"Have you people finally learned how to cook proper meat? Or make a decent cup of boh-cho?"

"You make a sky-dweller jest, I think," Ishnee replied. "Such things are not food fit to the court of the Gnomileshi Horde." He looked up, judging the sky with a practiced eye. "You may break your fast soon, as we all will. The swarm will rise early today."

"Go on! Get away, you death-hugging rot-sucker!" Sarqi kicked dust and pebbles angrily toward the face in the little hole.

"Many thanks, Ambassador. Such ire shall buy me a fine supper tonight, I think." Ishnee vanished back into his hole.

"Scumlings!" Sarqi shouted, banging a fist against the wall. It was so starvingly difficult to keep his emotions to himself in this place, and he suspected the little skites knew it too. They were always provoking him with their bland, expressionless behavior, and every time he lost his temper, more Gnomes would appear–like magic–crawling from out of the stonework to bask in his tirade. To them, emotions were like rich coin, and he was having a hard time *not* spraying his hosts indiscriminately with his treasure trove of riches.

For the hundredth time, Sarqi considered simply walking out, marching up the long slope to the Lip of the Throat, and pausing for a moment, to roll a dozen or so boulders back down the slope behind him, before heading home to the Anvil. But he had given his word to stay in his "embassy" until summoned by the King or a member of the royal court. And although the Gnomes had no bond-rings or honor rituals of their own, Sarqi's word and the honor of his father's House meant more to him than his freedom. So he hunkered back down against the clammy stone wall of his office to await his release.

Chuffich drew another small gobbet from the pouch at his waist and pushed it down into the warm, damp soil along the river bank. Like all Gnome crop seeders, he had his favorite spots, and he tried to keep his new offerings quite near to previous ones, so that he could monitor the long-term progress of his territory as he worked. The oldest dimple he could identify in the soil was perhaps three weeks old. Of course, the gobbets planted there had long since dissolved to join with the general muck of the embankment, but he was pleased to see that his more recent divots showed excellent development, crawling with plump, succulent maggots. He regularly fought with the urge to sample a little treat–purely for quality control purposes, of course–but in his heart, he knew that for every one he plucked in his greed today, the eventual harvest count would be shy by another thousand or even a score of thousands. Once established, the crop would multiply ferociously, but even this was only just fast enough to keep the balance–his kinsmen were voracious harvesters. Delicate and back-aching as the work was, the balance must be maintained. Chuffich drew another fly-specked morsel of flesh from his pouch and moved along to his next spot.

"Dark skies to you, Seeder Chuffich."

Chuffich whipped his head around, cursing at the interruption. "Who would sneak up on a– Oh. It's you, Urlech. How may this one assist the Reader of the Book?" By tradition, the keeper of the shrine of the dead was welcome anywhere. Even in the midst of your mucking workplace in the middle of your work day.

Urlech squatted down to join Chuffich, although he managed to avoid the squelchiest part of the bank, keeping his robes more or less unspattered. "Just Urlech, for this moment," he said. "The Reader is still deep within his Book, if you understand me."

Chuffich raised an eyebrow. "An odd hair to be slicing," he said. "But in that case, what do you want, Urlech? I'm busy." He waved another of his tantalizing strips of infected meat before the shrine-keeper's face and Chuffich was pleased to see that Urlech was a Gnome like all others. Even the Reader had licked his lips. But the temptation passed quickly, and Urlech once more wore his usual expression of peaceful authority.

"The bones give us much, Chuffich, and today they have given me a gift that must be relayed to... certain parties, yet I do not know with certainty who these parties might be."

Chuffich snorted thick, black, soil-laced phlegm from one nostril and hit his latest planting on the first try. Then he stood up to confront this unwelcome intrusion directly. "Look, I don't know what yer after, Urlech, but I've got wor-"

"You know that Velch has ascended of late, do you not? And that a bone of his was delivered into my keeping that same day? It is a very curious bone that has spoken of nothing but secrets and deceits. At the highest levels, no less... " Urlech let his voice trail off, but his meaning was clear and Chuffich's blood began to tremble.

"I uh, knew Velch," Chuffich admitted.

Urlech nodded. "As I was given to understand," he said. "Then perhaps you will be able to tell me the names of some few others who... 'knew' Velch. Hmm?"

Chuffich nudged at a planting with one toe and kept his gaze away from Urlech. He was certain the Reader would be able to read his thoughts, betrayed by the very bones within his body. The Reader of Ishig's Book was rumored to have access to all sorts of arcane knowledge, and many suspected that his powers were not limited to reading only the bones of the dead.

Urlech seemed to sense Chuffich's concerns and patted the seeder's arm reassuringly. "Be easy, Chuffich. You perhaps misunderstand my intent." Then he dropped his voice low, so that only Chuffich himself and the sack full of flapmeat could hear him. "I do not intend to expose the Resistance," he whispered. "My aim is to join them."

"Ah," Chuffich said, breathing a trifle more easily, but still not sure he could trust this conversation. "If that be your aim, then it might be I know someone who could perhaps be of some assistance, but I'll not hand over any names. Seems mayhap I could divine a way of getting word to someone who might know how to contact those you mentioned. Give it to me and I'll get your message to where you've aimed it. I'm sure if they be interested, one of 'em will be by to make a donation to the Book. In time."

If Urlech had a smile to his name, he would have gladly given it to Chuffich right then and there. "That will be sufficient, friend Seeder," Urlech said. "The message is this: The bones are unhappy. They tremble at new policies. I would offer my counsel to these 'friends of your friend.'"

"Well, that may be a *very* interesting message, Reader. I'll see that it finds the proper ear." Then Chuffich squatted back down in the mud and pulled another temptation from his pouch. When he'd heard Urlech leave, and was sure the shrine-keeper wouldn't be coming back, Chuffich dropped his pouch into the mud and ran toward the market.

A very interesting message indeed.

Urlech lay across his favorite rock. Alone in the darkness, he listened to the simple noises that only he could interpret. The clicks and plops of the cave around him, that to any other ear might signify a leak from the ceiling above or the settling of an unstable pile of rock or bone, were to him a quiet conversation unfolding among ancient neighbors, between generations out of time.

There was a scuffling sound near the entry hole and the ray of light that shone through it winked out. A moment later, a shape emerged and stood upright, silhouetted now against the light from the world outside.

"You seek the past," Urlech said. It was the ritual greeting of this place.

"I do not come for words from your Book," his new guest said. "I am told by the friend of a friend that the words I seek would come from the Reader."

Urlech recognized the voice, as most Gnomes now did, given the recent Contest for the Crown. "Fallen Contender," Urlech said. "Your presence is entirely unexpected."

"Do you mean that you were not expecting a reply so soon, Reader? Or that you expected one but are unsettled to find that it is me who brings it?"

"Perhaps both," Urlech admitted. "Although I judge that it is fitting. To share my message with one in such a position as yours will forestall many pointless discussions with lesser lieutenants who could only report and return. I confess that I had expected to go through this several times before finally offering my Reading to one who could act."

Qhirmaghen nodded. "Your thoughts reflect my own. The message you offered through our... friend suggested both import and urgency. I thought it best to set aside such tedious delays. Would it surprise you that your name is known at Court, Reader Urlech? It is a name draped in the sinews of respect. I judge that my secrets will remain my own, should our conversation not carry us any further than this place."

Interesting, Urlech thought to himself. As a Gnome accustomed to extracting the echoes of deeds, desires, lamentations and regrets from nothing more than the sound of a watery drip, Urlech could read much from veiled speech. Reading Qhirmaghen was no challenge. He comes alone, and offers flattery and threats. These are distractions, leading away from the question of why it was he who came. The Resistance is not as large as I had hoped. He comes because there *is* no other who could be sent.

"So, tell me Fallen One, should our words prove to continue beyond this place, would I be the fourth voice of dissent, or would I be only the third?"

Qhirmaghen, who was a relatively wealthy Gnome, having spent much of his life trading with sky-dwellers, spent a whole chuckle now. "You read the speech of the living as well as you do the reposed, my friend. And now that we have gamed our game of words, shall we talk plainly? Let me begin. Diminishing the count for Velch, your increase would bring our number back to five."

Urlech offered a grin as polite change and stood up, beckoning the Contender to follow. "Plain speech is not for the chamber of the Book," he said over his shoulder. "I have a damper hole where we might be more at ease. Come."

By the sounds of expensive robes brushing upon rock, he knew that Qhirmaghen followed after him. Good. Because they had much to discuss. And the first order of business was going to have to be growing their ranks. Risky as it may be, they would need to gather others who opposed the King into their fold, and quickly.

Or the war would be over before anybody could wet a finger.

"Do you know who I am?"

Sarqi looked up. It was a different Gnome today. This one was standing at the edge of the river bank, looking down at the waters that raced by, plunging down this final leg of their journey into the bowels of the Throat. Sarqi had not yet met this one.

"My executioner, at last?" Sarqi asked, unable to curb the sarcastic tongue that he now bit, punishing himself for not having mastered it before he spoke.

"I do not know of any executions in your future, Ambassador. No, my name is Qhirmaghen, last of the failed Contenders for the Crown. I am also the Overcaptain of Minor Works, and I serve as King Angiron's adviser. I thought it time to present myself and see if there is anything I might do to make your stay with us more comfortable. King Angiron is rather busy of late, and I'm afraid all of your demands to see him and your expressions of dissatisfaction have been routed to me. Until the King is free once more to consider his relations with your people, of course."

Sarqi eyed the adviser curiously. This was neither the lick-and-spit nor the kick-and-spit types of Gnomes that had visited before. Some had come to woo information from him with their assortments of promises and flattery, while others tried threats and even violence–now that such things had become possible again, with the collapse of the Dragon's Peace–but there was little the Gnomes valued that a Djin would value too, and there really wasn't much a Gnome could do to a Djin's body that would compel him to any traitorous action. So their attempts had all been more entertainment to him than motivation.

Yet this one was different.

"This sad rock you have given me for shelter does nothing to keep out the wetness." Sarqi gestured at the river racing past. A steady spray splashed in through the open side of his "embassy," which was nothing more than a pair of tall stones leaning together above his head. "Dampness may be sacred fun for a Gnome, but it could cause even the hardiest of Djin to sicken and die. Is that the kind of message your 'King' wants to send to mine?"

Sarqi watched Qhirmaghen calmly as the Gnome considered his reply. Probably trying to decide what kind of lie to tell. But when he spoke, the Gnome's response was another surprise.

"Your point is well taken, Ambassador Sarqi. I have to confess that I do not understand the reason for your confinement in such a place. The Djin are known to possess great strength. I must assume that you remain within these walls only because you have given your word to do so. And thus, since it is not the walls that confine you here, but the dictates of your honor, I see no reason why we could not permit you a larger territory to roam, were you to accept those greater limits under that same bond. Would that be acceptable?"

Sarqi had thought his captors to be rather dull witted, and completely ignorant of the Djin, but this one seemed to know a little more than most.

"It would be acceptable," Sarqi said.

The Gnome nodded. "If I have your bond-word that you will remain within sight of these walls that currently constrain you, then it is within my power to grant you that freedom."

"Then you have my bond-word," Sarqi replied. "I will stay within sight of these walls." With a nod of agreement from Qhirmaghen, Sarqi stepped out onto the slope of the riverside and stretched his lanky Djin frame until he thought his back might crack in two.

"How does Qhirmaghen, failed Contender, come to know so much of Djin ways?" Sarqi asked, as he bent forward to stretch another set of cramped and tired muscles.

"It has been my family's business for many generations to act as broker in transactions between sky-dweller artisans and the merchants of the Gnomileshi Horde. I have even been to your Anvil, and to the Wind Forge of your father, on several occasions. I am in awe, though I must admit, I was terrified the entire time I was there. I do not understand how any creatures can live so far from the warm, wet embrace of soil." Both men shuddered in vague distaste for the other's homeland.

Once his stretches were done, Sarqi looked around until he found a suitable grouping of rocks, clustered together, but of differing heights. He moved to face these, checking over his shoulder to be sure he could still see the walls, and then he began to ascend the rocks. He stepped lightly from one to another to the next, until he was at the top of his improvised stairway. Then he retraced his movements, descending back down without turning around. This he repeated a number of times, each time faster and more fluidly, until he had satisfied the needs of his legs and stepped easily down onto the riverbank.

"Thank you for the increase to my embassy," Sarqi said. The temptation to lace his thanks with scorn pulled mightily at the sour Djin, but he was determined to make some progress in his ambassadorial duties, even if he had to rip out his own tongue to do so. "Was there further purpose in your visit, or did you come only to see to my comfort?"

Qhirmaghen nodded. "There was, yes, there was. It is a delicate matter, but one that might prove to the benefit of both our people. It is said that there were three who warded the Wagon, yourself and your two brothers—the three sons of Kijamon—and that you bore the burden of two kings upon your honor." Sarqi's nostrils flared slightly. Qhirmaghen paused. "I see in your eyes that I tread dangerously, Ambassador. I assure you that I have no intent against the secrets of your House or of your people. I have only recently been confirmed in my new duties as adviser, and I would understand the full story of your ill-fated journey before deciding what course to recommend to my King. I had hoped you might illuminate some details for me."

Sarqi closed his eyes and slowly recited the oath of his House to himself. It was a method his mother had been trying to teach him for years, to master his thoughts when they threatened to master him. Did this wet-sucker really think that Sarqi would tell the story about how another rot-eater had outfoxed him and his brothers and consigned the honor of their House to the shame of rust? He repeated the oath to himself again, struggling against his own rising gorge all the while. Yes, he decided. He *would* tell that story. And he would tell it well, with humor, and many smiles, as though he were a complete donkey about the value of his laughter. Because, Sarqi realized, if he wanted to acquit himself of this "ambassador-ship" that had been thrust upon him–even though he had not asked for it–then he was going to need information of his own.

"I would be happy to share my memories," he said, as politely as he could manage. "Where would you like to begin?"

Their discussion lasted nearly an hour. At first, Sarqi had done most of the talking, but as time wound on, Qhirmaghen had inserted more of his own thoughts and interpretations into the conversation–interpretations that gave Sarqi the distinct impression that his Gnome visitor was leading toward something other than a simple accounting of Sarqi's encounter with the sprites. Why hadn't he asked how Zimu had managed to get free? Or why Sarqi had not? Or where Abeni and the girl had gone?

When the story had been told to its end, Qhirmaghen rose to his feet, promising to do whatever else he could to ease the Djin Ambassador's stay. Then Qhirmaghen glanced suspiciously toward the jailer's bolt hole, before turning to give Sarqi a direct and mean-ingful gaze.

"Thank you, Ambassador," he said. "You have given me much that I can use. Tasty flapmeat that my own King will no doubt crave." And then he left.

Sarqi watched the strange little Gnome make his way back up the path and out of sight. What had he meant by that? Flapmeat for the King? That was how Abeni had kept the water sprites off balance–by offering flapmeat to the "Kings of Night." But what did that have to do with Sarqi now? Or Angiron?

It was a puzzle, but what Sarqi needed was something to do with his hands. He always thought best when his body was busy, but what was there for a Djin to do when he was stuck in a moulder-ing prison cell? Sarqi turned slowly, surveying his shelter. Perhaps they wouldn't mind if he made some minor improvements. So Am-bassador Sarqi set himself to lifting and moving rocks for a while, distracting his body with labor, and giving his mind time to wander over the words of that strange conversation.

Qhirmaghen had definitely been trying to tell him something. But what?

———— ·· ————

The next meeting of the fledgeling rebellion was as if by chance. Just two respected Gnome elders, each touring the fragrant Harvest Yard alone, seemingly at his leisure.

"Greetings, Reader Urlech," Qhirmaghen said across the row of tables that stood between them. It had been some time since the Harvest had risen as high up the banks as where they now strolled, and the tables here were long dry from disuse.

"And you, Fallen Contender. I trust the burdens of your new office do not tax too greatly?"

"They do not, my friend. My responsibilities weigh my feet to the soil, as well they should. Neither taxing nor boring. Would you care to sample one of the fruits of my work?" Qhirmaghen asked, still playing the gracious benefactor, for the benefit of those few who wandered nearby. "The Horde has recently acquired a plentiful supply of deadwood from the slopes of the Anvil. Might I offer the Revered Ishig's servant a taste?"

Urlech ambled over to Qhirmaghen's side and made a show of selecting one of the rectangular sticks of gray wood from the small handful Qhirmaghen held out, and then he settled it into the corner of his mouth, enjoying the slow, heady release of vim that trickled from the deadwood as it moistened against his tongue.

"Highest quality," he said. And even though he too had spoken for the benefit of those nearby who might have marked their discussion, in truth it really *was* excellent deadwood. Urlech sat down on the gore-stained gravel and leaned his back against the base of the table, leaving room for Qhirmaghen to do likewise. Which he did.

Quietly, as though merely humming to himself, the Fallen Contender began the meeting.

"I have planted a crop," he said. The sounds of others moving around the Harvest Yard nearby and the buzzing of the food cloud above them masked his words from prying ears. "The Djin. I could not speak plainly, but I believe he took my meaning."

"Will he join cause with us?"

Qhirmaghen shrugged. "I do not know. But surely he must see how easily our new King gathers the Wasketchin. They are like maggots in a kitchen heap. No resistance. No violence. He just scoops them up, and they offer nothing but simple, dead-eyed compliance in return." Both Gnomes shuddered.

"So you believe the Djin will not want to see this power turned upon his own people."

Qhirmaghen paused for a moment, considering. "No," he said, slowly. "I do not think he considers that eventuality yet. Though surely it will be plain to him when his thoughts do finally turn that way. But no, for now, I think he speaks out of loyalty to his Wasketchin friends. House Kijamon is a friend to the Wasketchin Court. His is still the concern of a dutiful neighbor. But he will see the danger. I will go to him again in time. Perhaps there is a way he could get a message to his kin."

Urlech risked a glance at the Fallen Contender. "You think it possible? I had not heard this power of the unliving vim."

"It is only a possibility," Qhirmaghen replied. "We know little of the other magics. It would be unwise to consider any feat undoable." Qhirmaghen took the splint from his mouth and looked at it, considering its origin. It had been taken from the borders between Djin and Wasketchin lands. Owned by the Djin, harvested by a Wasketchin shaver. Even this tiny stick was a symbol of the easy friendship between the two sky-dweller races–a friendship that had not yet been dragged into Angiron's war. But it soon would be.

"What of the bones?" he asked, as he rolled the square stick between his fingers, feeling the bump, bump, bump against his fingertips as it turned.

"There is no change to the temper of the ancestors," Urlech replied. "They are of one voice. No good can come of this war he wages, and what ill we do will only be meted back upon us one thousand times over. It is all they will speak of."

Qhirmaghen shrugged. "Perhaps it is no surprise that the bones of our ancestors urge us to follow the paths of old. And what of you, Urlech? What are the urgings of the Reader himself?"

The chaplain of Ishig's Book made a show of splaying his feet out before him, pressing his heels down into the gravel-flecked mud. It was such a pleasant afternoon. He glanced up quickly toward the gray-brown haze of the crop overhead, but there were no wisps low enough to reach without standing, and he was too relaxed in the trickle of vim to want to stand. So he just sat there and wiggled his toes while he considered. Could this one be trusted yet? Urlech was not the trusting sort, even at the most casual of times, but these were not casual days. These were days of war and power, and he had a powerful secret. One that would not remain secret, nor powerful, for long.

"It seems the Ascendant has taken a wife," he said. If the Contender was surprised by this change of topic, he gave no hint.

"The signs indeed have been seen upon him," Qhirmaghen agreed. "But he refuses to reveal his brood-wife until all auspices have aligned, or some foolishness. It is a most troublesome point at Court–to know that there is a queen among us, but to not know at which shrine to lay the honors. He will not say, and none among us has seen these signs of queenly stature on any other–the elongated ears of blue. So we are vexed. And some few of us are troubled deeply by his secrecy in the matter. Most troubled, indeed."

"I have," Urlech said. The words were almost gone before they were spoken. All but a silent breath upon a buzzing wind.

Qhirmaghen turned and looked at his vim-lit companion. "You have what? You have been troubled?"

"No," Urlech said, with a quick shake of his head. "I have seen the signs. I know who the queen is."

Qhirmaghen did not respond right away. From the corner of his eye, Urlech could see that the news had startled the Fallen Contender, who merely stared forward with his face carefully vacant.

"Indeed?" Qhirmaghen said, after a short eternity had passed. "I would hear what you know."

"And you shall," Urlech said. Then he sighed. "But you will not believe me when I tell you."

———

"Water must be kept to the outside," Sarqi said. "Like so." He set a long flat stone over top of several vertical slabs arranged on the ground in front of him, forming a crude box. Then he picked up the gourd beside him and poured water from it, letting it splash all over his model. A handful of Gnome women pressed in around him, twittering and chattering amongst themselves as they watched the stream of water spatter across the simple roof.

"But the sand inside remains dry," one of the women said, poking at the dry sand within the model to confirm the fact for herself. "Won't your offal desiccate?"

Sarqi pressed his tongue against his teeth and clenched his jaw. Surely they were baiting him. Had he not just explained that very point less than a minute earlier? But whether it was willful ignorance or just the ordinary kind, Sarqi was determined to make progress. Since King Angiron had ignored him for days, the Djin Ambassador had resolved to put his waiting time to effective use, vowing to improve the quality of Gnome-Djin relations, somehow. And what better way to start than by teaching the basics of Djin culture to these dirt-born, filth-mongering...

A strained sigh escaped him before he could quite catch it, but then Sarqi drew in a slow, clean breath to replace it. Not dirt-born. Not filth-mongering. They were simply different, he reminded himself. He had every bit as much to learn as they did. But sometimes... Well. Best not to dwell on that.

Today's lesson was on the function of walls and roofing in proper Djin architecture. Relations with the Gnomes would take a welcome step forward if he could make headway on the quality of their guest shelters. And since the building of homes and living quarters was considered woman's work among the Gnomes, Sarqi had invited a group of them to come chat about architecture. It was something of a builder's group and gossip club, as near as he could make out. The desiccating offal woman was their leader.

"Yes, Oick. Offal *would* desiccate in a dry home, but recall that Djin do not keep such... treasures, in our living quarters. We are not able to appreciate it in quite the way a Hordesman might."

"Well there's your problem, Mr. Djin," Oick replied, bouncing lightly on her haunches and nodding at her friends as though she had gotten the better of the teacher. "It would be a lot less trouble to just leave the stones on the ground and learn how to decorate properly." Around her, other heads were bobbing in complete agreement.

Sarqi set his gourd down with a sigh. There had to be a way to explain–

But his thoughts were interrupted as another troop of Hordesmen and their captives crested the top of the Braggart's Arch. These parades had been happening more and more frequently in the last few days, and they never failed to attract a crowd, although Sarqi found them depressing. He had no idea how Angiron was managing to do it, but every squad of Hordesmen that went out seemed to return a day or three later with a train of Wasketchin prisoners.

Always there were just the three Hordesmen, but some squads had returned marching a line of as many as twenty captives, who all trudged along in utter sheepish tranquility. Sarqi had never seen so many fawn-eyed Vergefolk with so little to say.

The prisoners were always taken somewhere deeper down into the Throat, but to where, or for what purpose, he had not been able to discover. They just came across the bridge and then shambled past the Gnome ambassador, following their captors without complaint. Why did they not resist? Why did they not plea to their Djin friend for help as they passed by? They did not even make eye contact. Every time another group of them trooped by, Sarqi's heart withered just a little further.

This current group was a large one too, and the builder women he had been trying to instruct all turned to watch as the latest prize of the Horde paraded by. There was much chattering and giggling among Sarqi's students–if you could call them that–who seemed particularly smitten by the crook-backed Hordesman leading the procession. They called out to him as he passed and he puffed his chest out a little prouder for the attention, but he did not turn to engage his admirers.

Sarqi shook his head and turned away in frustration. Behind him, one of the Gnome women had scrambled up to the top of his embassy wall and was just now leaping into the air. He watched with further revulsion as she stretched up her hand and gathered a plentiful fist of lunch from the buzzing cloud these people so cheerfully called their "crop." In the normal course, she would have stuffed her reapings into her mouth before she had even regained her feet. Apparently, the longer you tried to hold them, the more of them escaped, which explained the hasty grab-and-swallow he'd become accustomed to seeing a hundred times a day. But even frequent repetition never robbed the ritual of its power to sour Sarqi's stomach.

This time however, the diner deviated the ritual. Instead of swallowing her catch, she pushed her way through the other ladies, past Sarqi, and rushed forward, toward the line of prisoners. A smallish Hordesman in the middle of the procession turned to look at her as she approached, and when she held out her squirming hand, he opened his mouth and she quickly delivered her buzzing payload, which he began to chew quite hastily. So hastily, in fact, that several unchewed morsels managed to escape through his nose, and he waved after them eagerly as they darted about his head before drifting back up to rejoin the crop.

"That boy would never eat if I didn't feed him constantly," the woman said, pushing her way back past Sarqi to rejoin her group. But Sarqi wasn't listening. His attention was fixed on the prisoners. One in particular. In the brief commotion caused by the Hordesman's frantic grab at his escaping lunch, one of the tall prisoners had stumbled aside, allowing the Djin Ambassador to see the Wasketchin woman who shuffled along beside him. It was M'Ateliana, wife to Lord Malkior.

The Gnomes had just captured the Wasketchin Queen.

Sarqi's first instinct was to cry out in protest. How dare they treat a queen so poorly? But in a feat of unrivaled courage, the Djin Ambassador bit down hard on his tongue. The sudden lance of pain in his mouth was worth it though. He'd almost let slip his first official state secret. Clearly, Angiron did not yet know he had captured her. There's no way she'd still be among the common captives if he did. And that could only mean that, so far, nobody else knew either.

With the parade now disappearing around the bend in the path further down the slope, the women were anxious to return to their teacher-baiting, but Sarqi had lost all interest and excused himself as politely as he could.

"I'm thorry, ladyth, but I have thuffered an injury and it now painth me to thpeak. Perhapth we could continue our dithcuthon tomorrow?" In his haste to keep himself from blurting it out, Sarqi really had bitten down too hard, and his tongue now throbbed in his mouth, feeling as though somehow, Zimu's tongue had been swapped for his own, twice as large and half as well exercised.

But tongues were not important now, and as the disappointed building and gossip committee wandered away, Sarqi's mind was already a'whirl. He found himself, quite unexpectedly, the sole possessor of information vital to this war. But what could he do with it? He was a prisoner here himself. Sarqi paced back and forth in front of the entrance to his flimsy shelter, heedless of the tiny model that he scattered into the dirt beneath his feet. And then he had it.

What he needed was an accomplice.

chapter 5

Tayna fell out of a milky white sky and slammed into a large padded chair. She bounced on the first impact, and soared back up to hang in the air for a moment, before thumping back down onto the cracked leather upholstery. Jets of dust that had shot out from the force of her impact now filled the air, and tickled her eyes and nose as they sparkled in the brilliant overhead light. A landscape wrought entirely of cloud and fog extended in every direction, as far as her startled eyes could see.

While she was puzzling at the scenery, a metallic ratcheting noise drew her eyes up, and an enormous stone slab fell out of the sky in front of her, snapping into position with the deep, authoritative boom and thunk of heavy machinery locking into place. But it was too close and too high, and Tayna had to crane her neck upward to see it. On its face, an image flickered and shifted, before finally settling into the face of a stern older man. Some kind of TV? His harsh mouth and angry eyes glared down at Tayna, and when he spoke, his voice carried the terrible rumble of a storm god cloaked in fury.

"The prisoner is charged with treason, sedition, and breach of faith. How does she plead?"

Tayna opened her mouth to speak, as the echos rumbled away into the surrounding cloud hills, but she didn't get the chance.

"Just a minute! I'm coming," called another voice. Tayna turned to look around behind her, in time to see an old Gnome trotting forward out of a featureless bank of cloud, waving a pile of papers in one hand. Several others trailed away behind him, slipping from the thick stack he held clamped under his arm. "I haven't had a chance to confer with my client," the Gnome said.

"Silence! How does she plead?" the Judgy voice thundered. Tayna could actually see the edges of the screen trembling from the intensity of the Judge's fury–an intensity matched only by that of the hatred in his glare.

Beside her, the Gnome flopped his stack of papers onto the armrest of her chair and turned to face the screen.

"Ot ilty," he muttered, nowhere near loud enough for the Judge to hear him.

Tayna turned to look at him. "I don't think he can–"

"SILENCE!" roared the Judge. "How does she plead?"

"Ot ilty!" the Gnome repeated, hissing the words between his teeth and rolling his eyes in a great exaggerated motion, first looking sideways at Tayna and then dragging around toward the screen, as though he were trying to tell her something with his pupils.

Oh. "Not guilty," she said to the Judge, finally realizing what the Gnome meant. Then she repeated herself, to be sure everyone had heard her properly. "Not guilty!"

For a moment, the face of the Judge hung there, motionless, his terrible eyes burning his fury down into her soul. Then, after an eternity of staring, the Judge spoke again.

"So be it. Call the evidence!"

Tayna felt the Gnome's fingers bite into the damaged skin of her wrist. "Ow!" she said, turning quickly toward him, but the Gnome's face was frantic.

"Ask him to sever the charges! Quickly, before any evidence is presented!" Tayna snapped her head back up to the Judge.

"Um, could you maybe sever the charges, please?" She glanced back at the Gnome to be sure she'd gotten it right, and he nodded tightly at her, then they both looked back at the screen.

The great red-gray eyes of the Judge considered her narrowly. Tayna could imagine that he was deciding whether to have her killed now or to wait until after the trial. Then his expression brightened and an icy smile crept across his lips without managing to touch any of the other muscles of his face.

"Motion to sever... granted," boomed the voice.

Instantly, the little Gnome had more instructions. "Now request a full audit of all counts," the Gnome instructed, still speaking out of the side of his mouth and under his breath. Tayna had no idea what was going on or where she was, but this didn't seem like the right time to start questioning the little guy's advice.

"And, I'd also like a full audit of all the counts against me," she said. "Please."

A low growl of irritation from the Judge rattled the screen and hurt her ears. If the screen had been rigged for it, Tayna imagined that bolts of lightning would probably have reduced her to an acrid stain at that very moment. But the Judge managed to contain his obvious fury. The old man's glare however, narrowed into razor slits of malice.

"Read the charges into the record," he thundered. And then the screen snapped off, and an off-stage voice began to recite a pile of legal gibberish. Tayna picked out a few words, like "malfeasance" and "dereliction," but the Gnome was grabbing at her arm again and wouldn't let her listen.

"Whew!" he said. "Well, that should buy us some time, at least. What's your name?"

"What's my name?" Tayna asked, her voice climbing in disbelief. "You're my what, defense lawyer? And you don't even know my name?"

The Gnome shrugged. "Well, seeing how I wasn't summoned until his fury-ness popped up into the air there, I think I'm allowed to be fuzzy on a few of the particulars. Got you this far, haven't I?"

Tayna wasn't sure how to answer that. Where was here, exactly? And how far was it from anything else? But it didn't look like she was surrounded by an army of friends offering to help, so she decided to cut the little guy some slack, and stuck her hand out. "Sorry. I'm Tayna. Now can you tell me where I am and what the hell is going on?"

The Gnome's name was Yama, he said, and as far as he'd been able to piece together, Tayna was facing a big pile of very serious charges. Even he didn't know what it was all about, but by having the charges audited and severed, they now had time to figure things out and mount some kind of defense before anything bad happened.

"Bad?" Tayna asked, not liking the way Yama had averted his eyes when he'd said the word. Now he looked up at her sadly.

"Well, the punishment for any of these charges is pretty severe," he said. Tayna glared at him, waiting for him to explain. Yama picked idly at the fragmented leather on the arm of her chair.

"If you're convicted, the sentence is automatic," he said. Then he swallowed hard and his voice dropped to a whisper. "You'll be neverwased."

Tayna's eyes widened. That did not sound good at all.

Eventually, the timid clerical voice reciting the charges ran out of accusations to make, and the screen flashed back into life. The Judge reappeared in mid-glare, staring down his nose at the entire world of clouds, and fixed Tayna in the cross hairs of his contempt.

"Having severed the charges *after* entering the plea, the defendant now pleas, post hoc, to each charge in kind. To the charge of treason, she pleads, 'Not guilty.'" The Judge then proceeded to rattle off a string of apparent legalese and mumbo-jumbo, but again, while he was talking, Yama grabbed at her hand.

"This is the worst one," he said. "You're accused of being an agent of the Dragon Grimorl. They say you're trying to sneak into the Forest, and that you are bringing a powerful magic here that you intend to use to throw open the rift between worlds and allow the Exile to return."

"What?" Tayna sputtered, but her eyes kept darting to the Judge on the screen, who continued to glare at her as he thundered on about due process and rights to appeal. She dragged her attention back to Yama. "I've been on the run for weeks! If I'm so powerful, why haven't I just... I don't know... vaporized everyone who's chasing me? Or turned them into guacamole? Hell, I can't even heal myself." She held her arms out, showing the bruises and the torn skin of her wrists. Then she turned her face, to highlight the bruising there, and a quick glance down at her knees showed that the unhealed hurts were extensive.

"That's good," Yama said, nodding thoughtfully. "If we can prove it, we can use it." Then he looked back behind Tayna and gave a quick whistle. When she turned, two figures had formed out of the cloud bank and were walking toward them. One was in the shape of a Djin, the other a Gnome. When the two cloud-folk reached Tayna's chair, they stood shoulder to shoulder, facing her.

"All we have to do," Yama said, "is show that you don't have the powers you're accused of having, but we have to be sure this will work, before I say anything to His Angriness. Just reach out and grab both of the v'ou du forms. If you have this completion magic they're talking about, you should be able to pull power from both of these and use it to heal yourself. Give it a shot."

Tayna reached out uncertainly, and felt the strange tingling again as her hands settled on the wispy cloud shapes. They looked insubstantial, but to her inner sense, each form seemed whole, and she could feel their respective powers throbbing under her touch. As she had with Angiron and the Wagon earlier, Tayna reached out from within herself and pulled. She felt the electric snap as the forces connected within her and then she turned her attention to the aches and throbs that peppered her battered extremities. As her attention passed each hurt, the power within her sizzled and moved on, leaving a numb coolness in its wake.

Yama's eyes grew wider. "Uh oh," he said. "That's not exactly a convincing display of 'I don't have any power.'"

Tayna looked down at her arms and was startled to see that the bruises had all faded, and the cuts and scabs had healed. Even the savagely twisted skin of her wrist was whole and unmarked. "Whoa!"

Yama flicked a glance at the Judge, who was still reciting relevant case law or something. "Well, we can't claim lack of power, so we'll have to see if you can get away with declaring lack of intention. Here–" Yama reached into the stack of papers and drew out a thin plate, flicking it with a finger and listening to it ring. "Dragon scale," he said. "Place your hand on this and pull power from it. Then, while you're drawing, simply declare your peaceful intention and promise to uphold the Dragon's Law, or something. That should be enough."

Tayna did as her guide asked, resting her fingertips on the scale that was both frigidly cold and searingly hot at the same time, yet warm to the touch. Again she felt the tingle of power and this time drew it within herself easily. "I, uh, Tayna, promise that I'm not here to wreck the Peace..." She looked at Yama, who nodded at her to continue. "...and that I'll, er, fight evil throughout the land, wherever it may be hiding. Good enough?"

Yama blinked in surprise. "You were actually able to do that," he said. Then he shook himself. "That's good. We can definitely use that. I thought for sure it would tear your arm off."

"What?" Tayna jerked her hand back away from the plate and cradled her fingers protectively with her other hand.

The Gnome shrugged. "The Dragon's Peace may have collapsed," he said, "and maybe folks can lie all they want now, but not when they're pulling power from a scale. It would either weld your mouth shut, or it would taint the vim. And if it did that, the backwash would rip you apart." Then he smiled sheepishly. "I'm glad it didn't though. Anyway, I think that should be enough to get this charge dropped."

Then her hairy little public defender stepped forward and began reciting legal gobbledygook at the screen. The Judge, who had seemed ready to conclude his lecture on caterpillar contract disputes, or whatever it had been, stopped talking and looked up from his papers. A moment later, Yama raised the dragon scale, which now glowed a shimmery yellow, and waved it under the Judge's nose. The man's eyes widened, and flicked once toward Tayna before returning to Yama and his evidence. Then he scowled and nodded.

"The charge of treason is hereby dismissed," the Judge intoned. But before Tayna could breathe even a breath of relief, the old man's face twisted in savage delight.

"Next charge!"

"Standing accused of sedition, the defendant has already pleaded, 'Not guilty.'" the Judge rumbled. "Sedition is defined as an intention to bring into hatred or contempt or to excite disaffection..."

"What?" Tayna hissed, as the Judge droned on with his definition. Yama patted her hand.

"It's when you try to talk people into rebelling against the government," he said. "Did you do any of that?"

The Judge's monotonous voice filled the air with a low-pitched rumble as he continued his lecture. "...duly designated royal court, or the person of the Dragon, or Dragons..."

"But I've never met the Dragon," Tayna said. "I don't even know if he exists. Not really." Yama rolled his eyes.

"Let's not get into charges of heresy too, okay? You're in enough trouble already. But you don't have to meet the Dragon to be guilty of sedition. You just have to bad-mouth him where other people can hear you. And it doesn't have to be the Dragon either. What about kings or queens? Have you complained about any royals in public lately?"

Tayna's face fell. "Oh crap!" she said. "Angiron! I haven't shut up about what a gutter rat he is. And lots of people have heard me say it. Is that bad?"

Yama's eyes had widened when she'd mentioned the Gnome King. "You don't like to pick easy fights, do you?" he muttered. "Why couldn't you have insulted Malkior or spilled soup on Mabundi? They're pretty easy going. But Angiron?" The Gnome shook his head sadly.

"But he's only been King for, like, a couple of days! And I've been... away since then. On the Cold Shoulder. Nobody out there could have heard what I said after he got crowned."

A glimmer of hope lit Yama's expression. "You were alone? That might be enough." But Tayna was shaking her head.

"No, I was with Abeni, but he'd never–"

The hope in Yama's eyes went out and he frowned. "Doesn't matter. Sedition isn't about whether the people agree with you, or even if they'll tell anyone. It's about whether anyone heard you."

"And it doesn't matter that I wasn't in the Forest when I said it?"

Yama shrugged. "You might be able to make an argument on that–if you had been talking to someone from out there. But you were talking to a Djin. And not just any Djin either, but one connected to a powerful family on the Anvil. You really want to drag them into all of this? The court might decide that it was a conspiracy and charge them too."

"Forget it," Tayna said, waving her Gnome lawyer away with her hand. "Abeni is the only friend I have left. I'm not going to get him and his family into trouble just to save my skin. What's the punishment for sedition?" But Yama didn't have to answer her.

"...punishable by torture, public humiliation, execution, and neverwasing," the Judge continued, and then he went on to describe the ways in which those sentences could be carried out.

Yama held silent for a moment, as the list of punishments reverberated in Tayna's ears. Then he sighed. "Well, what did you say, exactly. Can you remember?"

Tayna threw up her hands, exasperated. "What *didn't* I say? My stupid husband is a scum-sucking, child-snatching son of a–"

Yama's hand flashed out, slapping over Tayna's mouth so quickly that it produced a loud popping sound as he clamped down. "Are you insane?" he hissed. Then he paused to listen, with his head cocked to one side, but the Judge hadn't broken rhythm, and was still reciting in gleeful detail all the ways in which the court was permitted to torture the guilty. The Gnome breathed a sigh of relief.

"The court hears everything," he said. "Even if the Judge doesn't. So anything you say here can and *will* be used against you. Got it?" When she nodded her understanding, Yama removed his hand.

"I suppose we could beg for leniency," the Gnome said, but even Tayna knew how likely that was.

"Where I come from, kids can't be charged with serious crimes," Tayna said.

"It's the same here," Yama replied. "But you're not a kid."

"But I'm only thirteen," Tayna said.

Yama shrugged. "Do you know right from wrong?" Tayna nodded. "And you've already flowered, or you wouldn't have any powers. And in this world, that means you're an adult. Old enough to know it's wrong means old enough to punish."

"So you're just going to give up? That's it? Case closed?" Tayna pressed herself back into the leather padding of the chair, angry at her spineless lawyer. But after a breath or two, she realized she had no right being angry with him. This was all her fault. She'd been talking trash about the King. It wasn't Yama's fault that she didn't know— "Wait a minute," she said, turning to face her furry little adviser.

"When I said all those things about him, I didn't know he was King then. I thought he was still the First Prince."

Yama's whole body brightened, and he stood taller. "Say, that might work," he said. "Wouldn't matter if you didn't know it was against the law, but not knowing that the man you're speaking ill of is the King... Well, it's never been tried before, because most everybody knows who the Kings are, but with your special circumstances, that might... " The little Gnome turned away in mid-sentence and scuttled forward to address the screen, just as the Judge was finishing his lengthy explanation of the manner in which toenails could be pried off.

"The defense presents an argument based on ignorance of fact," Yama declared, fitting his words in elegantly, as the Judge drew another breath, and thereby not quite interrupting him.

Tayna watched intently as the Judge thundered his rebuttals. Each time, Yama waited patiently for the long-winded Judge to complete his replies, before launching into a riposte of his own. But eventually the words spiraled down, and with each rebuffed argument,

Yama's shoulders dropped lower, until, at last, the Judge ended the conversation.

"Defense rejected. It is not credible that the defendant did not know the identity of the King. The defendant is hereby found guilty as charged and will now be sentenced."

Tayna's jaw flopped open, and her heart stopped beating in her chest. What? Guilty? Just like that? She stood up and stepped forward, looking up at the great Judge face hanging in the air above her.

"That's it? I don't get to say anything else? I don't get to call any witnesses? Ask Abeni! He was there! He didn't know Angiron had been crowned either! He'll tell–"

"SILENCE!" roared the Judge. The thunder of his shout rocked Tayna backward, where she stumbled and flopped back into the chair behind her.

"The defendant is permitted one defense, and one defense only. The defense of ignorance has been entered and overruled. The verdict stands." There comes a time when you realize that you just can't win–that the deck is stacked against you, the odds too great. A time like now.

Tayna had lost.

"This court rules that the defendant, Tayna, is guilty of sedition against the ruling house of Angiron, King of the Gnomileshi Horde. She is hereby sentenced to neverwas. Sentence to be carried out at the setting of the sun. All remaining, lesser charges are hereby dropped. This court is now concluded."

Then the view screen went black, and shapes of burly guards stepped out of the clouds around them and began to close in.

"Well, that didn't go as well as I'd hoped."

The cloud guards had advanced until they'd formed an unbroken ring around her, but they'd come no closer. Apparently, their only concern was seeing that Tayna stayed put until her sentence was carried out. That left her sitting in her chair in the middle of the circle, with Yama leaning casually against the arm of the chair, at her side.

She was too weary to even turn her head to face him, though. All she could do was slouch her eyes to the side and glare at him through the hair that now hung over her face. Other than that, she said nothing. What did it matter?

Yama shrugged. "Sorry. I really thought we had him."

Tayna felt drained. "So that's all? At sundown, I'll just cease to exist?" The Gnome nodded. "And then what?"

"Well, the path of time will be unwound, and you will be removed from it. Then it will be wound forward again, and all will be as though you had never existed." At least he had the decency to sound sad about it.

"Pretty extreme punishment, isn't it? I mean, got kidnapped? That's too bad. Raised in hell by evil harpies? That's all fine. But say one word about the creep who did it to you and, 'Off with her head!' Does that sound fair to you?"

"Is that really what happened?"

Tayna flopped a hand at him in dismissal. "What do you care? I'm just another unlucky defendant. A tick mark in the 'cases lost' column. But so what if I mouthed off? Angiron's an evil, sadistic creep and he should be on trial, not me. But is that going to happen? No. Of course not. He's a king now. But we'll take care of that girl he's been victimizing. Oh yeah. She's trouble. And when I get neverwased, and all those mean things I said about His High and Ugliness get undone, who's going to be left to help my friends, huh? They're still going to have crappy lives, because that nose-monster is still out there, still in charge, still doing sick things to helpless people."

"And that really matters to you?"

Tayna rolled her eyes. "Of course it matters!" she shouted. "This used to be a pretty nice place, from what I can tell, but ever since the Peace collapsed, it's been getting worse and worse and worse, and I'd bet my butt that Angiron's behind every minute of it. Everything he touches turns to crap. For everyone except him. And now he's taking his diseased road-show into Grimorl too. Like there aren't enough pathetic orphans here to pick on."

Yama looked at her curiously. "So with all he's done, and there you are with all that power you're carrying... Yet you'd just ignore it? You're not tempted to use it to get rid of that kind of evil? Kill him? Or turn his Horde into a sticky puddle of goo?"

"Power? I don't have any power. You think fixing a few bruises gives me the power to heal the world? Don't be stupid."

"But if you did have such power?"

Tayna thought about it for a moment, and then let out a tired sigh. "No, probably not," she said. "I mean, it's fun to think about it, but dead is pretty extreme. I'd probably just send him out to live with the Miseratu or something. I mean, you have to do something with him, right? If you want the Dragon's Peace to come back? It only takes one guy to not care, to be willing to treat everyone else like crap, and the whole thing falls apart."

Yama nodded again. More confidently. As though he'd made a decision. Then he stepped in front of her chair to look her straight in the eye. Tayna looked back at him, puzzled by his sudden seriousness. And as she watched, the timid little Gnome seemed to melt and shift. A moment later, she was staring into the eyes of the Judge.

"Oh crap," she said.

———————

"So that was all a trick?"

The Judge nodded. His face had none of the furious scowl that she'd seen on the screen. It was definitely the same face, with the same deep creases in his skin, but now they told a tale more of laughing than of frowning.

"The trial? The sentencing? All of it?"

Again he nodded. "Not everybody gets the full treatment, of course. Takes too long. Besides, most folk hang their souls on their shirtfronts, so to speak. I can read them without even slowing 'em down. Most are already on the side they're supposed to be, so they bounce right back. Never even know I'm there, doing the bouncing. But a few I let through, like your Djin friend. He's good people, you know. You *are* traveling with him, aren't you?"

Tayna nodded, although a trifle absently. The conversation was running ahead faster than she could process it.

"Who are you?" she finally managed to ask, her voice pinched with exasperation.

The old man smiled gently. "My name really is Yama," he said. "Although most have forgotten..." His voice trailed off in thought, and then he seemed to remember her question, and he drew himself up more formally. "I am the Judge of Changes," he said. "I was set here by the Dragon Methilien himself, to stand as the line between tranquility and chaos."

But if he'd wanted to impress her with his job title or something, Tayna wasn't buying. Instead, she focused on the part that mattered to her. "So, you really are a judge, only you conduct fake trials."

"Exactly!" he crowed. Tayna's eyes narrowed. She hadn't expected him to agree to something that sounded so stupid.

"And this makes sense to you?"

He shrugged, and above his eyes, the white tufts of his brows danced merrily. "It is necessary," he said. "You feared him, didn't you? That great Judge, glaring down at you from on high?"

"You could say that."

"And fearing him, you vested him with all of your attention, yes?"

"You mean, was I riveted by the giant angry face as he ordered my death? Yes, I was vaguely interested."

"Precisely! And while you were so distracted by him and his judgments, how much attention did you pay to me? Hmm? Did you primp and preen to present your best face to your humble harried clerk? No. You spoke to me as you would speak to any other lesser being in a time of stress. To me you showed your natural self." Then he pointed up at where the empty screen still hung above them. "That Judge sees only what a candidate wants him to see, but me? I am shown something that many might prefer remain hidden."

"What? Terror? Maybe a little pants-wetting? Is that your thing?"

Yama chuckled. "No. I see truth–the candidate as he or she truly is. Although, to be fair, it is usually the darker colors of that true self that I am shown. Not every candidate is as genial with petty underlings as you might think."

"So, what happens now? We have another trial–a real one–and you drag out everything I said or did during the fake trial and use all that against me, too?"

"No. You are free to enter the Realm," he said.

Tayna's eyes bugged out a little. She'd been expecting more of a run-around than that. "I can? Really? This isn't just another fake part of the test, to see how I'll react?"

Yama's eyes sparkled. "No more tricks," he said. "I have seen your truth, Tayna of Grimorl. You have an honest heart and a great soul. Such traits will always be welcome within the Dragon's embrace."

He seemed to be waiting for something. A hug, maybe? Tayna

could feel the rage starting to build up in her ankles. She was tired of being jerked around. Tired of being danced through other peoples' hoops without ever being told what the show was all about. Something inside her snapped.

"So that's it? *Show's over, folks! Move along. We got what we wanted, so you'll have to get out now.* Is that it?"

Yama looked at her, bewildered. "I thought you would be pleased."

"Sure, yeah. Now I have your permission to go back to *exactly what I was doing before you pulled me in here!* Everything is so much better now. I really oughta remember to send you a thank-you gift."

"You are truly displeased?"

"Buster, I'm way beyond displeased. I'm... anti-pleased! Who the hell are you anyway? And no, don't give me your name and your job title again. I got that. You're the Dragon's lap-dog who gets to jerk people out of their lives and scare the crap out of them. Does that make you special? What did you do to earn this fancy job you've got, anyway? Did you babysit for Methilien when he was just an egg? Did your sister marry his brother or something?"

Yama shrank back from her blustering tirade, and Tayna stood tall, towering her Wasketchin frame over the little Gnome, and she was so deep in her righteous fury that she almost missed his answer.

"I died," he said.

She paused. "Come again?"

"I died," Yama repeated. "Myself and two others. We sacrificed our lives so that the Dragon could forge us into the three avatars of his Peace."

"So you're dead?"

"I thought you knew."

"I'm not from around here," she said.

That made the old Gnome smile. "Yes, Tayna. I know your tale. I wept when you left us and I sang when you returned. But you do not know mine."

"Oh. Sorry."

The old Gnome waved her apology away. "How could you? You were raised in a world not your own." Then he paused, and a look of irritation swept his face. "If only we had more time!" Then he took her by the shoulder. "We are three," he said. "Three Avatars of the Peace. One to preserve it, to repair it against all harm. Another to destroy it, to tear it down and grind it to dust. And myself, to test the suitability of the participants and hold the line between those within and without. As you said yourself, there are some whose very presence would taint everything."

"But that makes no sense," Tayna said. "There's some great dark minion out there who's trying to tear the Peace apart? And he was put there to keep the Peace going? How does that work? Is it suddenly Opposite Day?"

"It is actually quite wise," Yama replied. "No promise that is made in one age can be held in earnest by the folk of the next. To make a thing and then to walk away, expecting it to endure without change would be folly, and the Dragon Methilien was no fool. The only way that his Peace might be hoped to survive was to give it life. Allow it to grow and change. To *make* it do so. To endure, it must be forced to adapt, ever seeking its own weaknesses and pressing upon them. And occasionally it must fail, and then be built anew. Stronger. More resilient. But how are we to ensure its periodic destruction if we do not provide that destruction a champion? I am but the filter, keeping away those who would tip the balance irrevocably. But the pulling and the pushing–the necessary tension of the Peace–that is for the others. Mardu and Suriken. The Oath Keeper, and the Oathbane. Creation and Destruction."

"Jeez. They sound like fun. I hope I never run into them."

Yama clapped her on the shoulder. "Oh, but you already have. One of them anyway. And you will meet the other before long, I suspect." Then he glanced away, and when his gaze returned, it was full of sadness. "Our time is ended," he said. "You have passed through."

"Through? Passed through what?"

Then, with a puff of fog, Yama vanished, and he took the chair, the guards, the big screen, and the clouds with him. "Welcome home, Tayna," was the last thing she heard him say.

And then she was thirty feet above the ground and plunging rapidly toward it.

chapter 6

"More personal research, Detective?"

DelRoy nodded happily. "Maybe I should start paying rent around here, Doris."

"What? Your taxes aren't high enough? You want to pay more? You could always pay mine." He chuckled as the older woman ducked down below the desk for a moment and then popped back up and held out an old laptop. "You know the password?"

DelRoy accepted the computer and its dangling cords from her with a nod of thanks. "Wouldn't be much of a detective if I couldn't remember the word 'matronly' for longer than three days, now would I? Next month, what about, 'encyclopedic?'"

Doris rolled her eyes. "Oh yeah, that's all I need. Every teenager in the city would be lining up here nine times a day to ask, 'Whatsa password again?' and 'Couldjuh spell that?' I'd never get any work done." Her impersonation of modern teen speech was bang on, and doubly funny, coming from the mouth of such an articulate, older woman. DelRoy laughed.

"Right, I forgot about the kids," he said, giving in gracefully. "Thanks again, Doris. I'll have it back in an hour or so," but the librarian was already bustling down the counter to help a young mother and her child with a stack of books to check out.

DelRoy turned away from the long counter and headed toward the hall that would take him back to the reference stacks. Most people he knew had computers at home. Some even had several, scattered around for decoration, like high-tech throw pillows. But DelRoy lived alone, and he knew that if he allowed himself to buy a computer, he would never leave the apartment on his days off. At least this way, whenever he found something he wanted to look up, he had to come out into the world of people to find a computer. It kept him from getting too isolated. He stepped back against the wall to make way for the shelving kid, who was coming toward him down the hallway with a cartload of books.

The other advantage of not having a computer at home was that he was rarely tempted to work on his days off anymore. Years ago, he had enjoyed the work–back when it let him actually help people. In those days, he'd spent lots of his personal time down at the station. His work had made him feel useful. But these days, policing was more about reports, accountability, and blame assignment. What little helping he actually got to do anymore had to get crammed into those little bits of time left over between all the finger pointing and keester covering.

Not that his down time was any better, really. No wife, no real hobbies, no yard work to do, no family to speak of. When he looked at his existence honestly, DelRoy couldn't tell which part was worse. A working life that was slowly having all the joy sucked out of it? Or a home life that steadfastly refused to let any in? But at least it was balanced.

The light at the end of the hall was out, making it hard to read the sign on the door, but he already knew what it said. "Reference and Research. Quiet, please." He pushed the door open and went in.

It was a large room, filled with book shelves. The stacks. At the back of the room, two long work tables filled an open area, each surrounded with chairs. It was a quiet place where he didn't have to listen to the kids giggling and snorting, but where he could still get a decent network signal. It was his favorite room in the library. DelRoy eased himself around the shelves and made his way to the back.

One of the two long tables was unoccupied, so he took a seat there, near the electrical outlet, and set the computer down beside him. A middle-aged woman was sitting at the other table, facing toward him, but she had her head down, peering at what looked to be a legal text. Behind her, an elderly man was scanning carefully along the shelf of books about appliance repairs.

Not together, he thought to himself.

It was a game he often played when he first came into a room—watching the people he found there and trying to pick out who was connected to whom, before anybody spoke. It was the only foreign language he spoke, and a very useful one for a detective to know. Body language. And DelRoy had always had something of a knack for it.

The appliance man pulled a book from the shelf and studied the back cover for a moment, then he tucked it under his arm and wandered away, never even looking at the lawyer woman. Nope, not together. Chalk up another win for Detective DelRoy. Although, on second glance, the woman didn't seem to be a lawyer, after all. Her posture was wrong–as though the entire book was written in some alien script, and she was studying each word as she encountered it, teasing out its meaning from only the vaguest of clues. So not a lawyer. A professional woman of some kind though. Maybe considering a legal action?

But it was just an idle thought. He bent over in his chair, reaching under the table to plug in the ancient laptop. After a moment of fumbling, the plug slid into the socket and he was rewarded by the familiar, high-pitched whine from the electronics. As he sat back up to wait for the old beast to boot up, his chair scraped across the floor. The woman jerked her head up, startled by the sudden noise.

DelRoy smiled sheepishly. "Sorry," he said. She gave him a distracted smile in reply and then bent back to her reading. Obsessive and very intent. Considering legal action very soon then.

For the next hour, DelRoy busied himself on the web. He called it "research," but the truth was, he didn't really know what he was looking for. A hobby, maybe? A new career? What might someone have deduced from the list of websites he'd been visiting lately? He scrolled back through his browser history, and then laughed. Private security companies, alarm technologies, bodyguard training, banks, private investigators. "Looks like I'm planning a bank heist," he muttered.

"Excuse me?" The woman at the other table looked up at him with a slightly panicky look in her eyes.

"Sorry again," he said. "I was just laughing at my browser hist–Never mind. Thinking about suing somebody?" It was the first thing that came to mind–just something to change the topic from his own weird tangle of thoughts. But it hadn't been the right thing at all to say, and he watched helplessly as the woman's face seemed to shatter in front of him. Tears began to spill down her cheeks, and she could only nod.

DelRoy was out of his seat in a heartbeat.

"Oh, God! I am such an idiot!" he said, as he hurried around the ends of the tables. "I didn't mean to upset you. I was–"

"Right," she said, smiling up at him through the tears. "What you were was right. I've just never said it out loud until now, and it just..."

"So it's a family matter," he said, as he pulled up a seat next to the woman. And now he suddenly felt awkward. He wanted to put a hand on her shoulder, to undo whatever unhappiness his blunder had triggered, but he didn't know her. Instead, he put his hand on her book, and turned it toward him. Town Ordinances.

"How could you know possibly know that?" she asked. Del-Roy looked up from the book at her. "How could you know I was thinking about suing somebody over a family matter?"

"I'm a good guesser," he said, still trying to lighten the situation, but she shook her head, and her eyes narrowed in suspicion.

"Are you working for them?"

"Working for who?" he asked, but even as he did, he recognized that this was turning into one of those conversations where everybody talked but nobody really listened and nobody really learned anything either. His training took over and he raised his hands, palm out, to stop her.

"Let's start again," he said. "Hello. My name is Martin DelRoy. Detective Martin DelRoy. I'm not working for 'them,' unless 'them' is the city police. When I said I was a good guesser, I was being completely honest. It's my job, and even there, I'm known to have better instincts than most. Guesses. So if I upset you by seeming to know something about you, I'm sorry. I really was guessing. And I was also talking without thinking."

"That's three now," she said. Her eyes were a bit puffy, but the waterworks had stopped, and she was wiping at her face with a tissue she'd taken from her bag. Not blotting daintily, the way some women would, but actually wiping. For some reason, he liked that.

"Three what?"

"That's how many times you've apologized to me so far."

"Oh." Suddenly he felt self-conscious. What do you do when somebody accuses you of apologizing too often? Apologize? Instead, he grinned. "My quota for the day is seven," he said. "You've still got four more coming."

The woman laughed, and held her hand out. "Sue Nackenfausch," she said. "And I do believe I am glad to make your acquaintance, Detective. I wonder if you'd mind paying for all those apologies by answering some questions for me?"

DelRoy grinned. The conversation was darting like minnows in a brook and he was finding it hard to get his balance. Which meant that he was also finding it extremely refreshing. "I'd be happy to," he said. Then he leaned in conspiratorially and added, in a whisper, "But if you *are* planning to sue the department, I should warn you. I'd be willing to help with that for free."

"Really?" Sue said. "I'll keep that in mind. But for now, I was wondering if you could tell me about Missing Persons."

DelRoy's eyebrows shot up all by themselves. Now it was her turn to seem the shrewd guesser. How had she known he worked that desk?

Suddenly, it was looking to be a very interesting day.

They didn't stay in the library for long. What had been a comfortable silence for quiet reading, or for private research, had quickly felt too conspicuous for conversation–especially if they were going to talk about her problems. So they left the library and went across the street instead. By the magic of coffee shops, the constant din and clatter of the busy restaurant was somehow a much better cover for their private conversation than any silent library archive could ever hope to be. Although, "conversation" was a bit of a misnomer, because it was Sue who did most of the talking.

And the longer she talked, the odder things began to sound. Missing Persons was the biggest part of his job, and missing kids made up the largest chunk of the cases. About two thirds of the kids reported missing each year were runaways, and more than half of those were from orphanages and foster care.

So how come Detective Martin DelRoy of the Missing Persons squad had never heard of Our Lady of Divine Suffering's Home for Orphans and Evictees? It was like a baseball scout going half his career without ever learning that the local high school had a team. It just didn't seem possible.

But to hear Sue tell it, that was only the beginning. Apparently, the kids at this "Old Shoe" place were treated like they were living in some kind of Charles Dickens novel, rather than a care facility in a modern city. But that didn't make sense either. DelRoy knew the people at Children's Services personally. There was no way that any of them would have allowed that kind of facility to stay open for even a weekend–let alone the fifteen or so years that Sue claimed it had been in operation.

The waitress approached to refill their cups and DelRoy thanked her, then they busied themselves with the sugar and cream for a moment, until the woman had bustled herself out of earshot.

"So the kids do all the cooking and the cleaning?" he asked, leaning in close and keeping his voice lower than the background din. "You're sure about this? Could Eliza have been... exaggerating, maybe? Trying to impress you with the hardships of her life there?" But Sue was already shaking her head.

"It wasn't just what she told us. We actually *saw* it. Mr. Nackenfausch and I–Ned–visited one day to have lunch with Eliza, and we actually had to wait until she'd finished serving, and then cleaning the dishes, before she herself was allowed to eat. It was heartbreaking..." Sue's voice trailed off, heading toward another spasm of guilt and loss. DelRoy reached out and patted her hand. Somehow, being in a coffee shop made little gestures like that seem more appropriate than they would have been in the total privacy of the library.

"Well, kids in care are expected to do chores," he said. "It's good for them. Sets an expectation of making a useful contribution to society, and all that."

Again Sue shook her head. "Chores I agree with, but serve all the meals? Do all the cleaning? All the repair work? And always the same dozen girls, in a facility that holds sixty?"

DelRoy leaned back from the table and shook his head slowly. "I don't know what to tell you, Sue." Somewhere along the line, they had graduated to first names too. "I can look into it if you like, but if what you say is–"

"No!" Sue's hand shot across the table and clutched pleadingly at his own. "There's something going on. I'm sure of it. But if you start asking questions through your channels, word will get back to the Goodies and they'll know we're onto them."

"Goodies?"

Sue blushed. "It's what Eliza and her friends call them. The Sisters of Good Salvation. The order of nuns who run the place."

"I've never heard of them before," DelRoy said. He was getting used to saying that today.

"Nobody has," Sue said. "I've asked the Bishop and several ministers, priests, and whatnots, but *nobody* seems to have heard of them. I can't even find out what church they're affiliated with."

"Well, if the place is as bad as you say, I suppose that could explain why nobody knows about it. Or rather, why nobody will admit to knowing about it. Who would go on record saying they'd known something like that was going on, but hadn't reported it?"

"Frankly," Sue said, "I couldn't care less who's to blame. I just want my little girl back. I've been searching for so long. And then to lose her on the very day we were supposed to... What's the word? Become a family. How come we have words for getting married and getting divorced, for being born and for dying, but we don't have a word for that moment when that whole purpose of marriage suddenly comes together and the circle of your family closes into being? Where's *that* word? I find I need it a lot."

He couldn't help but smile. Even frustrated and angry, Sue kept coming at him from directions he couldn't anticipate. "I don't know," he said. "I've never been good at finding the just-right words for things. You were saying?"

Sue sighed heavily. "Oh, I don't know what I was saying," she said. "It just feels so good to be saying anything, and having somebody hear me, and acknowledge that it's weird, and that it's important."

"If even half of what you've told me turns out to be true, this might turn into a major case," he said.

"But you will be discreet, won't you?"

DelRoy sipped his coffee and thought about it for a moment. Sue was right. If something this foul had been kept under wraps for this long, they couldn't afford to give those responsible any warning at all, or their cloud of secrecy would probably just rise up again and swallow the entire case. Maybe even Sue along with it. He nodded.

"I'll be discreet," he said. "Do a bit of digging, check a few facts. First thing we'll want to do is try to find out who owns the building, where their funding comes from, that sort of thing. It'll give us some names and organizations to start digging into."

For a moment, Sue just stared at him, her eyes shining with tears. "Thank you, Detective. You cannot know how long I've waited for somebody in authority to say something like that." She stared at him intently for a moment, then she broke eye contact and gave a little laugh. "Sorry. I just wanted to bask in that for a moment. Now tell me, is there anything I can be doing while you're looking into all this?"

DelRoy was about to say no, but then he thought about the need for discretion, and realized that a city detective asking questions at a black-market orphanage wasn't exactly going to count as "discreet."

"You might try to talk to some of the kids there," he said. "If you get the opportunity. See if they've heard about any companies, or owners, or board members... anything. Even a name on a letter-head would be a start."

"I'll do that," Sue said. It was good to hear a ring of confidence in the voice of this woman who had seemed so lost just a short time ago. And it occurred to him that he was the one who'd put it there, which made him feel good about himself too.

By the time they'd settled up–with Sue insisting that coffee was her treat–DelRoy was feeling so energized that he decided to do something that he hadn't done in years.

He was going to go back to the station on his day off.

DelRoy sat still and placed the folder carefully back on his desk. Other detectives and clerks wandered around the room in their usual state of distracted intensity. But he couldn't make eye contact with them. Couldn't look at them. He couldn't *not* look at them either. It was as though he'd been paralyzed by the two conclusions he'd just reached. One: there really was something going on.

And two: somebody inside the department was involved.

His first task upon reaching the office had been to go back and look through the old case reports. Was it possible that an entire orphanage, an entire religious order, and a dozen different caregivers had all simply escaped his memory? But the records backed him up. It wasn't just his mind playing middle-age games with him. There was nothing there to remember. Not one reference to any of this in any of his files.

The simple explanation, of course, would have been that Sue was some kind of paranoid, but she hadn't seemed the type. And all her seeming aside, there was something else too. She had shown him a copy of the report she had filed when her daughter went missing. A report for which he could now find no trace anywhere in the system. Somebody had removed it. And not just from the computer. He couldn't find the paper copy either. He couldn't even find references to it on the duty sheets and shift reports. Every piece of paper and every mention of this case was gone. He wasn't naive. He knew that no system was invulnerable, and it was easy to imagine that hackers might have managed to wipe the digital stuff. But only an insider would have known where all the paper information was kept, and how to remove it.

So had Sue made up the whole story? If she had, then she had also made a perfect forgery of the standard missing persons form and filled it in correctly–even to the point of following the department's idiosyncratic practices, such as circling the year of disappearance, and jotting the complainant's email address in the "Country" box. Could she have forged that as well? In short, not bloody likely.

No matter how he looked at it, there was only one explanation that made sense of what he was seeing, and it sent a shiver of dread down his spine. The kidnappers were real, and somebody in this room was actively collaborating with them. As crazy at it sounded, it was the only explanation that fit the facts.

When he was sure that he had put everything back and that nobody was paying any particular attention to him, DelRoy gathered his things and headed toward the stairs.

"Clocking out early, Marty?" DelRoy rolled his eyes. Goreski. Every department had one. The guy who seems to think it was his job to watch everybody else's clock for them.

"Yeah, Jay," he said with a forced smile. "About nineteen hours early. It's my D.O."

"Well! Don't let us working stiffs get in your way, then." Goreski made an elaborate bow. "We'll see you again when you're actually *supposed* to be here."

DelRoy kept his smile in place. Robbed of any actual wrongdoing to call attention to, Goreski was the kind of guy who would simply switch to snide implications, just to maintain his sense of superiority. A couple of choice retorts occurred to him, but he couldn't be bothered wasting them on that goof, so he just grinned his way past the guy and kept going.

But the altercation got him thinking, as he clattered down the old staircase and headed out to his car. Could it be Goreski? Could he be the scurrying little weasel who had vanished Sue's case file? The guy was seven kinds of idiot, but DelRoy had never thought of him as actually *evil* before. Had he been wrong about that? And if Sue's file had been snuffed, then were there others missing too?

The sense of unease stayed with him all the way to the city records building. Whoever it was, they'd made a kid disappear, and then they'd done a good job of making all the records of the search for her disappear too. From an investigating perspective, it was almost as though they'd wiped Eliza Drummel from the universe's memory. With no person to look at, and no pieces of paper pointing at her, she might just as well have never existed at all. But there was one thing in all this that they couldn't disappear.

The Old Shoe.

It was a building. It had weight. Presence. It occupied space–in a formidable way–and it could not be shredded, redacted, or stuffed into the trunk of a car. It was unavoidably there. And one of the perplexing things about cities is that they tend to invest far more energy into tracking their own inanimate parts than they do their living inhabitants.

The records building was a grim, blank-nosed box of mostly concrete, tucked neatly in behind City Hall. People drove past it all the time without the faintest idea what it was. Those that did wonder, probably thought it was an insurance company, given its drab, unimaginative facade. But even insurance is a wild party compared to the plodding dullardry of municipal record keeping. This building wasn't going anywhere, and by extension, neither would your buildings, if you kept your records about them here.

DelRoy parked in the visitor's space and went inside, waving his badge at the little reception booth just inside the door. The radio in the waiting area had been tuned to the frequency exactly between the polka station and the Latin rhythms station, and the resulting sound of static, throbbing in and out to a syncopated beat while accordions wheezed all around, was enough to qualify that room as the first circle of Hell. A designation only confirmed by the zombifying light of the fluorescents above. He was glad when the girl buzzed the door and allowed him to escape that pit of damnation.

But as hideous as it had been, the waiting room had offered more warmth than the entire rest of the building, and he soon found himself sitting in the microfiche room on a hard wooden chair, zipping through the miniaturized records of land sales from decades past. The most recent transactions would be accessible by computer, but for anything older than ten years or so, fiche was the place to be. The ancient paper records of bygone eras had all been updated to the little plastic films, but those had not yet degraded anywhere near badly enough to make digitizing them any kind of priority. And Sue had said that the orphanage had been in operation for at least fifteen years, so microfiche it was.

Unfortunately, the files were cataloged chronologically, rather than by location, so he had to scan back through years worth of land sales, foreclosures, and auctions, and his eyes were getting numb by the time he had gone back thirty years, still without finding any mention of the lot and parcel he was looking for. He'd probably started too far back. So, with a sigh of resignation, he trudged across the room to the cabinets to find the more recent spools. Then he reversed his trudge back to his chair to repeat the search all over again.

When he found it, half an hour later, he was somewhat surprised. The orphanage had been in operation for fifteen years all right. But the nuns had only purchased it ten years ago.

"Who buys a five year old orphanage?" he muttered, as he leaned back from the table to stretch his aching neck muscles, cocking his head from side to side and straining until he heard a little popping sound from the base of his skull. There was something about these machines that always gave him a crick in his neck, no matter how good his posture.

Now that he'd found the title transaction, things got a little easier. That document had given him the name of the purchaser, Regina Finch. The name seemed familiar, although DelRoy couldn't recall from where. But with that thread to pull on, unraveling the rest had been pretty easy, and DelRoy was soon gathering his printouts and notes into a folder and heading for the door.

He couldn't wait to tell Sue what he'd found. Even the way they were registered was weird. You'd expect nuns to be set up as a charity, or as some kind of subsidiary of a church, right? But not these ladies. Nope. The Sisters of Good Salvation were set up as a for-profit company.

And business had been very, very good.

Sue sat and watched the front entrance of the Old Shoe from the shelter of her parked car, half a block away. All morning she had been sitting there, but with the cold wind blowing gusts of ice down the empty streets, not a single soul had ventured in or out. The weather was a cocoon of sorts, isolating the self-contained little universe where the Great God Regalia boomed and thundered and a dozen Harpy angels trumpeted her will to the wide-eyed and terrified masses: the children of the Old Shoe.

Meeting Detective DelRoy that morning had completely rejuvenated her, and for the first time since Eliza had gone missing, Sue felt like she was getting something done. Something constructive. On the detective's advice, she had taken up observation at the Old Shoe, and she planned to spend her day here, making notes of any comings and goings, and in particular, keeping her eyes open for a chance to make contact with the children. She had her camera, and a good, long-distance lens, and she was just going to watch. And take pictures, of course. If anything interesting happened. She was on a stake-out, and being here made her feel powerful again.

The afternoon hours crept across the dull gray sky, and aside from a slight change in the angle of the light, nothing happened. Nobody came out. Nobody went in. No faces appeared in any of the windows. No silhouettes peered over the edge of the roof. No deliveries. No visitors. No children. No nuns. No nobody. It was a singularly boring afternoon.

From time to time, Sue would take up her camera and peer at the building through the long, telephoto lens, bracing her hands on the steering wheel to keep the image steady. She took a picture or two each time, more for something to do than for any practical value. Sure, when she got back home, she would play with them in her editing suite, on the off chance that an enhancement might reveal something that she hadn't been able to see with her naked eye, but the chances of that were pretty remote. It was busywork really, but without it, there was nothing else to do at all but to wait and to watch.

She was flipping back and forth between the day's photos when a slight flicker caught her eye. Sue pushed the back button and reversed the shuffle. There it was again. Nothing exciting, unfortunately. Just one of the basement windows, at the far end of the building, at sidewalk level. All day it had been a dark hole of shadow, but in the last photo, it was suddenly lighter. Not light from inside the building, but the brighter grayness of a winter sky. Between one set of photos and the next, somebody had tilted that window open, changing the reflection. If she hadn't been desperate for something to do, she'd have ignored it completely, but she couldn't bear the thought of leaving with nothing to show for her day, so she set the camera on the floor and got out of the car.

What could it hurt to go take a look? After all, it was a basement window, and as she recalled, the basement was where Eliza and her friends had been relocated, shortly before she had disappeared. Maybe she'd be able to overhear something useful.

As she approached the orphanage, pulling her coat around herself against the biting wind and trying to act inconspicuous, Sue wondered if detectives ever felt this self conscious. She felt like she was a little girl again, sneaking out of bed to go sit by her cracked-open door so she could read by the hallway light. Only she wasn't a little girl, and this was not some cute infraction. Now she was a full-grown woman, sneaking up to an orphanage so she could spy on the children.

The thought sobered her and she quickly realized that she needed a more plausible pretense for being there than "just walking by." A squat red mail box stood on the curb, in front of the now-open window. That would do. Sue dug through her purse and managed to find a folded piece of paper and a pen. Hardly a letter, but she walked up to the mailbox as though it was, and paused there for a moment while she carefully wrote down an address, as though she'd been about to post a letter and had only just now realized that she'd forgotten to address it.

While she wrote, she listened, but strain as she might, she couldn't hear a word of chatter coming from the window. The rush of wind past her ears obscured whatever sounds might escape the open window. Sue paused and looked back toward her car, then the other way. There didn't appear to be anybody watching, but she didn't want to take any chances either. So, with an exaggerated jerk of her hand, she "dropped" her pen and then turned to watch it sail toward the window, where it banged the glass and then clattered to the concrete sidewalk.

"Oops," she said, to no one in particular, and then she scurried over to retrieve it.

She *had* remembered correctly. Just inside the glass and just below the level of the sidewalk, Sue could make out the top level of a bunk bed, its blankets pulled tight, like a hotel bed. Or an army cot. This *was* where the girls slept. And realizing that she was just inches from making contact with someone who might actually know something, Sue had an idea.

So she picked up her pen, unfolded her sheet of paper, and began to write once more.

chapter 7

"What a pathetic trio we are," Eliza said, as she pushed forward, following the course of a small brook. "One ancient ghost on a secret mission, who was totally hip a bajillion years ago, but has no clue about today. One ill-tempered crow with a cruel sense of humor, who knows where everything is, but doesn't know what anything is called. And then there's me, stone dead, naked as a seal–except for this *very* stylish tarp–and apparently my one big contribution to the team is that I'm the only one in the bunch with hands. All together we add up to one full moron. But just barely."

Hunger always made Eliza grumpy. She had no idea how much time had passed since she'd last eaten, but she did know it had been in the kitchen of the Old Shoe, so a couple of days at least, and her stomach was now clenched in a continual snarl of complaint. When she asked Mardu about food, the Flame of the Dragon had consulted Scraw's memories–the crow's name apparently was "Scraw"–and had found a hiker-berry hedge not too far away. Berries weren't pizza, but at this point, Eliza didn't really care what she ate. Just as long as it was soon.

"So what does a Flame of the Dragon do, anyway?" she asked, as she skirted past another of the strange, multi-colored local trees, twitching at the corner of blanket dragging behind her so it didn't get caught on the roots. Mardu and Scraw flitted off its lowest branch as she passed, and flapped ahead to another perch.

It is my duty to remake the Oath of Kings, Mardu replied, the words sounding clearly in Eliza's head. *For millennia, the Forest has known peace, ensured by the pact between the Peoples of the Forest and the Dragon Methilien.*

"The Dragon's Peace thingy, right? That big mojo that stopped working?"

Indeed, Mardu replied. *And with its passing I was awakened and sent forth to re-establish the Oath of Kings and renew the Peace once more.*

"So how does that work? You just need to find the king and get him to pinkie swear? Doesn't sound so bad."

Hardly. There is not one king, but three—one for each of the Peoples. Nor will a simple vow suffice any longer. Were the Oath simply to be renewed, I would need only assemble the kings upon the mountain and have them re-say the words, but the Oath has not weakened—it has been broken. To remake it will require more than words.

Eliza paused, leaning heavily against a rock for a moment as a wave of dizziness washed over her from the exertion. She could feel her knees starting to quiver and it was getting harder to keep herself from stumbling and falling with each step. "How much further is it?" she asked. "I might actually be starving now."

I am not certain, Mardu thought back at her. *Scraw only sees memories from above, yet we are down here. It is perhaps three wing beats further. Continue alongside this brook. I believe we are almost there.* Eliza pushed off the rock and resumed lurching from one aching, stick-poked foot to the other. Odd to be so driven by mindless hunger when you're dead, isn't it? But she hadn't thought that thought in the part of her thinker that broadcast thoughts to her... thoughtbird?

Eliza shook her head to clear it. "Keep talking to me," she said. "Help me stay focused. You said you need more than words to fix the oath. What else? Fairy dust? A magic donut?"

Sacrifices, Mardu replied. *Each king must bring with him a member from his own household, to be sacrificed upon the Bloodcap. They will join with the Dragon, their blood mingled with his, and with the Mountain, and with the Forest. In this fusion, the Peace will be enjoined once more.*

Eliza stopped in mid-lurch. "What?" She turned to stare at the crow with open-mouthed disbelief. "You have to get three kings to kill off members of their own families? As in 'dead?' Like me? How are you going to get them to agree to that? Or can they just toss in a slave or pay some sick dude to stand in for cousin Wilbur?"

Not dead—enjoined. And no, there can be no substitutions. It must be blood of the House. Each royal is bound to their House, and each House to their Peoples, and so by enjoining the blood of the king, the Peoples themselves are bound together, each to the other and to this world as well. That is the foundation of the Peace.

"That is totally crap-side-up," Eliza said, then she turned away to resume her stumbling progress, still shaking her head at the strangeness of this... place.

There is one other difficulty, Mardu added, as she and the bird flapped forward once more to their next perch.

"What could possibly be more difficult than getting three powerful kings to drag off a sister or a nephew to be slaughtered?" Eliza asked.

Those who would be enjoined must go willingly.

Despite her exhaustion, Eliza laughed. "You people are crazy!" she said, although the laughing had brought back the dizziness and she clutched at the tree for support. "Do you really think that's going to happen? That people will go *willingly*? As *volunteers*? What idiot would sign up to be slaughtered on a mountain so that everyone *else* can live happily ever after?"

For a moment, not a sound could be heard. Even the crow was silent. And then a quiet voice spoke in Eliza's mind.

I did, Mardu said.

The silence continued for some time.

"I'll see you chopped and stacked for that," Mehklok hissed.

The offending tree did not reply.

It had taken him all morning to work up the courage to try climbing the miserable thing, but had this tower of splintery arrogance given him any consideration? Of course not. Instead, it had shown gall enough to give way under his scrabbling feet when he had most needed its support, and dropped him to the ground without out the slightest bit of regard for his station. It was clearly nothing but an ignorant, ill-tempered tree.

The Gnome chaplain picked himself up and brushed bits of leaf and bark from his clothing. As he picked at the pieces tangled in his hair, he whimpered quietly at the little flares of pain burning down the long, continuous scrape that now decorated his left arm. The Forest was just as he remembered it to be: chaotic and unpredictable. But as much as he ached to be back in his warm, damp hole in Gash-Garnok, this was clearly where that wretched witch woman had fled, and if he was going to recapture her and get her corpse back where he'd found it, he was just going to have to live with a few inconveniences. This whole situation was so unfair!

And to steal the marrow from an already softened bone, his head still hurt too. Not from the fall out of the tree–although that had certainly not helped matters any–but from the thumping the witch woman had given him the night before, when she'd spurned his hospitality and run off into the night. If anyone was to blame, it was her. If she had just taken the food and eaten it, he'd have had time to redisanimate her and then he could have taken her corpse back where he'd found it, with nobody the wiser. But no. She'd had to get selfish about the whole thing and make his life a complete shambles. So now here he was, dragging himself through this sky-cursed Forest, terrified and alone, exiled from his comfortable home and the seat of his authority back in Gash-Garnok. The sooner he found the woman and set her back to rights, the happier he'd be.

Mehklok stopped picking at himself and looked up. He still didn't know which way she'd gone from here. Which is why he'd been forced to climb the tree in the first place. Wasketchin though she may be, the woman left a big enough trail in the Forest for even him–a Gnome–to follow. But somehow, he'd still managed to lose her. He had hoped that a higher vantage point might reveal some clue about which way she had blundered next, but the trees were not cooperating, and there was no way he was going to risk his neck for an uppity corpse. If she wanted to be found and taken back to where she belonged, she was just going to have to show herself. Uttering a curse for all women and trees everywhere, the chaplain of Garnok's Rage picked himself up and marched off into the Forest.

In a random direction, just for spite.

The news that Mardu herself had volunteered for some kind of religious execution was a jolt to Eliza. Where do you go with information like that? *So, you were a teen-aged cult sacrifice, huh? That must have been fun. Is there a support group for that?* Between the sweeping waves of stomach cramps, and the whole trying-to-keep-her-feet-moving-in-the-same-direction-as-her-eyes thing, Eliza just couldn't wrap her head around the enormity of that news, so they proceeded in silence until they rounded a rocky jut and Mardu suddenly called out.

There! Ahead! The red bushes with the golden thorns. That is hiker-berry. You will be nourished by–

But Eliza was already lurching toward the hedge as fast as her zombie shuffle would carry her. Mardu had warned her about the sharp thorns, but Eliza only cared about the clusters of large, purple berries those thorns were supposed to protect. She grabbed convulsively at the first clump she saw, and by a small miracle, managed to avoid skewering her hand in the process. The berries were ripe and three came off the branch easily, which she quickly popped into her mouth.

"Oh my god!" Eliza groaned. Sweet juice ran around the inside of her mouth, lighting up her tongue with a gush of liquid happiness. "These are fabulous!" Eliza all but attacked the bush, yanking off berries as quickly as she could and stuffing them into her mouth. Somewhere along the way, she started chewing them too, and was rewarded with another surprise. "Hey! They've got chewy centers!"

Indeed, Mardu thought back in reply. *That is why they are prized by travelers.*

"Kack!" said Scraw.

Scraw complains that the berries are inedible to his kind.

"All the be'ffer me," Eliza said around a mouthful of berry pulp.

By the time she had filled the hole in her belly, Eliza had worked her way deep into the red foliage–almost to the point of popping out the far side–and she might have done so if she hadn't been startled by shouts of laughter coming from beyond the hedge.

Cautiously, Eliza peered out, keeping herself hidden behind a final screen of leaves and thorny branches.

There are people out there, she thought, forming the words carefully in her head in the hope that Mardu would hear her. The response was a quick fluttering of feathers from behind her that passed over her head. Scraw glided into her field of view and lit onto the lowest-hanging branch of a tree that stood part way between Eliza and the laughers.

Wasketchin boys, Mardu reported.

The boys seemed to be engaged in the sort of good-natured rough play that fascinated boys everywhere. There were four of them and they stood in a circle around a low-burning fire, pushing and swiping at each other playfully. To their right was a large, strange looking hut that appeared to be woven together from the branches of a ring of living trees. Two more boys emerged from the hut, each with an armload of some kind of dry, brown moss, which they heaped onto the fire, causing it to flare up. The group jabbered at each other rapidly in a language Eliza didn't recognize, but it was clear that their conversation was in keeping with the jesting nature of their behavior.

They discuss the work they are here to do, Mardu sent, *and which of them will finish his tasks first.*

Sounds like boys, Eliza thought back. *Talking about work and boasting about it instead of actually doing any. What kind of work?* Her stomach grumbled loudly just then, no doubt joyful at having work of its own to do again, but Eliza pulled back deeper into the hedge, just in case any of the boys had heard it.

They speak of this place as a rest area for travelers, Mardu replied. *Their work is to visit such places and see to their upkeep.*

And maybe to have a party, while they're at it, Eliza thought.

Well, they are *boys*, Mardu replied.

"K-k-k-keh!" laughed Scraw, who approved of any disparaging comments made about any creature. Crow humor.

Eliza watched the hi-jinx around the campfire for a while longer. In a way, the boys and their banter reminded her of working in the kitchen at the Old Shoe. These hut cleaners were a bit more boyish about it, of course, but they showed the same easy familiarity as they moved around the site, gathering wood, and doing a dozen other little tasks. This was more than just a randomly assembled work crew. These boys were friends.

Much of their activity centered on the shelter itself. One boy was threading the newly-grown shoots and leaves on the side of the hut back into its outermost layer of woven greenery. Two of the others carried large armloads of moss back inside, although Eliza hadn't seen where they'd gathered it from. Perhaps they were replacing the dried stuff they had pulled out earlier?

I wonder if that hut has a bed, she thought, half to herself and half to Mardu.

Such shelters are not familiar to me, but Scraw has seen people sleeping within them on low beds.

Sounds great, Eliza thought. *I wonder if they'd—*

Suddenly, the bush just to her left shook and before Eliza could react, a face appeared among the leaves, peering in at her, accompanied by a grunt of surprise.

Uh oh.

The boy turned to his friends and called out something that almost certainly meant, "Hey guys! Come see what I found," because a moment later, the entire group was hurrying over to the hiker-berry bush. The first boy was talking to Eliza excitedly, but he was of course speaking that weird language of theirs, so she had no idea what he was saying.

Um, Mardu? What's going on?

They are puzzled. That one wishes to know why you are hiding in the bush and watching them.

What am I supposed to say? "Take me to your leader?"

Eliza pulled her blanket more tightly around herself. Great. Boys. And me in my frumpiest blanket. The original boy and one of the others talked rapidly back and forth between themselves, and then the second one turned to her and held out his hand. He seemed to be inviting her to come out. Eliza took a tentative step forward.

This may be fortunate, Mardu sent. *Perhaps they will assist in restoring the Peace.*

No! Eliza thought, trying to keep the sudden panic from her eyes. *These are not your new suicide buddies! Let's just... Well, never mind. Time for Operation Pylon again. When you don't know what's going on, shut up and play stupid.*

The boys pulled the bushes back gently, and assisted Eliza by unsnagging her blanket and hair from the thorns for her as she stepped out of the bush. She gave them one of her best "pylon" smiles and waited to see what they would do next.

There is no time for wait and wonder, Mardu said, and then a rush of black wings hurtled toward her and settled onto her shoulder. Eliza felt the pinprick of crow talons biting through the fabric of her blanket as Scraw found his purchase, and she looked quickly at him before turning back to the startled expressions on the boys' faces.

Which was the perfect moment for Scraw to puff himself up and begin to speak. So he did.

"Bow down before me, for I am the Flame of the Dragon returned. By my will, the Oath of Kings shall be restored and all who oppose me shall fall." He spoke the words in the local language, but their meaning echoed in Eliza's mind, in English or brainspeak or whatever it was, courtesy of Mardu. All around her, jaws flopped open and the boys looked back and forth between her and the talking crow on her shoulder. Suddenly, the naked girl wrapped in a blanket had mojo.

It worked! Mardu sent, along with a giggle of happiness. *I wasn't sure I could make him talk, but it was actually pretty easy.*

Great, Eliza sent back. *But now what have you done? Look at them!* Judging from the look of fear on their faces, the boys clearly believed that *Eliza* was the Flame of the Dragon.

Oh, Mardu sent. *That could be a problem.*

You think? Eliza replied. But aloud she said nothing. She simply smiled her cryptic idiot smile and tried to look all-powerful at the same time.

Piece of cake.

Eliza fought down a growing need to run away. The boys pressed in around her, babbling and excited, asking questions and pointing at Scraw, but Mardu could not keep up with the translations and everything was a confused smear of noise. A lesser girl might have screamed like a crazy woman and run off into the Forest, but Eliza and Tayna had been staring down Goodies with their hearts pounding since before they were old enough to talk.

We need to leave now, she sent to Mardu. *They're excited and impressed, but if we hang around, I'll just become a girl with a talking bird.*

I am not sure they will let you leave, Mardu replied. *Will they not simply follow you?*

Eliza grinned mysteriously. *Not if we do this right. We need to put on a show. Stay ready. When I tell you, start translating exactly what I say.*

Eliza turned and plucked a large berry from the bush beside her and then she took a step forward, bringing herself face to face with the boy who seemed to be the leader of the group. Without breaking eye contact, she crushed the berry in the palm of her hand.

Now, Mardu.

At her shoulder, Scraw began to speak as Eliza reached toward the boy's face. *I mark you now as Embers of my Flame,* she sent. At her shoulder, Scraw repeated her words in the local language, giving them eerie weight with the harsh birdness of his voice. As the bird intoned her message, Eliza swiped sideways across the boy's eyes, leaving a thick smear of pulp and juice across them. *Your eyes are now mine,* she sent. *You see only for me.* The boy stood mesmerized as though he were hearing the words of the Dragon himself, instead of some frightened foreign chick just making stuff up out of desperation. She dipped her fingers back into the sticky mess in her hand and reached up again, this time drawing her fingers down in a line over his lips. *Your words are now mine,* she intoned through the crow. *You speak only for me.* Around them, the other boys had fallen into stunned silence, watching the ritual with apparent awe.

When she was done, and with Scraw's words still ringing in the air, Eliza turned and pulled five more berries from the shrub, which she then handed to each of the boys in turn

Each of you is mine. Bound to my will. Champion of my duty. Mark yourselves, as I have marked the first among you, and remain here. Think upon my words and make yourselves ready. In the morning, I shall return, and together we shall straighten the words that have been twisted. We are its Keepers, and together we shall restore the Oath of Kings.

Then, in as dignified a manner as she could muster with a crow bobbing around on her shoulder, Eliza strode away from the boys and off into the Forest. For a time, she didn't dare look back, for fear of breaking the spell her words had cast over them. She had seen it in their eyes when she'd handed them the berries. They were actually buying it.

That was most... dramatic, Mardu sent.

You think we got their attention? Eliza asked. She couldn't help but let a mental giggle follow the question.

"K-k-k-keh!" said Scraw. At least the crow thought it was funny.

chapter 8

"Return her to Abeni!"

Leaves tore at Tayna's face as she plunged through them, and the only thing between her and the crushing bounce below was the Wagon of Tears, which she still clung to with one hand as it pulled her down.

Below that, there was only Abeni. But why did he look so mad? And why was he throwing enormous tree trunks around? Like that one there, hurtling up toward her now.

If a tree trunk, A, leaves Methilien traveling straight up at a speed of twenty miles per hour, and a girl's head, B, falls from the sky at thirty miles an hour, how long until tree A intersects head B?

Answer: Right now.

Most people think that when you're knocked out by a blow to the head, you remain unconscious for a long time. Blame Hollywood. In movies, the hero is often out cold for hours or even days before waking up in all his groggy masculinity. Usually tied to a chair, or stuffed in the trunk of a car. But that's not how unconsciousness really works.

Tayna woke up just before she hit the ground.

More precisely, she woke up just as the Wagon thundered to the Forest floor below her. So she didn't so much hit the ground, as the Wagon. It turned out though, that this was probably the better option. When a bajillion-ton block of solid granite and precious metals plunges out of the sky into an overgrown forest, ground-zero tends to explode with little jagged knives of broken wood and rock. Luckily for her, Tayna landed–ribs first–across the upper row of sky tubes, as the Wagon teetered precariously to one side, and she was able to grab hold of those tubes before getting flung off into the brand new forest of wooden knives when the whole thing settled back onto its runners. Her entire side was on fire from the impact, but at least she was puncture-free. Probably. In the distance, she heard a tree trunk crash to the forest floor.

"Hit by the pitch. Walk your base," Tayna groaned, although judging by the look of him, Abeni didn't even realize that last throw had hit her. He was standing there in dazed silence, with his massive arms half curled at his sides, mouth open, and his chest heaving like the bellows of a forge. His eyes still had a sort of post-rage glaze that was only just beginning to cool enough for surprise to show through. Around him, the forest floor was torn up as though an enraged bull had been staked to that very spot.

Tayna took all of this in as she crawled her way gingerly to the end of the Wagon–the part that was *not* surrounded by sharpened death–and slid to the ground. She was woozy, but she'd be okay.

With one hand clutched across her torso, delicately probing her battered ribs, Tayna picked her way through the wreckage toward her friend. Had he been worried about her? "It's okay, Abeni. I mean, *I'm* okay." Her fingers found a very tender patch of skin. It felt scraped and raw. "At least, I think I am." She pulled back the edges of a tear in her kirfa, revealing an angry, red weal of skin inside. "Crap! I just healed all that!" she muttered. Then she turned to her large friend. "What do you think? Does this look okay?"

Abeni glanced at the wound, but he seemed to have more pressing concerns, glancing repeatedly at the sky above them. "The First Prince does not follow?"

"Who Angiron? I almost forgot about him," Tayna said, realizing with a start how long it seemed since she had escaped him. "No, I doubt he'll be coming that way," she said. "I don't think Yama will like him."

"The Judge of Changes?" Abeni asked, with a jerk of his head, seeming to see her, truly, for the first time. "What does the Little Fish know of that one?"

Now Tayna was confused. "Um, cranky looking Gnome guy? Face about this high off the ground?" She held her hand way up over her head. "Kinda hard to miss. Didn't he talk to you on your way through?"

"Abeni has heard stories of the Judge," he said. "But to see him? To share words? Even in stories, few have been given such an honor.

It has not happened for many years."

"So if you didn't see him and you didn't talk to him, what did you do?"

"Abeni does not understand. See when?"

"When you came through the wall. It took forever. You must have seen something. Did you at least get an in-flight movie or something?"

But Abeni was still shaking his head. "The Little Fish pushed Abeni, and he passed through the White Wall, where he fell to the ground. Here." The big Djin pointed at the torn up ground around his feet. "There was no 'movie.'"

Tayna pursed her lips. "No trial either, huh? And it was fast? No long pause, floating in his waiting room or anything?" Abeni cocked his head, perplexed. "Well, that's weird. Then you didn't get the explanation. That big wall we came through? According to Yama, the Dragon's Peace is more than just some magical law or a set of rules or something. It's an actual place too. This place." Tayna winced as she spread her arms to indicate the entire Forest around them.

"The Peace is every *thing* and every *place*–the Throat, the Forest, the Anvil–all of it. And that giant bubble thing is supposed to keep other things out. Bad things. Or maybe just things that don't play well with others. That's what the bubble wall is for. It's the Judgment. And he is too. I think maybe I was just seeing a sort of puppet show. I mean, a television in Methilien? That had to come from my brain, right? I know it sounds strange, but I think the Judge *is* the Wall. You need big magic just to push through it. But even that's not enough. You also have to get past the him part. Apparently he let you through without a fuss, but for me, he wasn't so sure, so that's probably why I got the full treatment."

"So the Little Fish believes now as Abeni does? That she has power?"

Tayna sighed. "People keep telling me I've got game, magic-wise. Maybe they're right. After all, we didn't have any trouble getting through the Wall, and that's supposed to be hard, right? And I was able to heal all my bruises pretty quickly, once Yama showed me how." She looked down at her hands and feet, as though trying to convince herself that it had really happened. Abeni looked as well, and seemed almost amused by this new revelation.

"The Little Fish has too many surprises for Abeni," he announced. "We must speak with Kijamon. He will know what to do."

Tayna sighed in delight at the very thought. "Oh, that would be awesome," she said. "I'd love to meet somebody who knew what was going on that wasn't also trying to kill me."

Abeni laughed with her at that, but beneath their moment of humor, there was a note of unspoken tension that neither of them wanted to think about. They were still miles from home, with a forest and a mountain yet to conquer.

And if history was any indication, the future of their journey would be no easier than its past.

Eventually though, there wasn't much more they could discover about the Judge, and they had a more pressing problem. When the Wagon had come through, it had emerged twenty or thirty feet above the Forest floor. Voila! Instant Wagon-bomb. Surprisingly, the Wagon itself hadn't been damaged in the fall, but the Forest around it was a different story, and the great granite sledge now sat neatly trapped inside a spray of broken tree trunks, branches, torn earth, heaved rocks and general carnage. It was a mess, and Tayna could only watch helplessly as Abeni tried and tried to chant the Wagon high enough into the air to free it from its accidental cage.

Tayna wanted to help Abeni as he wrestled with that puzzle, but she knew nothing practical about Wagon operations, and even less about charm songs. And there was another puzzle that kept teasing at her, drawing her attention away from his efforts. Why had they come through the wall so high above the ground? They'd been standing on the ground on the other side. What was the point of the Wall teleporting them up into the air when they came through?

It was Abeni who figured it out though, when she mentioned her puzzle to him during a break in his own efforts.

"The snow is too deep," he said. Tayna looked at him for an explanation, and Abeni shrugged. "For millennia, the winds have blown across the Cold Shoulder," he said, "moving the snows from place to place, sculpting great drifts and deep chasms. Perhaps the snow has become very, very deep against the Great Wall."

As soon as he said it, Tayna felt stupid. Of course that was it! When she'd pushed Abeni–and then the Wagon–through the bubble, she hadn't been pushing them through a door on the ground floor–she'd pushed them through an upper-story window, high on the side of the dome. It was a wonder she hadn't killed them both!

"Um, sorry about that," she said, turning away to hide her sudden embarrassment. Stupid, stupid, stupid! But Abeni laughed loudly.

"The Little Fish is displeased." he said. "She rescues the Wagon and Abeni from the King of Gnomes, and then is angry that she was not more gentle."

Tayna locked eyes with him for a moment, but a sheepish smile soon reddened her face. "Okay, I get it," she said. "Stupid, yes, but I couldn't have known, so 'yay me,' I guess." Abeni's scowl did not soften though, and after another long moment of trying to avoid his gaze, Tayna sighed and threw her hands up.

"Okay, I get it! Really!" she said. This time Abeni's glare evaporated as though it had never been there, and he nodded happily. "I just don't like making mistakes like that. What if we'd been a hundred feet up?"

Abeni shrugged. "Then Abeni and the Little Fish would be dead," he said. "In battle there is always risk." And it really did seem to be just that simple to him.

Tayna watched as he went back to examine the Wagon, and she wondered how he did that. How could he just shrug and accept the fact that something he said or something he decided might just get him killed? Or her? How could you know that and not lose sleep over it?

But as perplexing as that was, she was beginning to run in circles around it, making herself dizzy without actually getting anywhere. Much like Abeni with the trapped Wagon. She'd watched him try over and over again, but he couldn't raise it high enough to get past the shattered stumps and branches. Tayna shook herself clear of her own mental merry-go-round, and decided it was time to try something different.

"Hey, Great Whale! Come sit down for a minute, would you? Watching you try not to get smashed into jello is giving me a headache."

Abeni could walk for days, singing the Wagon into the air and leading it across frozen wastelands without missing a step or even breathing hard. But there's something about frustration that just kicks the joy out of any half-wise competent person–Djin or otherwise–and the Abeni that surrendered and came over to sit beside her now was as worn and bedraggled as she had ever seen him. He was silent as he rolled a shattered stump over to point its dangerous shards down into the soil, and sat carefully on the safer end.

"Remember what you said the other day? After the fire trap?" Tayna said. "About me maybe having 'Little Fish' magic?" Abeni raised an eyebrow. "Well, I've never really wanted to be special, you know? I'm just a kid, and all I've ever really wanted was to be allowed to *be* a kid. Just an everyday, ordinary freak of a kid."

Abeni frowned. "The Little Fish is many wonderful things," he said. "But she is not to use this word: 'ordinary.' It is a lie. Abeni forbids it."

Tayna laughed. "Well, that's kind of what I'm talking about. See, what I mean is, I've always *wanted* to be ordinary, but that doesn't really seem to be in my cards, does it?"

"So what has the Little Fish decided?"

Tayna looked up at her big friend, and took a deep breath. "Well, this Little Fish has decided that maybe it's time to see just how not normal she can be. Wanna help?"

Abeni's face broke into a matching smile. "Indeed, Abeni would enjoy such a thing."

Tayna got up, wincing from the tightness that had gathered along her ribs as she'd been sitting, and picked her way carefully toward the jagged wooden cage that held the Wagon. She waved for Abeni to join her.

"I've been thinking about what happened back there with creepy boy, and then again with the Judge. I guess it's kind of hard for me to keep saying I don't have any power, huh? Maybe I do have something. And if I do, then I guess I'd better start figuring out how it works."

But if she was expecting Abeni to be surprised, or suspicious about her change of heart, she was disappointed.

"Abeni agrees with the Little Fish," he said. "Let us begin." Then he stood up and offered her his hand. "What will she do?"

Tayna took his hand and let him help her down the slivery slope of broken tree parts, and together they made their way through the last of the shattered wood to stand beside the Wagon.

"Well, it was actually pretty easy the other times," she said. "I just kind of reached out and grabbed it, like a battery. And then I could do stuff." Abeni gestured at the Wagon, encouraging her to try.

"But what if I break it?" she asked. There weren't many things she could imagine herself doing that would make Abeni angry, but if she accidentally snapped the Wagon of Tears in half, that might be one. Abeni however, just laughed, and spread his arms wide.

"The Wagon has fallen from a great height upon many trees and rocks, causing much damage," he said. "Yet even now, it is unmarked. Abeni does not think the Little Fish can do any greater harm."

Reassured by his vote of confidence, Tayna closed her eyes and concentrated. She found that place of calmness within herself, and then reached out from within, feeling for the power.

But she couldn't find it.

She opened her eyes and looked around, as though she might be able to actually *see* what was different, but it wasn't as though there was a giant electrical switch she could find that was inexplicably set to the off position. After a moment, she closed her eyes again. Concentrate! It was so easy earlier!

The world fell away, and Tayna could feel the wholeness of existence all around her. She could sense the broken bits of wood and stone. She could feel the heavy presence of the Wagon. She could even feel the eternal, heavy silence of the trees surrounding her, their ancient roots questing deep into the soil, and the rocks below that, thrusting even deeper down, connecting with the very core of the world.

"Aw, gimme a break!" she muttered, shaking her head in frustration. "Now suddenly I get nothing?" She opened her eyes. Abeni was still standing there, watching her intently.

"Before, it was just like breathing, or floating in water," she said. "I didn't have to concentrate, or make up fairy tales in my head about it. I just did it. I felt for it, found the power, grabbed it, and used it. Easy peasy!"

"And now?"

"And now, nothing!" she said. "It's like the power's turned off. Brownout in sector three. Emergency crews are working round the clock to bring you a better tomorrow today. But still, bupkiss!"

Abeni took a step forward and placed a consoling hand on her shoulder. "Perhaps the Little Fish does not yet understand her gift," he said. "Abeni will show her the chant. Then perhaps the Little

Fish can build upon that." With that, he tipped his head back and splashing music, wet and bubbly, erupted from his throat.

The Wagon shot up into the sky and vanished.

Getting the Wagon to come back down turned out to be easier than they'd expected–just a simple matter of modifying Abeni's chant. Instead of urging the Wagon to strain against the bonds of gravity as he had been doing, Abeni sang more about floating at a digni-fied height, above the heads of the Warders, but not so high that it couldn't be seen. A few moments later, the Wagon settled back down and did just that, although the two friends were rather shaken by the experience. With a single glance, they reached a silent agree-ment. They were not going to talk about this just yet. They each needed time to process what had happened.

So instead, they had a spirited debate about the best way to pro-ceed from here. Abeni wanted to travel in the usual manner, with himself serving as both Way Finder and Way Chanter, and with Tayna filling in as Way Maker. It would be difficult, he admitted. Tayna had no whip, so she would have to be nimble, darting ahead quickly to clear their path by hand, and perhaps this would cause her to get in his way from time to time, but if they took their time, and coordinated their efforts, he didn't think it would be too bad–provided the Wagon would allow her to help at all, of course, since she was not of the Djin nor had she been properly bonded to its service. And even if the Wagon would let her help, she would of course have to stop helping when they reached the Anvil, for fear of offending any of the more traditional Djin they might encounter on the steep mountain paths. And true, climbing a mountain with an untrained Warder would present challenges as well, Abeni acknowl-edged, but if Sarqi and Zimu could come down the mountain while in a great hurry, Abeni saw no reason why he should not be able to manage the upward trek, so long as they held to a cautious pace and the forces of randomness chose to be kind.

Tayna wanted to fly.

In the end, they settled on a compromise. Abeni was forced to admit that floating the Wagon above the trees would eliminate almost all of the twisting and turning that usually made Way Chant-ing such a demanding task. With no obstacles to navigate the

Wagon's bulk around, his job would become almost easy, except for the matter of seeing where his feet were going while he kept his wary eyes on that bajillion-ton granite death threat hovering over their heads.

The other problem was how the two of them could maintain skin contact throughout the journey. Several quick experiments suggested that Abeni's sudden ability to fire Wagons into the sun had something to do with the two of them actually touching one another. He was still able to raise the Wagon much higher than normal if they merely stood near one another, but his power wavered unpredictably, as their natural movements shuffled them apart or brought them closer together. Under these conditions, it was almost impossible for Abeni to maintain control. And if there was more than a few yards separating them, then he might just as well have been Chanting on his own. They needed to find a way to stay in physical contact as they marched.

Tayna solved both issue in one step. "With you looking up at the sky all the time, you're pretty much blind," she said. "So I'll just have to be your seeing-eye fish."

It worked beautifully. Tayna stood in front, while Abeni laid one enormous hand across the back of her neck. This way, she could guide him by simply walking, and it allowed Abeni to steer her too, as necessary, with nothing more than a gentle turn of his hand. Their essential communication could be completely silent.

Once they had worked all of this out and practiced it to Abeni's satisfaction, there was nothing left to do but loft the Wagon up into the air and get moving.

So they did.

chapter 9

The Flame Gang, as Eliza now thought of herself and her two-companions-in-one, walked on for a little while–just far enough to discourage any of the boys from coming to find the Flame of the Dragon. She wasn't ready to talk to them yet. And besides, she and Mardu needed time to figure out their next step. And if she was lucky, maybe some down time would give her the chance to find out what the hell was going on.

After a ten minute hike, more or less following the stream, Eliza still wasn't sure they'd gone far enough, but the shadows were now joining hands into actual darkness, and Mardu urged her to find somewhere to sleep. *A tree would be best, but we won't be able to find one in full darkness.*

Sleep in a tree? What, so I can fall out and kill myself? Then what will happen to your Dragon's Peace?

You will not fall if you choose the proper tree, Mardu replied. *I will show you.*

And to Eliza's surprise, she did. Sooner than she'd thought possible, Scraw had found her a tree with two adjacent branches that spread apart above a third, creating a secure bed pocket with a solid floor and walls and everything. After a short, easy climb, Eliza nestled herself down into the cozy little nook, hardly able to believe that she was ten or fifteen feet above the forest floor. It wasn't as comfortable as an actual mattress, of course, but she was young, and where an older person's bones might have felt pressed and uncomfortable, Eliza found that she conformed rather easily into the contours of her makeshift bed, and so she did her best to arrange her stupid blanket robe thing around her. Tomorrow she definitely had to find some clothes that she did not have to hold tightly with both hands to stay decent.

Once she was settled, Scraw flitted up higher into the tree, seek-ing the shelter of leaves, hiding himself from whatever it was that crows feared, and of course, Mardu went with him. Eliza closed her eyes, but even though she was tired, a troubling memory bubbled just behind her consciousness, and it held her up, not letting her drift down into sleep. After a few minutes of trying, and failing, she gave up.

Mardu? What you said earlier, before things got crazy back there... Did you really volunteer as a sacrifice?

For a moment, there was no answer, but then Mardu replied. Her mind-voice was quiet, halting. As though the memory disturbed her.

Long ago, yes. I was one of three. Sacrificed to enjoin the Oath. My father was Notawhey, King of the Wasketchin.

So you were, like, an actual princess? And you just volunteered to be his scape-girl?

No! Eliza could feel a wave of outrage flowing back through their connection. *You know nothing of the time I come from! My father was a great and just man. He did not manipulate me like some goat being led to slaughter. The choice was mine!*

I'm sorry, Eliza replied. *But I just don't get it. Why would you volunteer for something like that? Didn't you want to live?* Eliza worried that maybe she had offended her new companion, but then she heard—or rather felt—a sigh in her mind, and the anger seemed to leak away with it.

The world was not as you see it now, Mardu said. *Today it is peaceful and green... In the time of my walking, every day was a day of war and hardship. The Miseratu preyed upon our people, feeding themselves from our fears. The water sprites, with their tricks and illusions, owned the low, damp places. Kalupliks stole our children along the banks of the rivers, and the enormous xiucatl serpents would swallow entire families, whole.*

And always, there were the Dragons. To carry the bone of such a one was a prize beyond measuring. With such magic, one could stand against a hundred sprites or a thousand 'pliks, and suffer not a scratch. But even a Dragon's magic does not survive long after its body dies, and so always our hunters quested for another. Each clan contested with the other, and Peoples fought against Peoples, seeking the nesting ground or feeding pasture of another of the great beasts, so that they could bring back more bones or scales of another Dragon, and thus live in quiet once again, sheltered from the constant battling for a time. But the Dragons did not die willingly for our moments of calm. They fought us in every corner, wreaking havoc and destruction upon the Peoples at every turn. All was hardship and grief.

Then, upon one unexpected summer, the last remaining two turned upon each other. For days they fought until, in the end, the Dragon Grimorl fled the land, and only a single member of his kind remained. His brother, the Dragon Methilien. The largest and greatest of them all. Should Methilien ever die, there would be no other. No more scales or bones. No tooth or spine plate. No dragon-vim anywhere with which to stave off the predations of the other kinds.

It was my father who summoned the kings together to devise a plan. They must unite, he told them, and find some way to preserve this last Dragon, or all the Peoples might perish before the spring. But the other kings mocked my father. They thought him a fool, and they would take no part in his soft ploys, believing he meant to trick them from this greatest prize of all. So my father went alone into the forest, and put his question to the trees. Would Methilien come to parlay, that they might find a solution to the ever-turning wheel of battle, death, and vengeance?

To his astonishment, the Dragon came.

When my father returned from the forest, he was ablaze with his new purpose, for he and the Dragon had fashioned a plan. And what a plan it was! The Dragon no more wished to fight or to die than did my father, or any other. Together they had agreed that the Wasketchin would hunt him no more, nor permit others to do so. In return, the Dragon would cease his offenses against the Wasketchin, and against any other Peoples who would join their pledge.

And more, the Dragon would employ his magic to create for them all a realm of peace, where any Peoples who would take the Oath might dwell in comfort, as brother races. But to work this magic, the Dragon would have to spend all the vim within him. For a time after, he would be as weak as a babe. So he required three conditions of my father. First, that it was not enough for the Peoples to simply promise *to walk the paths of peace. He required that they must be enjoined to that promise, by the very magic that created their new realm, and that with the crowning of each new king, the pledge must be renewed by all. Second, that all creatures who did not take up the Oath with them must be banished from the realm, never to return. And third, that there be none remaining who were not enjoined. To do this, the Dragon required that the blood of each royal house be spilled in sacrifice, binding each and every person to the Oath through the vows they had already sworn to their kings.*

In addition to the peace so established, the Dragon further pledged that in time, when his vim had returned to him, he would spread it upon the waters and the rivers of the new realm, gifting it to the Peoples, so that with it they might hasten the creation of their new world of peace, and that, for so long as he yet lived, they might all enjoy the uses his magic might bring them.

So tell me, friend Eliza. I was oldest of my siblings, fated to be queen in my time. But a queen of what? Of hardship? Of scarcity and predation? In a world so filled with death and strife, how long might I have lived? A year? A decade? You simply cannot know, but to be offered such a chance, so simple a path for peace and happiness, with so much good to be gained and so much ill to be lost? How could a queen—how could I—do anything other than step forward? It was my duty, and I gave my blood—and my life—willingly.

Tears ran down Eliza's face as she lay there in the darkness. She hadn't just heard the words. She had seen them. Somehow, Mardu's memories of the horrors her world had faced had come through the link they shared, and for a few moments, Eliza had been there. She had seen the broken warriors dragged home by their defeated brothers. She had felt the cavernous grief of a mother whose child had been taken in the night. And then she had shared in Mardu's relief too. After so much pain, to be able to actually do something about it. She'd felt the fierce pride—the honor—of those final words. "How could I do anything other than step forward?" The simple humanity of those words, and the feelings that had accompanied them, left Eliza in awe.

I'm sorry, she sent. *I had no idea.*

But now some viper of a Gnome f'znat digs his fetid claws into my Dragon Lord and threatens to return our realm to those very horrors that were only narrowly averted? He seeks to gorge himself on the corpse of the peace I purchased with my very life's blood? I don't think so, sister!

As impressed as she was by the righteous anger of a queen whose people had been threatened, Eliza couldn't help but giggle just the same. *'I don't think so, sister?' How can you sound like a raging queen* and *an outraged chica, all at the same time?*

Because I am both? Mardu suggested.

Eliza sent a grin of companionable sisterhood back across the link. This was getting weird, and complicated, but for the first time since awaking in this strange afterlife, she wondered if maybe her problems weren't the biggest ones on the block. With that thought to guide her, Eliza wriggled one last time to get comfortable, and drifted off to sleep.

It was some hours later when the sounds of shuffling and muttering in the darkness awakened her. The boys. How stupid did they think she was? No doubt they were rooting around in the darkness, searching for her with a bag full of questions that simply wouldn't keep until morning. Well, maybe she didn't have any answers for them yet, and since she was pretty sure they couldn't see her in her hidey-hole from down below, she decided to just let them keep looking, so she lay there, silent in her tree-loft bed as they passed by right below her, never even thinking to look up.

Boys! Could they get any dimmer?

When the sounds of their shuffling moved on, back toward their camp, Eliza smiled to herself in satisfaction and went back to sleep.

Mehklok hid beneath a log and whimpered. All around him, the forest was making noises. Each was no doubt a creature waiting to kill him.

He'd been tracking the witch woman for days, and though he hadn't caught an actual glimpse of her, he knew the trail was hers. He could still taste the otherly tang of tiny decay that she left on the rocks and branches as she brushed past them. It's what drew him on, this certitude that he had not yet lost her, that there was still hope of getting her corpse back to where he had found it before its owner learned of his involvement.

Each morning he arose before the sun, drained and exhausted, to resume his search. And each evening, he pressed on as late into the darkness as his imagination would allow. But inevitably, the light would fail once more, and with it, the crackles and snaps, the chirrups and twitters, the burbles and croaks of the forest grew louder and louder in his mind, until each of them was a crouching... something, lying in wait behind the very next tree–and the tree behind him, too–freezing him in terror to the spot on which he stood, leaving him no choice but to sink to his haunches on the disgusting, dry soil and cover his head with his arms, quaking in fear against the night.

So this was how she had brought low the Chaplain of Garnok's

Rage. This was how she forced him to spend the restful hours of his nights. Not nestled deep in a damp hole, as he should be, surrounded by his familiar comforts, but out here in the night air of a foreign land, eyes wide with fear, throat closed with terror, crouching under whatever bugless shrub or life-starved log happened to be nearest when the sounds of the forest overwhelmed him. Unable to sleep. Unable to go home. Waiting for the snarl and the teeth that would end his journey.

What was that?

Eliza came awake in alarm. A short, sharp cry in her dream had awakened her. At least, she thought it had been in her dream, but it had been so brief that she couldn't be sure, so she lay there, listening intently for any echos that might tell her if the cry had come from her dream world, or from this nightmare world she actually seemed to be living in.

But there was nothing. It had been just a dream sound after all. She was just drifting back to sleep when her alerted ears caught a different noise. Eliza groaned. Singing? Really? At this time of night? What is wrong with these guys? Don't they have like, jobs in the morning? More huts to fix, or something?

She tried to shut their stupid antics out of her ears and thoughts, but everything else in this world was stupid, so why should their music be any different? The song had some strange, unfamiliar melody. Alien. As though they didn't even use the same sounds as real music. She couldn't make the words out at all, not that she'd have understood them, even if she could, but the chant's awkward, staggering rhythm tugged at her awareness, teasing her back from the edge of sleep each time she neared it.

To make things worse, she couldn't help but notice how badly voiced it was too. Full of screeching and barking, like a chorus of bats and wolves fraying at the tatters of night. The she realized what was happening. They were actually baiting her. They'd searched for her earlier and when they hadn't found her, they'd decided to annoy her awake. Make her angry so that she'd come back sooner than she'd said. And it was working. Frustration building, Eliza squirmed herself into a sitting position.

This was totally bogus! Were they really that selfish? Hadn't they seen how tired she was? What is it with boys? Why can't they just accept when they lose a battle of wits and let it be? Eliza swore under her breath and rolled out of the tree, lowering herself down to the ground in silence. The singing stopped soon after she let go of the branch. No doubt they planned to deny that there had been any singing at all, but it was too late. Hardly adults, these were clearly still *little* boys, and they were going to hear a thing or two about proper behavior, whether they wanted to hear it or not.

We're returning now? Mardu asked over their link.

I'll be back in a minute. Just some juveniles who need a good yelling at, Eliza replied.

Then perhaps your yelling parts should come with you, Mardu said, as she and Scraw flapped out of the tree tops and descended to their place on Eliza's shoulder.

"Good point," Eliza muttered, as she stormed through the trees, her temper rising rapidly as she marched back to the boys' camp. She knew where it was, and went directly toward it, through the trees, rather than going back to follow the stream.

And that's what saved her.

She was almost on top of the Gnome sentry before she even knew he was there. Had she been following the stream, she'd have been spotted easily, out on its open, mossy bank. But in the shadows of the trees, Eliza was nearly invisible as she drew herself to a sudden halt and held her breath when the sentry appeared suddenly in the darkness ahead of her.

A Gnome! Mardu cried out, over their link. *Hide! The Gnomes and the Wasketchin are at war! If he sees you he will attack!*

The Gnome looked around with darting movements of his eyes and head. Eliza froze and watched him from scarcely ten feet away. Even without Mardu's warning, terror crept its way up from her stomach, with its own grim reminder. The last Gnome she had seen had tried to kill her in some underground perv lair. What would this guy do if he saw her? She did not want to find out. Had he heard her approach? His eyes darted left and right as she watched him, but he did not pause when he glanced in her direction. Then he looked straight back toward the fire at the camp site, probably ruining any night vision he might have had in the process. Eliza thanked herself for her luck and slowly crouched down, sidling sideways as she did so, inching herself silently toward the deeper shadow of the large tree that stood off to her left. Scraw seemed to understand the situation, and clung to her shoulder as best he could, without a flutter or a squawk as her movements threatened to shake him free. Eliza kept her eyes on the Gnome as she made her way toward cover, but his gaze did not track with her. It seemed she had not been discovered.

Once she got behind the tree, Eliza leaned heavily against it, sucking air in and out, trying to calm her thumping heart. She pulled the blanket up higher, tugging its loose end up over her head, seeking its shadows to hide her face. And then a horrible thought occurred to her. The boys! What had happened to them? Eliza inched around her tree and risked a peek, but there was little she could see.

The Gnome guard appeared to have moved off, but how long would he be gone? *Wait here,* she said, meaning both Scraw and Mardu. *I may need backup.* Once the crow had stepped quietly off her shoulder, onto the branch beside her, Eliza sucked her courage up into her lungs and ventured cautiously out from behind her dark shield tree.

Gnomes normally have excellent dark vision, Mardu cautioned.

Not when they're stupid, Eliza replied. *This one kept looking back at the fire. I think he was scared.*

Eliza crept further forward, keeping her body low to the ground and her hood pulled down over her face. From her vantage, on the slope above the hut, she could see three Gnomes below her. Two were on watch, one upstream, to her right, the other downstream, back near the hiker-berries. The third stood at the stream bank, tying the boys together with a thin rope. But for some reason, they were happy to just stand there, with vacant expressions, allowing themselves to be bound.

Why are they cooperating? Why don't they run? Did they even put up a fight?

I do not know, Mardu replied. There was a quiet rustle of feathers and Eliza saw a dark shape flit down toward a tree near the bank.

It makes no sense, Mardu said. *They just stand together, waiting to be tied.*

When the Gnome had finished linking the boys, he wrapped the end of his rope around a branch–not even bothering to tie it–and then hobbled away toward the fire with his awkward Gnome-gait. Like the guard she had seen earlier, this one's eyes kept flicking about with apprehension, seemingly nervous of the leafy unknown beyond the reach of the fire's light.

What has happened to my people? Mardu asked. *Even when their captor's back is turned and his attention so obviously elsewhere, they do nothing. They simply stand, as though waiting to be led off to breakfast. Where are my mighty warriors?*

As much as Eliza hated to admit it, even boys were not *that* stupid. Somehow they must have been drugged into a stupor.

Maybe that's what happens when you give them a few thousand years of peace? Eliza asked.

No, Mardu replied. *Peaceful they have become, yes, but not sheep. They have been charmed.*

Great, drugged with magic, Eliza thought. *So they'll be no help at all. Not to us and not to themselves.* She rubbed at her arms in the chill night air. Her skin was still slightly sticky from the berry juice. She'd washed the worst of it off as she'd stormed away from the boys earlier, but she hadn't taken time for a full rinse, and she could only imagine that she still looked almost as scary as she had when she had first emerged from the hedge. Could she use that? Would she be able to frighten the guards for long enough? But long enough to do what? That slender thought of attacking died however, when a fourth Gnome emerged from the hut. Three? Maybe. If she was lucky. But four? Even at her most scary-looking, Eliza didn't like those odds.

This new Gnome carried something with him, but he stood in shadow and she couldn't make it out. A vaguely round shape, clutched tight under one arm. He shambled over to the fire and held a brief conversation with the rope-Gnome, who nodded in agreement. When the discussion was over, Eliza watched in confused silence as the junior Gnome snatched a burning branch from the fire and went over to the hut, where he set the flaming stick at the base of the dehn, next to the door, and walked away. Did he think he could burn it down? A living ring of trees? With a single, smoldering branch?

I do not know, Mardu replied. Eliza hadn't even realized she'd been sending.

Back at the fire, the fourth Gnome raised his round burden to the flames. It was a large container, she realized, as she caught a glimpse of firelight shining off it in winks. Metal of some kind. And polished. Then she recognized it. But how could that be? One of Regalia's urns? Here? After saluting the fire with his giant cup, the

Gnome brought it down and tipped his head back. He was drinking from it! Then he lowered the urn and turned to face the shelter, as he uttered a single snarling bark of a word.

Get down! Mardu shouted suddenly.

And the entire hut exploded in a concussion of flame.

———————

The burst of heat that erupted from the hut knocked Eliza to the ground. When she had scrambled back to her knees, she saw that one of the Gnomes had been caught off guard as well, and was now whimpering for help from the middle of the hiker-berries. But his companions did not go to his aid. Instead, they arranged themselves around the shuffling Wasketchin boys down by the stream, and with a tug on the rope to get them moving, marched their string of captives toward the blazing fire and the hill.

Toward her!

Little help? Eliza sent. *A distraction maybe?* But there was no response from Mardu. Had she been hurt in the explosion? But Eliza didn't have time to worry about Mardu right now. The Gnomes were still coming right at her. In a few seconds, they would pass the raging fire and begin to climb up the slope.

Hot yellow light bathed everything–the Gnomes, their captives, and even helpless Eliza, kneeling there in plain sight. The lead Gnome hadn't seen her yet, but surely even the slightest movement would draw his attention. She flicked her eyes–left, right, anywhere! But dammit, there wasn't so much as a stump to hide behind. If not for the dark blotchiness of her stained blanket and the fact that she was frozen motionless on her hands and knees, they'd have already seen her. She could already make out the soft downy hairs that covered the leader's face. The layer of fuzz glowed with reflected firelight in a golden halo that enveloped the great, flapping flesh-loaf of a nose that dominated his face. At any moment he was going to look up and see! His eyes would lock onto hers. . .

Remain calm. Think.

Mardu? Is that you? Again there was no reply.

But she was right. Eliza forced herself to breathe slowly and to think. Why hadn't the Gnome seen her already? The fire! It was in front of him, still searing his vision. But not for long. He was almost even with the hut now, and as soon as he passed it and put its flames behind him...

But she just could not bring herself to break cover and run. She just knelt there, facing downhill, her weight still carried on arms that quivered and shook with fear. She wanted to run. She *needed* to run. But she could not. Whimpering with mounting fear, Eliza watched and sobbed as the leader of the Gnome group advanced past the hut. Any second his eyes would adjust. Any moment his gaze would lock... But still she could not move. He was only twenty feet away.

Eliza's legs finally gave up waiting for orders from her brain, and slowly gathered themselves together beneath her, making ready to flee on their own. *Stop that!* she screamed at them inside her head. Crap oh crap oh crap! But it was too late. Already the leader's gaze was turning toward her, toward the movement of her legs.

"Scraw!" At that moment, a black shape spun crazily from the trees, out of control, and spiraled into the hiker-berries, more a desperate lurch and plummet than actual flight. An instant later, a high, watery screech rose from the berry hedge. A screech of Gnomish pain. All the Gnomes jerked around at the sound, and for a moment, Eliza looked that way too.

But her feet didn't.

They, at least, recognized this slender morsel of a chance, and before she could even murmur a silent thanks to her feathered friend, Eliza's body flung itself away toward the darkness. It took her brain a moment to realize that her body was now running away without her, and when she did, she wisely decided to join it, taking over the management job from her legs, calling in favors from her lungs and her arms and sprinting now with her entire body. Eliza flew across the face of the slope, crashing through the low ground cover, snapping twigs and branches, heedless of anything save the need to reach that nearest cluster of trees and the hallowed darkness they guarded behind them.

In her mind, she was as noisy as a nun falling down a flight of stairs, and she was certain that the Gnome leader would grunt out one of his spell-barks at any instant and set her ablaze, like the hut. But she heard nothing above the roar of the fire and the pitiful wailing of the injured Gnome in the berry hedge. No cries of alarm. No snarls of command. And thankfully, no shouts of recognition from the boys either.

At long last, after what felt like an hour of terror-propelled flight,

Eliza reached the cluster of trees and threw herself behind them, dropping to the ground in utter, exhausted surrender. If they had seen her, she was done. She was totally spent. Her lungs heaved in and out, clutching at the air in great sucking gasps. She strained her ears, trying to hear any pursuit, but all she heard was the hammering of her heart, the wheezing rasp of her lungs, and the steady, deeper roar of the flames.

Then she remembered her friends. *Scraw?* she thought.

We are safe, Mardu replied, and Eliza added a sigh of relief to the list of things she would do once she could breathe again.

For several long minutes, she just lay there, reveling in the relief of not being dead. After a time, when still no shouts of alarm had been raised, and no Gnomes had been sent to search among the trees, Eliza dared to push herself up and roll over. It was the hardest thing she had ever done, to lean her face out of the protective shadows and into the light of the fire. Hooded or not, she was sure she would be seen, certain that a Gnome face would snap at her the moment she looked around the trunk.

But there was nothing. To her left, at the top of the slope, she was just in time to see the back of the last Gnome as he disappeared over the top of the slope into darkness. At the base of the slope, the fire had exhausted most of its easy fuel, and the skeleton of the hut could now be seen through the smoke, black ribs, etched with embers of glowing orange. Beyond it, the hiker-berry bush looked as though it had been torn apart by wild animals. Apparently the Gnome who had been flung there had not wanted to be left behind.

Then it hit her. To her complete, and utter astonishment, they were alone. They were safe. "Hooray for us," she said weakly.

And then she began to shake.

Once the trembling had subsided to merely jackhammer levels, Eliza stood up and limped her way down to the stream. She needed to clean the cuts and scrapes on her arms and legs and her poor, bare feet. But when she got there, she was stopped short by a twisted shape lying across the rocks at the water's edge. Eliza swallowed hard. It was a body. She stood there for a moment, wondering what to do. Then finally, she sucked up her courage and took another step.

She could see the twist of a fabric-covered arm, and the swell of a hood. Whoever it was, he was turned face down. A strap trailed away from his leg and hung down into the water, twitching and tugging in the rippling current. Eliza took another step, peering through the pale moonlight. Scared to go closer, but scared not to, as well. What if he wasn't dead? But it could be a trap, too. Eliza took another step. And then she started to laugh.

It was somebody's laundry.

Three large pieces of cloth, freshly washed and laid out to dry. What she'd seen as an arm was in fact just an empty sleeve, and judging by the hoods and straps she could make out, it was probably a couple of the strange robes everyone seemed to wear around here. With a sudden giggle of relief, Eliza flung her tattered blanket aside and grabbed one of the garments. Now all she had to do was figure out how to get it on.

She was completely tangled in her unfamiliar new wardrobe when Mardu and the crow flapped down to join her, coming to rest on an old stump that jutted out over the water.

Eliza looked up and a more serious thought occurred to her. "We are going after them, right?"

To what hope? Scraw cocked his head in honest curiosity.

Eliza knew that it was really Mardu answering her, but it was still weird trying to match a crow's body language to the very human voice she heard in her head. "To rescue them, of course. I thought that part was obvious." She flipped a loose strap of fabric up over her shoulder, trying to decide if that's where it was supposed to go.

Scraw shook his entire body. *We cannot.*

Eliza stopped fiddling with the belt thing and looked up at him. "What do you mean, we 'cannot?' Of course we can. As soon as the sun is fully up, we march over that hill and go the same way they went. They're not exactly forest ninjas, you know. Even I can see that they leave a trail a blind man could follow, and this is the first time I've ever even been in a forest. We could *totally* do this."

Scraw stamped a foot and glared back. *Yet we will not,* Mardu said.

"But we bound them to your stupid mission! We *claimed* them! And you don't get do-overs on something like that. Where I come from, people like us stick together, because we're all we have. We don't turn our backs on each other, and that's what you're suggesting–turning our backs on them!"

You think I don't know that? You think I watched my father lead his warriors into battle after battle against Dragons and Miseratu and xiucatl and windigos and yet learned nothing about the duties of command? That I do not know how a general must love his warriors more dearly than his own eyes?

Eliza let out a deep sigh. "You're right," she said. "I forgot. I'm sorry." The memory of the horrors that Mardu had shared with her earlier came rushing back. Who was she to lecture a warrior queen on the etiquettes of leadership? "But do we really have to abandon them?"

Scraw looked down at the water and his shoulders slumped. *We must,* Mardu replied. *For now. Time is not our friend, Eliza. With every day, the Gnome King grows stronger and his enemies–our friends–grow weaker. We can risk no delays. We must find stronger allies if we are to change the flow of history. And we must find them quickly.*

"So how do we do that?"

Well, on this point, at least, I have a thought.

"K-k-k-keh!" Scraw laughed.

Eliza didn't like the sound of that.

But first, let me explain the kirfa. You have it on upside down.

Eliza groaned and let the stupid fabric pool around her knees. "I'm all yours," she said, and then a shudder of realization trembled through her. *I am so totally and helplessly yours.*

chapter 10

Djin adventurers do not use maps. They discover the way to all the places of the Forest by smell and by feel. They learn to recognize the shape of the land as one trail wends into a particular village, or the way a river skirts past an especially welcoming homestead. But with the job of both Way Finder and Chanter falling to him, and with the ominous presence of the Wagon now hanging above them as well, Abeni had little time to look around.

"We're lost, aren't we?"

It was late morning of the day after they'd left the Wagon crater. The two travelers were sitting at the side of a stream they had just forded, and Abeni was busying himself over a small fire. The Wagon stood on its runners at the crest of the river bank nearby.

"Abeni is not lost," he said, as he raised one powerful arm to point off into the trees, without even turning his head from whatever he was doing among the embers of his fire. "The Anvil is there," he said. "Two days' journey from this place. No more." But the tree cover was too thick for Tayna to confirm this.

They'd had glimpses of the Anvil, of course, and the Wagon had always seemed to be pointed straight at it when they had, but as far as she could tell, they didn't always seem to be walking straight toward it. For some reason, Abeni was leading her along an almost drunken zig-zag path.

"So why are we wandering back and forth then?"

Abeni pulled two small bowls from the fire and set them on the ground to cool. At their first stop, he had surprised her by digging into a muddy bank with his hands and pulling out a sticky wad of clay, which he had then fashioned into bowls and baked in their camp fire. Later that day, he had paused their journey in mid-chant to collect roots and leaves and bark, which he had then placed into the Wagon's tailbox with some obvious delight, but again he had answered all her questions with silence and a sly smile. But now

JEFFERSON SMITH

she caught a faint scent on the air and her face brightened with delight.

"Boh-cho! You're making boh-cho!" And before Abeni could even nod, Tayna snatched up one of the bowls and held it to her face with both hands, savoring the spicy aroma of the Djin traveler's brew.

There had been some roasted beet-like things, on the first day, and the two of them had eaten their fill of the tough little roots, breaking the long fast that had been forced on them by the Cold Shoulder, and there had been a thin leafy soup before sleep that night. But as nutritious and healthy as their diet had become, this was more than just nutrition and eight essential vitamins. This was boh-cho! And boh-cho was... civilized. Boh-cho meant they were okay. Boh-cho meant they were going to make it.

Tayna took a sip from her mug, and all the good things of the world slipped back into place, radiating outward in soothing waves from wherever the rich flavor touched her tongue.

They were only half-way through their mugs when they heard something–or someone–crashing through the bushes beyond the Wagon.

"There's somebody there," Tayna said, setting her bowl down and standing up to peer into the Forest. "Friend or foe? What do you think?"

Abeni moved to stand beside her, placing one hand protectively on her shoulder. "Abeni does not know," he said, drawing her back from whatever had made the sound. "It cannot be him. Not so quickly. But the Little Fish must wait here. Abeni will learn more." Then he dropped into a crouch and sidled his way past the Wagon, vanishing from her sight.

A few minutes later, Tayna heard more thrashing of bushes. And then a voice. "Who's there? I warn you, come no closer! I'm, uh, very sick. My brother... no, my entire family has died from it. I'll bet I'm going to die of it myself, very soon now. You'd best move on."

A Wasketchin. Then she heard Abeni. "What sickness?" But Tayna just rolled her eyes.

"He's a horrible liar!" she called out. "There is no sickness. He just wants you to leave him alone." By that time, Tayna had rounded the Wagon and could see Abeni's large back, jutting up out of a clump of merlhora shrubs, just beyond a line of trees. When she

115

got closer, she could see a slender Wasketchin man, cowering at the Djin's feet.

"Greetings, cousin," she said with a wave as she pushed her way into the shrubbery to join them. The man's eyes were wide with fright, but he seemed to relax slightly when he saw her.

"Don't mind my friend here," Tayna said, soothingly. "We're not going to hurt you. We just, uh, heard you moving through the trees and thought we'd come say hello. Maybe exchange news?"

The stranger did not seem mollified at all by her explanation, but when Abeni did not immediately attack, he at least paused in his efforts to scramble away.

"Who are you?" he asked, with a trembling voice. "What do you want? I have nothing of value." Then he coughed very unconvincingly into his hand. "And I told you, I'm very sick."

Tayna smiled. "Cousin, where I come from, even the preschoolers are better actors. You need a lot more practice. But really, we aren't going to hurt you. What are you afraid of?"

The man looked back and forth between Tayna and Abeni, as though trying to decide whether she was lying or just stupid. "You mean, you haven't heard? There's a war on! The Horde is everywhere! They're rounding people up and taking them back to the Throat to roast them and eat them whole!" When they just looked at him blankly, he waved his arms wildly.

"Have you not heard? The King has told everyone to flee! We're to seek shelter atop the Spine. It's our only hope!" Then he looked nervously past them, as though expecting a Gnome to leap out of Tayna's kirfa and throttle them all with his bare hands. Tayna and Abeni both turned to see what he was looking at, but when they turned back, the man was racing away through the trees. "Get yourselves to safety!" he called back over his shoulder.

And then he was gone.

"Well," Tayna said, as she gazed at the spot where the man had vanished. "That was weird."

"Truly," Abeni agreed, but he stared for a long time into the deeper dark of the Forest before he finally turned back to Tayna.

"Abeni thinks perhaps things have changed for the Wasketchin people since the Little Fish left them."

"You think?" she asked, as they left the shrubs and went back to their fire.

At that point, they still had no idea how right Abeni was.

Twice more they encountered refugees. One, a group of frightened children hiding in some bushes, and then shortly after that, they came upon a pair of old women helping each other through the trees. The women confirmed that yes, Malkior had sent word to abandon the dehns and villages. There was just no way to defend so many people spread so thinly. The King and Queen were moving the Court to the Spinetop and urged everyone to join them there. With one end protected by a narrow stairway up a sheer cliff, and the other end in Djin territory, they hoped it would be enough to hold the Gnomes at bay.

And that was where the women were heading. They knew they would never be able to climb the Zalmin Stair that guarded the southern end, so they were making for the north end. While the path that led to the Djin Plateau was uphill, it was not treacherous, and they were sure they would arrive in good time.

When they parted, Tayna was relieved that the children had asked if they could go with the old women instead. Even though he was a Djin, and not a Gnome, the kids were now scared of all strangers, and kept cringing from Abeni with undisguised suspicion. The two old ladies were not much pleased at the thought of caring for young folk, but at least they'd have some help with the more difficult terrain ahead. The last Tayna saw of them was a pair of hunched old backs hobbling off into the trees, waving their walking sticks in the air and shouting for the kids to slow down.

"Djin Forest?" Tayna asked, after the ladies had disappeared.

"The Plateau of the Anvil," Abeni replied. "A raised land, higher than the Wasketchin lands, but still richly forested." He waved his arms around, gesturing at the trees around them.

"What, you mean we're already there?"

"Indeed," Abeni said, with a laugh. "Does the Little Fish not see how much taller and more colorful the trees have become?"

Now that they had reached the Plateau, they were essentially in the foothills of the Anvil, he explained, so the base of the trail they were looking for lay only a day's journey further. Then they would begin to climb the Anvil itself.

It was late in the afternoon when the trees began to thin out and Tayna finally got to see the mountain itself, peering down at them between the treetops. At about the same time, the stream bank they'd been following veered aside, but Abeni continued straight ahead, angling over land toward the base of the mountain and the foot of their intended trail. Rather than continue as they had been though, he felt it was perhaps also time to reconfigure themselves into less conspicuous travelers–since they were now far more likely to encounter other Djin, who might widen an eye at his unconventional handling of the Wagon, floating high above the trees.

Not only would the more traditional altitude be more seemly, he said, but it would also allow them to keep the secret of Tayna's power a while longer. And since he knew these mountain trails like the tips of his own fingers, Abeni did not feel he would need her constant guidance either. This would allow Tayna to range ahead of him a little when they reached the trail. Not enough to get truly separated, but enough so that she would be able to scout obstructions or on-coming travelers and come back to warn him, long before he and the Wagon encountered them.

When they finally did emerge from the trees a little while later, they did so like a normal Warding party, returning to the Anvil with an empty Wagon after a long but stately journey. Well, except for the fact that Abeni Warded alone–a fact which both fascinated and alarmed the party of Gnomes waiting for them at the trail's base.

"Who travels?" came the sentry Gnome's challenge as he watched them approach. He was standing at alert with a sort of primitive spear held out in front of him. Three other Gnomes had all been loafing in varying postures of ease across the trail mouth, but they hurried now to join their leader, and soon had their own spears pointed at the two travelers.

Abeni allowed the Wagon to touch down on the trail. "Even a blind Gnome would know what he sees before him," he said, once the Wagon's weight had settled to the stones. "It is the Wagon of Tears upon the Homeward Trail. All others are in service to its need." He emphasized the word "all."

The guard made a quick gesture with his wrists–a familiar motion of respect that Tayna had seen others make in the Wagon's presence before–but he did not move to clear the path. "Many pardons, Master Warder, but this is... not expected." Then he leaned to one side, trying to peer past Abeni toward the tree line. "But where are your fellows?" he asked. "How have you come to be Warding the Wagon alone? Surely this little Ketch is no aid to a great Djin in this honorable duty?" He gestured contemptuously at Tayna. "Will the others be along shortly, then?"

Tayna didn't like where this was going. Forget the insult to her. This guy appeared to be asking if Abeni could expect back-up to come charging out of the woods. Or was she just being paranoid? Either way, the Gnome party had them out-numbered and out-armed, and recent events had taught her to be less than trusting of Gnomes. She fought the urge to bend over and pick up some rocks. But there are rocks and then there are rocks. So, while the guards were muttering over the subtlety of their sergeant's ploy, Tayna casually took two steps backward, until she felt the warmth of Abeni's hand settle onto her shoulder, and she let out a sigh of relief.

The Gnomes noticed. "That's a curious thing, that is," said the leader to his cohorts. "A little Ketch sprat looking to a mighty Djin for protection. And him givin' it too." Then he turned back to Abeni. "You need to learn about the changes that's been goin' on around here, Master Djin. They isn't fit for polite company, they ain't," he said, indicating Tayna with a twitch of his nose. "So we'll just relieve you of the shame of it all, and take her off your hands now. A friendly turn from your friendly neighbors. 'Sides, the new King's got special orders about this 'un, he does. Filthy she-Ketch found in the company of the Great Wagon. That's what he said to be watchin' for. She'll be comin' with us. But then you'll be free to be on yer way. So be a good neighbor."

The Gnomes all gripped their spears tightly and stepped forward, spreading themselves out wider in an attempt to flank their quarry.

"Go! In the Dragon's Peace," came the deep voice from just behind Tayna's head, "and Abeni will not harm his little 'neighbors.' But go now, before Abeni decides to teach them better manners." Then he began to chant again, and as the sound of dangerous waters rose around her, the Wagon rose with it some ten feet into the air and slid slowly forward, coming to a rest above the Gnome commander's head.

To his credit, the Gnome only glanced up briefly before responding. "Now, now, Master Djin–Abeni–we both knows you can't do no damage with that bloody great rock of yourn. *'Touch not, save with the hands of grief.'* In't that right? And as you can see"–he held out his gnarled Gnomish hands, still clamped tightly around his spear–"they's not exactly grievin'. Not just yet."

Tayna took a deep breath. Was that true? Had this Gnome jerk just called Abeni's bluff?

"This is true," Abeni said, and Tayna felt her shoulders sag. But behind her, the sound of Abeni's song shifted. The Wagon slid further forward, and then settled onto the stony path, just behind the Gnomes. Then the song changed again, and a flicker of movement caught her eye. A largish rock about the size of her head shot up from the side of the trail, behind the Gnome leader, arced up over his head, and then came crashing down. Tayna was sure it was about to cave him in from forehead to pelvis, and she squinted her eyes to block out most of the gory details. But it missed the Gnome's head and dove neatly between his two hands, snapping his spear in the middle, and slammed into the trail between his feet. Immediately another rose from the path in front of him. Menacingly.

While the Gnomes all gawped about, puzzling over this new development, another rock rose from the trail, taking position in front of the Gnome on Tayna's far left. And another for the guy on her right. Then a fourth arced up into the air and then slammed back down into the dirt at the feet of the last Gnome–the one who'd been edging around toward Abeni's back and thought the big Djin hadn't noticed. The sneaky Gnome gave out a squeak of fear and scrambled back to rejoin his comrades in a hurry. Tayna felt Abeni squeeze her shoulder in thanks. It was her power that was making all of this possible.

"Abeni does not wish to harm his neighbors," Abeni said quietly, but despite the softness of his words, there was no mistaking the threat within them, nor his willingness to make good on it, should the Gnomes not take heed. "But he fears that they may perhaps bring injury to themselves if they are left to play with dangerous toys." Once more he sang, and this time, all five spears and spear-halves darted as one into the center of the group, clattering to the ground like kindling. "Like a good neighbor, Abeni has now ensured that his new friends will not meet such accidental hurt." Then his tone turned dark.

"But now they go. And quickly. For those neighbors who would play games upon the Anvil must learn to beware the falling of its hammers." Then Abeni sang a few words, and all five stones lifted into the air, climbing up to hang above the heads of each of the five Gnomes, who looked from one to the other as they struggled to understand how they had so suddenly lost the advantage in this little ambush of theirs. But Abeni had lost all his patience and his angry roar woke them abruptly from their fugue. "Abeni said, '*GO!*'"

And like a shot, the Gnomes fled. As they ran past her, Tayna noticed that one of them was carrying something strapped below his pack. It was another of Sister Regalia's urns.

Abeni watched them warily until they had disappeared into the trees. Then he blew out a tight breath, releasing some of the tension he had held during the encounter.

"Mabundi will not be pleased," he said. "Gnome raiders upon the Anvil. Word must reach the King of all Djin at once."

"Wha- Um, yeah. To arms! And all that kind of stuff." But Tayna had a creeping feeling that they had missed the most important part. That urn... It was just too weird. Seeing it with Angiron was one thing, but seeing it here in Methilien with some random Gnome... Why would Angiron have given one to such a distant underling? There was something else going on here—something that nobody even suspected yet. And knowing Angiron, it was probably more bad news. But she couldn't argue with her big travel buddy. He was right—they needed to find whoever was in charge around here and fill him in. Fast.

"Well, we better get moving, Oh Mighty Rock Hoverer. The path is clear now. Come on."

But Abeni shook his head. "No. The need is great and time is little. Abeni must speak to Kijamon. Now." Then his hand came back down firmly on her shoulder.

Tayna's eyes widened. "What do you mean?"

The Djin Warder smiled at her confusion. "On this day, a whale and a fish must fly up a mountain," he said.

"Wicked!" Tayna shouted, punching the air in excitement. "Don't worry, big guy. You are so going to love this! Flying is only like, the most awesome thing ever."

"Abeni does not fear to fly," he said, as they walked up to the Wagon and clambered onto to its sturdy runners. His big face grinned down at her as he wrapped one arm around her shoulder, making firm contact with her magic. "It is ceasing to fly that Abeni fears." And with that, he began to sing, and the Wagon shot once more into the sky.

chapter 11

"Well, it's Sister Regalia, obviously," Sue said, as she got up to help Ned with the tray of coffee and cookies. "Cream and sugar, right Detective?"

"Please." DelRoy was sitting in the large, stuffed chair in the Nackenfausch's living room. With dinner over, they had moved to more comfortable seating to continue discussing what each of them had found. "Regalia? Regina? Could be," he said, as he accepted a cup and sat back. "The names are similar, but it might just be a coincidence."

"Regina who?" Ned asked, as he took his own cup and settled into the other large chair. The man wasn't at all what the detective had expected. Aside from the stressed vulnerability she'd been radiating when he'd first met her, Sue Nackenfausch had struck him as a competent, motivated woman. Ned, on the other hand, didn't seem to fit. Quiet. Almost timid. And extremely deferential to his wife. If he'd been playing his game, this pair would have been a quick, "Not together." There was something... odd about the guy. Out of place.

"Regina Finch," Sue said, filling her husband in on what he'd missed while he'd been in the kitchen. "Detective DelRoy was just saying that the entire Goody organization appears to be owned by a woman named Regina Finch, which sounds to me like a name that would go with 'Sister Regalia.' What do you think?"

Ned shrugged uncertainly at his wife. "You'd know better than I would. Dear."

"Well, I can't help thinking I've heard that name somewhere before," DelRoy said. "Either of you know it?" Ned shook his head almost immediately, but Sue took a moment to think before echoing her husband.

"Maybe the Internet?"

"I checked that," he replied, "but nothing. A few hits, but mostly just private folks, nowhere near here. Nobody famous. Nobody prominent. Certainly nothing that rang my memory bell. But the feeling just won't go away. I know I've heard it somewhere."

"Well, let it rest," Sue said. "It will come to you if you forget about it. Meanwhile, I had an interesting day myself." She pulled a folded sheet of paper from her purse and spread it out on the table.

"I made contact with the girls. Come see."

DelRoy leaned in to read the note. It was written in two hands. Sue's part was written in a flowing blue ink, while the responses between hers were in green pencil.

Sue: My name is Sue Nackenfausch. I am the woman who adopted your friend Eliza. But Eliza never reached my house. Nuns say she ran away, but I don't believe them. Can you help? I need information.

Kids: Hi Sue. The Unlovables are on the job! What do you need to know? Also, use window with smiley face. First window has a rat.
—Agnitha and Rachel

"I think the 'rat' means that the girl whose bunk I dropped the note onto can't be trusted," Sue explained. "There was another window further down that had a happy face drawn into the grime. I assume it's the one above their bunks. Or closer, at least."

"And who are these 'Unlovables?'" DelRoy asked, poking a finger at the first line of the children's reply.

"That is what those delightful nuns call the girls they force to cook and clean," Sue said. "They say it's because those girls aren't adoptable, but I think it's just a pretense to let them crush the spirits of the more resilient girls and put them to work."

"And the girls call themselves by the same name?"

Sue smiled. "Eliza was very proud of it. Like a badge of honor. She and her friend Tayna were sort of the leaders of the bunch."

"That's the other girl, the one who ran away, right?"

"According to Eliza," Ned said. "She talked about the girl non-stop, but the nuns say she never existed at all. That Eliza made her up and then blamed everything she did on this fantasy friend of hers."

"Oh Ned, don't be ridiculous. You don't actually believe that, do you?" Sue turned an irritated eye toward her husband, but Ned just held up his hands in surrender.

"To be honest, I don't know what to think," he said. "She does have some pretty wild stories, after all." Sue shot a glare at him that clearly meant, "We'll talk about this later." Then she looked back down at her note.

"Anyway, that was yesterday. This is what I got from them today."

Sue: So your names are Agnitha and Rachel. How old are you?

Kids: 12 and 5

Sue: Do you know where Eliza is now?

Kids: We thought she was with you.

Sue: When was the last time any of you saw Eliza? Where was she? What was she doing?

Kids: Last seen sitting on her bed. Waiting for you on pickup day. Jenny saw her.

Sue: Do you know any reason why the nuns wouldn't want Eliza to get adopted?

Kids: Because she's an Unlovable and getting adopted would make her happy.

Sue: Do any grown ups ever come around who aren't parents? Anybody who helps the nuns or maybe works with them?

Kids: Lots of people come to their parties every week, and there's a new guy, Lord Angerton or something. He's really skeezy. But nobody actually works with them. It's all Goodies, all the time.

Sue: Is everything okay? Do you need anything?

Kids: Send pizza!

"They're pretty young," DelRoy said, once he'd finished reading it.

"But they're tougher than most kids that age would be," Sue said, sitting back on the sofa and setting the notes on her lap. She ran her hands over the paper, smoothing out the creases while she talked. DelRoy doubted she was even aware she was doing it.

"Any idea who this 'Lord Angerton' is?"

Ned looked lost in thought, as though trying to recall, but Sue nodded. "Eliza did say something about a man who'd been visiting Sister Regalia lately, but she didn't mention his name and I didn't know it would turn out to be important, so I didn't ask."

"You mean the angry guy?" Ned asked. Sue nodded.

"Angry?" DelRoy said, looking back and forth between the husband and wife yet again, still confused by the odd body language he was seeing between them. They just didn't act... comfortable with each other.

"Just something Eliza said at lunch once," Ned said. "That the angry guy had shown up a few days before Tayna ran away. Although 'angry' might just have been a reference to his name."

"I'll look into it. See what pops up," DelRoy said. "You think her friend left to get away from this Angerton guy?"

"Eliza didn't say, but that would be my guess," Sue said.

"And what about these parties the kids mentioned?" But neither Ned nor Sue had any ideas. "Might be worth keeping an eye on the place for a few days. If they have regular visitors, maybe we'll get lucky and be able to tie one of the guests to something."

"I can do that," Sue said, patting her camera, which was on the end table beside her. "And what will you be doing, Detective?"

"Following the money lady," he said. "Something tells me we want to learn more about this Regina Finch person. See what else she's into, where she's been, and so on."

"Can we meet again in a couple of days?"

"Sure," DelRoy said. "I should have something by then. Meanwhile, you be careful. You probably don't want to be caught hanging around an orphanage taking pictures." Sue smiled.

"I'll be careful, Detective."

With that, DelRoy thanked the two of them for supper and promised to be in touch if he learned anything important. Then he said goodnight and went back out to his car. He hadn't said anything inside, but there was one other puzzle he would be looking into as well. No matter what they might say out loud, body language never lied, and he was sure of it now.

Ned and Sue Nackenfausch were not man and wife.

"No warrant, no information!" The nun's face vanished into the gloom and the heavy iron door clanged shut in his face. DelRoy blinked in mild surprise. Hardly the welcome he'd been expecting at a high school, but perhaps it had been predictable. In hindsight, he probably shouldn't have announced himself as a policeman at all. He'd known, of course, that at the first mention of the missing girls, the nuns would shut down completely, which was why he'd chosen a different story. Surely a school entrusted with educating and supervising vulnerable children would want to hear about about a suspicious man seen wandering the neighborhood, wouldn't they? He had fully expected that angle to get him ten minutes with the headmistress, or the principal, or whatever they called her.

But instead they'd given him the clang of doom. Could the entire Sisterhood really be that paranoid? The reaction did not bode well. Not only would it make any further inquiries more difficult, but it also suggested they had something to hide. Maybe even something sinister.

Whatever was going on, it might be bigger than just the orphanage. And if it extended to Holy Terror Collegiate too, did that mean that *all* the Goody businesses were involved? Something told the veteran detective that this was not going to be an easy investigation.

Still wrapped in thought, he went back and got into his car. The empty seat beside him twigged a thought, and a slow smile spread over his features.

What he needed was an accomplice.

"Thanks for coming with me," DelRoy said, as Sue got in and pulled the door shut. The sign on the lawn outside read, "The Barbington Clinic for Toyfolk, Dr. Susan Nackenfausch, Chief Surgeon."

"That for real?" he asked, tipping his head at the sign as he pulled away from the curb and eased the car into traffic. He'd done a little digging, of course, and knew the documented facts, but he was honestly curious to hear how Sue explained it.

She grinned. "You'd be surprised how many people think very highly of their toyfolk, Detective. Dogs and cats are not the only way people distract themselves from an unfulfilled longing for children."

He wanted to ask the obvious question, but he thought it might be a bit insensitive. But Sue must have seen the question on his face.

"And no, I do not include myself in that camp," she said. He could hear the grin in her voice as she said it. "Actually, my background is in anthropology. The doll hospital was my mother's before me. I grew up here. I've worked with dolls and toys my entire life, so when it came time to pick a topic for my doctoral thesis, it was an easy decision."

"So you really are a doctor, then."

"Yes. A Ph.D. I may not be an M.D., but I do still have patients. When academic life turned out not to suit me, I came back here, and eventually took over the Clinic from my mother."

"So you fix dolls for a living." He didn't mean it in a judgmental way, though. Far from it. It was such a quirky and intriguing job for her to have. It made her seem mysterious. Normally when DelRoy met people, he'd hear what they did for a living and immediately they would be painted by all the sordid details he'd learned about their industry in the course of his own job. But this was totally fresh ground. A doll hospital. Not an industry he'd ever given any thought to before. So it was paint-free. Totally new. Safe, unknown, and utterly charming. Three things that rarely went together in his world.

They continued across the city, chatting about her experiences working with the permanently dead. Their chatter was easy and light-hearted. Sue was an easy person to talk to. They were leaving the downtown core when DelRoy turned his head and gave her a devious grin. "So, who should we kill, then?"

He had told her on the phone where they would be going, and Sue easily shifted conversational gears with him. She didn't even pause.

"Oh, definitely your mother," she said. "I never did like her. Too controlling. And she's never going to let up. You know that, right? For as long as she's around, there won't ever be anyone else in your life—not in her view, anyway—and I'm tired of being shut out, Martin. It's been fifteen years and I still can't do anything right by that woman. I tell you, I can't take it anymore. And I won't. So you're just going to *have* to kill her."

DelRoy turned to look at Sue in surprise. He hadn't expected her to be quite that quick. Sue batted her eyes back at him, but said nothing. He cleared his throat. "So, my mother then. Um, Alzheimer's?"

Sue shook her head. "Total cliché. Besides, it's too sad. Your mother's a bitch. I want something nasty."

"Um, my mother is actually a very sweet woman, you know."

"Oh, don't worry," Sue said, placing a hand on the detective's arm. "I'm not talking about your *actual* mother, of course. I'm talking about that vicious harpy who locked me out of the church on our wedding day."

"Hey!" he said, flinching away from the hand at his elbow. "That was an accident! How many times does she have to apologize?"

"Accident? There were three bolts on that door, Martin, and all three of them had been locked. That's no accident. That's a mad old cow who– Oh! Say. Can it be mad cow disease? That would be perfect!"

"I don't know. Do people actually get that? I thought it was just for cows."

"People get something else. Cracky-Jacky Disease, or something like that. But I think it's the same thing. Besides, we're playing a married couple, not doctors. It's more believable if we make some mistakes. Don't you think?"

"Remind me never to play poker with you."

"I shall, sir. And your compliment is noted and appreciated."

They continued rehearsing their story for several more minutes, all the way to the edge of town and out to the empty lots full of snow and the factories beyond the train yards. Eventually DelRoy pulled the car into a slushy, unpaved parking lot in front of a squat little concrete bunker. The corners and edges were crumbling and it looked like it had been abandoned since the war. A hand-painted sign hung from a nail next to the door: "Gruesome Harvest Mortuary and Crematorium."

DelRoy shook his head in disbelief. "Holy Terror Collegiate? Gruesome Harvest Crematorium? The Old Shoe? It's like these women don't speak English at all."

"It's worse than that," Sue said. "Because they do speak English. They know full well how those names affect people, and they just don't care. Or maybe they even prefer it that way."

For a moment, the two of them sat there, unwilling to get out of the car. They stared at the low, brooding building, with its decaying, barely functional exterior, and its complete lack of anything gracious or comforting. It didn't say "dignified interment services." It said, "discount corpse processing." There was even a vaguely organic tang to the air. Relax. You're breathing in it.

Both "husband" and "wife" shuddered simultaneously, and then flung their doors open. Maybe it would be better inside.

But it wasn't.

"Whaddaya want?"

The barked question assaulted them before the door had even closed behind them. An ugly old woman glared out from her desk in the inner office. There was no reception area. Just a bare concrete floor off the entrance, leading to a bare concrete wall, with that single inner door and the black hole of an office beyond. The crone's eyes shone out of that pit, boring into his soul, burrowing after all his secrets. "Um, we're uh..." he stammered, caught temporarily off his game.

Sue rolled her eyes. "His mother's about to croak," she said, in a rough, nasal voice, hooking one thumb at her idiot husband. "We're looking for the cheapest way to ditch the old bat when she finally kicks."

For a heartbeat, he could only stare at Sue, but then his brain found the missing gear and he turned his shocked expression into one of hurt. "Susie, you promised to stop calling her that."

"I will, dummy. When she's dead and roasted and in a jar on the mantle." Sue turned back to the woman. "You the manager? Watcha got that's cheap and fast?"

"I am," the woman said, standing up and coming out to meet them. Well, coming to meet Sue, anyway. She ignored DelRoy completely. "Sister Gruesome's the name. Best come in, I suppose. I'll have you fixed up before hubby here finds his next clue." Then she turned and ushered Sue back into the office and closed the door.

DelRoy could only stand there gaping, wondering what had just happened.

"Sorry about that," Sue said, as they climbed back into the car. "I got the impression that sweet and innocent wasn't going to cut it with her. She's just like all the other nuns I've met since this whole thing started. The only mood they seem to respect is 'mean.'"

"Whatever works," DelRoy said with a shrug. He wasn't too pleased about being left out of the conversation, but at least one of them had gotten past the front door. "Did you get anything?"

Sue shuddered, and he was pretty sure it had nothing to do with the chill winter air.

"It's like... I don't know, like we've lifted up an old board lying in a field and found all these bugs and worms and stuff scurrying around underneath it. It's been right there all along, just hiding in a pocket of darkness nobody knew about, right there in the middle of all that light."

"That bad?"

Sue nodded tightly, obviously too disturbed to say anything for a moment, so DelRoy started the car and got the heater going. By the time Sue was ready to talk again, he had driven them back to a less desolate part of town.

"For a day's pay, they'll cremate your mother and put her remains in any jar you want to provide them with," Sue said quietly. "For half that, they'll just get rid of her. No jars. No remains."

"What do you mean, 'a day's pay?' How much do they want?"

"They don't care," Sue said. "If you're a doctor, pay one day of doctor's pay. If you bag groceries at the Super Saver, it's one day of *that* pay. I've never heard anything like it. And the worst part is, she bragged about how they don't do many jar-jobs. Most of their customers take the half-off service."

"And at those prices, I bet business is pretty steady," he muttered, as much to himself as to Sue.

"They do a lot of municipal work too," Sue added. "On contract with the city. Vagrants, people who die with no friends or next of kin. It's like some kind of garbage dump for human beings."

DelRoy suppressed a shudder. "Anything else?"

"Nothing she actually said. I tried to get her talking about the rest of the organization. Told her I wanted a better price and demanded to talk to her boss, but she just laughed and said she was the boss, and there was nobody else."

"But you heard something? Saw something?"

"Yes. Two somethings. First, I got a look at her phone. It was one of the ones with speed dial and the numbers written in pen on little slips of paper. The only number on it was one I recognized. And no wonder, because I've dialed it a hundred times myself in the last couple of weeks. It was the number for the Old Shoe."

"So, despite what she told you, she probably reports to Sister Regalia. That fits. What was the other thing?"

"I saw it as I was leaving. Next to the door. The business license was nailed to the wall."

"And?"

Sue looked at him with a strange expression on her face. "Well, it wasn't made out to Sister Gruesome, or to the Gruesome Whatsit Mortuary at all. It was made out to Regina Finch."

DelRoy drummed his fingers on the steering wheel in thought. "So there she is again, huh? Our mysterious woman behind the scenes."

"Have you remembered yet where you know the name from?"

The detective shook his head. "No, and it's making me crazy. Like it was the woman who lived next door to me growing up, or my fifth grade teacher or something. It's in there somewhere, but I can't seem to get my flashlight on it."

Sue patted his arm again. "Well, it'll come. Keep ignoring it until it just pops out."

He nodded his head absently, but he hadn't told her the part that bothered him most. Despite all his memory tricks and recall techniques, he hadn't been able to dredge up any inkling of why he knew that name, but he had found the remains of one half-remembered feeling. A sort of déjà vu. And it filled him with dread.

This was not the first time in his life that he had tried to dig up his memory of Regina Finch.

chapter 12

When humans build homes in mountain settings, they seek the lower places–meadows, glens, and dales. It's as though, instinctively, they know that they do not belong there. Everything within them yearns to settle as far from the lofty heights as they can possibly manage. Even that very word, "settle," suggests sinking, as though their full intent is to one day precipitate off of the mountain and drip down its sides, into the valleys below. To settle down.

The same was not true of the Djin. Were it not for their reverence for the Bloodcap, there would be Djin holdings even upon the very peak itself. Djin homes were not just *on* the Anvil–they were *of* the Anvil–every room, every chamber carved with a purpose from the mighty stone, and every shard removed was given its own purpose. There is no *negative space* in Djin architecture. Wherever one finds a gap or pocket of air that once held a volume of stone, the mass of that space has simply been transformed to some honorable other usage. The negative space of Abeni's sleeping chamber was the positive space of Zimu's table and chairs, and it formed many tools and furnishings as well.

Rather than select a convenient gap or chimney of rock in which to build, as most Djin did, when Kijamon had first set out to establish his now great House, he had not been satisfied to let the chance processes of wind, water, heat and cold choose his location for him. "Who is to say that this crack of rock or that overhang will be placed in the strongest light, or receive the greatest blessings of the wind?" he had often said. "And why must a Djin be content to live within stone that has been proven unsound by the very existence of those cracks? House Kijamon will grow where Kijamon chooses–not where the lime and the dew and the sun have chosen for him. House Kijamon will be strong, because it will be shaped from the very strongest stone of the Anvil, with the best light, the best wind and the best ore possible–because it will be in a place chosen by Kijamon for just such reasons."

And Kijamon had made good those words. After earning his third golden bond ring as a young Djin, Kijamon had gone to his father and asked leave to establish his own House, as is the custom among the Djin. "I will be gone for one month," he told his father. "And when I return, I will bear with me the seed of my new House, or I shall content myself to stay here within your House for the rest of my days, if you will still have me."

His father consented, and gave Kijamon leave to seek out his new House across any and all portions of the Anvil not already inhabited or anointed in the Dragon's name. And true to his word, on the 27th day after setting forth, Kijamon returned bearing a single perfect cube of granite, icy blue in complexion and one hand's breadth wide in each direction. This he bore into his ancestral home and placed upon the mantle of the great fire hearth. "I plant this seed of my House in the bosom of your own," he said to his father, formally. And then he strode out, never to return.

For five long years, Kijamon labored alone in his solitary domain, slowly working his way down into the shoulder of Methilien's Anvil, but even here he was not satisfied with the practices of other Djin. Of the few before him who had chosen this more difficult path—of revealing Houses that lay hidden within solid stone—each had simply removed large blocks and set them aside, first creating the large voids and then partially refilling them with walls and shelters and stairways fashioned from those waiting blocks.

Not so Kijamon. Instead, each day, the young Djin built for himself some three or five objects that would be needed in his new House. A fork to eat with, a chair to sit upon, a chest to hold his garments. For each such object, Kijamon removed only enough stone from the Anvil to reveal the item he desired—nothing more—preserving the power and strength of his mountain home as he progressed. The walls that he left in his wake were like none ever seen before—rectangles and blocks, facets and ridges. No span of greater length than a long Djin stride had been left smooth, and the walls of his House sparkled in the light that reflected on the millions of facets left upon the stone. And in this manner, over those five intensive years, the young Djin slowly revealed his first great wonder—the Wind Forge.

Kijamon had chosen his location well. With the searing blues of its stone, shot through with veins of icy white, the great studio that would become the seat of House Kijamon gleamed in the sun-drenched days and radiated warmth and serenity back into the cool nights. Wedge-shaped, and hanging within a wider V-shaped notch that he carved around it, the Wind Forge was as its name declared–an altar to the wind, set into the uppermost ridge of the Anvil's shoulder, just below the crimson stain of the Bloodcap itself. A perfect shrine to metalcraftery, for no fewer than four veins of precious metals laced its various walls and ensconcements, setting their colors afire in the brilliant mountain sunlight.

Winds that climbed the Anvil in their daily chases flowed into the empty notch below and raced upward, only to be channeled at the base of the dangling structure into the ducts and raceways that forced them into the heart of Kijamon's forge, serving instead of the bellows that other metalcrafters were forced to rely upon.

But the Wind Forge was only the start, and below it, a thriving community took root, spreading downward into the mountain stone. As each year passed, new voids were cut, extending the original notch to make space for more windows and doorways to be carved into the descending faces of the V, and back from which hallways and chambers were dug from the stone. All of it was capped by the crowning jewel of the Wind Forge itself, suspended from the two great buttresses that Kijamon had left in place to support it.

Nor was Kijamon's vision limited to architecture alone. As others came to see this marvel that he was wresting from the living rock, some felt a resonance with him and his teachings, and begged leave to join him. At first, these had been other artisans of stone and metal, but in time, interest widened, and before long, the city that was growing in the cleft around the Wind Forge became known for other kinds of craftery as well, and ultimately, for the crafting of artisans themselves. For is it not said that any can go to Wind Forge, but only artists come out?

So now, on this beautiful winter's day, with the wind rising fresh and cold through the channels of its studios, and sunlight dancing from the jeweled faces of its stonework, Kijamon's jeweled city was in its fullest splendor. Musicians wandered the soaring walkways and lingered in the salons, playing their instruments or singing for the joy of simply being. Painters drank boh-cho on glittering balconies and dreamed new visions to reveal. Sculptors and jewelers worked their metals and stones, both precious and lesser, fashioning beauty for the pleasure of others. All was harmony, tranquility and delight. Kijamon's jeweled city hummed with the chorus of crafting.

Until the wonder-struck cry of a small child directed the gazes of the artists, musicians, the dancers and their patrons, up to where a missile of silver and granite was streaking toward them, inbound, from out of the dazzling clear blue sky.

———⌄———

"And still he sits, fawning like a kitten. Just look at him," Shaleen said, glaring from their viewing balcony, down into the Hall of Flame. Zimu came to join his mother at the rail. Below them, Mabundi, King of the Djin, was leaning forward on the Anvil Seat, chatting happily with the Gnome Ambassador, while courtiers and attendants flitted about the room, fussing over tiny adjustments to things that needed no adjusting.

"He is King. It is his duty to hold court," Zimu said, still not seeing what had sparked his mother's ire.

"Two weeks he has been here, my son. Two weeks. Having only just returned, you cannot know what we hear from the other Houses. How restless they grow. When will he grace *their* Halls with the honor of his court? When will he hear the grievances and joys of *their* folk? None who think themselves great will travel to seek the King's ear–not when each believes that Mabundi will come to them next when he leaves here. So they wait. But still he does not leave, and while he lingers, their grievances only multiply and fester."

Zimu nodded his understanding. She was right. This was not good. A Djin King was expected to be everywhere, constantly moving his court from one holding to another, giving each House access to his ear and counsel. It was not uncommon for court to linger at the larger holdings–Sunhome, The Warrens, and yes, even here at the Wind Forge. With so many Djin congregated in places such as these, it was sensible that the Court would linger to provide time for all to avail themselves of the King's justice. But today the Hall was empty, as it had been for the three days before, save for the Gnomileshi Ambassador. Any who wished to seek Mabundi's counsel had long since done so. Zimu could not recall the old King, Jallafa, ever having stayed with Kijamon for longer than four days. So for Mabundi to have been entrenched here for fourteen... It was no wonder the other Houses were muttering.

"Has Kijamon–?"

"Oh, your father takes no notice of such things. You know that. He says that the bond ring circling Mabundi's brow still dazzles and has not yet born down with its full weight. If Mabundi wishes to drape himself with the glitter of our walls for a time, it is to be expected. Being new to the Anvil Seat, he must be allowed to enjoy such trappings, which he will tire of soon enough, and then he will surely take up the full burdens of his duty, as he has sworn to do." Shaleen sighed. "Sometimes, your father can be such a fool."

Zimu grinned. His mother and father loved each other fiercely, he knew, but it always tickled him just a little to see the sparks of that devotion, still hot and fiery after so many decades of marriage.

"And the Hall of Flame?" Zimu asked. It was customary for foreign delegations to be received in the more formal Hall of Wind. This should have been especially true for the Gnomileshi delegation, given the rumors of their recent aggressions.

Shaleen rolled her eyes. "Mabundi says he does not care for the... discomforts, of our Wind Hall. And since your father has not seen fit to remake them to royal liking, all court functions are being held in the Hall of Flame."

"Truly?" Zimu asked. This was even more surprising than the over-long visit. For a King to reject the traditions of the Anvil Seat in favor of his own comforts... Such tidings did not put a shine on these early days of Mabundi's reign. And they did not portend well for the days to come either.

"Can we not–?" But before Zimu could complete his question, his mother raised a hand, and turned to look at the window behind them.

"Whatever is that commotion?" she said. Through the window, they could hear shouts of wonder and excitement from outside.

Zimu watched his mother as she went to the window slot to look. "Oh my!" she said, and turned back, her own face suddenly wide with that same wonder. "What has that boy...?" But the thought trailed off as she hurried toward the stairway.

"Come, Zimu! Your little brother is about to upend our world. Again."

Zimu moved to join her, but he could not hide his smile as he did. Abeni was home!

"Bulletman blows chunks! This is the *only* way to fly!"

Tayna held tightly to Abeni's arm as the Wagon descended out of the air. They rocketed down past the red blur of the Bloodcap–the peak of the Anvil–with its bright red stone that some said was infused with the blood of Methilien himself. But if the Dragon was present, he showed no objection to their passing, and they plunged down past the red-gray slopes, toward a tiny chip cut into the shoulder of the mountain. As they got closer, and the chip grew bigger, Tayna had to shake her head to readjust her perspective. The chip wasn't little at all–it was huge–and there were actually people in it. As they came closer still, she could make out graceful flying arches and delicate ramps of stone criss-crossing the face of the V-shaped city that had been set back into the mountain's face. Closer still, as the Wagon slowed and dropped into the notch itself, she could see faces raised in wonder. On the rampways and on the balconies and from the jet-black rectangles of windows cut into the stone, curious Djin pointed up into the sky. At them.

All around her, the faceted walls of the city sparkled in blues and whites and glitters of silver, and it was all so bright that Tayna had to shield her eyes with her hand. Abeni pointed up to the massive wedge-shaped building that hung over the entire city like a brooding god, suspended there on two thick buttresses that joined it to the faces of carved stone on either side. "The Wind Forge!" he yelled into her ear, pausing briefly from the song that held them aloft. "Abeni's home!" Then he lowered his hand to point down to the lowest part of the city, where the tip of its V-shape was blunted into a level plaza. "That is the Garden of Mothers," he told her. "Abeni will take the Wagon there!" But there was something lacking in Abeni's tone. She'd expected him to be happy, now that they were finally at the end of their journey, but even his song seemed to become more sombre as they descended toward their landing spot.

Others in the city seemed to have guessed where they were heading, because everyone she could see now seemed to be heading down toward that lower garden. And by the time Abeni had made a pass, giving clear warning of his intended landing place, and slowed the Wagon to a more stately speed, a crowd had begun to form on the plaza, although they stayed well back, leaving plenty of room in their midst for the Wagon's enormous bulk to set down.

As soon as it had, Tayna hopped down off the runner and swiped quickly at the wild tangle of her hair, which had been blown into a frenzy by the rushing wind. Abeni stepped down beside her, but if he said anything, it was devoured by the murmur of voices from the crowd pressing in around them, full of questions and shouts of surprise and delight. Abeni did his best to answer the few who were close enough to hear, but he said nothing of Tayna's role in the adventure. He didn't even mention her, and allowed everyone to believe that she had simply been a passenger–a mere witness to his latest achievement. But Tayna was not offended. This was what they had decided during their short flight. Until they knew more about what was going on, she would be a nobody. Just a random girl tagging along for the ride of a lifetime. The less attention brought to her right now, the better. And Abeni seemed to be holding up his end of that plan just fine.

He pushed his way through the crowd, politely, but persistently, making his way toward the edge of the Garden. Tayna followed along behind him. It seemed that everyone here knew her big friend, calling out to him by name as he passed, or placing an earnest hand on his arm if they were close enough–everyone trying to engage him with their questions before he had the chance to slip by. But he excused himself repeatedly, keeping a grim expression on his face and begging their leave until later. There was much to tell, but not until he had paid his respects to Kijamon.

"Not the King?" somebody asked.

Abeni seemed surprised to learn that the King was still in residence, but he nodded. "Of course. Abeni will pay respects to Mabundi as well," he said, and then he pressed forward once more.

The crowd thinned as they neared the edge of the plaza, fed only by a slender stream of latecomers trickling over from the Trail of Sky–the delicate lacework of stone walkways and arches that soared upward, connecting all the levels of the grand mountain city. But these latecomers did not know that it had been Abeni who had flown in, so they pushed past with little more than a wave of casual greeting before hurrying on to learn what the excitement was all about.

Abeni had just led her onto the lowest ramp when a familiar face emerged from the traffic coming toward them. "Zimu!" Tayna shouted, and she raced forward, throwing herself into a happy hug that only reached part way around the waist of Abeni's older brother. "How did you get here so quickly? Where's Sarqi? How did you get away from the sprites?"

"It is good to see the Little Fish once more," Zimu said, smiling at her firehose of questions, even if he didn't actually answer any. Then he turned to grip forearms with his brother, reaching past Tayna to do so. But Abeni took his brother's offered arms only briefly. His eyes locked momentarily on a brown band of cloth tied around Zimu's upper arm, and then he lowered his eyes again. His usual infectious smile was nowhere to be seen, and the grimness that had been growing in him for the last ten minutes was now almost palpable.

"Abeni! What is the matter with you?" An older Djin woman stepped out of Zimu's considerable shadow and scolded Abeni with her eyes. "You dishonor your father's House with such a greeting for your brother." She could only be Abeni's mother.

"The dishonor has already been done," Abeni said.

Zimu placed a hand on the woman's arm and she turned her face toward him. "Abeni has a duty of honor to complete," he said, pointing to the band of iron that still encircled his younger brother's arm. "He fears Kijamon will judge him harshly for his handling of it."

"But he *saved* the Wagon!" Tayna said. "Wasn't that what you were all bonded to–"

"No," her big friend said, cutting her off with a chop of his hand. "Abeni did no saving. It was the Little Fish who did this. Abeni must now inform Kijamon of his dishonor." And then he pushed his way past both his mother and his brother and trudged up the Trail of Sky, with his head hung low and gloom crowding around his shoulders. Tayna moved to run after him, but Zimu put a hand on her shoulder.

"He must attend to his honor alone."

Tayna turned to look at him. "Alone?" Zimu nodded, and at his elbow, the older woman echoed his movement. There was concern on her face for a moment, as she watched Abeni climb the ramp and disappear around the first turn. But then she turned back, and her expression melted into a smile.

"So you must be the Little Fish," she said. "Zimu has told us so much about you. Come. I am Shaleen. Mother to House Kijamon. We will speak of Abeni's troubles at another time. For now, you will be a guest in my home." Then she took Tayna by the arm and led her back up the ramp, with Zimu matching pace behind them.

From a balcony far above the plaza, a tufted face with a bulbous nose peered down from out of a tall window. A Gnome face. Its owner watched carefully as the little drama unfolded among the members of House Kijamon and their guest, standing on the Trail below him. He watched as Abeni stormed away, and saw how none chased after him. Not even the girl. Then he nodded to himself, already calculating how this apparent rift might be used to advantage.

"Ambassador! The Queen would see you in her study."

The Gnome turned away from the window and nodded to the young Djin who had been sent to pester him. "Then we had best not keep her waiting," he said. "Lead me. I still have no idea where anything is around here."

But as he strode from the room, his mind was a whirl. The girl was finally here. And now, at last, he could carry out the *real* purpose of his visit.

chapter 13

"Never mind all that, boy. I'd much rather know how you managed to fly the great Wagon."

Abeni blinked. He had just told his King that the flanks of the Anvil were crawling with Gnome Hordesmen–invaders who were harassing honest Djin travelers within their very own lands. "Surely the King of all Djin will wish to expel the outsiders," Abeni said. But again Mabundi waved such thoughts away with a casual hand.

"I tell you they are no matter," Mabundi said. Standing imperiously beside the Anvil Seat, Queen Yoliq glared down at Abeni, her face narrowing into a frown.

"Do as your King commands you, young man. Reveal the secret of how you lifted the Wagon of Tears into the sky. It is a great sacrilege. You should be ashamed! Tell us now, before your disgrace grows any deeper."

Abeni's confusion took a turn toward anger. "The Wagon is entrusted to House Kijamon," he said, trying hard to keep his tone polite. "Only the Mizar, or Kijamon himself may make report of that duty, and Abeni is not Mizar. Does the King truly plan to do nothing about the Gnomileshi stain that spreads upon the Anvil?"

Mabundi rolled his eyes. "Are you deaf, boy? I know all about that. Quishek asked if he could have a few of his Hordesmen patrol around the borders to make sure none of his more excitable Hordelets ventured too far, causing trouble for us. It was a rather neighborly gesture, I thought, so I allowed it."

"But, that makes no sense!" Abeni said, unable to keep the frustration from his tone. "The Gnome King is permitted to place his people within our lands, to be sure that none of his people come within our lands?"

Yoliq jumped to her feet. "You forget yourself, Abeni, son of Kijamon! It is not for you to question the wisdom of my husband!" Mabundi leaned over and placed a calming hand on her arm. "He only expresses his concern, my dear." Then he turned to look at Abeni.

"It is not so grim as you suggest, my boy. I have allowed Quishek four of his Hordelets to serve as buffer, but only on the Plateau. They may not set foot upon the Anvil itself. On that you have my word."

By then, Abeni had managed to rein in his surprise and was in better control of himself when he replied. "As the Queen has said, it is not Abeni's place to question. He has told his King of the Gnomes. His duty is complete. Abeni must now go to make report to Kijamon." But Mabundi raised a hand.

"There is still the matter of your iron debt," he said, pointing to the dull black band of metal around Abeni's upper arm. "You were bound to the Wagon, and to the care of two fallen kings. I will hear your report on this before you are released to your lesser duties."

Abeni stared intently at the King. "The duty was bonded by Kijamon," he said. "Abeni may not speak of it to any save Kijamon."

"Dammit boy, that's a technicality! I am the one who told him to bind you. The bond is mine, in truth. You will report to me."

But the young Djin shook his head. "Mabundi is wise, and perhaps Abeni is foolish. He knows only that his bond oath was spoken to Kijamon and so only Kijamon may hear the tale of its keeping and judge the mettle of Abeni's honor. Or his shame." But in his heart, Abeni had no doubt of which it was, and having delivered his urgent message, he turned to go. Since he had not been summoned to an audience, and had come voluntarily to report on the presence of the Gnomes, he was not bound by any protocol and did not require Mabundi's permission to leave. But this never even entered his mind. His only thought was about how he would ever stand the humiliation of disappointing his father.

Without even realizing he had done so, Abeni turned his back to his King and wandered from the Hall, drenched in the sweat of his own misery.

And behind him, Mabundi's face folded into a frown.

Mabundi watched the son of Kijamon stride from the Hall. Beneath his hand, he could feel his wife tensing, preparing to shout out for the guards to bring the boy back, but Mabundi squeezed her arm gently. Leave him be. He heard her snort with contempt for his weaknesses, but let it pass. At least she wasn't shouting for the boy's head. Off to the side, a door opened.

"You see how brash that House has become, do you my lady?" The Gnomileshi Ambassador slipped into the Hall, closing the door behind him. "Even its younger sons now dare to question the Crown." As always, he spoke to the Queen whenever he had something unpleasant to say.

"So you've been eavesdropping, have you, Quishek?" Mabundi was still irritated by the boy's news. "Well, what say you about this charge, then? Abeni tells me he was stopped by Gnomes on the flanks of the Anvil itself. That was not our agreement."

The Gnome's hands came up in a flutter of protestation, patting at the air as if he hoped to soothe the King's anger by creating a pleasant wind. "The boy was mistaken," Quishek said. "I have had reports already from those involved. They were merely resting in the shade at the foot of the trail. Upon the Anvil, yes, but only by a matter of strides. When they halted the Wagon, it was still on the Plateau. No Djin have been disturbed or waylaid upon the mountain itself. All is conducted as we agreed."

"Well, that sounds fine then," Yoliq said, straightening herself and seeming to gain her confidence now that her Gnome toady was once more at her side.

"There is another matter I would raise..." the Gnome began, looking as much at the Queen as at the King.

"What matter is that?" Mabundi asked.

"There is a girl," Quishek said. "A Wasketchin girl, here upon the Anvil." Mabundi raised an eyebrow in curiosity.

"What of her?"

Quishek rubbed his hands together in the Gnome gesture of pleading. "She has committed crimes," he said. "Back in the Throat. Crimes against the Crown itself. King Angiron would... greatly appreciate her return."

"A Wasketchin trouble child? Why bother me with this, Quishek? Present your petition to whichever House holds the lands on which she's hiding."

Quishek lowered his head. "Under normal circumstances, I would not trouble the Crown over such a matter," he said. "But I felt you might wish to be informed before I present my petition."

"Why?" Mabundi said, one eyebrow rising slowly in suspicion.

"Because the House in question just strutted out your door,"

Quishek said, inclining his head at the doorway through which Abeni had just left. "And the girl in question came here with him."

Mabundi cocked his head. "*With* him?"

"Yes, great King. *With* him. The girl was riding upon the Wagon of Tears, and is now being harbored by House Kijamon."

"What?!" Yoliq sputtered, leaping to her feet. "House Kijamon, again?" She turned to her husband with fury now burning in her eyes. "Having lost the Fallen King, and desecrated the Wagon of Tears, they proceed to amass magics of unknown power, they defy the Crown, and now they are harboring unsavory foreigners? Criminals? How much more do you need, Mabundi? How much more proof?"

"Proof of what, my dear?" Mabundi tried to pat her arm gently, but she jerked away from him, backing toward the Ambassador.

"You idiot! Can't you see? Kijamon is plotting to take your throne!"

Tayna could only sit back and watch the great Kijamon. The scene around him reminded her of a taxi dispatch office. Once, when she had been out doing her weekly chores for the Goodies, the taxi that had been hired to drive her around the city broke down, and she and the driver had walked seven blocks back to the dispatch building to wait for a new cab to become free. As she sat there in that grubby little office, Tayna had watched an entire world unfold around her. Cars came in and went out, drivers arrived and left, packages and passengers were dropped off or picked up. Voices called out and horns blared, and behind it all, some mechanized tool whined and burped in continual bursts, like a gassy mosquito with a bullhorn.

In the midst of all that, in that large, grimy garage, a cage of chickens had been set down, waiting for its rightful owner to come claim it. But somehow the cage door had sprung open, and for two or three minutes, Tayna and a rumpled older woman in a sarong and wearing too much makeup had chased the frantic hens around the concrete floor, herding them into a pair of large garbage pails before they could get stepped on or crushed by an arriving taxi. It had been pure, fascinating mayhem.

House Kijamon was like that.

Not that there were any chickens or belching tools, but the Wind

Forge had a similar energy all the same. While Abeni himself had gone off to report the Gnome incursions to the King, Shaleen and Zimu had led her up to the family home to wait, and to meet the famed Kijamon himself. It had taken them twenty minutes to climb the Trail of Sky all the way to the top, and all the while, her hosts had kept up a steady hum of conversation, describing the wonders that passed around them. They were clearly proud of Kijamon's city, and they showed it to her with all the love and reverence with which one might display a newborn child.

When they reach the summit of the long climb and marched across the great buttress that flowed seamlessly out to the main level of the Forge, Tayna found a busy hub of activity, with people coming and going every which way. Not at all the quiet, restful refuge of a master artisan that she had been expecting.

There must have been a dozen projects under way at various stations and benches around the area, but unlike the grubbiness of a taxi garage, this had the feel of both elegance and functionality. More like the kitchen of a busy hotel maybe, only carved from quartz. The entire main floor was devoted to Kijamon's work. The family lived on the floor above, and there were even more benches and booths on the levels below, where any number of assistants and apprentices labored over the many wonders and contrivances that would eventually bear the mark of House Kijamon and be sold or bartered to the world outside.

From the big studio, they ascended up to the private family level, where Tayna had expected all that activity to die down, but even here, the definition of "family" and "private" seemed somewhat fluid. They found Kijamon deep in discussion with two completely different groups of Djin, here in what he called his "little" shop, even though it comprised fully half of the family level.

Off to one side of the space, a clutch of older Djin stood together near the forge, deep in discussion, while other people came and went around them. The oldest and most animated of them all was a slender man, somewhat shorter than the rest, and whose once-dark skin had paled to a brownish gray. His hair was a nest of bristly silver coils that clung to the sides and back of his head, but avoided the top completely, save for a tight, circular knot at the crown. But this silver had nothing of the salt-and-pepper color that Tayna had been accustomed to seeing on older men in Grimorl. This was *silvery* silver, shiny and metallic. Hypnotic almost, as the longer tuft at the top-knot bobbed and waggled in time with the man's movements.

But as Tayna and the family stood by patiently, waiting for the discussion to end, a steady stream of younger Djin darted in and out of the room. As they arrived, the old man would turn aside from his conversation to ask a question or examine an item carried by the youth, and then send them on their way again–often without even breaking the stride of his original discussion. It was like watching a machine–No, a computer–and Tayna could not imagine how he managed to coordinate such mayhem as it orbited around him.

By the time the guests had said their say and been shown out, and the door at the back of the studio had been closed–a signal that the master was no longer available to those who worked below– Tayna had settled herself into a corner and begun to doze in the brilliant, sparkling light that filled the room by way of the windows, making everything warm and hazy.

"Aha!" said a voice, jolting her back from her slumber. "A wise girl. A wise girl indeed! Sleep when you can, eh? For an idea may take you at any time, and then you're off! Am I right?" Tayna grinned sleepily at the silver-framed face peering down at her.

This was Kijamon.

If Tayna had expected family life for clan Kijamon to be any different from the mayhem she had seen earlier, she was disappointed. The old man seemed to be a force of nature, greeting everyone, giving instructions to Zimu, and answering questions posed by his wife, all at the same time. And even so, his glittering eyes still found time to dart regularly back to Tayna long enough for him to ask perceptive and penetrating questions of her. He was like a switchboard operator, handling a dozen conversations at once, and never seeming to drop the ball.

"By all means boy, take them a twentyweight sample and see if they'll contract for five hundred. Send Abeni to find me when he returns. No dear, I leave food plans in your capable hands. And you must be tired after your long journey." This last statement was aimed at Tayna, but it took her a moment to notice. Apparently, you had to watch the man's eyes. It was the only clue he gave as to which sentence was addressed to which person, and she quickly discovered that it was best to ignore the conversations he carried on with the others and wait for his eyes to snap back to her before she started listening, although Kijamon himself appeared able to listen to everything at once and sort it all out just fine.

"Um, overwhelmed rather than tired," she said, in answer to his question.

"You're Wasketchin, clear enough, but your tongue is not limber in the language. You were raised apart from your kin?"

"Yessir," Tayna said, adding the "sir" more out of sheer awe than any conscious attempt at respect. It was absurd that he could have picked up so much from just the few words she had spoken, wasn't it? Especially with so much else going on around him at the time? But his eyes had snapped onward while she was thinking about it, and she resolved then and there to do her best to keep up.

"I don't remember my folks," she said, when his gaze next snapped to her. "I was raised... somewhere else. But now I'm looking for them and I think they might live here on the mountain somewhere."

His attention went around the group again, before coming back to Tayna with a snap.

"There's any number of Wasketchin living on the Anvil," he said. "Some are known but many are not. Do yours wish to be found?"

Snap.

"I think so," she said. "I think they might be in trouble, and I'm hoping I can help."

Snap.

"All Wasketchin are in trouble these days, it seems. Will your kin still be where you left them?"

Snap.

"I don't know, but it's the best place to start."

Snap.

"Then tomorrow we'll see about finding you some help in the matter. Bosuke is the Master of Histories. You can start with him."

At that point Shaleen raised her hands and brought the conversation to a halt. Abeni and Tayna had only just arrived, and it was time they be given something to eat. Or did Kijamon mean to stain the honor of their House? But the old man only grinned and nodded at his wife, saying how hungry he was and how welcome a meal would be.

As one, the family began making their way toward a side door, ushering Tayna along between them, which was good, because she was still completely bewildered by it all. She could barely believe it, but after a week on the run, she had been here for little more than a half dozen sentences and she had already made more progress on

147

her *family yours* problem than she had in all the days since she'd first learned about it. And to her astonishment, she was pretty sure that during the course of that same conversation, Kijamon had also organized a dinner party, negotiated two sales contracts, interrogated Zimu on the condition of the Wagon, and reminded Shaleen to prepare a room for their young guest.

The man was simply exhausting.

"Yes, my King. She is here." Quishek stared vacantly at the blank wall in front of him as he spoke. At his side, the tall Yeren assigned to him stared equally blankly into the center of the room, but Quishek ignored the beast completely, save for the fact of clinging tightly to its pink-skinned hand with both of his own.

"Indeed I do, my King," he continued after a moment. "The girl you seek arrived today, with the Wagon, and the Djin." Then he paused, as though listening to a sound only he could hear.

"Very perceptive of you, my Liege," he replied. "Yes, they arrived sooner than expected. It seems she has rediscovered the power of flight." Another pause.

"And what report is that, my Lord?"

Quishek shook his head tightly. "It could scarcely be the Djin, my Lord. He has been known to us for a goodly time. Is it not too curious that he might discover such gifts only now? No, power is not always where it looks to be, my King. It is hers, not his. I am certain of it."

Then the Gnome Ambassador bowed formally toward the wall. "If that is your will, your Greatness. I will report further news to you tomorrow. It will be–"

Irritation flashed across the Ambassador's eyes for a moment, and he let go the Yeren's hand. "Stupid f'znat!" he muttered to himself. "Is he blind? He sees only what he expects to see. Not what is. Unless. . . " His eyes lost focus again as he wandered toward the windows, lost in thought. Something in what he'd just said was tickling at him, like the lure of an unsolved puzzle.

A moment later, a slow smile crept across his Gnomish features. "No, truly," he said, as the smile grew. "Power is sometimes not where it looks to be at all."

With excitement in his eyes, the Ambassador turned and rushed from the room to summon his servants. The time had come at last for the game to change.

chapter 14

For the next two days, Eliza's cock-eyed Flame of the Dragon team did their collective best to raise an army from among the Wasketchin villages, but no matter how hard they tried, they were never able to repeat the success they'd had on that first night with the boys. They tried repeating the hiker-berry ritual, they tried heart-felt speeches, they tried commanding obedience by daylight, they tried begging for help by firelight. Yet in two whole days, and in half a dozen villages or more, they never once picked up so much as a single new follower. The only thing they'd managed to attract was pity, and one badly worn pair of boots for Eliza, that were at least one size too big and made the cuts on her feet hurt even more when sweat pooled inside them, making everything damp and salty.

She felt pathetic.

After watching yet another group of wide-eyed villagers gape at her in embarrassed disinterest, and seeing that once again, nobody was going to step forward, Eliza simply nodded, mute as ever, and strode majestically off into the Forest, which, with the lowering sun, was now dark and ominous. They had agreed earlier that it would be better to sleep in a tree with mystique and dignity intact rather than accept the hospitality of pity. Not because their pride was too great, but because Eliza was pretty sure that people would never join a cause led by pathetic hobos. Their plan to spend another night wedged into a tree however, was abandoned when Scraw flapped back out of the darkness after scouting ahead.

There is an empty traveler's dehn just a little ways further on, Mardu sent, and Eliza was only too happy to alter course toward it.

Like the hut the boys had been tending, these simple shelters were scattered throughout the Forest as part of a network of way-stations, free for the use of any traveler who came across them. They weren't as fancy as the dehns that were maintained in the villages, but they were decent shelter, and best of all—

"A bed!" Eliza shouted, when she pulled the door-flap open to reveal the low, moss-filled luxury inside. The Body of the Flame flopped herself down onto the moss and groaned in tired satisfaction as the earthy scent of clean soil and greenery puffed up around her. She hadn't actually *seen* the bed, of course. Not at night, in the shadowy interior of a leaf-covered hut. But Scraw had seen it for her, which was almost the same. Over the last few days, the group had worked out a way to share some of Scraw's sensory perceptions with her directly, and it turned out that the crow had better night vision than she did, which they'd been using to good advantage by traveling later into the evenings than would have been possible relying on Eliza's vision alone. They'd covered a lot of ground in two days.

But not anymore.

"That's the last time I'm doing the spooky prophet routine," she said, as she pressed her cheek against the cool, dry moss. All she could think about was how nice it would be to sleep tonight on a pillow that was not made of bark-covered oak.

Scraw pecked at the ground, digging between the roots of one of the wall trees. Suddenly, Eliza got an image of a fat, juicy grub in the soil, along with the sensation of delight. *Culinary* delight.

"Eww! Scraw, you are so gross!" Eliza dialed down the flow of imagery coming from the hungry bird and rolled over onto her back.

Why are you here? The simple question caught Eliza off guard.

"No idea," she said. "I'm still not even sure I believe in here."

"K-k-keh!" Scraw laughed.

It is a serious question, Mardu sent. *Why have you come to this world?*

"Come?" Eliza sputtered, rolling back over to face Scraw's general direction in the darkness. "Sister, I did not *come* here. I was *brought* here. Sincerely Yours wasn't even consulted."

Truly?

"One hundred percent, truly. One minute I'm following the scariest nun in history out to the car, and the next thing I know, I'm waking up in some dark wet stink-hole with a monkey-perv leaning over my face."

A Gnome.

"Yeah, I know that. Now. But we don't have Gnomes where I come from. We don't have anything–just us and animals. So imagine waking up, thinking you're safe in your own bed, in a world that has nothing that could possibly be standing over you except another person, and seeing *that* reaching for you instead." Eliza sent Mardu her memory of that terrifying moment. She knew now that Gnomes weren't anywhere near as big as he had seemed at the time, and she knew they didn't really have glowing eyes or fangs dripping with blood either. The only thing accurate about the image was the matted fuzz on his face, and the size of his nose. But it was an honest memory. It really did show what she had first seen–and felt– when she'd opened her eyes. Eliza felt oddly satisfied when she felt Mardu shudder in understanding.

How did you escape him?

"Using Eliza's patented Pylon Law of Threat Management and Information Gathering: when you get confused, just stand still. Pretend to be a deaf mute and wait. People aren't very careful around someone they think is an idiot, and sooner or later, they'll slip up. Monster boy didn't speak my language, so he couldn't exactly tell me anything useful, but I did convince him I was hungry. So when he went off to find something disgusting for me to eat, I hunted around for anything big enough to hit him with that didn't go squish when I touched it–not an easy task in a Gnome hole, let me tell you–but I did it. And when he came back, I clobbered him and took off."

Which is when I found you.

"Yeah. Pretty much."

So you were truly a stranger here. You knew nobody, you had no stake in the people or in the events, yet you agreed to assist me. Why?

Eliza shrugged in the darkness. "I got tired of playing pylon in this perv-infested wonderland, I guess. You seemed to know what was going on, and you looked like you could use the help."

I looked like a crazy crow fighting for control of his own body. And losing.

"K-k-k-keh!" Scraw said. Eliza laughed with him.

"See, that's the reason right there. You speak Eliza. And I guess I kind of needed that. I'm used to being a second banana. Lone banana never really worked for me." Eliza couldn't help leaking images of Tayna and her own warm feeling of happiness, knowing that T was enjoying her new freedom. Probably somewhere exciting.

"Besides," she added. "Once it started to look like I might have to topple a king or two to get out of here, step one became finding a partner. One who speaks the same language, and ideally, one who could point out which kings I need to topple. So see? We were made for each other. How could I resist?"

Then in your mind, it is me who is helping you.

"My agenda, your agenda. Pfft! Who cares? We like each other and we're both getting what we want. Isn't that what great partnerships are all about?"

But if you really do not wish to continue in our efforts...

"Right." Eliza sighed as the wind came out of her sails. "But if I don't, I won't really be much help to you anymore, will I?" Then she shrugged to herself. "Okay. I get it. So I guess we *will* be repeating the carny barker and her silver-tongued crow act. But it's not getting us anywhere. Why keep trying?"

Because we have not finished, Mardu sent. But there was something else too. Eliza could sense it as a sort of flavor, underneath the words. Mardu was waiting for something, but when she asked, the Flame of the Dragon was not sure. She knew only that there was... something, still to come.

But if you had to guess? Eliza sent.

A sign, Mardu replied. *I would say I am waiting for a sign.*

But of what, or to what purpose, she could not say.

Mehklok wriggled himself deeper into the soft, damp soil along the edge of the stream and sighed. It felt so good to have its oozing caress around him once more. For two days he had been tracking that blasted sky witch, and where had she gone, first thing? Why, straight up out of the Throat and into the crop-starved trees, that's where. Selfish witch didn't have the decency stay in a place where he could at least find some real food.

It was getting harder and harder to track her too. As the ground had become flatter, the witch had started making better time, and she no longer seemed to be wandering aimlessly either. Her track now moved in straight lines, as though she had rediscovered some forgotten errand and now hurried to attend to it. But it still made no sense. She was moving quickly, yes, but in seemingly random directions. First to one squalid little skyfolk village and then to another, but crossing back over her path time and again. It was like she was hurrying to find something, but had no idea where it might be. And the faster she moved, the faster *he* had to move too. To keep pace. No consideration at all for his aging legs or his Gnomileshi complexion that couldn't be out in the air all day without some decent mud breaks.

The little Gnome reached out and plucked a centipede from the rotting stump that jutted from the bank beside him, and popped it into his mouth. Without the convenience of the sky crop, nor any time to scavenge, he'd been reduced to eating wild bugs as he could find them, but it wasn't enough. He'd been feeling dizzy and dreamy lately. A good mud soak was just what he needed. Just an hour or two. Just until the sun was up high enough that the forest leaves would shade him properly. Then he would find her. But until then... Mehklok closed his eyes and sank blissfully into a damp and happy dream of dead things.

"Scraw!"

"Mago spiss, barg flummic ambusgarrent!"

The sound of feet crashing through the brush and an argument of some incomprehensible kind dragged Mehklok back up from his slumber. Just his luck. He'd closed his eyes for no more than ten seconds before some local bird harvester... Then his eyes snapped fully open.

It was her!

Mehklok struggled to sit up, but the squelching mud resisted his sudden movement and held him firmly in place as the witch woman stormed by along the opposite bank. A crow swooped past her, squawking and garbling at her, and she spouted back some gibberish or other in turn. As though either one could understand the pox-rotting blather they were spewing. But there she was! Almost close enough to touch!

Oh curse her and all her sorcery! She had done this on purpose, he just knew it. She had waited, just out of sight, until he'd gotten himself good and properly buried in his lovely little muck, and then she'd popped out, just to tease him with her damnable proximity.

Mehklok didn't want to draw her attention though. No. Now that she'd gotten the surprise on him, he'd have to wait, let her think she'd gotten away with it. But he was a Gnome with a mission now. He knew where she was, and he could see what direction she was heading. As soon as she was gone, he'd hop up out of this hole and go after her. Crow or no crow, by high-sun he would catch her and get his world back in order. And by day's end, she'd be safely back in that blasted merchant's cart he'd found her in. Let that cloud-strutting skite have her, for all the trouble she'd caused. And the sooner done, the better for it.

Yes sir. Tomorrow, Mehklok would be a free Gnome. Of course, he still had to redisanimate her. Couldn't return a live body where a dead one was expected now, could he?

As the sorceress disappeared into the trees, still squabbling with her bird, Mehklok lifted himself up from out of his hole, as quickly as the mud would allow. There was no time to waste. He had work to do. The little Gnome reached down and patted the harvesting blade that still hung from his belt. At least it would be happy work.

With the sounds of distant crow calls leading him on, Mehklok took up the pursuit, and plunged on into the disgusting forest.

"... and together we shall restore the Oath of Kings!"

Mehklok watched from cover as the witch-girl lowered her arms. His mouth hung slack with the revelation he'd just heard. This changed everything! He could scarcely believe his own eyes and ears. Such power! The bird had actually spoken for her! Not only was she a terrifying sorceress, as he had suspected from the beginning, but an actual warrior queen as well, come back from death to lead her people into battle in their hour of need! Mehklok had to lean against a tree for support. His head was swimming with awe. And to think he'd been planning to redisanimate her and return her body to the f'znat he'd stolen it from. What a fool he'd almost been!

The villagers surged forward at the end of her speech, gathering around the woman as though transfixed by her message, but what did they know? Only one such as he could appreciate... Wait a blink. Had she said she was a queen? Returned from death? That stirred a memory somewhere. What was it about dead queens... ? Mehklok massaged his nose with his fingers, squeezing the flesh, trying to force more blood up into his brain, to make it think harder. There was a memory in there, buried deep, and it had the taste of something important. What was it?

The girl smiled at the ignorant peasants pressing in around her, yet despite their enthusiasm, Mehklok noticed that she remained silent. A smiling mute, gesturing, pointing– That's it! The prophecy! The sky reeled around the little Gnome and the trees spun. His knees melted into water and his heart hammered in his chest. Delirious with hope, the Gnome chaplain lurched forward out of the underbrush.

"The prophecy was true!" he wailed, as he fell to his knees in the dirt before her. With hands raised up in divine supplication, Mehklok shuffled forward on his knees. Tears streamed down his face. Real tears! Spontaneously wept! Yet another miracle to prove the truth of this revelation. "You've come back!" he cried. "Oh holiest of days! You've come back to us! Tell me how I may be of service."

The witch woman screamed and hit him with the bird.

For the first time since they had started making these speeches three days ago, trying to drum up support, Eliza lowered her arms and looked out at the crowd to see something she hadn't seen before. Hope. Not on every face certainly, but it was there. Most of the villagers still stuck to the usual script, wandering away quickly when she was finished, and refusing to make eye contact–the kind of behavior most people reserved for crazy folks encountered on a sidewalk. But this time, two or three of them actually came *closer* when she was done. Mardu did her best to interpret their words for her as they all spoke at once.

"Is it true? Can the Oath really be restored?"

"Don't we need all the kings to agree?"

"My sister and her boys were taken. I-I'd like to help. Somehow."

What's different today? Eliza sent.

You are, Mardu replied. *You sounded different today. Like...*

Like what?

Like you believe. It is no longer a game you play to fill your day.

But that was a bit more truth than Eliza wanted to think about, so she changed the topic.

We better get to the ritual then, before they change their minds.

Turning her attention back to the villagers pressing in around her, Eliza gave them a silent smile, and gestured toward a small sack lying on the ground behind them. It had been given to her at one of the previous villages, although more out of pity than any urge to support their cause. To its supply of dried travel foods, Eliza had also added a handful of hiker-berries, earlier that morning, but people were pressing so closely to her now that she couldn't step past them to reach the sack. She finally managed to make herself understood to one young man, who turned and looked back where she was pointing.

"The sack? Why of course, Prophetess. Let me just–"

But they were interrupted by an terrifying shriek that rose from the shrubbery behind her. From the corner of her eye, Eliza saw a shape lurch out of the undergrowth and then fall to the ground. She turned slowly, hampered by the press of bodies around her, but at last she managed to get a clear look at the newcomer.

"It's him!" she cried. And then, acting on pure reflex, she grabbed the heaviest thing she could find, and threw it at him.

The monster Gnome-perv had found her.

In the ensuing confusion, three things happened, more or less on top of each other. First, Scraw bounced unceremoniously off the Gnome's face. In his haste to get away, the terrified crow managed to beat the little creep mercilessly with wild, flapping wings, and he didn't hold back on the scratching claws, either. But Eliza didn't see much of that, because she was already looking around frantically for something bigger and heavier to hit him with.

The second thing that happened was that, upon seeing a Gnome come stumbling out of the bush at them, the villagers ran. All of them. Most ran away, toward the forest or back toward their huts, but the man who had talked about losing his sister did not. He made a beeline for the Gnome, and the look on his face spoke plainly. Eliza saw no reason to interfere.

And then the third thing happened. It was a voice. An exasperated, irritated, frustrated, and above all, an angry voice, that barked an unintelligible command.

As though he had been shot, Scraw folded up and dropped to the forest floor, where he lay unmoving. The little Gnome pitched forward onto his face, whimpering and whining, either unable or unwilling to look up. The villagers also collapsed, as though they had suddenly changed their minds about fleeing, and had called a spontaneous stage-dive practice on the forest floor instead.

Through the confusion, Eliza stood tall and did her best to not look shocked by what was happening. The voice had been Mardu's, of course, speaking some mystic command directly into the minds of everyone in sight. But since everyone thought the command had come from *her*, Eliza had to play the part. Quickly drawing her face into a fearsome scowl, she glared around in all directions as she took one large step toward the Gnome and drew back a foot to kick him.

Be still, Mardu sent. Eliza set her foot back down.

Why? He deserves it. He's the one who–

Not now. Trust me. There is still much for the Flame of the Dragon to do. Scraw, I release you. You may rise. I'm tired of staring at the dirt. Hopefully none of the others saw that.

On the scrub grass next to the prostrate Gnome, the crow shuddered and then got to his feet before flapping indignantly off toward the trees, but half way there, he jerked in the air and then turned, coming back to alight on Eliza's shoulder. He did not look happy about it.

I am sorry, friend crow, but it was unavoidable, and you must now resume your place as Voice of the Flame. In a little time, we will hunt succulent grubs together, but not yet.

"Scraw!" He shouted this right into Eliza's ear, and she was pretty sure it was not by accident.

Unavoidable? Eliza sent. *Why didn't you throw me down like everybody else with that magic judo attack?*

It would not do for the Flame of the Dragon to flop on the ground, victim to her own magic, would it? The only way I could think to effect everyone except you was to speak the charm in the Forest Tongue, directly into their minds, but alas, Scraw understands it too, and there was no time to be more selective. Still, I do not think anybody noticed that your charm felled your familiar as well as the others.

My charm? My familiar?

Yes, yours. Remember, to them, you are all there is. You are the Flame of the Dragon, and there is only you. And your bird servant, of course, who speaks for you. Your familiar.

Right. So when can I start with the kicking? Eliza nudged the Gnome's butt with her foot, and was rewarded with louder whimpering as the disgusting little wretch trembled in fear.

Leave him be, Mardu said, this time a bit more sternly. *He is important.*

Him? Important? What's he going to do? Kidnap more children for us? Strip them naked like he did me? Eliza shuddered at the thought of having been so... alone with him.

He did not bring you to this world, Mardu said. *Nor was it he who removed your clothes. I can see that much in his mind. That was how he found you. He believed you were dead, and that your body would bring him great riches.*

Oh. So he only grave-robbed me? Some sort of pimp of the undead? You're right. That is so much better.

Think, Eliza. In doing so, he removed you from the power of the one who did *snatch you into this world. Do you not think he may have done you a service in this?*

Eliza didn't like the sound of that. She was still in favor of blaming the little grunt for everything, and now Mardu was messing with the good mad she had going, leaving her with little more than a frustrated seething. *You didn't answer my question, O Great and Powerful Oz. That's what he did* before. *What makes him so important to us now?*

I do not know, Mardu admitted. *But he is important. He is the sign we have been waiting for.*

Him?

Yes, but there is no time for further discussion. We must act quickly now, or we will lose our gains. I have an idea.

Under Mardu's instruction, Eliza moved around the clearing, releasing the Wasketchin villagers from the charm with a touch. When they were all standing again, they could have gone back to their homes and tasks, but they could see that the Gnome had been captured too, so most of them stayed to see what would happen next.

We will perform the ritual now, Mardu said. *We must claim those who would join our ranks, and it will be good for the others to see this, and to spread the word. Perhaps in time, more will seek us out.*

Unfortunately, now that there was a Gnome involved, none of those who had pressed forward after the speech were still willing to follow the Flame. Eliza stamped her foot in frustration.

All is not lost, Eliza. One still waits. Do it now, Mardu sent, along with a mental image of the groveling Gnome.

Wait... What? Him? No way! I don't want that little–

Now, Eliza! Quickly, before the villagers leave. Don't you see? Restoring the Oath is more than simply re-saying the words and spilling new blood. We must show the people–all the people–that there is goodness in their neighbors. We must restore more than an Oath–we must restore their faith in peace, as well. And we can begin today, with him. Let them see that the first to join our cause, the first to stand against Gnome predations upon the Wasketchin, was in fact himself a Gnome. Swear him in allegiance to the Flame. I can hear his thoughts. He burns inside for permission to do so. He fears you will not accept him. Let him stand and he will swear to you eagerly. We must not let this opportunity pass.

So, against her better judgment, and resisting the very strong urge to simply strangle the little sniveler, Eliza reached down and touched him on the shoulder.

"Rise, Chaplain of Gash-Garnok," Scraw said, from his perch on Eliza's shoulder, and the Gnome got slowly to his feet, eyes wide and quaking so badly with fear that Eliza had to fight down a smug grin. If she had to put up with him, at least his devout worship put her on the power side of the relationship. So at least that was cool.

There was a bit of awkwardness when she reached the point in the ritual where she was supposed to wipe berry juice over his mouth. How was she supposed to get around the great floppy Gnome nose that hung over his lips? For a moment, she didn't know what to do, but then she realized that in Gnome culture, the nose was probably a very important feature, so instead of going around it, she adapted her ritual, adding a bit about "Your nose belongs to me. You scent the air at my command." Then she simply lifted it out of the way and did the part about "speaking for me" over his mouth.

And then the ritual was over. The little runt had become the first voice to join the Chorus of the Flame.

But he would not be the last.

chapter 15

In the few days... hours?... since Calaida–his only friend down here–had been silenced, Elicand had made little progress on scouting out his environment.

The blackness of the cave was total, and the roaring hiss that filled his ears had not abated for even a heartbeat in all the time he'd been here. He couldn't hear himself talk, he couldn't hear himself shout, he couldn't even hear the quiet clicking of his back when he stretched. So with no eyes and no ears to help in his task, he'd been forced to explore with nothing but his fingers.

When Shondu had first brought him to these strange, dark caverns with his stupid Brownie prank, Elicand had made a game of his investigations, giving names to every feature and every half-dreamed avenue of escape. That first cavern he had christened Ouchyville, in commemoration of the numerous minor injuries that had plagued his blind explorations. Although, in full honesty, those injuries had probably saved his life, forcing him to be more cautious than was his normal habit. But in *this* cavern, without even his ears to aid him, his fingertips had proven much less effective. Not that there was much for them to see.

He knew he was on a shelf of rock, perhaps five body-lengths long and three wide that hung out over, well, nothing. The air around him was the same cool dampness it had always been, and just the tiniest bit... oily, although none of that oiliness seemed to linger on his fingers at all. It was more an idea of filminess than an actual feeling of it, which made no sense, but that's how it felt. There was nothing but this flat jut of stone and the empty space around it.

Like a tree branch with a flattened top, jutting out from the trunk and broken off cleanly at the end, the rock he stood on was a long and narrow platform that seemed to have no purpose other than to delay his eventual plunge into oblivion. Emerging from a tall, impassible wall of stone at one end, and surrounded by a leap into the dark unknown on the other three sides, it was as much a prison as anything else. A tabletop with no way down, and no sign that there was anything below him except air to plummet through.

Continuing with his practice from Ouchyville, Elicand had given names to all the features he discovered. At the end of his prison was the flat, cold face he called the Unclimbable Wall, for what should be obvious reasons. Opposite that, perhaps ten long strides away, the rocky floor just stopped. This was the furthest extent of the Featureless Lip of Plunging–a smooth edge that ran from the Wall, out into the darkness, and then back to join the Wall again. All of it utterly without crack, bump or crevice. Well, almost utterly. There was one particular section, right at the tip, that had been drawing him back like a tongue drawn to a sore tooth. The Slightly Not Completely Featureless Feature of the Featureless Lip. He could always come up with a better name for it later, if he survived.

The Featureless Feature was a single knobbly bump on the face of the Lip, perhaps half an arm's length below where he knelt. It wasn't knobbly enough to provide any actual support, but pressing his fingertips against its slippery hump, he could almost convince himself that it would serve as a brace, allowing him to reach out just a little further. There was *something* out there, in the damp and empty air beyond the Lip. He had been over every inch of this jutting prison of stone, and aside from a few loose pebbles and a crumbly patch of dust–all that remained of the protective cocoon that had healed him–there was just nothing else left to try. It was either the almost-knob or wait for starvation to claim him.

Elicand knelt once more at the Lip and eased his hand down its slick face, feeling around for the bump. When he found it, he took a deep breath and then tried to will the ridges of his finger-tips to bite as he pressed them against the smooth stone. Carefully, he reached forward with his other hand, probing outward, stretch-ing, until he felt himself on the very verge of tipping. There it was again. He could sense a changing in the air around his wavering hand. Gingerly, he shifted his left foot, spreading his toes out just a tiny bit wider, and then he stretched forward again, maintaining his precarious balance with nothing more than wishful thinking in his fingertips, and waved again. There! It was–

(aloneness negation question)

A wall of water grabbed at Elicand's fingertips and yanked his whole hand downward. It would have jerked him into the abyss–it *should* have jerked him into the abyss–but the downward movement broke his contact with the raging torrent. Elicand shot his legs quickly back behind him as the lower half of his stomach crashed onto the rocky floor, leaving his head and chest and the upper span of his tummy projecting out over the not-floor, held there, defying gravity by the sheer willpower of his fingerprints on the wet... slippery... The fingerprints let go of the bump, skidding down over it, and Elicand could feel his body beginning to shift forward. If he'd had anything to eat lately, anything at all, he would have been that much more top-heavy and probably *would* have plunged headlong into death. But the palm of his hand ground onto that vaguest of bumps...

And held.

With his heart screaming an ancient curse at him that he could not hear, but could only feel, throbbing at his temples and pounding in his chest, Elicand, managed to wriggle one foot ever so slightly further back, away from the edge. And then the other. Maybe. He wasn't sure if it had actually moved, or if he'd only hoped it had moved. The wild card was his free hand. It still dangled below him, limp against the featureless face of the rock. If he pressed it against the Lip as he so desperately wanted to do, the pressure would only thrust his upper body further out into the air, beyond his precarious balance point, and that would be all. But there was nothing for him to brace it against either. What he needed was to get that arm back up onto the floor without toppling himself in the process.

Slowly, in what might very well be the slowest of panicky movements ever made by a Wasketchin at any time in history, Elicand curled his free arm upward toward his stomach, keeping his hand and forearm as close to the rock as he could. When his elbow was above the edge of the Lip, he began to unfold it again, drawing first the elbow and then the forearm back and then at last turning his hand palm down to grab at the dusty rock floor beside his hip. It wasn't much. It felt like nothing at all. It had taken him a hundred heartbeats. A thousand. But it was enough. The grip of his palm on the floor was enough to allow him to wriggle his body back from the edge, until at last, with a whoosh of released air that he had not realized he'd been holding, Elicand withdrew his other palm from the Featureless Feature bump and rolled away from death.

It was almost an hour later, after the jubilant pounding of his life against the walls of his body had slowed to a more decorous tempo, that a curious thought echoed in his mind: (aloneness negation question)

The voice had been Shondu's.

⸺⸺

His experience with the Featureless Lip had taught Elicand three things. First, that he was not alone–Shondu was somehow, miraculously, gloriously still here. Somewhere. That knowledge was useless however, until he was able to find a way out of his current predicament and then go find the little guy. Second, he was only going to be able to do that by taking chances. They would be carefully weighed and considered chances, of course, but there simply was no safe route off this rock. And third? Elicand was now certain that his end, whenever it might come to seek him, would do so after a terrifying plunge into an abyss. But strangely, all three of these revelations were comforting to him.

As with all education however, his new knowledge left him with new questions. Which of the pointless, clueless, featureless directions available to him would lead to an escape? Would he be able to reestablish contact with Shondu? And if not, would he ever find the little guy? Somehow, his furry little friend had spoken to him when his own hand had touched the water. There was no way he was going to try *that* experiment again, but was there some other way to make the connection? Or somewhere else where he could reach the river without risking his life?

It all came down to a single puzzle that taunted him for hours. If he could find a way to communicate with Shondu again, then he might learn of a way off this rock, or, if he could somehow get off this rock, he might be able to find Shondu again. Each solution seemed to require the other one to happen first.

Elicand had been over each and every inch of the stone platform, and in all of his searching he hadn't found even a hint of a way off, nor any other access to the sky river. All he had was the general clamminess of the air and the thin sheen of wetness that coated everything he touched. It hadn't been until his almost death, when he'd made fleeting contact with the torrent of water thundering past him in the darkness, just beyond his reach, that he had even known there *was* any water nearby. Of course, now he felt stupid. The roaring and raging of water crashing all around him should have been his first clue. But it had surrounded him since before he had first regained consciousness here however many days or maybe weeks ago that had been. It was so loud, so penetrating, that it had numbed the parts of his brain that might have wondered more about it, just as it had numbed his hearing. It wasn't a sound, it was a thing, physical and suffocating, crowding him out from the center of his own mind. And such a *thing* had no connections to those happier, everyday ideas like rivers.

Contact with the film of water that coated his current world did nothing to reestablish contact with Shondu. He had tried several times now. Clearly, communication would require touching the flow itself again, so that was out. At least until he found another river, or a less death-causing way to touch the one he already had.

Once again, in a sort of ritualized refusal to give up, Elicand tried to invoke the charm for light, but as before, it simply refused to catch. The vim had never been particularly strong for Elicand–it was one of the reasons his family had always chosen lives of service, because their vim was not usually strong enough to contribute in more conspicuous ways–but it wasn't like they were dead to it either. Still, no matter what pleas he sang, nor how convincingly he sang them, Elicand couldn't muster up so much as the glowing nose that he had often used to entertain the little ones.

Which only left escape. And that meant taking some further risks. But instead of fearing such risks, he was surprised to discover that he felt elated by them. Perhaps it was the utter surprise–after the terror had worn off–of finding the river arcing through the air a mere finger's-breadth beyond the world he had previously explored. It forced him to wonder. What lay just another fingernail above the highest point he had yet reached on the Unclimbable Wall? What ridge or foothold might lie just one inch further down the Featureless Lip than the furthest inch he had yet explored? Well, he wasn't ready to think about the Featureless Lip option again. Not yet. But finding a river in the middle of the sky had been a curiously invigorating experience, so Elicand went back to the Wall with a renewed sense of hope.

Try as he might however, even with his newfound ambition, there wasn't a crack deeper than a fingernail nor a bump thicker than an eyelid to be found on the entire expanse. Every feature that might once have been there had been worn away by untold centuries of running, dripping dampness. For hours he had been trying to reach beyond the limits of his body, running from several paces away and flinging himself up the Wall, slapping at it with out-stretched fingers. He was sure that if he could just reach a tiny bit further, some finger would catch the crease of some ledge and he would have found his way out. It was the technique he had used to find the Scary Tunnel of Wind when he had first become trapped here in Shondu's "pocket," and even though the success of that find was still in question, it *had* been a find. But with no way to quiz Shondu about hidden exits, and literally no other inch of rock left unexplored, the old Leap and Slap had to work. It simply had to. So he kept at it, long after he'd lost the feeling in his fingers, and long after the repeated poundings against rock had split the skin and added the slick grease of his blood to the dampness of his prison wall.

Eventually though, his body simply gave out. Elicand launched one last, pitiful assault upon his imprisonment, and then lost con-sciousness when his face and chest slapped once more against the stone. It was a good thing he was not near either end of the Wall when he did so too, because an unconscious Wasketchin body is neither graceful nor particularly careful about where it sprawls–not even when it is trapped and all alone. He had tried, to the limits of his abilities, and he had failed. So it was a good thing for Elicand when, in the end, both of his problems took pity on his efforts and solved themselves.

Shondu found him.

———————

Elicand was happy beyond stories when he heard Shondu's voice bubble into his own thoughts like laughter.

(healing-place stay reason question)

Their previous contact had tasted to Elicand of loneliness and fear, but it had been so brief that it hadn't even had time to register before it had disappeared. What he felt now was an impish tittering delight. It washed over him like a gentle summer breeze, and the unexpected warmth and familiarity of contact with another soul, after so much time spent alone in this crushing darkness, took Elicand completely by surprise, wrenching an unexpected sob of relief from his chest. Alone for days, blind, and deaf from the constant oppressive roar of the water echoing throughout the cavern, the feeling of proper contact was like birdsong in his skull, even if it was a trifle mocking.

"I'm stuck here statement," Elicand said. "How do I get off this rock question?"

(tumble fall glee statement)

"Great," Elicand replied. "I'll tumble off this rock and fall to my death while you laugh your little laugh of glee then, shall I question?"

(correction tumble fall thou statement) (tumble thou fun play statement)

While Elicand was puzzling over how it could possibly be fun to fall to his death, he was startled by a furry touch at his elbow. Before he even knew what he was doing, Elicand had scooped Shondu up into a furious double-armed hug that threatened to overwhelm them both, and though he tried several times to put his feeling into empathought, Elicand found himself speechless. But Shondu seemed to understand and for several very satisfying moments, the two accidental adventurers simply held onto one another, communicating all that needed to be said through the warmth of their skin and the firmness of the grip with which each held the other.

"So, tumble fall not die question?" Elicand said, when he was finally ready to let go of his friend.

(follow show feel statement)

Elicand felt Shondu's hand tug at his own and allowed himself to be led toward the Featureless Lip, although he insisted on taking the last few strides on his hands and knees. Shondu guided Elicand's hand in the darkness, along the Featureless Lip, but Elicand could feel nothing special about the stone. Perhaps it was the tiniest bit smoother than it was elsewhere. More polished, perhaps. But the difference was too slight for him to even be sure it was real.

(tumble place statement) Then Shondu let go of his hand and toppled off the ledge.

"No!' Elicand screamed, even though he couldn't hear it, and as he screamed, he instinctively reached toward the empty air where his friend had just disappeared.

And plunged headlong after him.

chapter 16

"Would you like some wine?" DelRoy held up a bottle of red wine and a bottle of white.

"Yes, please. The red looks good."

He pulled the cork on the red and left it to breathe on the table while he went to find some glasses. He left Sue doing the woman thing, wandering around the sitting room, inspecting. Normally a fairly private guy, this was the first time he could ever remember having a house guest, and he was feeling a little nervous as he went into the kitchen.

"Your place is very tidy," Sue called, from the other room. "Except for your desk. You really should dust more."

"Can't do that," he called back, as he hunted through the drawer for the good corkscrew. "Might lose an important clue that way, and then where would I be?"

He only had the two wine glasses and one was all he'd ever used, so he ran the water in the sink. They just needed a quick rinse.

"Hey! You've been holding out on me!" Sue called. She sounded a bit excited.

"What do you mean?"

Sue came into the kitchen waving her hand in the air. "This!" she said. "As if you didn't know. You've put together an entire Regina Finch file. Why didn't you say so?"

DelRoy smiled. Sue Nackenfausch had the most disarming way of playing characters. Like this afternoon at the mortuary. Too bad she was still hiding behind that married woman front. "You got me," he said, nodding playfully at her empty hands. "I confess. But it's written in code. You'll have to read it to me."

Sue gave him an odd look, but then she smiled, and proceeded to page through the imaginary docket.

"Oh, say! This looks interesting. Seems to be a letter to you. From you."

He laughed. "You don't say. And what, pray tell, did I have to say to myself?" With the glasses clean, he set them on a little serving tray and dropped a folded towel over his arm. With a wave of his arm, he ushered Sue back out toward the sitting room, where he'd left the wine, and followed along behind her as she began to read.

Marty, I think something screwy is going on, and if I'm right, you'll have no idea what I'm talking about, and no memory of ever writing this down. Hell, I'm not even sure you'll be able to read this. But before I continue, it's crucial that you believe me, so I'm going to prove that this note is really from you, no matter how weird what I tell you seems. Okay?

Here's the proof: Rebecca Calveigh. Tupperware.

DelRoy was startled by the sound of shattering glass. Sue whirled around to look back at him. "Martin? Are you okay?"

He could feel the heat of two emotions surging through him: shock and shame. How had she known about that? It was impossible! "Um, yeah. Fine," he said, not wanting her to see his embarrassment. Rather than face her, he pulled a broom and dustpan from the closet by the door and then stooped to gather the broken bits of glass from the floor. Sue bent down to help.

"You really didn't know what was in there, did you?" Sue's voice was still bright, but edged with concern. Was she worried that she had revealed too much? But how could she have known to say exactly those words? However it was she'd found out, now his reaction had proven that her information was correct, so there wasn't much use in trying to hide it. Besides, it wasn't like it had been illegal or anything. Just stupid. And young.

"It's nothing," he said. "Not really. Just a dumb thing from the past that probably means a lot more to me than to anybody else."

Sue grinned. "And maybe Rebecca Calveigh, I'm guessing?" There was a playful twinkle in her eye, but when he didn't react, it turned more serious. "You don't want to talk about it."

He laughed nervously. "You could say that."

"Then we won't," Sue said. "But we should probably read the rest of that letter, don't you think?" Why was she still going on with this? Why the game? He couldn't think of any reason, so he just nodded his head.

Sue handed him the dustpan full of glass shards and crossed back to the desk, while he went to dump the remains of the old wine glasses and set about looking for replacements. There was no sign left of the trembling in his hands when he returned, just as Sue began to read again.

Okay, so you know it's really you. But trust me, that little escapade is nothing compared to what seems to be going on around here. Let's see. What do you need to know for background? Well, it's June now. You've... I've... We've been working Missing Persons since April. Remember Arun Singh? He's been showing me the ropes around here. Anyway, you know how Arun had a thing for cold cases? Had that stack of them on his desk? Well, he was talking about one of them a few days ago. The Regina Finch file. The one you're holding now. Said he'd found something that connected her to a group of women running a home for abandoned kids. Check it out. It's all in the file. Anyway, yesterday he decided it was time to go have a chat with these women, but when he got back, he was acting kind of weird. Didn't seem to know what I was talking about when I asked him how it went. And here's the really weird part. When I showed him the file, he pretended he couldn't see it. Or at least, I think he was pretending. He kept asking why I was waving my hands at him, but I wasn't. I was waving the Finch file at him.

"I remember that," DelRoy said, as a cold shiver ran up his spine. He quickly set the new glasses down on the table. Before he dropped them as well. "But how are you doing this? How could you know any of these things?"

Sue looked up at him in confusion. "I don't know anything, Martin. I'm just reading what's written here. What *you've* written here." She looked back down at the nothing in her hands, then her eyes widened with realization and she looked back up at him. "Wait a minute! You can't see this folder either, can you? Like your friend, Arun." She waved her empty hand in the air again.

He stared at her for a long, hard minute. But he wasn't really looking at her. His eyes were just focused in her direction as he hunkered down into crunch mode, and began working the problem. Things were not adding up. He couldn't tell whether Sue was being sincere, or whether she was a master actress in the midst of some elaborate head game. Earlier, he wouldn't have given that possibility any consideration, but given how quick-witted she'd been at the mortuary, now he wasn't so sure. Was this just more of the same? Was she playing him? But why would she? This was *her* case. What good would it do her to confuse the guy trying to help her?

And then another thought occurred to him. Maybe she actually believed there was something in her hand. But that just raised more questions. If it was true, then somebody *else* was feeding her information–information that nobody else could possible know. No way in Hell. Not a chance. There was only one person alive who knew the significance of those words. Not even Rebecca herself knew the full story. No. So, once you have eliminated the impossible... There was only one conclusion. As improbable as it might be, he himself had written the note that Sue now held. And, just as improbably, there must really be papers in her hand–papers that he could not see, and that he had no recollection of ever having written.

DelRoy could feel his heart racing and sounds were getting distant. Fumbling for the arm of the couch, he flopped himself down. Then he poured a full glass of wine and drained it off in a single gulp. After pouring another, he raised the bottle to Sue in a silent question, hoping she couldn't see how badly the bottle shook in his hand. Sue nodded, so he poured her a glass too. When they were both settled back onto the sofa, Sue prodded gently.

"You okay?"

"Well no," he admitted. "Not really. It's... disturbing." He waved his glass at her empty hands. "You got the people right– though I don't know how–but the way I remember it, Arun and I got into an argument about proper documentation. I must have said something stupid to him. I don't remember what. Because shortly after that, he asked the captain to reassign me. So I got handed off to Trina Wyatt for the rest of my orientation, and then spent the next year trying to stay out of Arun's way. Until he retired." He let his voice drift off, unsure whether to risk saying anything else.

"There's more here," Sue said gently, tapping one empty hand with the other. "You want me to keep reading?"

DelRoy felt completely lost. Could she really believe there was something in her hand, even though there clearly wasn't?

"So just to be clear," he said, "you're actually reading this. From a piece of paper. Lying inside a file folder. Which is right now in your hands. That right?" Sue nodded. He could only shake his head. "By all means then," he said. "Keep reading."

Sue looked uncertainly at her "papers," and then glanced back up at him. "You sure?" He nodded. Sue held his gaze for a moment, and then turned back to her fingers and began, again, to read.

... waving the Finch file at him. Well that was a week ago, and ever since then, I've been going through these notes. All kinds of crazy things. Missing Person files that vanish without a trace. Calls to Children's Services that don't get documented or followed up. Social workers who lose kids in the system. And all of it pointing back to that one common element: Our Lady of Divine Suffering's Home for Orphans and Evictees. That's where Arun went, just before he stopped being able to see the file.

And it's where I'm heading tomorrow. With Judy Chan. Apparently they have these little shindigs regularly, and because she works in Children's Services, she's been to a few of them. I managed to get her to invite me along this time. Don't think she knows I was fishing for it.

Anyway, I don't know what we're going to find when we get there, but I don't want this file to just disappear, so I'm leaving it here on the desk. Right on top of the keyboard. That way if it does disappear–

"But I don't have a computer," DelRoy said, gesturing at his desk, which was obviously free of any technology. "They just suck you into working at home, so I never got one."

Sue gaped at him. "But, of *course* you have a computer, Martin. It's right there on your desk! That's where I found the file. Lying on top of your keyboard, just like the note says."

DelRoy looked back at the desk. No keyboard. No screen. Just a mess of paper. And a couple of pens. "Okay, then. Touch it," he said. Sue looked at him oddly. "Touch it!" he said again, this time through gritted teeth. His temper–normally nonexistent–was rapidly rising. Someone was playing very unfunny games with him, and he was having trouble figuring out who to blame. He was pretty sure it wasn't Sue now, but that just made it worse. DelRoy jumped to his feet and began to pace. He could feel the tension climbing up his arms from his clenched fists.

Keeping one eye on him, Sue got up slowly and went to the desk to do as he asked, as DelRoy just stood there, trembling. With a shrug, she reached out a hand and patted at the empty air. DelRoy watched her fingers as they flattened against the nothingness, like a mime playing the trapped-in-a-box game, only inside-out. But this was too much. There was no way an entire computer was sitting on his desk. One that he'd just never noticed before? No way! There were limits to how far a guy's gullibility could be stretched and this was about ten yards too far. To prove his point, he stormed across the room and shot his hand out, punching at the empty air under Sue's hand.

And a jolt of pain raced up his arm.

"Martin!" Sue gasped, the shock plain upon her face. "Why did you... Are you okay?" DelRoy sucked in air and clutched his screaming hand to his chest. Sue reached out a hand of her own, but he twisted away from her, too confused–and embarrassed–to accept her sympathy.

"We'd better get some ice on that," Sue said, then she stepped past him and went into the kitchen. She came back a minute later with a towel folded around several lumps of ice from the freezer, but he ignored her and continued to probe at his desk with his good hand, forcing himself to lower his fingers over every square inch of its surface. And even though he couldn't see anything other than the clutter of paper he'd always seen, there was an obvious computer-shaped region of space where his hand would not go, along with a matching monitor-shaped space, and a keyboard-shaped space as well.

"What the hell is going on?" he said, scarcely noticing how much his voice shook. Sue took his throbbing hand and placed the bundle of ice on it, holding it there between her own. "What's wrong with me? Why can't I see it?"

Sue looked at him. Her eyes were filled with sympathy. "I don't know, Martin. At first I thought you were teasing me. Saying that you couldn't see the file. Couldn't see the computer, even though they're both right here, plain as day. Then I though you must be lying, but how could you be lying about something so blatantly false? Although it's pretty obvious now that you really can't see it. Nobody would have punched that CRT screen the way you did. Not if they could really see it."

"CRT?" he said. "It's that old?"

Sue nodded. "And I wasn't going to say anything, but it's covered in dust too. The rest of your place is nice. Tidy, for a man. But the desk is filthy, like you haven't even set so much as a coffee on it since some time last century."

"You might be more right than you know," he said.

"Is your hand okay?"

DelRoy looked down. A hot ache still pulsed through the knuckles at the base of his fingers, but he was able to wiggle them without awakening anything more than a dull flare.

"I don't think anything's broken," he said. "What else does the note say?"

"Not much," Sue said. "Just that you were going to leave the file on your keyboard so that you'd be forced to confront it, even if you did suffer the same amnesia as your friend, Arun. But that's all you wrote. The note ends there. It's signed, 'Be careful. Love, Yourself.' "

He grinned weakly. "Well, at least I was playful about it." Sue had picked up the invisible folder again and was flipping through it, her eyes as round as watch faces.

"It's all here, Martin. Regina Finch. Her Missing Person report. Interviews with her neighbors and co-workers. High school records. Photographs. Newspaper clippings. Whoever compiled this was very thorough."

"So who is she? Master criminal? International child smuggler? Psycho-hypnotist?"

"Oh dear," Sue said. A hand came up to cover her mouth. "Look at this," she said, pointing at another invisible page. Then she realized that he still couldn't see it. "She was a mom," Sue said. "A foster mom. And fourteen years ago, she inherited some money, then she vanished. And all five foster kids with her. The investigation was fierce, until... Oh no." Sue turned to look at him with such sorrow in her face that he could feel the bottom fall out of his own chest.

"It says here that she was probably murdered."

" 'Probably' murdered? Or 'was' murdered?"

"It says 'probably.' Written on the last page. It looks like the same handwriting as most of these other notes. Except for yours."

"Probably Arun's then," DelRoy said. "And he'd be guessing. If he had any evidence, he'd have said so."

DelRoy sat back down on the sofa, one hand throbbing and the other wrapped around his wine glass. "Well, you're going to have to read it all. Try and learn as much as you can from the notes. The more we know, the more likely we'll be able to connect it to something. Is there a picture?"

"Of Regina? Yes, a couple. There's a family photo of her with her kids, and a newspaper photo."

"Show me the family photo."

Sue held up a sliver of nothing between her fingers. DelRoy sighed. "Figures. Describe her to me, would you? I feel like I've been chasing a ghost through my memories, and this isn't helping."

Sue looked at her hand. "Well, she looks like a nice woman. Kind eyes. The kind that seem to smile, even when she's tired. And she is. Tired, I mean. Fairly thin, and plain looking, but tired. Although who wouldn't be? The girls in the photo are all young. Not one of them looks older than five. That would be enough to drive any mother to exhaustion."

The detective nodded. "So it's one of those cases then," he said, setting his wine down on the coffee table.

Sue wrinkled her brow. "What do you mean?"

"Oh, you know. The sweet, devoted mother of five who inherits a ton of money, buys a crematorium, kills the kids and disposes of them, then, in her guilt, buys a private high school and an orphanage to make amends. You read about it every day."

"Are you seri–?"

"Sorry," he said. "Cop humor. What would this case be without another impossibility before supper?"

DelRoy stretched back on the couch and scrubbed at his hair in exasperation. It had reached the point where this was no longer just a case. No longer just about Sue and her missing daughter. It had become personal. Martin was no longer just a nice-guy cop helping an attractive woman with her problem. Now he was involved. Personally. And he was getting angry.

"Read it to me," he said, keeping his eyes closed so he could concentrate. "Read me every single word."

So she did.

It was two days later, and DelRoy sat in his car, half a block from the Old Shoe. Sue sat quietly beside him, drinking her coffee in cautious little sips. The gray afternoon sky had already grimed itself into the darkness of night, and a chill wind blew down the empty street around them. The car was running, to keep the heater going, but all the lights were out.

They were on a stakeout.

Yesterday, Sue had managed to get some information from the girls about the parties. Apparently, the Goodies held one every Friday night. The kids didn't know what went on there, and had no idea who attended them, but they were certain that they happened every week, starting promptly at eight. Every Unlovable knew the schedule, because it was the one day when they got a bit of a reprieve from the constant badgering of the nuns, who were always too busy with their guests on party nights to spare any more than a single Sister to watch the entire place. So even though Failing Light came early on Fridays, the girls could lie in their beds and talk as much as they wanted, without fear of being shrieked at, or punished.

When he had announced that he was going to go watch the party guests arrive, Sue had quickly insisted on coming with him, and now here they were, alone together. Again. And the more often it happened, the more uneasy he grew.

"If you'd asked me last week," he said, trying to fill the silence that was anything but comfortable. "I'd have sworn up and down that I've never even seen this building before."

Sue patted his hand. "Well, when it comes to the Old Shoe, your memory isn't exactly the most reliable thing going now, is it?"

DelRoy grimaced, but he couldn't argue the point. "At least I can see it," he muttered.

Sue laughed. "That would have been awkward, huh?" Despite his irritation, he chuckled.

"It's almost seven. According to the kids, people should start arriving soon," he said.

"So who is it we're looking for, exactly?" Sue asked.

He shrugged. "Nobody specific. This is more fact-finding than a witch hunt. Sure, it would be nice to get some hard evidence on whoever it is in my department that's involved, and it would be even better if we got a sighting of Regina Finch, but we still have no idea what's actually going on. So the best I'm hoping for is that we'll get a few leads, based on who shows up."

"It's too bad Ned and I never got an invitation," Sue said. "If we had, then you and I might be sitting somewhere warmer now, instead of freezing here in the darkness waiting for clues to parade past us."

She was making light, DelRoy knew, trying to fill the drab hours of waiting, but how could she not realize that she was sending mixed signals, too? Talking about Ned, and in the same breath talking about himself and her sitting somewhere warmer? More intimate? He sucked angrily at his coffee and felt himself slumping down into somber thought. What could she be thinking?

"Something wrong, Detective?" Sue asked, after a moment of silence had stretched into three.

DelRoy jerked his head up. "What? Oh, sorry. No, nothing's wrong. Just thinking."

Yes. There *was* something wrong, dammit. This was the fourth time they'd ended up in some intimate little situation while discussing the case. And every time, it had been without Ned. Without *Mister* Nackenfausch. DelRoy had been certain for several days now that Sue and Ned weren't actually married. Not only because that's what his instincts told him, but also because he was a detective, and he'd done a little detecting. There was no marriage license on record. No joint taxes filed...

Granted, none of this was proof, really. Not ironclad. But it was enough for him. So why the charade? He wanted to ask her. Wanted to tell her that he had penetrated her game. Wanted to hear her explanation, and to be reassured that it didn't have anything at all to do with her missing daughter, or with any of this other craziness they were unearthing now. Only he couldn't ask. Because he was afraid he'd learn she really was mixed up in it all. Or find that the question drove her away.

Most people who lie build a shallow story. They don't plan out all the details. So if you want to catch them at it, all you had to do was ask about a specific detail that they *should* know about, if their story were true. Sure, Sue probably had an answer ready for where and when the wedding had taken place, and for where they'd been when Ned proposed. But had she prepared other details? Like, where they'd held the wedding rehearsal dinner? Or where she had registered for her china? Probably not. When people get an unexpected question like that about their past, the truthful ones get drawn back into reminiscing, trying to recall the answer. But the liars panicked and got defensive about the question. Not always, of course. Especially not the accomplished liars. But with the garden variety mom or pop who gets caught up in events that are spiraling out of their control? The ones who reached for that lie as a desperate bid to gain back some of their control? Well, they didn't reminisce. They panicked. And when they did, they often lashed out too.

So yeah, he was pretty sure that he could get the truth from her, and he needed to. He couldn't go on pretending not to know. She might not feel it, but it was becoming a barrier between them. A barrier for him, anyway. Which is why he'd agreed to let her come along. To confront her. To shine his trick question lamp in her eyes and watch her squirm in the light. Only now, as he sat there, sipping his coffee and watching its steam fog up the windshield, he realized that he didn't want to use his professional techniques. Not this time. Not on her. This wasn't professional interest. This was off the clock. And more importantly, it was getting personal too–in a number of ways–and his usual tricks of the trade suddenly felt cheap.

"Why are you pretending to be married?" he asked. The question just blurted itself out of him.

Sue's answering sigh of relief almost shattered him.

"Oh, thank God," she said, setting her own cup back on the dash. "I've been trying to figure out how to tell you, but I was afraid it would..."

"Make you look guilty? Of something?"

Sue nodded and began to fidget with her scarf. "But I'm not!" she added. "We're not. Or, at least, not what you must think."

"Sue," he said, resting his hand over hers, stilling her sudden nervousness. "Just tell me what's going on."

She looked away, then she nodded tightly. "It's a bit of a long story," she said. "And a weird one. And kind of personal too. I'd have told you sooner, only I couldn't be sure you weren't part of the conspiracy."

DelRoy laughed. "Which is exactly what I told myself about you," he said. Sue turned back to face him. There was a weak smile on her face, but mostly, she looked nervous. "So spill. Who is Ned, really? Is he making you do this?"

"What?" Sue's shock was plain. "No! Of course not!"

"Then why...? I mean–"

Sue looked at the confusion that must be painted all over his face, and then she burst out with happy laughter. "Oh, you goof! Ned Nackenfausch is not my husband, and he's not some manipulative master villain. He's my brother!"

The detective's brain came to a screeching halt.

"Your brother."

Sue nodded.

The detective shook his head in a tight shudder, as though trying to dislodge some idea that had gotten stuck. "And you needed your brother to pretend to be your husband because... ?"

"Because the Sisters of Good Salvation do not accept unmarried women as parents," she said. But before he could press her further, Sue gasped and pointed.

"Look at that!" she said, reaching for her camera. "There goes the Mayor."

And just like that, the case took a different turn.

chapter 17

All that night, Sarqi puzzled over what to do next, and finally, as darkness began to wane, he decided there was only one way to respond to his new-found knowledge that the Gnomes had captured the Wasketchin Queen.

He would have to tell Angiron everything.

So, the next morning, when the crop had fully risen and the oppressive humidity had sludged itself up into the air, clutching at him like a fever-drenched blanket, Sarqi called out to his jailer.

"Ishnee! Get up here, you miserable fly squisher! The Djin Ambassador has an urgent message for the King!"

"Another one?" The Hordesman's worn and tired face poked itself up out of the bolt hole next to Sarqi's embassy, and blinked twice in the light before freezing still–the closest a Gnome ever came to showing spontaneous emotions. The sight before him clearly was unexpected. During the night, and for the early part of the morning, Sarqi had wrestled with his thoughts, trying to plan a way out of his dilemma. And since he always did his best thinking while working with stone, Sarqi had put his hands to the task of improving his accommodations, leaving his brain free to puzzle over his deeper problems.

Building from the original pair of rock slabs, which had leaned against each other like two exhausted books, the Djin Ambassador now had a serviceable, four-walled structure with a roof of overlapping slats. Lacking the tools to make a proper door, Sarqi had left a gap between the walls at one corner, which he had faced directly away from the river, giving himself a dry and comfortable diamond-shaped building in which to receive any further diplomatic inquiries.

"Yes, another one," he said, trying to keep the scorn out of his voice. "Tell your King that I have news that will change his war plans."

Maybe it was the tone of his voice, or maybe the jailer was still startled by the transformation that had swept through the rocks above him while he'd slept, but for the first time, Ishnee did not argue. He scrambled up out of his hole and ran off to deliver the message.

"Tell him to hurry!" Sarqi called out to Ishnee's scurrying back. Then he turned to consider his new shelter. "I think it needs a balcony."

It was long into the blackness of that following night, much closer to sunrise than sunfall, when the stars were stretched out in brilliant promenade across the sky, that Sarqi heard a scratching sound from inside the walls of his embassy.

He'd completed the balcony that now thrust out over the raging water late that afternoon, and he'd been sitting on it ever since. Waiting. Wondering who would come. Would it be Angiron? He hoped not. Qhirmaghen had said that all Sarqi's requests ended up going to him, so Sarqi had trusted that the king himself was still too busy for the grumbles and complaints of a Djin ambassa-prisoner. But even if his message had been shunted to Qhirmaghen, would he come? Might he send somebody else? Might he ignore it? Sarqi's message had been carefully worded to entice the man to come himself. "News that will change his war plans." It sounded important. Surely anyone who heard that would want to judge the news for themselves, wouldn't they? But he'd been sitting here for most of the night with no sign of a visitor.

Again a scraping noise reverberated from within the walls of his newly remodeled prison. Sarqi rose up on his long Djin legs and went inside to investigate.

The small stone that Sarqi had used for his dimlight charm now glowed a steady blue-green from the corner of the single-room structure, oozing a cool bath of light around the floor of the room. In the corner, to the left of the doorway, a head-sized hole now glared its black gaze at him from the floor.

"Who comes?" Sarqi hissed. He glanced quickly over his shoulder to be sure Ishnee had not taken a sudden interest in the night air.

"A friend," came a muffled voice from the hole.

At night there was no buzzing from the airborne crop or any natter of people coming and going along the path, but the river still cast enough of a din to mask casual conversations. If they were careful. Even so, Sarqi did not want to risk any more than he must, so he kept his voice as low as he could and moved closer to the empty void. "I have no friends here," he replied.

There was a pause. "I have come for more of your... flapmeat," the voice from the hole said. "I was told you have a very fragrant piece to share."

Ah. So it *was* Qhirmaghen. Sarqi felt himself relax a little. "Come up," he said. "We are alone." It would be best not to speak his visitor's name. Ishnee was probably asleep at this time of night, but there was no sense trusting in probably. A moment later, the Gnome's head pushed up through the hole, followed shortly by the rest of him.

"You waited a long time," Sarqi whispered. "I did not think you would come."

"I've been here since sunfall," Qhirmaghen replied, "but I had to be sure your message had not reached... its original target." Sarqi nodded. That made sense. The last thing they wanted would be for the Gnome King to arrive late and find them plotting together. "You took a grave risk, sending the message the way you did," the Gnome added.

Sarqi shrugged. "If Angiron had come instead of you, I would have spun him tales enough to worry his war-loving heart."

Qhirmaghen nodded briefly. "So tell me, Ambassador. What news reaches a man exiled in a house of stone that does not reach a man in my position?"

Sarqi paused to consider his answer, and was surprised to feel a tremor of apprehension clutch at his stomach. He believed that Qhirmaghen was earnest in his opposition to Angiron, but still, what if he was wrong? This whole concept of lying and deceit was still so alien. Without the Dragon's Peace to ensure truthfulness, how was one supposed to know when a man's words did not align with rightness? So far, they had been speaking in code, making only veiled references, as each felt for strands of trust delicately reaching out from the other. Time was crucial if there was to be any chance of taking action, but he was also painfully aware that he was gambling with somebody else's life, and must place his feet with great care on this political scree of oily tongues and slippery agendas.

"Before I give answer," Sarqi said, "we must speak plainly, you and I. Once said, my news cannot be unsaid. If I trust unwisely, I will have betrayed all. So first, tell me what you intend to do."

Now it was Qhirmaghen's turn for silent consideration, and Sarqi watched the Gnome administrator wrestle with his own doubts. Would the Gnome rebel feel that he could trust Sarqi? For all Qhirmaghen knew, Sarqi had been placed here by Angiron for this very purpose–to ferret out those who opposed the King's war. Sarqi didn't even know what trust would look like on the face of a Gnome. Their stinginess with emotion made them so hard to read. But whatever doubts or fears might be giving the Failed Contender pause, he must have found reason to set them aside.

"We mean to topple the King, and beg the Wasketchin Crown for peace," Qhirmaghen said. "This war is wrong, and it can do nothing but ill for the Horde, or for any other peoples of Methilien."

Surprised, Sarqi drew a deep breath and let it out. He had not expected Qhirmaghen to speak *that* plainly. But in a way, it was good that he had. Sarqi could feel an almost child-like sense of release relaxing its way through the muscles of his body. Qhirmaghen's bluntness had been more than simple expedience. It had been a gesture of trust. Both men had much to lose if they were caught, but it felt so good to let the walls and barriers of suspicion down– to be free of the second guessing, the silent examination of every utterance before allowing it breath.

It felt good to be trusted.

And being trusted, so openly and so entirely without reserve, Sarqi realized that the honor of his House would let him do no less. He squared his shoulders and drew himself up to full height.

"Your squads have captured the Wasketchin Queen," Sarqi said. "And we must free her before your King learns of it, or the Wasketchin King will collapse."

Outside, nothing could be heard but the crashing of the river.

—

"I release you from your word," Qhirmaghen said. "You are free to roam freely, or even to leave the Throat if you wish."

Sarqi heard him, but did not respond. He was standing on his newly constructed balcony in the late morning sun, gazing out at the hypnotic crashing water that, despite its thrashing violence,

seemed almost to not be moving at all. Humps and valleys of wetness bounded over rock while somehow remaining static in their
shape just the same. Like me, he thought. Worries and fears cavort-
ing under my skin, but on the outside, still the same, skinny Djin.
Which is the real me? The thoughts I think, or the shape I fill?

So much had changed in recent days. So much of *him* had
changed. Where was the acid tongue that had been his shield?
Where was the reluctance to risk? He felt so different now, yet
still himself. He was a new him, but where had the old him gone?
That Sarqi–the one who had been happy to let others make decisions for him, so that he could sit back and criticize without fear of
responsibility–that Sarqi didn't seem to be in here at all anymore.
Was he a new river now? Or merely the same old one, with a few of
the rocks rearranged?

It had been only hours since they had concluded their quiet
scheming in the night, and here was Qhirmaghen, back already. The
fact that he came now, openly, in the daylight, suggested that the
Gnome had cast his lot and was ready to commit. Everything lay
in readiness, awaiting only the two of them to set things in motion.
It was a simple plan. The Fallen Contender was known among the
Horde, and known to be a trusted adviser at court. If he made a
journey now to choose a prisoner to bring before the King, who
would argue? All they had to do was go get her, and then flee. But
didn't some of the rocks define the river? Weren't some of them
unmovable?

As he stepped away from the railing, Sarqi accepted the truth.
Their plan was not going to be as easy as they had thought. "You
cannot release me," he said, and as he turned to meet the Gnome's
startled gaze, Sarqi realized that he had spoken truly. "I gave my
word to the Gnome King, and then again to you, his Aide, but in
this, you do not act for your King. The Qhirmaghen who does this
is not the Fallen Contender–he Contends anew, and cannot unspeak
the words of his former office. I must remain within sight of these
walls."

Sarqi could hear the gnashing of the Gnome's teeth even from
a distance, but to his credit, Qhirmaghen did not argue. After a
drawn out pause while they each considered their options, the new
Qhirmaghen, Resistor to the Crown, nodded once to the Djin Ambassador, and then turned away to scuttle down the path, toward
the prisoner pens, deeper down into the Throat, and toward an act

of treason that he would now undertake alone.

Sarqi sighed in frustration as he watched the Gnome disappear behind the bulk of the embassy. At his feet, a splash of water slapped against the new balcony and he looked down in time to see it dislodge a pebble that tumbled into the foam and vanished.

Hopefully it had not been an important pebble.

For almost an hour, Sarqi fumed. Rock dust and splinters! Why had he given his word? To stay within sight of the embassy walls until "summoned by the King or a member of the royal court?" He regretted that promise now, but he had given it, and so far, the King had shown no signs of summoning him, so he would just have to sit here, while another risked his neck to carry out a plan that Sarqi himself had conceived.

Three times, the Djin Ambassador strode down the path, each time intent on testing his own resolve, but every time he approached the point where the embassy walls threatened to slide out of sight behind the curve of the path behind him, his feet would come to a halt and refuse to go on. This was no binding of magic, no charm of family magics. It was simply his honor. He knew, deep within himself that if he willed it, he could continue down the path. But he also knew that it would shame him like nothing he had ever done before. He had spoken his word, had given stony substance to his honor, and *that* was the true bedrock of his river. It was the weight each Djin must bear if he was to remain himself. A load he must carry on his back.

Then Sarqi stopped, his mouth hanging agape for a moment, before it closed into a thin smile. Yes, perhaps there *was* a way.

"Hurry up!" Qhirmaghen shouted loudly enough for passers-by to hear him, but his impatience was not entirely an act. It had taken longer to find the woman than he had anticipated. One sky-dweller female looked much like any other to his Gnomileshi eyes, but eventually he had spotted the markings he had been told to watch for. A curled, red line, like a tiny vine, beside her right eye. The Djin Ambassador had mentioned the woman's distinctive a'dinesh as part of his description of her. And there she'd been, standing vacantly, like all the other fawn-eyed captives, not moving, not talking. Just standing there, as though awaiting an invitation that would never come.

Every time Qhirmaghen brushed up against one of the new King's magics, it left him feeling too clean, as though all the vims of rot and decay had been flushed from his body by a harsh dunking in the river. He shuddered now, even at the thought of it.

Once he'd found her though, she'd been easy enough to lead. The brilliant wedding mark next to her eye was unmistakable, almost regal in its elegance. But her high rank had given her no special powers to resist the new capture charm, and when he'd tugged at her hand to draw her out from the crowd of prisoners, she had followed placidly along behind him. Vacant, null-willed baggage. For now, that idle complacency was a boon, allowing him to lead the woman quickly through the crowd of both prisoners and guards alike. Her dull-eyed expression was so commonplace that, so far, nobody had asked him a thing. Soon enough though, they'd be away from the prisoner pens, where she would suddenly become entirely too conspicuous. Keeping her hidden would require more than just gormless obedience—she would need to actively cooperate. Hopefully, by that time, he'd have found a way to break the charm that enthralled her, and convince her to take an interest in her own escape.

"Just a little further," Qhirmaghen said. He didn't even know if she could hear him, but it made him feel better to think of her as alive and alert and simply ignoring him, the way sky-dwellers usually did. Somehow even that was better than this mindless complacency.

As they climbed higher from the prison yard, the rocks rose steadily on either side of the path, until they were in a deep channel between two facing banks of stone. This section of the trail received only infrequent traffic, and for the moment, they were alone. They were getting close to the branching point, where the trail into Ishig's Book would break away from the main road, but before they reached Urlech and his precious bones, Qhirmaghen stopped to get a good look at his companion. She did not look in any way harmed. At worst, she had been the victim of indifferent treatment. Her clothes, once made from fine, tightly-woven fabrics, had worn thin and were actually tattered in places. She had a good layer of dirt smudged onto herself, but as much as he himself approved, he knew that neither she nor her people would agree. He suspected that she would be aghast at her appearance if she could see herself, thin and underfed. He wondered how long it had been since she had eaten. But clearly she was not in danger of sudden collapse, so food could wait. He took her once more by the hand and continued up the trail, looking for the way marker that would announce their turn.

But when he found it, he stopped and looked around in confusion. Signposts always stood directly across from the trail they announced, but this one faced nothing but the same, continuous stone bank he'd been following for the last ten minutes. Where was the path to Ishig's Book?

Qhirmaghen turned a slow circle, as though perhaps the path would appear if he caught it from the right angle of his eye, but after a complete turn, he was still confounded. Could somebody have moved the signpost? Leaving the woman standing on her own for a moment, he trotted up the main trail a bit further, but there were no more indications of a side-path up there than there had been at the post. Almost frantic, he turned and scurried back. He had been to the Book a hundred times before, but now, today of all days, he could not find his way. And their timing could not be better now. The road was completely empty. If they could find the trail and get out of sight quickly, unnoticed by any others, it would make their escape that much more likely to succeed. But where was the rot-sucking passage?

The woman was still standing where he'd left her, and even without the signpost, his memory told him that the passage should be right there! Was his mind playing tricks on him? Cautiously, he took a step forward, reaching out his hand to touch the rock wall. Yes, here was the funny little nose-shaped protrusion. He'd noticed it many times when coming to consult his ancestors, even as a boy. It had always amused him that the last sight he saw before speaking with his elders was a large rocky nose. The nose-rock marked the entrance for him, just as clearly as a bonfire or dancing sprites might have done. "It's supposed to be here!" he growled, slapping his hand against the rocky flatness that now blocked his way.

And the rock pushed back.

Qhirmaghen stumbled backward, his eyes opened wide, as the rock wall began to press toward him. He quickly snatched at the Queen's hand and pulled her back with him, away from the shifting stone. A moment later, a great arm poked out from behind the sheet of rock and waved at him urgently. "Hurry! Inside. Both of you!" Then an even greater head poked out, near the arm.

It was the Djin Ambassador.

Not waiting to ask questions, Qhirmaghen pushed the woman ahead of him, through the narrow gap, and then followed her in. Behind him, Ambassador Sarqi set the massive slab back into position. This was the side path that Qhirmaghen remembered–little more than a crack in the surrounding wall of stone, really. It was scarcely two paces wide at the mouth and then narrowed quickly as it zigged its way back into the rock, leading to the shrine of Ishig's Book.

Qhirmaghen pushed forward, herding his Wasketchin sheep ahead of him, and was just about to round the first kink of the gully's crooked path, when the Djin called out.

"I can go no further," Sarqi hissed, keeping his voice low, as though Hordesmen already hunted them in every corner.

Qhirmaghen halted the Queen and turned back, confused at the Djin's sudden reluctance.

"First no, then yes, then no again... Make up your mind, Ambassador. Are you coming with us or do you stay here? We must get into hiding quickly, and to do that, we must go a good many paces further before we stop."

Sarqi shook his head. "The path is too narrow. I couldn't possibly drag it any further, so I can't go past that corner where you stand. But if you'll wait a moment, we might be able to solve that." Then he turned and addressed himself to the woman. "My Lady M'Ateliana, you will not remember me. My name is Sarqi, of House Kijamon. I would offer my services to you and to the Wasketchin court. You have but to summon me into your service."

The woman stared off into empty space. She didn't even look at the Djin, and the Ambassador's face began to slide into a frown as Qhirmaghen watched. How simply they did that–contorting their faces from joy to sorrow, from hatred into laughter. It was all so easy for them, for dark feelings as well as for light. But even though he could not feel it himself, Qhirmaghen knew despair when he saw it. Clearly, the Djin had not seen the effects of Angiron's magic up close before.

"She does not rebuke your offer, Ambassador. She is still held thrall to whatever magics our King has unleashed. Her mind is not her own, if indeed she still has one left at all. Come with us to the Book. Perhaps we can get her head cleared there, and then I am sure she will accept your offer."

The Djin shook his head. "No. It must be done here. By my word I can go no further."

Qhirmaghen looked around, confused. "But, obviously you have set your word aside. Come with–"

The Djin threw back is head and roared his rage at the sky. "I have *not* broken my word, you snuffling little wound-licker! She must release me, and it must be here, before you round that bend!"

In the storm of emotions being displayed before him, Qhirmaghen felt almost rich, and allowed himself a dismissive chuckle. "Of course you've broken it," he said. "You yourself said that I could not release you. I doubt that King Angiron has done so, and I don't see your embassy around here, so clearly, you *have* broken your promise. But what of it? They are just words. Let's get into–"

A loud thump shivered the air. "*This* is my embassy wall!" Sarqi shouted, forgetting to keep his voice low as he pounded his fist against the great slab of rock that blocked the gully entrance. "I have *not* left sight of it, nor will I. Not until I have been released."

The Gnome walked slowly toward the Djin and the rock wall that hid them from prying eyes. It was impossible. How could he...? But now that he looked closely, Qhirmaghen could see that the color was wrong–it did not quite match the walls of the crevice around him. "You... brought the walls with you?" Qhirmaghen could not imagine how he could have done such a thing.

"One wall, yes," the Djin replied. "And it very nearly killed me, but I can go no further. The slab is too big for this narrow passage." To demonstrate his point, Sarqi reached out to either side, but his palms met the walls of the gully before his arms were even half extended, and he dropped them again in disgust. He stood there, fuming for a moment, but his anger soon passed and he looked again toward the Queen. Sarqi stepped forward and took her hand in his own. It lifted easily in his grasp, effortlessly, as though she neither permitted nor opposed the action.

"Is there no way we can return her to herself?" Sarqi asked. He was speaking quietly now, as though the woman's presence had calmed him. Qhirmaghen could see no rage left. No frustration. Only sorrow.

"I don't know the manner of this magic," Qhirmaghen said. "And even if I did, it's more powerful than anything I've seen. Perhaps the shrine keeper will know of something." But he didn't believe that, and his words rang hollow for all to hear. Sarqi didn't believe it either.

"Then I must remain," Sarqi said. "Go. I will keep the passage blocked to delay pursuit. Get her out of the Throat and back to her own people." Still he clung to her hand and stared into her vacant face, hoping she would awaken. But she did not.

Qhirmaghen edged past them both, taking the Queen by her free hand as he did, and pulling her to follow after him, further up into the crevice. For a moment, the Queen stood there, her hands pulled to either side–one by the Gnome trying to lead her to safety, and the other by the Djin begging her not to leave him behind. But at last, Qhirmaghen gave a final tug, pulling the Queen's hand away from the Ambassador's, and then she followed him easily down the path toward Ishig's Book.

Toward freedom.

Sarqi watched as M'Ateliana and the Gnome disappeared around the bend of the gully. He hadn't wanted them to leave, hadn't wanted to be left behind, a prisoner of his own conscience. His place was with them. With her. He knew it, he could feel it, like the swirl of grain in a granite beneath his fingers. He could not see it, but he knew it just the same. M'Ateliana needed a guide. She needed a Djin at her side–him–or this entire escape plan would come crashing down before she could reach safety. But she had just left.

Without him.

Sarqi twisted around to glare at the stone wall of his embassy, furious with himself. He'd come so far, and now, to be trapped here, helpless, bound by something as insubstantial as a breath of words. Words that had forced him to stagger and drag an enormous slab of rock two hundred paces down the Gnome road, and even that had not been enough. It was never enough, and now he was here instead of there, and just as trapped by those words as he'd been when he'd started. There was nothing more he could do. It had taken two hours and all of his strength to come this far, and that had been with a wide path and no traffic. There was no way he could bring the wall in here–not even as far as the first corner. The crevice was too narrow, and even if it were a thousand paces wide, he doubted that he had enough strength left in him. He was near to exhausted.

Yet still that truth burned at him. He wanted to snap off a piece of the rock and run after them, carrying a fragment of the wall with him where he could always see it, no matter how far he might go, but he knew that such a ploy was a stretch beyond reason, and that it would shatter the very soul of his honor. He'd already strained it beyond caution by coming even this far. When he had promised to stay within sight of his shelter walls, he may not have promised to leave them where they were, but his honor nagged at him that even this was scree-talk, slippery words that seemed sound, but would only shift under weight and plunge him to his ruin.

He knew what his word demanded of him, but word or no word, he also knew where his duty lay, and it was not in bowing to the whims of a faith-breaking Gnome kinglet. His duty had just marched off into darkness, vacant and heedless, led by a shift-cloak Gnome. Sarqi's duty was to go to the aide of the only true Djin-friend he had seen since being brought here. A real queen, leading an honest people, with dignity and poise. Or so she would be once more, once he had discovered how to release her from the Gnomish magic that now clouded her. Sarqi could still feel her need, the warmth of her hand, tugging at his while the Gnome had tugged at her. But honor held him fast in this place, anchored to that thrice-blasted wall of stone.

"Grind me to dust!" Sarqi bellowed in frustration as he whirled to face the wall-slab behind him, his lungs heaving with the ferocity of his shout. Then, with a snarl of purest rage, Sarqi punctuated his fury, slamming both of his great Djin fists into the middle of its span. Whether he was overcome by a great power, or merely lucky, striking the stone upon a vulnerable twist of grain, the stone wall shattered under Sarqi's rage, and collapsed into great shards at his feet.

But still, honor would not let him leave its sight.

No son of Kijamon had never dared to hate their father's honor before, but Sarqi did so now. There was right and there was wrong, and this was wrong. Duty and honor were meant to *serve* rightness, not to obstruct it. Yet here he was, bound by that honor to watch over a pile of rock chips and to reject the full-throated scream of his duty.

Sarqi was miserable. He stood there in the stony corridor, oblivious to whoever might pass by and see him, head bowed, as though he bore the weight of his entire embassy upon his slender neck. Who will guide her to her people? The Gnome? And would he also free her from the bewitchment that was upon her? If only she hadn't pulled at him. If only she had just let her hand slip placidly from his own...

The thought hung there, echoing in his bowed head for a long second, daring him to think about what he'd just thought. And then, slowly, his head rose, eyes widening in a bloom of pained realization. Oh, rock splinters!

"Wait for me!" he yelled, and then Sarqi, Djin Ambassador to the Gnomileshi Horde, abandoned his embassy without any further thought and bolted down the path in pursuit. The Queen of the Wasketchin *had* summoned him. With every fiber of strength she could muster, she had begged for his help.

And now she was gone.

chapter 18

It was a very different Kijamon who summoned the family to gather around the forge that evening. This Kijamon was not the man Tayna had seen earlier–the seemingly unstoppable idea machine who juggled twenty conversations at once. This was a softer Kijamon. A quieter, more contemplative Kijamon. He'd been that way ever since Abeni had returned from reporting to Mabundi.

"Matters of honor have been brought to the family," Kijamon said, his gaze flicking toward his son. And then to her.

Tayna stepped back from the forge. "I, uh, should leave you to discuss it," she said, but Kijamon raised a hand.

"Please stay," he said, gesturing her back to her place. "As the closest witness in these matters, you honor our House by bearing witness to our decisions as well." Tayna glanced around uncomfortably for a moment and then shrugged and resumed her place at the forge.

While there were several small clusters of furniture scattered around the perimeter, the middle of the room was empty, occupied only by the massive stone forge. Apparently, it could be moved around the workshop, to suit whatever Kijamon wanted to work on. Although how he moved something that big, Tayna couldn't imagine. Until she remembered the Wagon.

The floor of the room was dotted with circular rings–caps that covered wind ducts, Zimu had explained. Each duct was a separate channel for the winds that raced upward through the Wind Forge from below. Each time the forge was moved, one of the covers would be removed and the forge centered over it, allowing Kijamon to harness the very wind itself to serve as his bellows. Hence the name: Wind Forge. And the actual forge at its heart had always served as the centerpiece to all serious family discussions in House Kijamon, as it did again now.

The entire family was in attendance, except for Sarqi, who, the

Gnome Ambassador had been happy to inform them, was now a guest of King Angiron, although nobody seemed sure just what that meant.

Standing here now, included in such a private family meeting as this, Tayna felt a number of conflicting emotions. She felt sad that Sarqi wasn't here, although glad that he was okay. She felt lonely, being an outsider in an unfamiliar place. She even felt a pang of jealousy. *Family yours, peril great,* and all that.

But most of all, it made her feel short. These people were huge.

"We gather the House to decide matters of Honor," Kijamon began. "Since the first days of this dwelling, this forge has been the very crucible of our House, giving heat, and light, and work. Giving honor. Every matter of duty has been sworn by its light. Every judgment has been warmed by its heat. The very name of House Kijamon has been hammered and shaped in its flame. And so now today, do we forge honor again."

Beside her, Abeni shifted awkwardly on his feet, as though *he* was the stranger here. Poor guy. Tayna reached out and patted his hand. Around the forge, the gesture was noticed, even drawing a smile from Abeni's mother.

"We begin with a matter of duty," Kijamon continued. "Abeni, youngest son of this House, stands in iron. Bonded to the Wagon and to the Warding of the Seekers Royal."

With all attention focused on him, Abeni looked miserable, and he hung his head with shame, refusing to even meet Tayna's gaze. It was heartbreaking and stupid, she decided, but she knew better than to say so.

"So my son," Kijamon said. "Have you anything more to say? Anything you left out when you spoke your report?" When Abeni had first returned, he and Kijamon had spent a long time speaking quietly together in the corner. Abeni had seemed to do most of the talking. Tayna hadn't heard what he'd said, but from the sadness and guilt on his face it could not have been anything good. Now though, in response to his father's question, Abeni snapped his head up and his eyes blazed.

"To not say a truth is to say a lie! Abeni would not do this." Then, apparently embarrassed for having let his temper get the better of him, he lowered his head once more.

"So you say. So you say." Kijamon tapped his fingers on the forge. Then he turned to Tayna. "And you, Little Fish. Would you add anything to your tale?" After speaking to Abeni, Kijamon had asked her a few questions as well. Mostly to clarify details of things Abeni had not seen for himself. "Any other wonders that slipped your mind? Invisible Gnomes, maybe? Or talking beavers to throw into the story pot? The stew is already quite filled with amazement, but another morsel or two would not be amiss."

Tayna looked quickly at Abeni, but her friend was still in his "just shoot me" position, and Zimu wasn't much help either, offering nothing but a shrug when she looked his way. Great. Flying blind again. Tayna drew a deep breath and then turned to face the master of the house. She wasn't sure exactly what Abeni had told him, but "everything" seemed the most likely. There were lots of things she wanted to say. Things to make her look less like an idiot, or to make Abeni look good, but she didn't know the rules for this kind of thing, and the honor in question was Abeni's, not hers.

"I don't think it would be good for me to add anything," she said. "I hardly know what's going on here, and since nothing that happened makes sense to me, it would probably make less sense to you. Or I might say the wrong thing and make things even worse. I don't want to get Abeni into worse trouble because of my stupidity. So no, sir. I think I'd better shut up now." Then she did.

Kijamon nodded at this and then turned to address his family. "If none will speak further," he declared, "then, having heard the deeds of Abeni, son of this House, Kijamon, of House Kijamon, will now speak honor's word." Abeni drew himself up straight and raised his head to meet his father's eye.

"Abeni. You were charged by my bond–at the behest of Mabundi, King of the Djin–along with your brothers, to see the Wagon of Tears upon its sacred journey. In this task, you were further charged to bear with you the bodies of two fallen kings: Jallafa of the Djin, and Grinyak of the Gnomileshi. Now you have returned to my House, with no brothers, and an empty Wagon, which you flung down upon us from out of the sky, riding it, clutching it with the bare of your hands, like one who would wrestle a common bear. Do you deny this?"

"No, honored father. Abeni does not deny these things." Firelight from the forge glittered brightly in Abeni's shame-filled eyes.

"Then I must judge in accordance with the laws of honor. Abeni, third son of Kijamon, of House Kijamon, I declare that the honor of this House has been most well served." There was a musical "clink" as the iron band on Abeni's arm twitched and transformed into silver, as the honor charm of House Kijamon completed its process, guided by the binder's pronouncement.

Shock stood starkly on Abeni's face as he looked down at the new band on his arm. When he looked back up, tears spilled down his enormous cheeks. "But Abeni does not understand... He has touched the Great Wagon in flight. He has ridden within its sacred chamber while he yet breathed. In so many ways has Abeni dishonored his duties. Abeni begs Kijamon. Do not compound these failures with those of a father's blindness. Unsay these words and say those that *must* be said."

Kijamon looked at his son fiercely, but Tayna quickly saw that it was the fierceness of pride. It was Shaleen who spoke. "Abeni, do you question your father's wisdom?"

Tears still running down his face, Abeni shook his head. "Nor does Abeni question the heat of the sun, nor the wetness of the river."

Shaleen nodded. "Then think upon what he has said. What you did, you did in the moment that action was needed. Do you think honor requires you to act with the wisdom of having hours or days to think upon your course, when the world offers you only moments to consider? Would that be honorable of honor?" Abeni stared at his mother as though she were offering him a rope to safety, but it was one that he could not see.

Kijamon sighed. "Look, boy. Now that the preachy words are over, I'll put it plain. You got handed a slimy stick. Sure, you got a bit of it on your fingers, but you grabbed it, you hauled it in, and you delivered it to where it was needed." The old man began to count on his fingers. "First, you delivered both kings to the Gnomes. A bit unusual in the how of it, but it got done, and it wasn't an easy thing. Second, somebody bashed you on the head and stuffed you into that chamber. Soon as you woke up, you climbed out. Wasn't anything more you could have done, and even then, you didn't pack your hammers and head for home. You always were a rock head. Third, you saw signs of trouble with the Gnomes, you recognized them as important, and then you came straight back to report them. And doing all this, you never abandoned the Wagon or left it unwarded. At no time did you take the easy way of giving up, and each time, it seems to me you found creative solutions to sticky situations. If there is one thing that does House Kijamon proudly boy, it is creative thinking applied to difficult problems. Were it up to me, I'd have given you gold for this, but I knew you wouldn't be able to accept that, so the silver stands. I will not compromise further."

"But ours were not the hands of grief!" Abeni protested.

Kijamon rolled his eyes, and his wife burst out in laughter. "Oh no!" she said. "I knew that was going to backfire one day." Abeni looked back and forth helplessly between his parents, so his mother shook the laughter from her face and tried to explain. "Oh, Abeni! You were all so young at the time. Little boys getting into little boy mischief. Your brother Zimu had taught Sarqi to practice his signs in the dirt, and Sarqi... " But she couldn't finish, and burst out into a fresh spasm of laughter.

"Filthy little ninx," Kijamon muttered. "Your brother Sarqi made a most unfortunate sign on the silver of a chamber. This big, with mud," he said, holding his hands shoulder-width apart and smiling, despite his fatherly duty to be stern about such things.

"What symbol?" Abeni asked.

Laughter had stolen Shaleen's air and she could barely get the words out. "The sign of the Void!"

"Can you imagine if we had reached the next town without noticing?" Kijamon chuckled. Tayna didn't get the joke, but she smiled politely and tried not to look as confused as she felt.

Finally, Shaleen seemed to regain her composure. "You see? We had to think of something. We couldn't risk that one of you might find some new mischief, one that escaped our notice until it was too late. So your father came up with that rule about the "hands of grief," and it worked like a wonder. We never had a single problem with mischievous tampering again. So we began to teach the other Warders this rule as well."

Abeni looked at her as though she had sprouted demon wings.

"Oh, don't be so serious, Abeni! It *is* a good rule, but rules are there to guide us in our thinking–not to stop us from it. You touched the Wagon, but it carried no Seekers at the time, so what of it? And do you really think there are rules for how to respect the Great Wagon when you are *flying* in it? That is a new thing, my son. There *are* no rules. And if there will be any, it will be you and Tayna here who speak them."

Abeni did not look completely convinced, but he no longer looked scalded either. Beside him, Zimu smiled and reached up to pull the brown kerchief from his arm. Earlier, he had explained that when two people involved in the same duty were to be judged independently, it was customary that those judged first should cover the sign of their judgment until the others in the group had been judged. Zimu was now revealing that he too had served the honor of his House. But where Abeni had done so with silver distinction, Zimu had apparently earned a mere copper. Satisfactory. Abeni opened his mouth to protest, but Zimu shook his head.

"It is correct," he said. "I did not call the sprites. I did not vouchsafe the Wagon. I did not find and protect the Little Fish. I did as I thought best, but there was no great honor in my trials nor in their solving. Only competence." Abeni opened his mouth to disagree, but Zimu simply shook his head once more, tightly. The message was clear. I'm okay with this. Please do not dishonor my satisfaction. Abeni closed his mouth and nodded to his elder brother.

Seeing that her son was going to be okay, Shaleen stood up and excused herself, coming back a moment later with a large pot, which she set on the edge of the forge to stay hot. Tayna could smell it, and her mouth could smell it too, watering in anticipation. Boh-cho.

"So you accept my judgment?" Kijamon asked, as Zimu dipped mugs into the steaming pot and began passing them around.

With one last look at his brother, who truly did seem untroubled by the situation, Abeni nodded cautiously to his father. "Abeni accepts these things. He is honored by the wisdom of House Kijamon. And perplexed by it also."

"Ha! That's the spirit, boy! Think sharply, act boldly, and speak plainly. That's the way of this House!"

The boh-cho brought a welcome respite from the solemnity of Abeni's honor ceremony, and Tayna relaxed as the family seemed to unwind. She was just beginning to relax herself when Kijamon set his mug on the hearth and clapped his hands. "And now we must attend another matter of honor," he said. Then he turned to face Tayna with a grimace of distaste.

"We must deal with the crimes of the Little Fish."

The uproar that followed was unexpected, with both Zimu and Abeni protesting loudly. "Who dares say such a thing?" Abeni roared. "He will answer to Abeni!"

"The Little Fish has committed no crime," Zimu added, looking at his father curiously.

The Master of House Kijamon nodded. "Indeed," he said. "But so the House has been petitioned, and so the claim must be examined." Zimu nodded his understanding, but Abeni was still furious.

"Kijamon must not believe such a thing! The Little Fish has been an honorable and fast friend to Abeni. If not for her..." But it was Shaleen who calmed her son.

"Of course she has. We know this. Do you think your father such a dullard as that?"

That took the puff out of Abeni's sails, and his shoulders sagged. "No. Abeni does not think Kijamon dull-witted."

"Well, that's a start," his father said. "Now, can we commence with the matter before the family?" Abeni nodded, and held his tongue.

"There are actually two problems concerning the Fish-girl here," Kijamon continued. "First, there is the matter of the Gnomes. Quishek came by this afternoon to speak a formal claim. King Angiron demands her return. She has been found guilty of crimes against the Horde and against the Gnomileshi Crown–" Abeni tried to interrupt again, but Kijamon fixed him with a glare and he backed down, allowing the old man to continue.

"Clearly, Quishek is within his rights to present his petition. The girl is unbound to any House and has taken shelter on stone held by House Kijamon. Without standing, she must be delivered to her accusers–"

"But Kijamon cannot–" Abeni sputtered, but this time he was interrupted by a roar.

"SILENCE!" The fury in Kijamon's face was there for only a brief moment before the old man composed himself, and then he brushed at his robe in apparent embarrassment for his outburst. "I'm sorry, boy. It's not you I'm angry with. You have every right to defend your young friend, and more credit to you for doing so. But if you'll let me finish, we'll see what can be done, shall we?" Abeni let out a long breath and nodded.

"Now, where was I? Oh, yes. Without standing, she must be delivered to her accusers and bound over for honor court among them. But I find that there is a second matter, which according to the laws of this House, must take precedence and be dealt with before considering claims from outside the House." Zimu and Abeni both looked up, with curiosity on one face and confusion on the other. Shaleen patted Tayna's hand and smiled, but she said nothing, allowing her husband to continue.

"So, Little Fish," he said. "There is a matter of honor between us that I would discuss with you now."

"Um, okay," Tayna replied, unsure where this was going.

"It has been reported that you have rendered a number of services in recent times–services that have made it possible for a son of this House to return, and to bring honor with him."

"I guess so," she said. "But he's done way more for me."

"And honor to him for doing so, but that is in a different valley. It is you who now stands before us, and it is you to whom House Kijamon owes a debt. I would ask a boon of you."

Tayna grinned. "You owe me a debt, and now you want to ask me for a favor? Shouldn't it work the other way around?" Abeni's eyes grew wide that she would talk that way to Kijamon, but the old man merely chuckled.

"You have the tongue of a jay-hawk," Kijamon noted. "Quick and bold, yet full of laughing. Hold it still but a moment longer while I explain my boon. And *then* you may set it free, so that all might see where it may jab next."

Tayna shrugged. "Okay. That's fair. Ask away."

"On three occasions you have stood by House Kijamon and rendered great service. In the first, you revived a son of this House from the brink of death by flame, snatching him back from the Grey Shepherd's flock. In the second, you rescued that same son of this House from capture by another grim keeper–a Gnome King, no less–who has turned against all the Peoples of this land. And in the third, you preserved a great trust of this House–the Wagon of Tears–and held it safe from those who would use it to disrupt the Djin." All around the table, heads were nodding in agreement as the old man concluded his list and looked around. Then he drew a deep breath.

"Do you–?" He paused and leaned his head toward Abeni, pitching his voice in a loud stage whisper. "What's her true name? Surely it isn't really 'Little Fish?' "

Abeni smiled. "The Little Fish does not know the full name of her House," he said. "She seeks it still, but the name of her heart is 'Tayna.' "

Tayna couldn't remember if Abeni had ever actually said her

name before, and much as she liked their playful bantering and mutual name-calling, it made her feel good to hear him say it now. But she had to pay attention, because Kijamon was going back into preachy mode.

"Do you, Tayna, attest these services to be true? That they have been rendered of your heart, without expectation or deceit?"

"Well, sure. I guess. But Abeni did lots of great things for me too. You should have seen him tackle me out of the flames, and then when we were in the Cold-"

"It is well that you would share honor, but do not diminish that portion which is your own. You attest these services to be true?"

Tayna nodded. "I guess so." Kijamon cocked his head at her and then flashed a stink-eye of mock irritation. "Okay. Yes." Tayna put one hand over her heart and raised the other in the air. "I, Tayna, do solemnly swear that these services were true and honest and wholesome, like little kids, and oatmeal." Kijamon smiled. She had no idea where this was going, but she got the sense that they were trying to do something nice for her, and since that didn't happen very often in her life, it wasn't something she wanted to miss. Maybe they were going to give her a souvenir boh-cho mug. She liked those.

"Having attested to these services, freely rendered, I, Kijamon, Lord of House Kijamon, extend to you the Keshwa-Ji. The Inclusion. Will you, Tayna, known in this House as Little Fish, do honor to Kijamon and Shaleen, and take their House to be your own? Will you stand as honor-daughter to House Kijamon?"

That's when Tayna lost it and started to cry.

Celebrations continued around the forge for several minutes, as each member gathered Tayna into an embrace and welcomed her into the House. It was not an adoption, they explained. She was an adult, and as such, had no need for the protective swaddlings of childhood. There was nothing similar to it in Grimorl customs that she knew of. It was something like a business merger, except warmer and more personal, involving people instead of companies. But the two sides did not become one. It was an alliance in which each became a part of the other. Tayna had joined House Kijamon, and House Kijamon had joined House Tayna, should she ever start a House of her own. Technically, it did not extend to her family, should she ever find them, but in practice, they too would be treated as members of House Kijamon until Kijamon found reason to declare otherwise. But Tayna didn't get far in her exploration of all the maybes and mightbes. When the hugs and smiles had all been shared out and enjoyed, Kijamon raised his hands.

"Now we must return to the other honor matter before the House," he said, and the family settled themselves back into place around the forge, although Shaleen couldn't help but reach over and squeeze Tayna's hand, offering her a warm smile to go with it.

"The Gnome Court has made petition," Kijamon said. "They claim that there is an unbound criminal hiding on the lands of this House, and that, without standing, she must be delivered to them and bound over to the honor court of the Gnome King." Everybody around the forge was now beaming. At her. At Abeni. But most of all, at Kijamon, now shown to be a Master Sneak of the highest order, in addition to his other lofty accomplishments.

"After considerable search," the shining-haired old man continued, "it is the finding of this House that no such unbound person could be located. The only girl present who could fit the charge is fully bound to House Kijamon, and therefore has its protection. The matter must be sent to the King of all Djin, for only he can deliver an entitled bondsman into the hands of a foreign realm. The honor of this House has been satisfied. This discussion is concluded. The King will be informed in the morning."

Then Kijamon clapped his hands together and the preachy expression was gone, leaving an impish grin in its place. He leaned over to pat Tayna's shoulder. "That ought to buy us some time at least," he said. Then he dipped his mug back into the pot to get some more boh-cho.

———⌄———

The sky was still brilliant out through the window slots when Tayna excused herself from the chatter around the forge and stepped through the door that divided the open workshop from the living quarters. But night sets quickly in the mountains. One moment, the sun is low in the sky, blinding you with its cheeky glare, and the next, you're plunging off a ledge you missed in the total darkness. So she was surprised to find Shaleen already preparing for bed.

"I'm sorry," Tayna said, backing quickly out of the room.

"Come in," Shaleen called. "Let's get you settled."

Tayna stepped cautiously back in. The room looked comfortable. Big enough for two, but not ostentatious. "I'm not really tired," she said, fumbling around for something to say in what still felt like an awkward moment. "It really isn't very late yet and I-"

"Two squares to dark," the older woman said, gesturing high on the wall behind her. The roof of the Wind Forge was a vast arch that spanned the entire structure, sloping back to catch the full warmth of the sun. Along its lowest extent, evenly spaced holes in the stonework allowed natural light into each room of the studio, casting squares of brilliant light onto the stone walls above Tayna's head. In this room, two identical magenta squares were visible where the reddish evening sunlight gleamed onto the blue of the stone. As she watched, Tayna could just see that one of the squares was getting narrower, as the sun set behind the mountain ridge and its shadow crept slowly across the face of the Wind Forge.

"Not much accustomed to the high places, are you?" Shaleen asked, conversationally. "Days last longer up high, but they start and end more suddenly. Best come along before you bang your nose in the night. Don't want you looking like a Gnome now."

Tayna followed her through what appeared to be the master bedroom, into another, smaller room beyond. This one had no sun clock on the wall–just one narrow slot of a window to let in air and the diffused, indirect light of a sunset sky, but this end of the studio was already in the shadow of the mountain, and it was only dimly lit.

"Dark rooms are best for busy young Djin boys," Shaleen said. "This was Abeni's room, when he was small. You'll be comfortable in here, I think." Tayna looked around. Like the other rooms of the studio, it was tidy and simple. Not much decoration, but then, when the walls are made of blue stone and etched with intricate veins of gold, silver, and crystal, how much extra decoration did you need?

The only ornaments at all were a few small shapes–toys by the look of them–arranged on the low table beside the bed. One, a round leather orb, caught Tayna's eye. It was the size and shape of a baseball. When asked about it, the woman looked at her curiously. "You've never seen a coverlight?" she asked, and Tayna shook her head. "Odd. I thought they were common."

So Shaleen showed her that the leather had a seam, which could be opened and closed, much like the seam on her boots. When the orb was open, a pale whitish light spilled out from the glowing stone inside, lighting up her hands and the walls around her. Shaleen explained that too much darkness was sometimes difficult for Djin children, especially before they could work magic of their own. So parents often placed coverlights like these in their rooms. With one, any child had power over their darkness, and this helped them to overcome their fear of it quickly.

There were a few other oddities on the table, but Tayna didn't want to get that look again. The one that said, "What kind of weird kid are you that you've never seen one of these?" So she thanked Shaleen again. "Everything looks fine." Then she yawned, surprising herself and earning a laugh from her hostess.

"It is as I told you. Little more than one square now until dark. Sleep will find you. You'll see." It only took her a few moments to show Tayna the low, hard bed, with its single blanket and strange bag-of-gravel pillow. Shaleen had turned and was about to leave when Tayna had a sudden, horrible realization and stopped her.

"Um, Shaleen?"

The woman turned back into the room. "Was there something else you needed?"

Tayna wanted to die of embarrassment, but she knew there was no way she could wait until morning. "Er, is there, um, like, a bathroom?"

"You wish to bathe?"

Tayna's cheeks reddened. "Uh, no. Maybe you call it a washroom?"

Shaleen cocked her head, apparently bemused over what Tayna could possible be talking about, but having realized her need, Tayna's situation was now suddenly urgent and she unconsciously began the dance of the full bladder. Shaleen burst out laughing.

"Oh! You mean the Void! Come girl, this way."

So ten minutes later, after what were, without doubt, the three most embarrassing questions Tayna could ever remember having to ask, she was finally alone in her bed, just as shadows of sunset plunged the room into darkness. And as Shaleen had predicted, the darkness of night and the chill of the air wrapped themselves around her and dragged her quickly down into sleep.

She did not resist.

Later that night, Tayna woke again. "Damned boh-cho," she

muttered, and she fumbled around on the low table beside the bed, feeling for the coverlight. Her hand closed on something, and immediately, a shock ran through her body, but the soft blue glow that crackled from between her fingers lit the room. Not the same coverlight, but it would light her way to the void just as well.

When she climbed back into bed, she set the coverlight back on the table, but it did not go out. Tayna was pretty sure this one hadn't had a cover. It had been bare and cold when she'd picked it up. But there was no way she was going to be able to sleep with that glaring in her face all night, so she pulled the second blanket from where it had been folded at the end of the bed, and tossed it over the light. Voila. Instant darkness. Without giving it another thought, Tayna rolled over and went back to sleep.

This time, her dreams were entirely waterfall-free.

chapter 19

Eliza sat in the crotch of a tree, near the traveler's dehn, watching the creepy little Gnome– Check that. Watching *Mehklok* wriggle his delighted little tush into the mud of the river bank. A shudder of revulsion ran through her, but Mardu had made her promise not to reveal how much she hated the disgusting little worm. Because they *needed* him. So Eliza would just have to suck it up and play nice-nice with her former abuser. Figures.

Beside her, Scraw was doing his best to be even more revolting than the Gnome, working his pointy little beak up a long branch, digging and poking under the loose bark. Occasionally he would throw back his head in delight as he choked down another grub. Eliza shuddered every time. She was convinced his whole grub fetish was just more crow humor, meant to freak her out. So with the others occupied, this might be their last chance to chat without interruption for a while.

Where next? she sent.

I have given this much thought, Mardu replied, as Scraw found another package of ugh! and choked it down. *We must convince three kings to set aside their war and return to the Anvil–to the very Bloodcap– and there to renew the Oath.*

And don't forget about the part where they sacrifice family members, Eliza added. *That should make it easier. Everybody loves a family barbecue.*

Mardu twisted Scraw's head around and threw a glare of resentment at her.

Oops. Sorry. I forgot.

The problem, Mardu continued, as though nothing had happened, *is how to convince them of our cause. To their eyes, we are but a mute girl, a cross-tempered crow, and a Gnome, and it has been the slaughter of Dragons even to assemble this many. Without followers–without a visible people behind us–we will appear as little more than a deluded rabble, demanding*

207

concessions from our betters. Not leaders of men, treating with equals.

You mean Captain Creepytime is part of the team now? He's not, like, a follower? To pick grubs for Scraw or something?

"Scraw!" the crow interjected, voicing his approval of the suggestion.

Don't you see, Eliza? Friend Mehklok may be key to our success. He is an ordained chaplain of an ancient order, who has built his life from convincing villagers to align themselves with hopeless causes. His are the skills that will complete our company and bring success to our mission.

But how does he help? We almost had four new recruits today, but dingus scared them off. What about that do-what-I-say magic you did back there, when you froze everybody? Can't you just do that instead, but you know, bigger? Make them obey you? And if you did that, then we wouldn't need him for anything.

Eliza tasted Mardu's frustration and a hint of sadness over the link. *No*, Mardu replied. *An oath made under compulsion has no substance. And what is more, the Flame of the Dragon That Was draws vim from Methilien himself, and from the remnants of the original Oath, but something is wrong. Something has changed. Even with the Oath in tatters and the Dragon withholding his vims from the Peoples, there should still be vim aplenty within the world. Enough for me to command the entire Gnomileshi Horde to sing songs of love and bake pies, yet there is not. I should not have used what little store I had. We will lament its loss before long, I think.*

Great, so your batteries are dead. I get it. No hocus-pokus-take-the-oathus. Not any time soon, anyway. How long will it take to recharge?

I do not know. None of this is as it was supposed to be. I am having to... wing it.

"K-keh" Scraw said, lifting one of his own wings to salute the joke. Eliza smiled with him.

Okay, so no recharge, Eliza said. *What about new batteries then? Can you switch to alkalines? Or car batteries or something? Maybe plug into a wall socket back home? Or maybe we don't even need magic. What if we built up a big group of foll—*

Hold, Eliza.

What? Oh. Sorry. I tend to just spout garbage when we're brainstorming. That's kinda what I do. And then Tayna usually stops me in the middle and says—

Yes, that might work.

Eliza's eyes widened with surprise. *How did you know? That's*

208

almost exactly what–

You were jesting, but there is wisdom in the words, even if you did not intend it. Suddenly, Scraw stopped his grub hunt and flapped back down to perch in front of Eliza. *I must seek something upon the wind,* Mardu sent. *Scraw and I will return shortly. Hold here until our return.* Then they flitted off the branch and vanished through the foliage. Eliza didn't even have time to ask where they were heading.

When fifteen minutes had passed and still Flame Girl and Robin had not returned, Eliza began to wonder just how long they might be gone. Was she supposed to wait here for an hour? Or a week? As she was pondering that, Mehklok grunted in satisfaction and began splashing muddy water up over his head. His back was toward her, and he was completely oblivious. His hearing would be impaired by all that mud and water. It would be one minute's work to hop down from this tree, and sneak up behind him... There were plenty of fist-sized rocks scattered around by the river... Not that she would ever do that, of course. But it was a fun way to pass the time, and she soon lost herself in dreams of violent revenge.

What are you doing? A flutter of wings startled her out of her fantasy, announcing that Mardu and Scraw had returned. She opened her eyes and smiled guiltily.

Um, nothing. But you first, she answered. *Where did you go and what did you find?*

Scraw cocked his head at her, curiously. *As you will. Your earlier words hinted at a solution. A possible source of vim. In honesty, it was not one I would ever have considered, yet you said we might 'plug into a wall socket back home.'*

Eliza laughed. *You mean you've figured out how to power magic with electricity?*

No, but there is one thing your world does have that might give me power. Power enough that we may yet bargain earnestly with kings.

Ooo! Is it Pop Tarts? I miss Pop Tarts.

No, Mardu said, shaking Scraw's head at Eliza's burst of silliness. *It is the Dragon Grimorl.*

We will draw our strength from the other *Dragon.*

They were heading south and west, toward the distant tug that only Mardu could feel. From time to time, Scraw would flap off, up into the forest canopy, and beyond, seeking altitude. Up there, separated from the confusing scatter of Methilien vim trickling in and around and through everything around them, Mardu could open her senses to the wind and seek out for that... otherness. She still couldn't say what it was, exactly. Only that it was a relic of some kind. Some token of the Dragon Grimorl. It called to her from the south-west. Perhaps two days distant.

And it shimmered with power.

If Eliza had taken the time to think about things from Mehklok's point of view, she might have been surprised by what she saw. To him, it was just he and the crow following their enigmatic young woman leader through the Forest toward their holy duty. Like a stone thrown straight and true, directly along the path of greatest good. But sadly, she did not take the time. All Eliza could see was herself stumbling around half blind, stared at by a lecherous mud monkey as she lurched along behind a schizophrenic crow with delusions of godhood.

Paradoxically, it was Mehklok's perspective, more than her own, that would have made her feel better about herself. But for that to happen, she'd have needed time free from the plague of distractions and delays that hounded them.

All of the Gnomileshi variety.

It seemed they couldn't march an hour in any direction without having to take cover at least once to allow a Gnome scouting party to pass by. Each time, Mehklok volunteered to simply talk their way through. After all, he was a powerful and well-known church official, and the Hordesmen would do his bidding without question. Probably.

But each time, Eliza had declined his offer, using Scraw to tell him that one should not question the Ways of the Flame. She hadn't meant to capitalize the phrase, but hearing Mehklok repeat it many times over the course of the journey, the capitals had crept in there somehow, and now everything she did became part of the secret body of mystic lore being codified by Mehklok as "The Ways of the Flame."

Through their near-encounters with the roving bands of Gnome scouts, they noted a few recurring themes. Each band was comprised of either three or four Gnomes—one of whom always carried a Goody urn—and most groups had one of the tall, white gorilla-like creatures with them as well. These were the Yeren, according to

Mardu. A peaceful and utterly harmless folk, although quite rare. In her day, they had been connected somehow to the dragons, but nobody had ever figured out how. All that anyone knew was that whenever a dragon lair was discovered, there was usually a family or two of Yeren living in the same cavern. But the creatures of Mardu's recollection had not been as pathetic as these she saw now, being led around on a leash by Gnomileshi Hordesmen, shuffling dimly like confused old men. *They were quite dignified creatures,* Mardu had said. *Docile. Gentle. But not stupid. To see what they have now become is sad.*

On the evening of the second day of their march, Mardu called a halt. *What we seek is just ahead,* she said. *I can taste it from here, even above the Methilien vim that should drown its flavor with ease. To sense it should not be possible, and yet it is. Another puzzle for us to unravel, perhaps. But for now, remain here. Scraw and I will seek ahead.* And with a flap of black wings, they were gone.

Earlier, Mardu and Eliza had decided that, in order to maintain the illusion of mystical presence, Mardu would not speak directly into the minds of any of the Followers unless absolutely necessary. Instead, everything said to them by the Flame would be in pantomime from Eliza, or from the screeching throat of the crow. So, with Scraw off reconnoitering, Eliza simply sat down in place, crossed her legs, and resumed the Praying Mantis pose. Another of the Ways of the Flame. This one meant, "I have no idea what's going on either, and I don't know what to tell you, so I'm going to look all magical and divine and stuff and let you guess." The Gnome took up position beside her and amused himself by trying to contort his stumpy Gnome legs into a semblance of her pose.

Scraw returned a few minutes later.

It is here, Mardu said. *But it is buried. Ahead there is a clearing, and through the clearing, a small brook flows. In the center of the clearing, the brook divides to flow around a circular island. From legs, it appears normal, but from the sky. . .* Mardu included a crow's-eye view of the clearing. With the sun nearing the horizon, the view was etched with deep shadows, but Eliza recognized the ring shape instantly.

A bullseye.

An eye? To see what? Mardu asked.

No, not an actual eye. A 'bullseye.' It's a mark you draw to practice shooting or throwing things. You put a bunch of circles around each other and then try to hit the middle one.

211

And these are drawn on a bull?

No. Forget about the word, Eliza sent. *I only meant that it looks like a target—as though someone was planning to throw something. Something hella big and really important. Must have wanted to be sure they hit the right spot.*

Perhaps they threw the dragon scale, then. It is not large, but it is buried deeply beneath the center of the island, which is the center of this bull's eye. A circle of trees, surrounding a circle of grasses, around a circular bulge in the stream that contains a circular island.

Buried deeply? How deep?

Many strides, Mardu replied. *I think. It is hard to be certain. I do not see it. I can only sense it.*

So now we have to start digging. Great.

Yes. After we dispatch the Gnome guards, Mardu added.

Eliza shot to her feet. *Guards? There are guards? Do they know we're here? Why didn't you tell me? That part should have come first!*

I assumed you had seen them in the sky-view, Mardu said. *But all is well. We are not discovered.*

Great, Eliza replied, as she wrestled her heartbeat and breathing back to normal. She looked again at the mental image of the clearing and yes, she could see that there were three Gnomes standing still, arranged around a camp fire they had set in the middle of the island. They stood so still she had assumed they were rocks or stumps or something. *Is there anything else you haven't mentioned that might be useful? Any rings of fire around it? Does the dragon scale have a money-back guarantee? Will I get a free all-expenses paid trip to Tahiti if I circle the smiling monkey and act now?*

You are very strange, friend Eliza.

Thanks, Eliza said, sticking her tongue out at her crow-shrouded friend. *I love you too.* Beside her, Eliza noticed that Mehklok was now staring at her in confusion. Oops. Gotta watch that whole talking to myself thing. Hopefully he'd just write it up as another mysterious Way of the Flame. Then she called Scraw to come settle on her shoulder.

It was time to tell the midget about the next step in their crazy plan.

"But I am certain they will do as I instruct," Mehklok said. Again

Eliza shook her head.

"Too risky," she said, through Scraw, who was perched on her shoulder. "Need them scared. Running away. Not curious."

But internally, she was much less confident. *Any idea how we're going to do that?* she sent. Scraw shivered his entire body in a quake of uncertainty. *Better let me see then. Take Scraw up ahead and show me what's what.*

Scraw flitted off into the night and Eliza turned to look at Mehklok. She still didn't trust him, but she needed to see what they were up against. After a moment of silent contemplation, Eliza stepped past him, placing her back against a large rock that thrust up out of the forest floor. Then she settled herself down into her lotus position. She was just going to have to trust the little creep. With her back now at least partly protected against treachery, Eliza closed her eyes and reached out through her connection to the bird, leaving Mehklok to puzzle it out for himself in the growing darkness.

"You see through the eyes of the bird?" Mehklok asked, after a moment. His voice was quiet with awe. Eliza nodded her head. "That is truly–" Eliza held up a hand to cut him off. Scraw had reached a branch overlooking the glade and she needed to concentrate on what he could see.

As in the earlier mental image Mardu had shared, there were three of them, but seeing it live, sort of, rather than a memory, everything was much clearer. They really were guards. That much was obvious now. They stood in a ring around their watch fire, completely still, gazing outward into the surrounding gloom.

They're not fools, Mardu sent. *See how they stand with their backs to the flame? They protect their night eyes while the light of the fire illuminates any who would approach.*

But why guard an island? Do they know about the magical whatsit underneath? Then she scoffed at herself. *Yeah. Right. They're in the middle of nowhere guarding a damp clump the size of our kitchen so that nobody steals the mud. Of course they know about the dragon thingy. But why leave it here and post guards? Why not just dig it up and take it back to Gnome-land with them? It doesn't make any sense.*

I do not know.

At least they don't seem to be armed.

Do you not see the long pole each of them holds?

Well yeah, Eliza sent, *but I was worried about, you know, actual weapons. Arrows or machine guns or magic phasers or something. Clubs don't scare me so much.*

Not even a magical club, forged from the wing bone of a dragon? The bone lance of a Gnomileshi Hordesman was a weapon much feared in my time. Capable of grievous charms over considerable distance. You truly do not fear it?

Eliza shuddered. *Well, now that I know it's not just a stupid club I do. Nobody told me the bad guys got magic spears, too. This just keeps getting better and better.* Eliza's inner eye flitted around the image, looking for anything else that might be useful. *Hello, there's the Tupperware.*

The what?

That giant metal bowl on the grass. Beside the big guy in front. We keep seeing those. Every group of scouts we've seen has had one just like it—even the group that first night, back at the traveler's dehn. And I've seen them in my world too.

Truly? What are they used for in your world?

For burying dead people.

So it is a thing of death.

Yeah. Pretty much.

"What's going on? What can you see?"

Eliza shook her head to clear the crow's vision from her mind, and opened her eyes to find the Gnome peering at her anxiously, with an almost reverent awe. Even though she was sitting on the ground, Eliza did not have to look up very sharply to meet his gaze. She shook her head briefly and then held up a hand in the international goddess gesture for "leave me alone you little twerp, I'm busy." Mehklok bowed his head in apology, and Eliza closed her eyes once more.

In a moment, she had reoriented herself to the full-surround crow-o-ramic vision, and as she examined the scene, it occurred to her that something was missing. *Where's the Yeren?* They had asked Mehklok why every Gnome squad seemed to include a Goody urn and one of the tall, white-furred creatures, but he had been just as perplexed as they were. Or at least, he'd *said* he was.

She is asleep in the forest, Mardu answered. *They have tied her to a tree and left her with their packs and supplies.*

"Tell me what you see in the flames!"

Eliza sighed. *Doesn't look like there's anything else to see here. Let's regroup and figure out a plan. I think Junior's wet himself or something. He doesn't seem to be able to go five minutes without somebody telling him what a pretty monkey he is.* She opened her eyes and then let out a yip of fear. Frustrated at not knowing what was going on, Mehklok had leaned in so close that he appeared to her opening eyes as a touring menace, looming over her, as his voice still echoed in her memory. "... what you see in the flames!"

And suddenly, Eliza knew how they were going to get rid of the Gnomes.

***

It might work, Mardu agreed. *But I am so weak. I should be replenished by now. Or Scraw should be. Something is very wrong. There is scarcely any vim left in the world and we have gathered but little. I do not know if it is enough to work a fire charm from here.*

But it can't hurt to try, right? If you can't do anything, there'll be nothing for them to notice.

After discussing Eliza's idea for some time, Mardu admitted that she knew a charm that might work. Something called a "fire puppet." It was a simple charm that parents often used to entertain and even educate children–making characters and shapes appear in the flames of a cookfire, where they could be moved about to re-enact great battles or demonstrate a difficult task. But Mardu was not optimistic. A full fire puppet, she admitted, would require a lot of vim, and a lot of concentration too. It was considered quite an art to be able to sculpt the flames using nothing but your imagination, and she did not believe she was strong enough for it. But there was a much easier version of the charm, and that's the one they decided to try with the guards.

The difference, she explained to Eliza, *is where the image comes from. I do not have even a portion of the vim that I would need to create visions from nothing. But if there were a model. Someone to pantomime the move-ments... Then I could simply project the sights before me to guide the flames. A much simpler charm. As soon as we know what we are going to project.*

Surprisingly, it was Mehklok who provided that last part.

"It is said that when a sky-dwe... when a *Wasketchin* faces a great problem, he will speak his question to the trees, seeking the wisdom of the dragon. Is this true?"

It has nothing to do with dragons, Mardu said. *But yes. My father put his great problems to the trees, as did his fathers. Trees are much wiser than any dragon.*

Eliza nodded at the Gnome. It was true.

Mehklok seemed pleased. "My people also have problems," he said. "Though we do not have so many trees. In the Throat of the Forest, when one has a great difficulty, one speaks his question to the flames."

Eliza raised an eyebrow. Oh really? Do tell.

"There is much to hear in the roars and whispers of fire," Mehklok explained. "It is the Dragon speaking with tongues of flame and the voice of fire. All Gnomes are taught to fear the fire voices, and to obey. To do otherwise is to spurn great wisdom and play games with the future. Some have even seen visions in the flame. Visions that tell them to do all manner of things. Sometimes terrible things. I myself would not trust the urgings of a burning stick, but these guards are simple. They will fear. And they will follow."

"Fire puppets," croaked the bird. "K-k-k-keh!"

Eliza grinned. This was beginning to sound like a plan.

chapter 20

The next morning, Tayna emerged from her room to find most of the family engaged in a heated discussion.

"That cannot be!" Zimu said. "Does he not see that the Gnome manipulates him?"

Tayna joined them at the small table in the kitchen, where Zimu had been bringing Abeni up to speed on everything that had been going on among the Djin. Tayna took a seat next to Abeni, and Shaleen greeted her warmly, handing her a hot mug of boh-cho with a dense, nutty cake set across the top. Tayna smiled her thanks and then they both turned their attention back to the discussion. Apparently, Abeni had just told his brother the details of his audience with Mabundi, and Zimu was none too happy about it.

"What service to the Djin is offered by leaping at Gnomileshi bidding?"

"He believes he is sparing us all from the Gnome King's war," Shaleen said.

"That is a false bargain," Zimu said. "Mabundi was a fine teacher, but he was lenient. Too readily he accepted tardiness and shallow excuses from those who did not wish to work at their studies."

"Perhaps he was allowing them to confront the consequences of their efforts," Shaleen suggested, as she settled herself into a chair across from her boys and set her own cup on the table. "Or their lack of effort. It is a worthy lesson, and one every person must learn."

"But shall a king treat his people so?" Zimu countered. "Does he mean to teach us by delivering us to the Horde? No doubt there are many worthy lessons such hardship can teach as well."

Shaleen shrugged. "I do not–"

"Divide and conquer," Tayna said, as she bit into her cake. All three faces turned to look at her.

"What is to be divided?" Zimu asked. "The Djin are united,

even if poorly led."

"Not the Djin," Tayna said. "The opposition." But still her table-mates seemed perplexed. Then it hit her. "Oh right," she said. "I keep forgetting how much you guys don't know about fighting. Where I come from, this is all pretty basic. It's how you beat an enemy who's bigger than you are. Rule #3 for how to beat Goodies. Never let them work together."

When she saw that they still weren't following, she turned to Abeni. "Look, how did you control the sprites?"

"Abeni does not see how—"

"You offered a prize to each one of them, right? Individually. Those 'tasty morsels' of flapmeat. And that got them fighting each other instead of you, remember?" Abeni looked at her thoughtfully, as she turned to Zimu.

"That's what Angiron is doing to the entire Forest. He knows he can't beat both the Wasketchin and the Djin—not if you team up—so he's trying to keep you apart."

Abeni began to nod and Zimu's eyes widened with sudden understanding. "It is the same with a large task," he said, and Tayna could see the wheels clearly turning behind that large face of his as he put the idea together. "It is as Kijamon has always told: when one cannot do a large, impossible thing, do many small possible things instead."

"Right," Tayna said. "Divide and conquer."

"Perhaps he divides more than simply Wasketchin from Djin," Abeni said. "Everywhere, Wasketchin flee throughout the Forest. They do not resist together."

"The Houses!" Shaleen said suddenly, and everyone turned to her. "Mabundi has remained here with us for much longer than other kings. Already we have had complaints from House Xenek and House Bashee."

Zimu nodded. "As you told me yesterday. Perhaps the Djin are not as united as I had thought. The Wasketchin stand divided from the Djin, and it seems that both Peoples stand divided among themselves, as well."

"And while everybody's standing around wondering what's going on, Angiron's scooping up all the Wasketchin he can find," Tayna said. "Soon there won't be any of them left for the Djin to team up with."

"Then he will come to the Anvil," Abeni said.

"But what can be done about it?" Shaleen asked. "As Zimu says, the Peoples are already divided."

"We must undivide our people," Zimu said. Then his eyes narrowed. "But first, we must remove the knife that divides us."

"But where is the knife?" Abeni asked.

"Not 'where,'" Shaleen said. "The question is 'who.' It is Yoliq who divides us."

Abeni's shock was clear on his face. "The Queen of the Djin seeks to divide her own people?" But Shaleen shook her head.

"No, such is not her aim. The Queen does not seek to divide Djin from Wasketchin, nor House from House. She sees no further than her own wants, and what she wants is to join herself to power."

"It is true," Zimu said. "Our King is but a chalice, filled with the liquor of his Queen's ambition."

Shaleen sighed, shaking her head sadly. "I had hoped when we named him to the throne that he would have time to grow into his wisdom," Shaleen said. "We did not know he would need it so quickly upon the heels of his Oath. His love has closed his eyes to her hunger."

"It makes him thin," Zimu said. "And now we see through him, to the hand of an ambitious Queen upon his spine. She sees her chance of greatness held out before her eyes by the hand of the Gnome King, and she cannot look away from it. If we are to bend Mabundi at all, we must first bend the Queen."

"Or oppose her," Abeni said, but Shaleen shook her head.

"There is nothing to be gained from opposing," she said. "Not alone. We must seek the mood of the other Houses. Many think as Mabundi does–that we must appease Angiron now, and draw out for time–but all do not agree. We must find another way."

"And we must find it quickly," Zimu said. "Before the true hand behind the King is revealed, and found to be clenched about the spines of all Djin."

"The Queen," Abeni said, and the others nodded. Except for Tayna.

"No," she said, surprised that they had missed it. "The real hand is Angiron's."

And slowly, three pairs of eyes around the table began to widen in understanding. House Kijamon had finally recognized its true foe.

———

"They dare stoop to such tactics? For a 'Ketch girl?'"

Mabundi watched as his wife raged across the floor. The Gnome Ambassador stood by as well, watching quietly now that his news had been delivered.

"And you're sure there has been no mistake? They've Included her? Offered the Keshwa-Ji?"

"That was their answer to my petition," Quishek replied. "No unbound has been found on their holdings, they said. And when I asked about the girl who arrived yesterday, they informed me that she has been formally accepted into House Kijamon. She is bound. And so the matter falls to the King to decide." Quishek bowed and stepped back.

"They mock you, my husband!"

Mabundi turned from the Ambassador to look at his wife. She had stopped her pacing and was now twisting and clenching her hands in fury.

"Do you not see? Having been told that you would let the matter be settled by traditional laws–between their House and our esteemed neighbor Gnomes–they seek to defy your wisdom! They've Included her simply to show you that they can do whatever they wish. They forge laughter from your crown!"

"They do seem to have twisted the King's intentions..." Quishek added.

Mabundi frowned. Could House Kijamon really be making such mockery of him? He hadn't thought the Master of the Wind Forge capable of such low politics, but then, maybe he'd never seen the true face of Kijamon's ambition before. Still, he must not rush to judgment.

"Summon her," Mabundi said, waving at an attendant who had been standing near the door. "Have her brought to me. Here. After full sun, tomorrow."

"Here?" Yoliq shouted. "You would honor their treachery by receiving the girl in the Hall of Flame?"

Mabundi raised his palms, trying to ward off the worst of his wife's temper. "She has been Included. She must be welcomed in a manner suited to her House," he said.

But his wife's fury only deepened. "Oh, of course," she cried.

"You sent a plain and simple message only to have it flaunted in your face, so now that you send another, by all means, permit them all the privileges their deviousness has earned them. Concede defeat before they even come."

Was she right? Had Kijamon really been playing him the fool?

"Whether the Keshwa-Ji has been performed or not, who can say?" Quishek said. "Were the proper forms observed? Has the Inclusion been recorded in the Hall of Histories?" Then he stepped forward and knelt formally before the Anvil Seat, and Mabundi pulled back just a trifle. "Can a Wasketchin even *be* Included?" the Gnome continued. "If not, it would be a dangerous precedent to establish. But none could fault the King of all Djin for receiving a common Wasketchin in the Hall of Wind. That he received her at all should be honor enough."

Mabundi sat back in the Seat and pondered. Had there ever been a Wasketchin Included before? He could not recall. Perhaps Yoliq was right. It was a minor enough concession to keep peace in his marriage. And besides, she might be right about this matter as well. She had a much better head than he for these kinds of subtleties. Mabundi waved his hand. "So be it," he said to the attendant, who had been standing there, waiting for a final decision. "Have her summoned to the Hall of Wind."

When word reached Kijamon that Mabundi had summoned a member of his House to a meeting in the Hall of Wind, the old man did something entirely unexpected.

He closed the Wind Forge.

For the first time in memory, the great manufactury that hung suspended over the Djin's prized city of artisans and craftsmen stood silent in the morning sun. All assistants, porters, suppliers, and tradesmen were sent away. No forges burned. No hammers rang. No voices called out in the friendly camaraderie of creative production. House Kijamon was closed for the day.

Then Kijamon did a second unexpected thing. He called his family to attend him upon the great balcony that surrounded their now-silent home.

To speak of politics.

In order to understand the full import of these two events, one must be reminded of Kijamon's history. On three separate occasions in the past, a cluster of aging Djin had made their way up the Trail of Sky to stand before Kijamon in his forge. Each time, their mission had been the same. They had come to offer him the crown, to make him King of all Djin. And each time he had refused.

Kijamon had no patience for the petty squabbling of critics and cowards. "Politics is chickens in a hen house," he often said, "writing policies and protocols for the governing of foxes, when only the chickens can read."

More importantly, each time he had refused them, he had done so with a single word–"No"–after which, he would refuse to speak any syllable more on the matter. He had not even done his guests the courtesy of turning away from his work to hear their pleas. The forges ran, messengers and helpers came and went, and all around the wise heads, the foxes of Kijamon's enterprise continued their pace of production.

But today, Kijamon had closed the forge.

To speak of politics.

Tayna and Abeni arrived just behind Zimu, and followed him out onto the sweeping terrace that emerged from the buttress ramps on either side and stretched outward, surrounding the Wind Forge in a grand gallery. They found Kijamon waiting for them near the middle, gazing up along the shoulder of the Anvil at the Bloodcap, which towered above them, a deep red wedge holding up the sky. Shaleen stood quietly by his side.

"It comes to my mind," Kijamon said, not looking away from the mountain's peak, but beginning to speak as soon as the family was gathered around him, "that the time has come for the House to take action."

And with those words, Kijamon began to outline his plan for securing the honor of the Anvil Seat and all Djin.

This was not the kindly and somewhat distracted father figure Tayna had seen around the family table. This was the imposing Kijamon she had observed when she'd first arrived. This was the Kijamon of legend. The Kijamon who had three times been offered the crown. Questions and answers swirled around him as he drew each member of his House into the web of his penetrating intellect. Once more, Tayna felt as though she had been plugged into some vast computer system that extracted information from her and hundreds of other sources with surgical precision, sorted it all together, analyzed it, sought new updates, refined it all, and ultimately, shaped it into a vast and glittering whole. A sculpture of understanding.

When he first began to speak, Tayna had been surprised that he did not want to talk about the snub Mabundi had offered his House by summoning her to the Hall of Wind. "It is a sign only," Kijamon had said. "A sign of how gravely Mabundi stumbles. To respond to the sign would be folly. We must seek the cause of his stumble and attend to that instead." So this is what he had proceeded to do. And when he was finished, House Kijamon had a plan. Six people, each with a task, and each task uniquely suited to their skills and to their current situations.

Sarqi, appropriately, was charged with remaining in the Throat and serving as Ambassador. The family had no illusions as to their son's true status in Angiron's Court, of course, so there was no point in setting him any task that his captivity would preclude him from performing. But as Ambassador, it was possible that he might gain access to useful information, so it only made sense to confirm him in that duty. Unfortunately, it was beyond Kijamon's power to appoint Sarqi as Ambassador to the Anvil Seat, so he had made the appointment that he *was* empowered to make, and had declared Sarqi to be House Kijamon's ambassador to the Gnomes.

To Shaleen was given the daunting task of trying to establish communication with the House's new ambassador. "Not much point in acquiring the information if he can't get it back to the rest of us," Kijamon had said. Upon being given the task though, his wife had simply nodded, announcing that, while she had no idea how this might be accomplished, she would put her question to the Dragon and see what answers might come. To Tayna, that sounded an awful lot like praying for help, but it was Kijamon himself–the ruling champion of reason and self-sufficiency–who corrected her. "Shaleen does not appeal to a higher power to solve her problems for her," he said with a laugh. "No, putting a question to the Dragon is simply a way of focusing the mind on a single problem, and then opening yourself to the solutions that are being whispered at every moment by the world around you. It is a practice rich with inspiration, and one that every artist uses, whether they know it or not."

But if Tayna had been surprised by his support of prayer, she was doubly startled when he had turned his gaze next on her, and given her a project too. And it was not some little "keep busy" task either.

"The Anvil Seat has shown its misguided back to its friends and neighbors for too long," Kijamon said. "While it is understandable that the weight of a new king's crown might sometimes cause him to stumble, we who are loyal to that crown must not let it strike the ground if it should bobble from his head as a result."

The upshot was that Tayna had been charged with seeking out maps of the undertowns. In the old days, before the Dragon's Peace, many Djin had lived in stone caverns, dug into the rocky bulk of the Plateau. But since the terms of the Peace had ceded all holdings lower than the surface of the Plateau to the other Peoples, most of the subterranean villages had long been abandoned by the Djin. Rightfully, they now belonged to the Wasketchin. But aside from a few wanderers–scatterlings, the Djin called them–those neighbors had never taken up their claim, because the undertowns could only be accessed from the surface of the Plateau, which was entirely within Djin territory. Those difficulties now seemed trifling, of course, so the time had come for the rightful owners of the undertowns to take possession, even if only for a short while. And to do that, they would need maps and information.

Tayna gulped when the duty was assigned to her, but she accepted it. Nobody had ever trusted her with something important before, and her skin was buzzing with excitement as Kijamon's attention swept past her, and the plan continued to unfold.

To Abeni had fallen the task of reaching out to the Wasketchin King. Not as an official emissary of the Djin People, but as another ambassador of House Kijamon. While Tayna was busy acquiring the necessary maps, it would be up to Abeni to outfit a relief mission, and to that end, Kijamon had pledged the full resources of the House. With such backing, Abeni would be easily able to produce whatever goods or equipment he might deem necessary for helping their scattered neighbors to their new lodgings. Once the maps and the equipment were ready, Abeni and Tayna would then seek out the Wasketchin King, where they would present him with the support of at least House Kijamon, and help him to get his people to safety.

And defend them.

Kijamon himself took a task, as well, and one that only he could accomplish. It would be his delicate job to survey the great Houses of the Djin. Discreetly, and at all times with the firm intention of aiding their struggling King. But it was imperative that he learn the hearts and minds of the other Houses, and ensure that all moved as one to protect the honor of the Crown. In all likelihood, most of the Houses did not even know of the King's struggles and would no doubt be dismayed by the news. Coming from any lesser messenger, they would surely waffle and debate over how much credence to give the news, and there was simply no time for such chicken-talk. Therefore it was of utmost importance that it be Kijamon himself who made this contact with them. The very fact that he had stepped out from his forge to engage in the politics of the realm would speak with far greater urgency than any other courtier or emissary could hope to convey.

And this left Zimu, to whom Kijamon had charged the direst of burdens, because to him was given the task of finding ways and means by which Mabundi might be removed from the throne. In all the long years of the Dragon's Peace, it had never before been neces-sary to unseat a ruling King, and while there were many rumors and stories of how this had been done in the distant days of warring and strife, none of the family could recall with certainty which of those stories were true and which had only been fancy. Nobody wanted it to come to this, of course, which was why so much of the plan must be rooted in supporting the throne. Or at least, not working openly against it. But if necessity should demand it of them, House Kija-mon must be both willing and prepared to take that loathsome step. Zimu accepted the bond with wide searching eyes, scarcely able to believe the words as his father spoke them to him. But accept it he did, and all around the group, Tayna felt a shudder of dread ripple among them.

"So that is our plan," Kijamon concluded, casting his gaze over each of them in turn, making sure everyone understood the import of what they were about to do. "We must gather what information we can," he said to Shaleen. "We must rush to the aid of our friends, before Mabundi's stumble in this regard becomes a great fall." This he spoke to Tayna and Abeni, and then his eyes glittered darkly as he turned to his eldest son.

"And if strife demands it of us, we must be ready to pull down a King. If we are to save the world."

Kijamon raised his hands and spoke a phrase in a rough and guttural tongue. When he finished, Tayna heard a series of metallic clanks around the table and felt the weight of an iron ring magically drop onto her own wrist too. She looked down at it in wonder.

"My own bond ring?" she asked. Abeni smiled and nodded, raising his own arm to point to the ring of dark metal that had been added to his own arm.

"Let none among us bear the shame of rust," Shaleen said. And with that, the official meeting was over. It was an ominous thought to end on, but Tayna couldn't help but ask one more question. "What about tomorrow?" she said. "What should I do about Mabundi's summons?" Kijamon's eyebrows rose in surprise.

"Mabundi is King," he said. "You must attend him."

"And if he orders me to leave with the Gnomes?"

Kijamon's face split into a happy grin. "By the time you have entered the Hall, your name will already be written into the Scroll of Houses, so again Mabundi must bring his petition to me. And while I debate him on the wisdom of his actions, you will continue with your assigned duties."

Now it was Tayna's turn to grin. "Which just happen to take me away from the House for a while, where I won't be able to receive a summons."

Kijamon nodded. "Clever, aren't I?"

Tayna nodded in agreement, but inside, she couldn't manage to calm the trembling of her nerves. Nothing that seemed good for her had ever worked out the way it was supposed to.

Especially when kings were involved.

chapter 21

"I haven't seen any of these nuns before," Sue said, as she snapped a photo of the group of nuns now scurrying up the front steps.

"That's Sister Inquisita at the front, I think," he said, peering through his binoculars. "She runs Holy Terror. The high school. The others are probably her staff. See how they all sort of cringe behind her? Looks like a submissive posture to me. Like underlings."

Sue turned away from her camera to look at him. "Submissive posture? They just look like women on a staircase to me."

DelRoy shrugged without taking his eyes off the steps. "I'm good with body language," he said.

Sue's gaze held on him for a moment, before turning back to the activity at the orphanage. "So that's the mortuary and the high school both accounted for then," she said.

"And that woman getting out of the taxi looks like Judy Chan," he added, swinging his binoculars around for a better look.

"The one who brought you to this party? Your social worker friend, from Children's Services? "

"Director of Children's Services now," he replied.

"Oh," Sue replied. They were both getting punch-drunk from the repeated surprises of just who was attending these parties.

By the time the parade had ended, they were both exhausted from the shock. The list of party-goers seemed more appropriate to a high-society wedding or a red-carpet gala somewhere. Not some tawdry little elbow rub with a roomful of cloistered nuns.

In addition to the Mayor, they had counted thirty-seven other guests, including a Bishop, the Superintendent of the School Board, and to DelRoy's own utter despair, the Chief of Police and two of his most senior aides. There had also been a good smattering of people that neither he nor Sue could identify, but given the company they were keeping, something told him that those folks were probably equally powerful players in the city's infrastructure. Perhaps just not as visibly so.

"What have we gotten ourselves into?" Sue asked, once the big doors to the building had closed and the train of guests had stopped arriving.

"I don't know," he replied.

Just then, a limousine came around the corner and slowed as it approached the orphanage. The two of them watched as the rear window slid smoothly down. They could see the steam of breath puffing through the open window as whoever it was took a long look at the closed orphanage doors. A moment later, the window slid back up again, and the car pulled away. Nobody got out. Apparently, once they had closed, you did not go thumping on the doors and yelling for late admittance.

"I wonder who that was," Sue said.

"I got the plate," he said, hastily jotting down the numbers on a small pad of paper, "but it was a rental. I might be able to get something from the dispatcher later, but they're pretty protective, and I haven't got any official standing."

"And you can't ask for any either," Sue said, nodding toward the police car that the Chief and his friends had arrived in.

"Right. But none of this makes any sense," he said, drumming his fingers on the steering wheel. "I mean, these are some of the most influential and politically connected people in the city. The kind of people who only got where they are by having excellent scandal radar and an itchy trigger finger on the 'run away' button. Not one of them should be stupid enough to be here. In a building full of nuns and underage children? After dark and on the wrong side of town? It just doesn't add up. Hell, the photos you took alone would be enough to topple the entire city infrastructure."

"So why *did* they come?"

"I have no idea," he said, shaking his head.

"You mean you don't remember."

DelRoy sagged. "Right. I don't remember."

And somehow, that made it worse.

The next day, after a sleepless night worrying about all the powerful people who seemed to stand between her and her daughter, Sue returned to the scene of the crime. Most things look better by day.

Happier. Less threatening. But to her eye, the Old Shoe hadn't lost even a shade of its midnight evil. If anything, it was even worse now, standing there in the crisp morning sunlight with all its callous indifference on display, blind to the plight of the children it was supposed to be sheltering.

Sue strolled confidently down the alley beside the old brick building, and plucked the folded scrap of paper out from between the bricks next to the rear door. This new drop location that the girls had suggested was more secure, but it made Sue a little less comfortable. Scuttling around behind the dumpster made her feel more like a criminal than a mother searching for her lost child, but the girls had insisted on finding a better place. There had already been one mishap, with one of Sue's notes being picked up by another girl, but the next time they might not be so lucky. The window drop was just too risky.

She pushed the note down into her pocket and turned to head back to her car, but a dark figure stepped into her path from the shadows. Sue let go of the slip of paper and made a fist around her car keys, ready to fend him off if he attacked. But for the moment, he just stood there, peering at her. His hands came up, almost distractedly, rather than threatening.

"Don't come any closer," Sue said, trying to sound more confident and dangerous than she felt.

The man's hands patted at the air, his fingers dancing around her as though they bounced along a surface that only he could sense. Sue had to suppress a smile as she took in his wardrobe. Hip waders that had been intended for a much fatter man covered him from toe-tips to arm-pits, and a dusty pink trench coat was tucked haphazardly into the waders. On his head he wore a baseball cap to hold his wild, stringy hair at bay. It wasn't until he turned to follow his finger-dance off to Sue's left that she saw the hat's yellow bill and googly eyes. She coughed suddenly, in an attempt to hide her laughter.

"Ah, hello. Am I in your way?" Sue stepped aside, hoping that his private pat-a-cake game somehow didn't involve her. Perhaps it was just a coincidence. Maybe she was standing in the middle of his invisible sculpting studio or something. But as she moved, he moved with her.

"Well, I don't want to be rude, but you're blocking my way." Sue had always tried her best to be civil and respectful to the homeless.

She couldn't begin to imagine what nightmares of perception this poor man lived in, but she wanted to get back to the car and read the note from her young cohorts. She took a step forward, showing him that she intended to move along now, and he brought up a hand abruptly, signaling for her to stop.

"I'm afraid I don't have ti-" His other hand had fumbled briefly in a pocket of the trench coat, but he brought it out now, clutching something between his fingers, which he thrust out, obviously intending for Sue to take it. Another note.

Sue took it from him warily, keeping one eye fixed on him as she reached out. She had to fight hard to not grab it and snatch her hand away, as if he was filthy or radioactive. Instead, she took the piece of paper calmly and said, "Thank you." Then she put his note in her pocket and moved again to step past him. But he plucked at her hand, almost politely, so she turned and looked at him. His eyes bored into her with intensity and he pointed at the pocket she had pushed the note into.

"Yes," she promised. "I *will* read it. But not here. I have... somewhere I need to go right now. But later. Yes." That seemed to satisfy the poor man and he stepped aside, allowing Sue to continue on her way. When she reached the sidewalk, she turned and looked back, but he was no longer there. Poor, poor man, she thought. I wonder what he sees.

When the finicky engine finally started and her seatbelt was secure, Sue reached curiously into her pocket and drew out both notes. "I feel so James Bond," she said to herself, raising her voice over the blowing of the car's heater, as though there might be somebody listening.

Hobo first, she decided, and she unfolded his note. Her first thought was that the hand was surprisingly crisp. She had expected some cramped and palsied rambling, but this looked almost like laser printing, though clearly it had been hand-written. "It's like he was trying to mimic Times New Ro-" Then the words registered.

And Sue began to scream.

chapter 22

To Elicand's relief, the fall did not kill him. In fact, it wasn't even a fall at all. Not really. More of a terrifying, death defying slide. After a short drop from the Lip, ridges began to rise on either side of him, keeping Elicand channeled between them as the cliff face arced out away from vertical, pressing against him, and eventually, under him. He had no idea how far he slid, nor how fast, but a year or two after he'd tumbled off the edge–at the very most–the slideway had carried him as far as it would and he'd come to a rest some vast, unknowable distance from where he had started. Or maybe only a few strides distant. It was impossible to say. He'd been too busy screaming.

(fun play tumble fall statement) (confirmation query)

"Piles of fun statement," Elicand replied, standing slowly and rubbing at his backside. That part of him had received the worst of the scrapes, during the parts of his journey that had actually included contact with the rock, although those had been fewer than one might imagine. With every bump or rise along the route, Elicand had been tossed abruptly into the air, certain that he had come free from the track at last and was now being flung aside to his certain doom.
"Where are we now, question?"

(sadness family mother group live place statement)

Elicand wasn't sure he'd caught the gist of that one. "This is where your mother lives question?"

(correction mother family group live place time-past statement)

"And where are they now question?" A sense of dread bloomed in Elicand's belly. He was afraid he knew the answer to this already.

(big-nose-people steal people-mine time-past statement)

The Gnomes. Great. Why would Gnomes want to take these gentle people hostage? What use could he–
"Wait a minute," Elicand said, out loud. "How is it that you can do empathinking? Where did you learn to do it?"

(talk-teach time-past lesson-mine mother-give statement)

"But how does she know? Where did she learn to do it?"

(mother-mine friend-yours statement) (memory-share (DAN-GER DANGER FLEE SELF-THOU TIME-PRESENT-NOW)) (sadness-mine-ours)

Elicand recognized the shared memory right away. It had been playing over and over in the back of his mind ever since he'd first heard it. From Calaida. Just before she and her people had suddenly– And then, like a brilliant light had shone down, illuminating everything, Elicand realized what had happened. When he had gotten himself trapped in the Scary Tunnel of Wind... Shondu hadn't wandered off and left him to die. He'd gone for help–gone to the one person every child runs to when they're scared. He'd run to get his mother. Empathinkers were adult Brownies and Calaida was Shondu's mom!

"Oh, what have I done?" Elicand groaned. He stumbled then, banging his shoulder against a rocky cave wall and then leaned against it, sinking slowly to his haunches in despair. "And ow!" he added, rubbing at his latest bruise. "Are all stories this painful question?"

The darkness did not reply.

———————

They had been wandering about blind and in the roaring silence for days. No matter where they went, they never seemed to get far enough from the cascading river to diminishing its ravenous appetite for sound. The only time Elicand had heard any sound at all had been the few times he had banged his head on low rocks, or the one time he had fallen painfully, striking his knee on a raised ridge of stone. And while these occasional reminders that he was not in fact deaf were reassuring, he decided he would rather live without them, if that could be arranged. Hearing the sound, "Clunk!" conducted to his ears by way of his skeleton was just not worth the bruises.

Their explorations however, were much more productive than they had been in Ouchyville, because here they could communicate more clearly. According to Shondu, they could only "think-talk" in the caverns that were filled with "river-breath." It was apparently something about the dampness of the air that permitted this unusual way of talking. But even though empathinking was better for conveying emotions than conversations, Elicand preferred it greatly over the "fun play, eat now" style of chatter that had been the extent of their conversations on the surface, before this adventure had begun.

The biggest problem confronting them was that Shondu did not know his way around the caves. Apparently, young Brownies were educated by sending them out into the world to roam free and have fun, learning about the peoples of the world and exploring whatever places, things or ideas captured their interest. Brownies considered themselves the only well-educated people in the entire Forest, and indeed, Shondu's knowledge of the Wasketchin, the Djin and the Gnomes did seem quite extensive. Especially his knowledge of their curse-words.

But that education came at a price. Until they reached maturity, Brownies returned to River-Home rarely, and even then their visits were brief. Shondu knew next to nothing of the politics or daily life of his Brownie elders, so he could not explain anything about the relationship between his mother's people and the Horde. And he knew absolutely nothing of the local geography, so he was as lost down here as Elicand himself was.

When young Brownies visited home, they did so in the same way that Shondu and Elicand had arrived–by doing what Shondu called "pocket-turning"–a phrase that conveyed a sense to Elicand in empathink of something like both "door-opening" and "door-closing." As best he could tell, it meant both, and this was their problem. Before Shondu could open the door again to the out-

233

side world, he must first close the door he had opened when he'd brought Elicand here, by taking him back out again. But he was powerless to do so without the pikabu bag that Elicand had lost. It was hard to know exactly what the problem was, given the oddness of this emotion-based communication, but clearly, if Elicand wanted out of the caves, they either had to find the bag, or find their own way out.

So that's what they were doing now. Exploring the caverns and tunnels of the Brownie territory, trying to find their way to the surface. It wasn't entirely hopeless however, because Shondu at least could see down here. He'd been able to see in Ouchyville too, of course. Elicand had worked that out for himself at the time. But Shondu had been different then. More frivolous. Caught up in a joke that only he had found funny. When they talked about it now, Elicand was surprised to sense that Shondu seemed genuinely embarrassed by how immature he had been. Apparently, his little friend had done some growing up recently. Maybe hearing the screams of your mother being dragged away by invaders had that kind of effect.

Since Shondu could see though, and since they were now actually cooperating in their mutual exile, things were going much more smoothly. Elicand did not have to crawl about on hands and knees, making little cairns of stone to orient himself by. He simply stuck out his hand and Shondu took it, to lead him through the tunnels, avoiding the most dangerous places. Consequently, their progress was much faster than it had been before. And safer too.

They were sitting on a comfortable stoop of rock, sharing a bitter helping of the papery-tasting moss that Shondu assured him was safe to eat, when Elicand caught wind of something strange. Literally. He had been in sensory isolation for so long that at first he couldn't even name the sense that had disturbed him. Oh yes. Smell. For the first time in week-long days, his nose brought him a hint of something that was neither damp air nor rock dust. It was a high-pitched odor. Sweetish, but somehow oily too. And it left an unpleasant tang on the back of his tongue. It was unlike anything Elicand had ever put nose to before.

"What is that smell question?"

(ignorance unpleasantness dislike statement)

"Can you at least tell where it's coming from question?"

(uncertainty statement) (everywhere statement) (avoid suggestion)

"Well, if you don't know where it is condition, and you can't even tell what direction it's coming from condition, how do you propose we avoid it question?"

(nose-close eyes-close run-away suggestion) (laughter question)

"Did you just make a joke question?" Elicand asked. "In empathink? I didn't even think that was possible statement."

(laughter-thought time-always possibility statement)

"Trust a Brownie to say that," Elicand replied. "But it's the first thing we've smelled down here in forever statement, and it might be coming from outside suggestion, so I think we should try to find it decision."

After arguing about it for several more minutes, Elicand finally convinced his tiny guide to continue leading in the direction they had been going. Since the source of the smell was not clear, there was no more specific direction to choose, and the only wrong way would be back the way they had come. Finally, Shondu took him by the hand and began to pull him forward again, but not quickly.

(tongue-sticking-out statement)

"Be that way if you want to suggestion," Elicand said, "But thank you for helping gratitude statement, just the same."

They continued like that for some time, moving forward through the caves. For a time, Elicand wondered if they had lost the trail. The smell had receded and even the incessant din of the river seemed somehow less oppressive, but Shondu assured him that there had been no branches or side trails that they might have missed, so they pressed on. While the sound and smell had diminished, the air seemed to be getting wetter and Elicand wondered if perhaps the smell and the dampness flowed differently in the air, refusing to mix—perhaps the odor had risen higher above their heads and was forcing the watery parts of the air down lower, or some such explanation? But then they rounded a bend and were suddenly overwhelmed as everything came crashing together–the smell, the dampness and the noise–all of it. The tang of the smell suddenly felt thick enough to lick–like a gel forcing its way into his nose and throat, while droplets of spray spattered across his face.

Elicand spat and coughed, trying to clear the sickly mist from his mouth and lungs, but a new breath followed every cough and just pulled more of the stuff back in. His sightless eyes burned in its stinging presence and he lurched away, losing track of Shondu's hand and stumbling about, gagging. Something smooth and cold banged against his leg and he fell, reaching out with his hands, but his fall was broken by more of the smooth hardness, which somehow, writhed beneath his weight, skittering away to either side, and left him to drop face-first onto the cave floor. His hands and cheek struck hard against the gritty stone, but there was a squelch too, as though he had landed partly in the thick muck of a river bank.

((water-hole rushing-speed place-here caution statement) intensify)

Gagging and retching, Elicand scrambled to his feet and backpedaled, trying desperately to get away from whatever creature had tripped him, before it could attack.

(negation creature place-here statement)

"Are you sure?" Elicand wheezed. "It felt like a snake. A giant snake."

(smell horrible place-here statement) (iron-stump number-many place-here statement) ((negation creature place-here statement) intensify)

Elicand brought his hand up to wipe away the gravel that seemed to be stuck to his face, but he immediately regretted the move. His hand was covered in a tar-like, gluey mess and all he succeeded in doing was getting the gravel stuck to the goo on his hand and smearing it all on his face.

With a gentle tug on his clean hand, Shondu guided Elicand forward.

(water-hole rushing-speed hand-clean place-here suggestion) (movement speed-slow caution suggestion)

The hand tugging at him pulled him down into a crouch, and then Elicand felt the cold rushing of the river envelope his hand.
And suddenly, he could see.

The image that swam before Elicand's blurry, burning eyes was the strangest thing. Another Wasketchin hung in the air, staring down at him in disbelief. The face was close enough to touch, too close, and as he reached out to push the stranger away, the stranger made a lunge toward him. Elicand cried out in the deafening silence and jerked himself away.
Blackness enveloped him once more.
"Where did he go? Where is he? Did you see who it was?"

(negation person-other here-place time-now statement) (puzzlement statement)

"But I *saw* him," Elicand said. "Another Wasketchin. He was right in front of me. He tried to kill me."

(laughter statement) (understanding statement)

"What's so funny?" Elicand demanded, but Shondu's calmness, his certainty that he knew what had happened, helped to calm the frightened story uncle, and eventually Shondu managed to explain what had happened. (soul-blending statement) Apparently, the river was more than just a convenient flow of water for the Brownies. It was the entire reason they lived down here–to be near it. Because when two people placed their hands in its current, their minds became one, allowing them to hear, taste, feel and think as one. They could see as one too, which is what had happened. Elicand hadn't seen another Wasketchin looming over him. He had seen himself, looming over Shondu, but through Shondu's eyes.

At first, Elicand hadn't believed, but eventually Shondu convinced him to come back to the hole in the floor where the river peeked through and they had plunged their hands back into its powerful flow. This time, Elicand was prepared for what he saw, and it did not frighten him. But it was still a very disquieting thing. To see himself as Shondu saw him. Impossibly large and threatening, looming over him and blocking his view of the world. But there was humor there too. And kindness. Trust. What Elicand saw was not limited to the content of Shondu's vision–it was a blending of all that Shondu saw and felt about him, laid together on top of what he saw. Soul-blending.

It was the most powerful experience Elicand had ever had.

When at last the wonder of that experience had receded, and the stench of whatever it was that lived in this cavern reasserted itself upon him, Elicand allowed Shondu to hurry him along. He paused briefly to scrub as much of the filth off his face and hands as he could manage–which had been Shondu's original purpose in leading him to the crack in the floor that exposed the river coursing beneath the rock under their feet.

What he had seen through Shondu's eyes had been as perplexing as the smell itself. More than a dozen cylinders lay scattered about the cramped cavern. Like the sky-tubes that bore Seekers in the Wagon of Tears, but not as long. Those standing on end came as high as Elicand's chest. Each had a hole on its upper face, and each had several raised ridges running around the circumference of the cylinder, like bond-rings around the arm of a Djin. Had *they* brought these things here? But the stench of the containers, and its assault on his eyes would not allow him to linger, and since he couldn't examine them without taking his hands from the water and plunging himself back into darkness, there wasn't much more he could learn about them. Elicand allowed Shondu to take his hand and lead him onward again, away from that strange place.

Two moss meals later, and after walking an unknowable distance, but one that should surely have been enough, Elicand was disappointed that the stench still hounded him. He had done what he could, rinsing and scrubbing at his hand and even plunging his face into the river water, but he had not been able to completely remove the traces of whatever it was that he had stuck his hand into, and the smell lingered there with it. By this time, Elicand was exhausted. He had no way of knowing how much time had passed since he had awakened on that little jut of rock, but it felt like ages upon ages, and the more he thought about it, the less enthusiasm he could muster for standing up and pressing on into the dark. So Elicand wrapped himself more tightly in his kirfa, and leaned back against the papery moss that they had been eating, and which grew along the base of the tunnel wall here where they had stopped to do so. Shondu seemed to approve of this new course of action.

(sleep-ours place-here time-now statement) (happy statement)

Soon, the two of them were cuddled together against the cold and damp, dreaming fitful dreams, and neither of them stirred for the longest time, until Elicand reached up to scratch his chest and then awoke with a frightened cry.

He could not move his fingers.

Once more, Elicand strained to flex them, and once more, they refused to bend. The sticky mess that had coated his left hand the day before had now hardened into a shell of sorts, like a tight-fitting glove of stone—one that was virtually impossible to bend or close. He felt around blindly in the darkness until he found a small round rock, about the size of a fist. Then he pressed the center of his palm flat down on top of it, pushing hard as he tried to close the hand into a grip around the stone. But nothing moved. In frustration, he slammed the hand down on the rock, but the armor held, absorbing the shock of what should have been a very painful blow, and distributing its force around his entire hand. It took a dozen repeated slams of his palm down onto the rock before he finally felt a slight give in the shell. Huzzah! He could now, with great effort, fold his thumb very slightly toward his fingers. At this rate, he would have to smash the bones of his hand entirely into dust before he'd be able to flex it enough to do anything useful. Elicand sighed and slumped back down.

"Well, one thing is certain," he said. "Being me has become much more interesting since the Wayitam sent me home."

(fun-time self-you-feel time-now question) Shondu asked.

"Oh, yeah agreement," Elicand replied. "Lots of fun statement." He reached up with his good hand and rubbed at the spot on his cheek that had stiffened along with his hand. There wasn't much he could have done with the side of his face, even at the best of times, but the stiffness he felt there bothered him even more than the rigidity of his hand. The skin of his cheek tugged at him incessantly– when he talked, when he swallowed, when he smiled or frowned. Even rolling his eyes at his own predicament came with a slight twinge of tightness. What good is a failed story uncle who can't even smile without looking like a cripple?

A moment later, Elicand felt Shondu's fingers on his good hand and then felt a few clumps of moss pressed into it.

(food-eat person-you time-now suggestion)

"Right," Elicand said. "Do you think I can use this club-hand as a dinner plate question?" He placed a large piece of moss on the up-turned palm of his left hand and brought it up to his mouth. But in the darkness, his little finger bumped against his nose, and he felt the moss hit him on the lip and then bounce away into oblivion. Elicand reached forward and began to pat at the ground with his good hand. The least he could do was refrain from throwing his food around after Shondu had gone to the trouble to fetch it. But this rock-falling, tree-blasting, perpetual blackness of night was getting to be extremely not fun anymore.

Once again, Elicand sang his charm-song for light. He was no longer trying to make light, of course. It was a song of defiance. It was a song of frustration. It was a song to sing against the forces of everything that was wrong in the world and declare his complete lack of caring how many victories those forces might take–he was never going to bend to them.

So of course, this time the charm worked.

Elicand winced at the sudden brightness of light after so many, many days without it. His eyes watered and tears ran down his face, and even though he could not feel their wetness where they passed over the stiffened part of his cheek, it was still the most wonderful thing he could ever remember doing with his vim.

He had long ago given up trying to charm light into a rock or stick. For days now, Elicand had been trying to simply bring light to himself, hoping that if the vim didn't even have to leave his body, then maybe it would more readily do its work there right inside of him, but even that had never produced anything before.

Curiously though, now that it *had* chosen to work, it only did so from within the armor casing of his left hand. How odd.

Elicand waved the hand around him in the air, delighting at the harsh shadows it threw around the tunnel where they had slept. Shondu's eyes sparkled and blinked in the sudden glare, but he too seemed happy at this new development.

(fun-play shadow-scare delight statement) Shondu bubbled, turning to face the tunnel wall and then raising his hands like the claws of an attacking bear. The shadow on the wall did indeed look like a great and terrible bear, but the sight of a short-furred Brownie wiggling his behind to make the great bear look threatening was more than Elicand could take and he doubled over in laughter, folding at the waist and holding his stomach as though he might die from the hilarity. With his hand covered by the fold of his body and the fabric of his kirfa, its light vanished–and so did the great and terrifying shadow bear. Shondu turned to look at him, disappointed that the game was over so quickly. With his hand mostly covered, Elicand noticed that there was also a bit of glow coming from somewhere else and he held his non-glowing hand out, moving it closer and closer to this second source of light until he had located it. His face, of course. His cheek did not glow as brightly as his hand, but it too shone with the slightly greenish light of the charm. Something about the armor shell seemed to help magic to work, but why that might be, he had no idea.

The two of them played with the light for a little while longer, making silly shadows and following them around the tunnel, seeking better walls to throw their shadows at. But soon enough, they tired of the game and resumed their journey. With Elicand's light, he was now able to see without the need for Shondu to guide him, and so they were able to walk properly, without Elicand half-stooped over to reach his little guide's hand.

The only problem they encountered was that, while a brilliantly glowing hand was a good lamp to light Elicand's way, it also did an excellent job of blinding him. Eventually, he settled on a strategy that seemed to work, by placing his hand on top of his head, where its light could not reach his eyes directly, but could still light the way in front of him. It was odd, but it worked, and their progress from that moment onward was much faster.

Each time they came to a branching of their path, or entered a chamber with more than one way out, Elicand elected to move upward. He hoped that sooner or later, they might possibly reach a tunnel that connected to a cave that finally emerged somewhere into the world above ground level. There were plenty of blind alleys and dead ends, but Elicand had been happy to learn that they did not need to mark each path with a cairn of stones. Shondu had an unerring ability to recognize the places they had already been, and to steer them to a different, untried path so that they could continue their exploration.

As day followed day—or at least, as sleep followed sleep—the pair of explorers wound their way up higher and higher in the system of caves—never freeing themselves of the oppressive sounds of raging, hurtling water, but eventually it dawned on Elicand that he hadn't actually seen the river in some time. Perhaps as long as a day. They had been making a habit of stopping whenever they'd found an exposed flow, and after taking time to drink, they would often share a moment of soul-blending. It was so much easier to communicate when all you had to do was think your thoughts and they were shared by both thinkers. Ideas did not have to be spelled out in full, or converted into words—they just had to be thought. Conversing with Shondu at such times was as easy as talking to himself inside his head.

But now, he felt the need to blend with his friend again. Shondu had wandered off ahead to explore a side-tunnel, leaving Elicand with a moment to rest, but he found too many worries percolating in the silence to let him rest. Sooner or later, they were going to have to make some decisions. How long could they continue with nothing to eat but moss? Was it possible that heading down would have been the wiser course? And why could they hear the river still, if it had been so long since they had seen it? How did that make any sense? There were so many questions, and even though Elicand liked the emotional honesty of empathinking, he had to admit that he wasn't very good at it—certainly not good enough to hold complicated discussions about the practical questions that now pestered him.

He was still running in mental circles on a half a dozen worries when Shondu's thoughts broke into his own.

(Dragon-breath Dragon-blood secret-place excitement state-ment)

But what sent a jolt down Elicand's spine and chilled him to his soul was the voice that followed–not an empathought that tickled inside his mind, but an actual voice that spoke in the air all around him.

"Come to me, story thief. Come and take *my* story. If you dare."

In that moment, Elicand was certain who that voice belonged to. He had been hearing it in his dreams for his entire life. He had sought it over and over again on the hills outside his own village, and again at the Heart of the Verge with the Wayitam, and always it had eluded him in the waking world.

It was the voice of the trees.

It was the voice of the Dragon Methilien.

And then that voice let loose a roar of agony, and the rocky world around him began to shake.

chapter 23

None may speak against the King, Kijamon knew. To do so would be treason. But any Djin could choose not to speak *for* him. This was the logic behind the Chorus of Silence, though it was a song that had not been sung in half a thousand years. The old Djin wormed his way down the narrow tunnel, inching forward on his belly, toward the small room that awaited him ahead, set deeply into the stone of the mountain behind the Wind Forge.

Sometimes called the Dragon's Sinus, it was a chamber in which those who sought his voice could come to seek it in stillness. But for those who knew the secret, other voices could be summoned there as well, and that's what he sought now, crawling forward in the darkness, as he had not done for many years. Kijamon paused and lifted the coverlight to shine into the tunnel ahead, peering after it into the darkness. He sighed. Still no sign of the chamber wall ahead. Once more the Master of the Wind Forge cursed himself for having dug this passage so deeply, and pushed the coverlight back into his vests. But curses would shift no gravel, so with his hands free once again, he put them to use and resumed his awkward slither into the gloom.

When he at last reached his destination and brought out his light again, Kijamon muttered in displeasure. He had forgotten how small the chamber was. All the better to hear, of course. The smaller the sphere, the more precisely it could be shaped to focus the sounds. But even so, he had carved the room large enough so that his own ear would rest at the precise center of the space when he stood upright.

Although, that had been when he was a young Djin, in the prime of his life. And the prime of his height. The old man grumbled irritably as he looked around and found the thick stone on the floor, which he dragged into the center of the chamber. It's what it was there for, of course. But he had never imagined having to use it himself.

Stepping up onto the stone, Kijamon had to bend his knees a trifle, but eventually, his ear was at last centered in the room, and the dim and distant sounds of the Djin city fell away, leaving only the crushing silence of the world beyond. It was the soundless sound that had always filled the center of the chamber, and it waited there, patiently, ready for new sounds to be placed into it by others.

Kijamon leaned back slightly, bringing his mouth to where he felt his ear had marked the center. Then he puckered his lips and whistled. It was a low, steady note, but not quite right. Working on instinct, he raised the pitch of his whistle slowly, and shifted his weight to the left a bit. In a moment, he was rewarded with a rich, resonant sound, as though the Dragon himself whistled back. Such a thought was nonsense, of course. It was just his own tone reverberating in harmony with the sphere of the room. But such fanciful beliefs were fun to think sometimes, even if they were silly.

As the tone reverberated through the space and then trailed away, the blue stone of the cavern around him began to glow. The summons had been sent. Soon, the Masters of the other Great Houses would be alerted to a similar glow in their own chambers, and they would rush to find out who it was who had summoned the Chorus.

And the best part was, since there was only one such chamber in the entire city and he himself was standing in it, Mabundi would have no way of listening in on the discussion that was about to take place.

Kijamon pushed the cover light back into his vests and then settled himself to await the Chorus.

All the way down the Trail of Sky, Tayna wondered if she would ever get the chance to go back to searching for her family. She wasn't complaining, exactly. It was awesome that she had been given such an important job, finding old maps to help her people and all that, but she couldn't help feeling that it was just another distraction keeping her from *family yours, home come.* And she was close now. They were here, somewhere on the Anvil. She just knew it. But it was Zimu who put it into proper perspective for her when she grumbled about it.

"Will they still be at home when you reach them?" he asked. Abeni had been busy making a list of the things he wanted to take with them to the Wasketchin, and another list of things that should be prepared and sent along later. So he had been delighted when Zimu had offered to guide Tayna instead. And since he had questions of his own for the old historian, it only made sense.

Tayna blinked though, in response to his question. "You mean, do they still live there? I don't know, but a girl can hope, right?"

Zimu smiled, but he shook his head. "No, I mean, with all that is happening in the Forest, and to your people, do you think that you will find them at home *now*?"

And of course, as soon as he asked, the answer was obvious. "No," she said. "You're right. They could be anywhere today, running from the Gnomes, or even captured already. They won't go home again until all this is over. Probably."

Zimu nodded. "So if you wish to find them, the best course for you to follow would be?"

And now Tayna had to grin at this crafty son of an even craftier father. "Let me guess. I should help bring all the troubles to an end maybe, so they can go home again?" Why did everything always sound so much more logical when a Djin said it? But curiously, now that he *had* said it, Tayna felt a sense of relief. She wasn't avoiding her mission at all. She was actually doing it. Just not the way she'd expected. She was still puzzling over this latest wrinkle of thought when Zimu led her up to a large door and stopped.

"The Hall of Histories, I presume?"

Beside her, Zimu nodded. According to both him and Abeni, behind that door lay a vast room filled with delicate old scrolls, heaped in scholarly disarray, but rich in the smells and even the artifacts of the stories they told. Tayna could almost see the famous sword, lying chipped and dented next to the scroll that recorded its tale. All waiting for her, just beyond this door. Well, not a sword, maybe. Not in a world that had known thousands of years of Peace. But a famous shoe, perhaps. Or the Grand Gem of Something Awesome. Whatever they were, the room she saw in her head was filled with the trinkets and treasures of a thousand tales, each one a touchstone that would launch the wizened old traveler who now cared for them into another tale of past exploits and lessons learned. It was this very warehouse of adventures, curated by Bosuke himself, that had first ignited the imagination of a young Abeni. And Tayna was about to see both for the very first time. Her skin prickled with anticipation. "I'll take what's behind door number one please, Zimu," she said, waving her hand imperiously at the entrance in front of them.

What they found, once Zimu had pulled the great door open however, was nothing at all like what she'd expected. Here, the walls were lined with rows upon rows of boxes, each set deeply into the stone, each the same depth, and each holding exactly one curled spool of paper. If there were any trinkets, keepsakes or touchstones, they were not visible. This was not the tantalizing explorastorium that Abeni had described to her. This was a records office. A cold and emotionless storage depot for scraps of paper, each to be filed and counted, and perhaps rolled a quarter turn clockwise, once each half year.

Tayna could feel Zimu tense up beside her as he too looked around, startled into blinking rigidity. Clearly, the room was not as he remembered it either.

"Have you made an appointment?" said a voice. Tayna had to look around twice before she saw the middle-aged Djin, stooped over near the back wall, making marks on a board as he counted the cubby-holes. He had not turned to face them.

"We have questions for the Master of Histories," Zimu said.

"Come back later," the man replied, still counting the holes in the wall in front of him. "I'm busy just now."

Tayna caught the unmistakable aura of no-sayer coming from the guy. Like the Goodies and most of the adults she'd ever encountered in connection with them, there were some people who just seemed to live for the chance to say, "No." As if saying it gave them power. *"Hello, dear. How was your day?" "Delightful. I gave out 38 'nos' today, and 17 'not until next week at the earliests.' " "Oh, what fun! Let's celebrate!" "No." "Ha ha ha ha ha!"* Tayna hated no-sayers.

While Zimu stood there fuming by her side, clenching and unclenching his massive fists in an effort to calm himself, Tayna marched into the Hall, walked up behind the man, and 'accidentally' knocked the board from his hand.

"Oh, I'm sorry," she said, bending over to pick up the board and then holding it out sweetly in front of her. "If you could just tell the Master of Histories that we're here..."

The officious Djin straightened himself up and sniffed indignantly as he snatched the board from her hands. "I *am* the Master of Histories," he said. "Wijen. Now I told you, I'm busy. Come back later. Tomorrow, perhaps."

"You are not," Zimu said, his tongue finally jolted into action by the insolent tone of the box-ticker in front of them. "Bosuke is Master of Histories. Summon him."

"You really have been living in a pit, haven't you, boy?" Wijen drew himself up to full height, as though he thought to intimidate Zimu, but he quickly abandoned that ploy when he realized just how big Zimu really was. "I tell you again. Bosuke is not the Master of Histories. He was, but now that duty is mine, and I mean to do it properly. Now leave me. As I said, I'm busy." Then he turned back to his wall of holes.

"But where is Bosuke?" Zimu demanded.

"Don't know. Don't care," Wijen responded, waving a hand at them over his shoulder. "The door's back there somewhere. Use it. And begone."

Tayna could sense Zimu's rising anger, but before he could work himself to a full boil, she put a hand on his arm. She knew how to deal with no-sayers. Stepping past Zimu, she addressed herself to the historian's back. "Oh, we are sorry to have bothered you, Mr. Wijen. Yes, of course we'll let you get back to your work." Then she turned back toward the door and pulled at Zimu's arm, urging him to follow her lead. "I'm afraid Wijen can't see us just now, Zimu. We'll come back tomorrow. I just hope they aren't all dead by then. I'm sure the King will understand."

They had almost reached the entrance when Wijen's voice called out behind her. "The King?"

"Oh, it's nothing," Tayna called back over her shoulder, as she pushed Zimu ahead of her toward the door. "Just something about wanting to gather the scatterlings. And about getting them out before the attack. Bye, Mr. Wijen."

"Wait! That's absurd!" the historian shouted. Tayna heard his counting board clatter to the floor again, dropped no doubt in his haste to rush after her. A moment later, she felt his hand grab at her arm. She allowed herself to be turned back toward the man, and greeted him with a smile of concern.

"Mr. Wijen? Is something wrong?"

"Gather up the scatterlings? It can't be done!" he said. "And what attack?"

"I'm afraid I don't know," she said. "I just know that we were to ask you where those poor people could be found. Before it's too late. But I don't know anything more. We'll come back tomorrow, as you suggested." Once again, she turned her back on the man, and again he grabbed at her arm.

"But girl, they can't be gathered up! Not in a day. It would take weeks. Possibly months. They're called scatterlings because that's what they are: scattered. They're everywhere. Strewn about the flanks of the Anvil, scattered across the Plateau. There are even some living down in the undertowns. But never do they gather in large numbers. There's only ever two of them together, or four or three. Never more. Here, look," he said, then he scurried to one of the holes in the wall and came back. At the low table beside her, he rolled it out. "See? Look here at this map. See? Here, and here, and all those over there. And up here. These are all undertowns. The Plateau is infested with them. And there could be scatterlings in every single one of them, not to mention a thousand other places. You'd never gather them in time."

"Really?" Tayna said, pursing her lips and looking down at the map in feigned concentration. Then she lifted the scroll out of the historian's hands to squint at it more closely. "As many as that, you say?"

Wijen nodded.

"Well that will certainly upset Mabundi's plans," she said. "Will you come with us to tell him yourself? I'm sure he'll want to thank you for pointing out his error." The Djin's face paled in horror.

"Oh, no! I mean, I've got so much to do here, and it's all quite plain on the map, really. Just take that and show him. I'm sure he'll work out an even better plan once he sees it."

Tayna pursed her lips, as though frowning in unaccustomed thought. Then she looked up. "Well, I don't want to take all the credit for correcting him," she said. "Are you sure you won't come?" By this point, Tayna could barely keep her laughter contained. The look of horror on the man's face was just too much fun. But on the outside, she just smiled sweetly when he again refused. "Okay then. Well, thank you so much, Mr. Wijen. You've been so helpful. We'll just take this and let you get back to your important work."

She turned away from the flustered Djin, tucking the map neatly under her arm, and headed for the door. Zimu fell into step alongside her, and a moment later, they were in the corridor, with the Hall door closed firmly at their backs.

"The Little Fish is well named," Zimu said. "She is very slippery, and darts quickly in unexpected directions." There was laughter in his voice, and Tayna laughed along with him.

"No-sayers are all the same," she said. "Just start talking about secrets and important people, and they all turn into yes-men."

"But where is Bosuke?" Zimu asked.

To that, Tayna had no answers.

Most people Shaleen knew liked to seek the quiet heart of the Sinus when they had a question to put, but she herself had never understood how such a dark and isolated little cave could be expected to connect her with any great current of inspiration. How could you foster new ideas by shutting yourself away from all the currents of the world? When Shaleen needed insight, she much preferred the Dowager's Leap–the proud jut of stone that erupted from the back of the Anvil's shoulder, just a little ways downslope from the notch of the city. Tradition had it that the Dowager Queen, Xolile, had spent many long days upon that spar of rock, seeking answers to *her* pressing questions. If any Djin had ever been plagued by doubts and a need for inspiration, it had been Xolile, widowed queen to the king who had forged the Dragon's Peace–and then died, leaving his widow to forge a nation. If the Leap had been good enough for that fabled queen, who had hammered the rough iron of a hundred power-hungry warlords into a single peaceful and honorable society of artisans and craftsmen... Well then, it was plenty good enough for a heartsick mother too.

Shaleen had not yet told her husband, had not wanted to pile her troubles atop his own, but she had not been sleeping of late. Not since word had first been brought of Sarqi's capture by the Gnome King. And it had only worsened since Abeni and the girl had arrived, adding their own stories of Angiron's malice to what she already knew of him. She had met the First Prince of the Gnomes on a number of occasions, and not once had she come away feeling anything other than itchy. The Gnome prince made her twitch, in her heart. It was a feeling she could not describe, but there was something about the way he spoke, the way he stood, the way he breathed. Everything about him made her... itch. As though his very presence had scratched a wound somewhere inside her, and her mind could not leave alone with its poking and prodding at it. And now, to think that her most sensitive and complicated son was captive to a being such as that. Well, surely it was understandable that a mother could not sleep with her son in such peril.

The journey from the Wind Forge to the Leap was not a difficult one, but it was not easy either, and when Shaleen finally reached it, she stood there for a moment to gather herself. The long, black finger of dragonstone erupted from a field of loose scree, stabbing into the eye of the sky like an accusation. The field of dusty rubble from which it emerged had flaked from the grayish slopes above, but there wasn't so much as a single black pebble to be found that might have fallen from the Leap itself. Dragonstone simply did not appear to weather or age. It was an otherness, curious and distinct from everything around it. Shaleen had often wondered why this might be so. What could cause a spear of such different stuff to emerge from out of the mountain like that, with no sign of kinship to any of the stone around it? Not that the question held any great import, one way or the other. It was just a passing curiosity. Part of the litany of thoughts she wandered over whenever she prepared herself here, making herself ready to ascend the tower and throw her question to the winds. Already she could feel them flowing around her, tugging at her vests and shawl, teasing her with a hundred different thought-tastes at once. It was time.

Quickly, before the feeling could pass, Shaleen clambered up the finger of stone–damp with rocksweat, as dragonstone always was– and stood proudly upon its tip, a flattened area no larger than her bed. From this place, there was only Shaleen and the sky and the wind between them. A wind that had scoured the world, touching upon every being who lived, snatching up their breath, and their sweat, and the particles of their skin, and even their ideas, then flinging it all up into the sky and carrying it here. To where she now stood. Her own mind was an unmoving nexus in the cacophony that swirled around her. A cacophony that she now gave shape, channeling the winds and the sweat and the ideas into threads, and the threads into voices, and the voices into harmony. A symphony out of chaos. A symphony of raw inspirations that washed over her. Around her. Through her.

And into this symphony, she called out her question. "Hear me, Song of Life! Wind of the World! Hear the plea of a mother, worried for her son. Of a woman, worried for her people. I have need of news, but no place to seek it. The world boils in a kettle with no spout, and soon it will burst. I must know of Sarqi and of the Gnome King, but I have no messengers to send to my son, nor he to me. How can I hear the words that cannot be sent? How can I learn the thoughts that cannot be spoken?"

Then she stood still. And listened.

In truth, it was as much meditation as listening, but she liked to think of it as listening. She tried to detach herself from her pressing need for answers, and instead, open herself to the voices of suggestion that flowed past her on the wind. It was as Kijamon had said. "The spirit of invention is not a muscle one can clench, nor even a place one goes in the mind. It is an opening. An emptying. A removal of the self, to be replaced by an awareness of the else. One does not create an idea—one becomes aware of it. Like a mouse nibbling grain in a corner, one cannot see or hear it until one has settled all the noises and commotions and distractions from the world. Leaving only the mouse. And in that stillness, his nibbles will become his roar."

So Shaleen stood there, on the fingertip of the Dowager's Leap, with her eyes closed and her arms stretched out, touching all of the winds she could gather. She emptied her mind of all that she could jettison, save the one question on her mind.

And she waited.

Waiting for an idea is not like waiting for a friend, or waiting for soup to boil. One always knows that, in time, the friend will come. If not today, then tomorrow. If not for lunch, then perhaps for supper. So too, the soup will eventually boil. But inspiration carries no certainty. One can stand for an hour, or a day, or even a lifetime, and never be certain whether an idea will occur in the following minute, or never at all.

So waiting for inspiration, especially regarding a question so entangled by love and fear and need, was an ordeal of its own.

Shaleen waited patiently, for half a day. It was not a test of endurance. From time to time, she would lower her arms and walk around in a small circle, flapping blood and warmth back into her fingers against her sides, but such respites were always short, and as quickly as she could, Shaleen would resume her posture and let her feelings flow back out into the streamers of the wind. How does one send messages over distances? The wind could carry shouted words over many strides—one hundred, two hundred, perhaps even more–but Sarqi was many *leagues* distant. Much too far for a voice to carry on the wind.

She wondered too, about Kijamon's Chorus of Silence. Some special charm he had devised for speaking across great distance, among the more powerful Houses, but she did not know the how of it, and he would say little, only assuring her that it could be of no assistance in her present quest. Was it some charm of mind-touching?

It was said that, long ago, before the Peace, some creatures who then walked the world had possessed the power to speak mind to mind over great distances. But none of their kinds had been known since the time of Xolile herself, if truly they had ever existed at all.

Round and round her mind whirled, spun in the currents of wind and cold, and the further she wandered in her thoughts, the more frantic she became, fearing that there *was* no answer. That Sarqi truly was alone in his misery, and she in hers. Oh, Sarqi, how can I reach you?

And then he was there.

"Mother?"

The surprise of his voice settling upon her mind, with such force and such abruptness, rocked Shaleen backward on her heels, and she stumbled. "Sarqi?" she said, whispering the words into the wind.

"I am..." But the words faded. For a moment, Shaleen feared that he had somehow come and gone before anything could be said. But as his voice faded, the images began, flooding her in rapid succession as his mind skimmed in chaotic fashion. He had tasted of some Gnomileshi elixir and it flowed through him now. Quickly his story unfurled in her mind. Impossible memory images of a giant white-furred beast, and a battle with Gnomes. The Spinetop. A pile of stone slabs beside a river. Of capture and escape. Tunnels in darkness. *Of rescuing the Wasketchin Queen!* But all too quickly, the images faded away, and Shaleen opened her eyes to see the sky teetering before her. She reached out to her son again, only to find what she already knew.

He was gone.

The elixir had swept him beyond the place where he could touch her mind, but it had been enough. More than enough. Oh my son! My beautiful and capable son! To think that she had dared hope only that he survived. And then to learn this. Such wondrous news

beyond hoping! More than alive, he was free! And from his captivity, he had dragged a powerful gift. A mighty gift! M'Ateliana, captured by Gnomes, but then delivered from them before they learned
of their fortune. By her wonderful, wonderful son! This was news
that must reach the Wasketchin King.

Shaleen turned and scrambled her way back down the Leap.
Abeni and Tayna must leave at once!

⸻

When Tayna went to bed that night, it was with the jangling accom-
paniment of an electric current burning through her skin. At least,
that's how it felt. So much seemed to be going on, and as usual,
most of it seemed to be orbiting around her. Since the family had
gone into action mode, things were happening quickly now, and it
was hard to keep it all straight in her head. She need to talk it out,
put it in some kind of order.

Or write it.

And who better to write to, than a powerless god who listens to
frightened children but does nothing useful about what she hears?

But lying there in the dark, her head whirling too fast to let
sleep slip through, Tayna realized that maybe all those old letters
to Shammi really had served a purpose. She had always been so
focused on the suspicion that nobody was out there listening, that
she forgot there was one other important person who needed to
hear it all laid out too.

Herself.

Only, she didn't exactly need to write it down for that to happen,
did she? All she really needed was to think it through, in logical
order, as though it were a letter, but without all the accessories.

With that, Tayna rolled over onto her back and began to "write."

Dear Shammi:

*So here I am at Abeni's house, at the top of the Anvil, and things
are going so fab! It's such a cool place, and there's so much to tell,
but I'm too excited to go over all the old news. Let me just say:
Miseratu, ice fields, Judgment, Gnomes, refugees, more Gnomes,
kings, Keshwa-Ji, and more kings. There. You're now up to speed.
(grin)*

Okay, seriously. I'll tell you about all of that later. Right now I've

254

got to tell you about the really *important stuff.*

Most of it's all chuckles, but the Hall of Histories turned out to be totally lame. I was really looking forward to meeting this Bosuke guy everyone keeps talking about, but it turns out he flaked, and now they've put some office-bozobot in charge. Imagine, running a library like a bank! Anyway, tomorrow morning, we'll ask around and see if we can find out where Bosuke went. I totally foxed the map from Wijen, but Abeni thinks Bosuke probably knows more useful intel that hasn't even been marked down yet, and Zimu really needs to talk to him too, so finding him will probably be good. Plus, having something to do in the morning will be extra helpful, because if I don't have something to do, *I'll probably flip a squirrel, worrying about this whole Mabundi thing tomorrow. (See above. Specifically "kings" and "more kings." Don't worry about it. I'll fill you in later.)*

Speaking of Abeni, you should see this enormous list he wrote. It's like he wants to take half the Anvil down to help Malkior and the Wasketchin. Kijamon told him he could have it all, if he really wanted it, but that it would take six months, so he should probably write a shorter list and just concentrate on what he needs first. So now the big goof is all grumpy, and he's still up, making a smaller list. But he'd better hurry. We're supposed to be leaving first thing, the day after tomorrow, and somebody is still going to have to build and pack whatever we're taking. It's kinda funny seeing him here with his family. He's so much more like a kid than his usual wise and powerful adventure Djin. Turns out the "wise and powerful" bit is sort of a family thing.

So is crankiness, now that I think about it. House Kijamon doesn't like stupidity much. It makes them all growly. Like, today Kijamon went to sing his Song of Whispers, or whatever it was he called it. Well it worked, so "Yay!" But it turns out the other Houses are kind of dragging their heels now, and Kijamon's having a fit, but can you blame them? They've been moaning for weeks about how Mabundi seems to spend all his time here, and then the guy in charge of here contacts them on the bat-phone to tell them the King's insane and we might need to put a bullet in him. Okay, those are my words, not his, but you get the idea. What were they supposed to say? "Oh, okay, Kijamon, go ahead and whack the King and take over yourself. We've got your back?" Yeah, right.

But I can't really blame Kijamon either. The other Houses want to talk and talk and talk about what to do, but they don't get how bad things are, and how fast they're getting worse. Still, he's a pretty impressive guy, so he'll probably get it sorted out. Everybody pretty much worships him around here, and you should see him work a crowd. Everyone talks, and everyone answers, and somehow, it all gets processed.

Oh, that reminds me. You will not believe what Shaleen found out. Sarqi is alive! And not just alive, but it sounds like he's throwing down with Angiron and the Gnomes all over the place, and kicking hairy butt! Not only did he manage to break out of Gnome prison, but he got somebody else out too. Somebody important. You ready for this?

Who could Angiron have in his prison camp that would absolutely destroy Malkior and kick the sails out of all the Wasketchin? Queen M'Ateliana, right? Well that's exactly who they had! Only they didn't know it. So Sarqi tosses around some wocky-socky-hiya! action, and soon he's strolling around, free as you please, with Queen freaking M'Ateliana along for the ride! You should see how proud everybody is. Even me! I mean, Sarqi is a bit of a sourball, but I gotta admit, he came through big time on this.

Now all he has to do is figure out where Malkior is, and then he can get her home, safe and sound. But don't ask me how Shaleen got all this, because it sounds like fairy dust and wishing to me. She goes up to some middle-finger-in-the-sky rock and asks it questions, and it answers her. I don't get it, but everybody else does, so I've gotta trust them on that.

Anyhow, that just leaves tomorrow, and I'd tell you all about it, but I don't want to scare you. Or me. Let's just say I'll fill you in after it's all over. Okay?

And that's it. Did you know that mountains have thin air and long days? Well they do, and now I've gotta get me some zee-time. I'd ask you to write back, but we're past that now, right? So if you do have any questions, just wake me up and ask. I'll be the doofus drooling on the bed with her eyes closed.

See ya when I see ya,
Tayna of the Mountain.

With her skin still crackling and buzzing like she was on fire, Tayna rolled over and pulled the pillow up over her head. She'd sleep now for a while. If she could.

And tomorrow she'd find out if she had sparked a civil war.

Flee now!

Tayna came awake blind and confused. The darkness around her was absolute and the tendrils of sleep were slow to withdraw. She could almost feel them pulling away from her, like a silk scarf being dragged across her face, leaving confused questions in its wake. Where was she? Could be anywhere. The Old Shoe? Veest's dehn? The Cold Shoulder? She had been dreaming of voices in the night... Slowly, the scarf withdrew further and the answers began to swim up out of the dark. Kijamon's house. Abeni's old bedroom.

There was a scratching noise, but she couldn't see. It came from the far side of the room, over near the corner. Wasn't that where the window was? It would have been visible if there had been any light in the sky to see by.

Tayna rolled off the low bed as silently as she could, and felt around the table until her fingers settled on the coverlight. She snatched it up but she couldn't find the seams of the leather cover. "Dammit, I need light." The seam must have popped at that point, because now a faint blue light flickered in her hand, revealing the dim shapes of the room. She waved the lamp around three times, peering long and hard into the corners before she was satisfied that nothing was crouching at the edge of vision, waiting to jump her. Just a dream, then.

She was about to turn over and go back to sleep when she heard the scratching again, along with a hoarse whisper. "Come! We must flee. Now!"

The voice had come from the open window.

Tayna held the light in front of her as she slipped from the bed and advanced cautiously toward the window.

"Who's there? What do you want?"

"It is Abeni. Come! Quickly!"

"What? Abeni? What are you talking about?" Suddenly, his big face pushed in through the window, where coverlight lit him from below, making the expression of near-panic on his face seem all the more sinister.

"Abeni has spoken to an old friend," he said, his voice wavering between fear and anger. "Mabundi denies the Keshwa-Ji. He has given the Gnome permission to take any Wasketchin girls found within House Kijamon."

"What?" Tayna hissed. "How can he–?" But Abeni shook his head.

"There is no time!" he urged. "Quishek comes at any moment. Perhaps even now. We must flee!"

"Just a minute," Tayna whispered. "I'll go tell Shaleen."

"No!"

"No?" Tayna said, cocking her head as though she hadn't heard him right. "Why not? Shouldn't we at least tell your parents?"

"It is very important," he said, shaking his head sadly. "All must be able to deny knowledge. To defy Mabundi's decision would be. . . bad. For any of my House who had knowledge. Abeni has left signs. They will know. But they will not *know*. Now come!"

So just when she thought she'd get a chance to explain things to Mabundi and settle everybody down, now it was all sliding down a mountain again. And even faster than anybody had guessed too. Why did trouble always have to come in Gnome clothing?

Tayna dressed quickly and then hopped up onto the low sill of the window, taking a last look back into the room to be sure she wasn't forgetting anything. Abeni pointed at the light in her hand and shook his head. Great. Now she'd have to run away in total blackness too. Tayna sighed and tossed the coverlight back onto the bed. "Sorry Shaleen. It's been nice." Then she eased herself through the slot window and followed Abeni out into the darkness. It was official.

Now they were running from *two* kings.

chapter 24

Eliza was never going to be able to scrub the images of that night from her memory, no matter how long she lived. It had started out innocently enough...

We are here, Mardu sent, once she and Scraw had reached their chosen spot. Scraw had settled himself down onto the bank of the stream to watch, directly across from the island, half way between two of the Gnome guards. Neither had seen him approach. The island was higher than the surrounding bank, so Scraw was little more than a black ruffle in its shadow. Even so, Mardu still felt badly exposed, and despite the crow's assurances that he was much faster than a Gnome, Mardu remained unconvinced. In the end, she had no choice. They needed this to work if they were going to gain access to the power idling beneath that island, and every step closer Scraw brought her to the fire would make it that much easier for her to control the flames. She grumbled something about risk-taking males, but resigned herself to the situation. Scraw laughed at her in his head.

Hearing them bicker over their shared connection, Eliza was struck by how familiar her crow friend's sense of humor seemed. He'd have made a good Unlovable. Eliza smiled at the thought as she pulled her attention back from the remote team and opened her eyes to check the physical world around her. Mehklok loomed above her, on top of a large knob of rock, swinging his arms into different positions, searching for his scariest pose. Any of them would be fine. *We're set,* she replied. *Ready when you are.*

It was an odd sensation for Eliza, as she sat there, watching Mehklok through her outside eyes, as he puffed and pinwheeled in anticipation, while her inside eye showed her a large fire, flanked by two enormous Gnomes, which she also watched, carefully, looking for signs of change in the flames. It was like trying to watch two movies on the same TV at the same time.

Dimly, she was also aware that she could hear Mardu's inner voice as the Flame of the Dragon cast her charm, muttering to herself in a quiet kind of sing-song voice. At first, nothing seemed to be happening, but after a while, the fire did appear to be somewhat less than it had been.

Are you having trouble? Eliza sent.

Not yet, Mardu replied. Her low singing dropped into a background murmur when she spoke, but somehow she was able to maintain it in the back of her thoughts. *I want them to think the fire is dying naturally. If they suspect a charm, they will be on guard for trickery. We need them to look at it, not peer more grimly out into the night with suspicion.*

Good point, Eliza sent. *We're standing by.* She raised her hand in a halting gesture to Mehklok, indicating that he would be needed shortly. He nodded to her and settled himself into readiness.

Through the crow-cam, Eliza watched the Gnome's fire continue to lose energy as the flames licked and danced. Little by little, as one moment followed the next, the brilliant tongues dipped, bowed and then guttered. Not too quickly, not all at once, but with steady regularity. Within five minutes or so, the light had dropped low enough to catch the attention of one of the Gnomileshi guards–the one on Scraw's right. The guard turned to glance over his shoulder at the fire. Eliza couldn't make out specific words, but she did hear a guttural grunt of some kind as he turned to investigate.

It's working, she sent to Mardu. *Hold it there a moment. Now that somebody's watching, we don't want him to notice anything weird.* The background murmuring stopped, and Mardu watched along with her, scarcely daring to let Scraw even breathe.

Excitement edged into Eliza's thoughts. *Look! That far guy is glancing at it too.* Sure enough, the Gnome on the far side of the fire had twisted around to see what was going on, but the third one, to Scraw's left, remained solid, as though rooted deep down into the soil.

And then, as if out of nowhere, Eliza had an idea. Here they were, standing on top of what Mardu had said might be the most powerful magic battery remaining in this world, and they hadn't even considered trying to make use of it.

Oh my god, she sent, sharing her sudden revelation with Mardu. *I know how to make this loads better.* But for the moment, she didn't want to distract Mardu, who had gone back to her charm song and

260

seemed to be having to concentrate more intently now. *Just don't run out of juice for a little bit longer,* Eliza sent. *Stay ready. That last guy looks a bit peeved. Things should happen any second now.*

With her hand, she motioned at Mehklok to go into his pose, and the little guy didn't miss a beat, stretching up onto his toes and glaring down at her, arms curled in front of him as though he were lifting a heavy rock in front of himself. He looked every inch the angry fire demon. He even seemed to be wreathed in flames already, on account of the weird double vision thing she had going. This was going to be stellar!

Steady... she sent to Mardu.

The guard on the right had now turned fully around to watch as the far one poked a stick at the coals, trying to get the fire to come back up, but the guard on the left was still facing away, looking out into the night. More guttural comments were exchanged between the two fire-tenders and then a louder demand. They both looked toward their companion as though waiting for his opinion. The entire Flame gang had agreed that they needed all three guards to see the fire ancestor, because anyone who did not might not believe what the others had seen and might choose to remain on guard duty instead of obeying the flames.

Eliza gripped Mardu's hand over the link–or it felt like a hand grip, anyway. Whatever it was, she sent some kind of squeeze of reassurance and shared excitement. *Steady...*

Time seemed to stand still for one eternal heartbeat and then the last guard–the one Eliza had come to think of as the boss–spat out a reply and turned around to face his cohorts.

Now, Mardu! Now! Grab power from the dragon thing! Use it to make a huge flame ancestor puppet guy. Here comes Mehklok! And then she threw her vision of the towering Gnome chaplain down the link–but not just the one posturing in front of her now. She could not help but mix in her recollection of the leering, salivating Hell-beast that had greeted her back in his cave when she'd first opened her eyes, so many days ago. It was a truly terrifying sight.

She felt Mardu recoil at the image, but then steady herself. Then she felt the Flame of the Dragon reach down into the soil, deep beneath the fire, questing, reaching, until she touched it. Pure power. She could feel Scraw preparing to speak.

And then the night exploded.

chapter 25

Sister Diaphana set her bags down on the gritty front steps of the Old Shoe and let her arms just hang there, exhausted. A long, weary sigh chased ghosts of frost into the air around her. She was home. It had been a long walk. Much longer than she had expected it to be. With no money in her pockets and the credit card declined, a taxi had been out of the question. Busses too. So she had been forced to walk all the way back from the toy shop, through the cold late-winter afternoon, and her load had been much heavier than she had expected it to be too. At first, she had wondered if maybe some kind stranger would offer her a ride, or if perhaps a youngster or two might offer to help carry the dozen or more bags that hung from her arms and around her neck. But no such offers had come.

Still, the trip had been worth it. Today was a good day. In fact, it was the best day she could remember in quite a long time. Despite all her struggles, and despite having had to pawn her mother's necklace to pay for all the toys until Regalia could pay her back... Despite all of this, today she returned home bearing gifts for the children. Toys and dolls and games and crafts. It was almost like a dream, really. A dream of Christmas. Let the day be cold and miserable. Nothing could dampen the tingle of delight she had been feeling ever since Sister Regalia had first told her the good news.

"We need toys, Sister. Lots of toys. It's time we had more fun for the children around here, don't you think?"

Diaphana had been so startled by the suggestion that she had only been able to nod a timid response. Was the Sister Superior really agreeing with her? Finally? After all these years?

"Well, let's not delay then, Sister. Here is the credit card. Go now. Get as much as you like. The more the merrier. When you think you have enough and you think it's time to stop, just imagine the smiles of joy you'll see when you come back through that door. Then buy a few more."

"But Sister! That is– I mean, really? How wonder–"

"Not now, Sister. You can thank me when you return. Now go. Time is wasting and you have a lot of shopping to do."

The giddiness Diaphana had felt then, as she'd run out the front door of the orphanage, was still with her now. She could still feel the tingling in her legs, and the fluttering in her stomach. But that was nothing compared to what was about to come. She lifted her weary eyes to look up at that heavy front door. When she imagined all the excited little faces that were about to explode into delight, like on a birthday morning–a birthday for every girl in the entire place... Well, it made her heart want to burst from her chest and dance on the steps for joy.

Picking her parcels up one last time, the bulky Sister made her way up the steps and shouldered her way through the front door. "Hello! Come see, my darlings! Come see!" Diaphana's voice rang out as she stepped into the warmth of the front hallway. But no sparkling eyes were there to greet her. Oh darn. How silly of me. It's late. They'll all be in classes still. Sister Diaphana hefted her bags once again and shuffled down the hallway toward the classrooms at the back.

"Surprise!" she called, as she burst through the junior classroom door, managing an awkward flourish of her arms for show, despite the bags and parcels that hung from them.

But the room was empty.

Now where on Earth can they be? Oh. Of course! Sister Regalia had taken them all down to the dining hall in the basement. That's what she'd done. They would all be down there having a late lunch. What a perfect place to surprise them all with gifts! With her heart beginning to race in anticipation, the large nun gathered up her bags–and her stamina–one more time, and went back down the hallway toward the basement stairs.

It took her several minutes to struggle her way down that narrow, rickety flight of steps, but in the end she managed it, without having to leave even a single package behind. Marshaling her reserves for one last big push, Diaphana launched herself into the dining hall. "Hello my lovelies! Hell–"

But this room too was empty.

Now this really is odd. Where could they all have gotten to? With no young faces around to see her exhaustion, Sister Diaphana dropped her bags where she stood and slumped her sweating frame into the nearest chair, letting out a satisfied whoosh of breath, and tugging at the collar of her habit for ventilation. Then she just sat there for a while, breathing heavily and enjoying the tingly feeling as the circulation returned to her fingers and arms. And she listened. The Old Shoe was normally a buzz of activity during the afternoons. Classes in session, babies and toddlers being put down or taken up from their naps, the sounds of pots and pans banging down here in the kitchen, as the Unlov– as the rambunctious girls helped prepare dinner. The Old Shoe might be many things, but it was never quiet. Not like this.

After a few moments mulling that over, Sister Diaphana dragged herself back up to her feet and went up the stairs to see where everyone had gone. She'd already checked the ground floor, so she went up further. No sounds of laughter or cat-calling from the Sisters' floor. Up further, and nothing on the junior floor, nor the senior floor above that, nor even anybody on the fifth floor, which had once been the home of the rambunctious girls, but was now being used for storage.

Wherever could they all have gotten to?

Sister Diaphana paused in the stairwell. Could it be? Possibly. Maybe. Sister Regalia had been going to the zoo a lot lately. Maybe she had been arranging a big tour of the place for all the children. The portly nun smiled at that. Yes, that seemed likely. The zoo. Something had changed Sister Regalia for the better, it would seem. First all the new toys, and now a trip to the zoo. Life in Our Lady of Divine Suffering's Home for Orphans and Evictees was finally starting to look up. Everybody was at the zoo, of course!

And when they got home, they'd be hungry, yet there they were with nobody on hand to get the dinner ready. Well, nobody except one exhausted Sister. How hard could one dinner be? So with her smile back on her face where it belonged, the Sister with the heart as big as all the world toddled back down the stairs to get dinner going. For sixty people.

When she got to the kitchen, she found that there wasn't really much to work with though. Sister Disgustia obviously hadn't done the shopping in far too long. Still, Diaphana put herself to work and managed to find a cupboard full of bread. And they still had an enormous tub of peanut butter. So she rolled up her sleeves and set to it.

There was a scary moment when the table had lurched under

her hands and she wondered if the whole building was going to fall on her, but it passed quick enough. Probably just a truck going by, she decided, and she had a good laugh at herself for taking such a silly fright. Then she picked up her knife and went right back to sandwich-making.

A few minutes later, she had a hundred and twenty sandwiches ready, and milk poured for everybody. Well, ninety of the sandwiches were peanut butter, but she'd run out, so she'd made thirty more with plain margarine, just to be safe.

Diaphana was just tidying things away when she heard a bang from upstairs. That's them. Her eyes flicked immediately to the pile of bags and boxes that she'd arranged along the back table. They're going to be so happy! She could already hear them shouting, and their heavy stomping as they ran down the hall above.

"Unit two, basement level! Three and four, upstairs! Move it!"

That was odd. Had they brought people home with them from the zoo? Perhaps a zoo keeper to teach a class on animals? That would be nice.

A moment later, the swinging kitchen doors flew open, and dark men stormed into the room.

"In the kitchen! We've got one!" Army men of some kind. Or policemen? They rushed forward, rifles raised to their shoulders, pointed at her, as they fanned out around her.

"Down on the floor, lady! Now!"

"Do it! Do it now!"

Diaphana looked around, bewildered.

"Knife! Knife! She's armed!" The big man on her right darted forward suddenly and punched viciously at her hand. The butter knife jangled away into a corner. Diaphana's eyes went wide and she turned to see where the knife had gone. What was–? Then the pain shot up her arm and she cried out. But what did I do?

"The man said 'down,' lady! And that means DOWN!"

The shorter man on her left waved his hand, and Diaphana turned to look at him through teary eyes. What did he want? But then she sensed a motion from the first man and she turned slowly back to see what he–

The heel of his rifle came rushing toward her face.

"Hostile neutralized. The kitchen is secure."

chapter 26

"Out of my way, Goreski!" DelRoy pushed past the nosy jerk and hurried toward the stairs.

"You don't clock out for another hour," Goreski sputtered, behind him.

"Family emergency. Bill me."

"But you don't have a family!"

I do now, DelRoy thought as he thundered down the stairs, but he didn't want to give Goreski the satisfaction of that kind of revelation. Besides, he wasn't even sure where that had come from. Family? All he knew was that when Ned had called and said that something had happened–that Sue had been attacked by some homeless man and was now in hysterics–something inside him had clicked. Something ancient, and kind of scary even. Someone he cared about had been threatened. And now here he was, racing to protect her.

It was a funny way to learn how he actually felt.

"She won't thank you for that in the morning," DelRoy said, pointing at the bottle of sedatives on the side-table. Ned was coming out of Sue's bedroom and he paused to pull the door shut quietly behind him.

"I know my sister, Detective. If I hadn't done something, she'd have gone back down to that place and torn it apart. And how do you think that would have ended up? Yesterday she comes home and tells me that every powerful bureaucrat in the city is dancing in secret with those nuns, and then tomorrow she gets arrested for breaking in? Maybe hurting someone? You think they'd just slap her on the wrist? They're making people disappear!"

"So she's kept you informed."

"Of course she has! I'm her brother!"

"That's not what she tells people."

Ned looked away. "I know. Not our brightest idea, maybe." Then he looked back. "But it worked. You gotta give her that much."

DelRoy shrugged. He was still wound up tight. He'd arrived less than an hour ago to find Sue frantic, alternating between tears of frustration and screams of rage. It had been all Ned could do to keep her in the house until DelRoy had arrived, and the first thing he'd done was hand over the note.

the fire is here but it sleeps soon it will not they will all be taken many will die if you would see the girl again follow nafosh

It looked bad. That much he could admit, but Sue was more than just scared. She was like a caged panther. A raging kettle of boiling oil, looking for someone to spill on. After reading the note twice, he'd suggested a drink, to calm her nerves–not to mention his own–but he hadn't twigged to what Ned had done until Sue's eyes had begun to droop. And now that she was down for the count, he could only stand there, looking at the brother with frank curiosity.

"I don't know what to make of you, Ned. No apparent job, but no criminal record either. No history of paying taxes, or having a phone, or a car, or a bank account. But you do have childhood records. Classic paper trail of a guy who grew up here, but then moved away."

"Except...?" Ned said, smiling in a curious way.

"Except that Sue says you've visited a few times, only I can't find any passport or visa information. No consistent pattern of long distance calls on Sue's phones, and judging by that odd accent of yours, wherever it is you live, it is a long, long way away."

Ned laughed. "Very far indeed," he said. "But just a few miles up the road."

DelRoy glared at the guy and counted slowly to himself, before he felt calm enough to continue. "Look Ned," he began. "I'm trying to help, but maybe you don't understand how this is shaping up. You've falsified documents in an attempt to gain fraudulent custody of a minor. A little girl. Who has now gone missing. On top of that, we now have threats of additional serious crimes on the horizon–arson, murder, who knows what all? These are not petty. They're as major as they come. Which means that when I leave here, I have to notify the feds, who are going to show up here with their paper-sniffing proctology equipment. And when they do, you are going to stick out like a corpse in a chorus line. So maybe this would be a good time to drop the cute and mysterious. Don't you think?"

Ned dropped his gaze to look at the floor. He looked like a five year old boy with his hand caught in the candy drawer. Then he seemed to melt. "Oh crap," he said, running his hands through his thinning hair. "I need a drink." DelRoy watched him wander out to the living room again, snatch the gin bottle from the table, and take a long pull from it as he flopped himself into the overstuffed chair.

The detective followed and sat on the sofa beside him. Ned held the bottle out and DelRoy accepted it, taking a small gulp himself. Then the two men sat there in strained silence for a while, passing the bottle back and forth between them.

"She trusts you, you know," Ned said, breaking the silence.

"Who, your sister?"

"Yeah." Then Ned shifted in his chair and turned, peering at him from behind those old fashioned glasses. Ned was sweating–probably from the gin–and his wispy white hair was clumped and damp around his temples and across his forehead, hanks of darker silver-gray plastered against his flushed, pink skin.

"That's important," Ned said. "Me, I just don't get people. Not here, anyway. Never have, so I've always relied on Sue's instincts. Even when we were little. And she trusts you."

DelRoy recognized the signs of a witness talking himself into a confession, so he just nodded and let Ned continue.

"The thing is," Ned said, nervously, "I'm pretty sure you won't believe me. And then where will we be?"

Ned was the bookish sort, and he'd already said more words today than DelRoy had heard from him over the entire week since they'd met. Which was good, because guys who didn't talk much didn't get much practice at lying either. The detective took another slug of gin and shrugged. "In the last couple of days," he said, ticking his observations off on his fingers with the bottle as he spoke, "I've learned that somebody may have brain-wiped me, the city is effectively run by nuns, and hobos deliver hand-printed death threats while wearing clown costumes. In light of all that, I'd say I am unusually receptive to weird right now. Try me."

Ned chuckled nervously. "Well, you see, the thing is, I don't actually live in this world."

DelRoy looked at him with one barely raised eyebrow. "That's it? I just told you pretty much the same thing, myself. Of *course* you don't live around here, Ned. Everything about you says that you're a long, long way from home. India or Asia somewhere, I'd guess so it–"

Ned shook his head. "No, when I say 'this world,' I don't mean this *society*, as in this city or this country. I mean this planet."

DelRoy snorted a laugh, and then choked as the mouthful of gin tried to jet from his nose.

"I know," Ned said, waving a hand at the detective's obvious amusement. "I know exactly how it sounds, Detective. Like I'm a complete nutter, right? So I guess I'm just going to have to show you."

DelRoy reached up with the bottle to scratch at his head, watching with wry curiosity as Ned held his hands together in front of his face, and spoke quietly into his palms. Like he was praying or something.

"Creepy, isn't it?"

The detective reeled back in his chair and looked around in a panic. "What the–?" The voice had come from right next to his ear, but there was nobody there.

"Down here, dumbass."

He looked down at the bottle in his hand. "That's right, genius. Not ventriloquism. It's really me."

DelRoy flung the bottle across the room, and backpedaled himself right up out of the chair, and fell hard over the back, crashing to a heap on the floor. Because while he had been watching, the open rim of the gin bottle had spoken to him.

And just to prove he was crazy, he'd even watched its lips move.

———

"I'm what the Wasketchin call a 'kincraft,' " Ned said.

DelRoy was standing with his back to the wall. At first, he'd drawn his gun, but that had just been a panic reaction, and he'd quickly shoved it back into his shoulder holster. But that didn't mean he was prepared to believe what he'd seen.

"You put something in the gin."

Ned shook his head. "I've been drinking the same stuff you have, Detective."

"In my glass then," he tried.

Ned smiled. "You weren't drinking from a glass." He waved a

hand at the mostly-empty gin bottle lying on its side in the corner. "And you can take that away and have it analyzed if you want. I promise you, there's nothing in it that shouldn't be."

DelRoy quickly flashed on a dozen other explanations, hallucinogens in the air supply being the most plausible of them. So in the absence of a rational explanation, he fell back on his training. Collect more evidence.

"Show me again," he said, but Ned just shook his head.

"That was all I had in me, I'm afraid. I can't create magic over here. I'm limited to what I bring with me when I come back, and that was it."

But that gave him something to pounce on. "You can do magic, for real, and you put all your cards into the talking gin bottle trick?"

But again Ned shook his head. "No. That would be too specific. Not much chance a mugger or a gang banger would happen to be carrying gin, is there? Before I cross back, I prepare a fairly general purpose charm. It lets me animate any small object in the vicinity. Make it talk. It only lasts for a few seconds, but it's enough. Most people react the way you just did, and by the time they calm down, I've had plenty of time to run away."

"So you've done this before?"

"Two other times," Ned replied. "This city isn't as safe at night as it used to be."

"And this is, what did you call it, your kink?"

Ned laughed nervously. "No, not 'kink,' Detective. 'Kincraft.' It's what they call my kind of magic over... there. I never even knew it existed until I discovered my way into Methilien, but it turns out I'm really good at it. Back here, I was just a creepy guy who liked dolls, but over there? I quickly became Kincraft to the King of the Wasketchin. Can you blame me for wanting to make a life in that world instead of this one?"

DelRoy glanced at the bottle again, but his eyes snapped back to Ned just as fast. He was in full-bore detective mode, and for now, the bottle wasn't the issue. Ned was. He had to listen to Ned. Find the flaws in his story. Poke holes in them.

Only he couldn't.

Sure, there were gaps you could fly a cargo plane through, but the problem wasn't really Ned. With a story like his, what *you* think is or isn't possible is irrelevant. What matters is what *he* thinks is possible. So you pay attention to that. But listening to Ned was like listening to a foreign tourist talk about life in his village back home. You can tell by the expression on his face and the light in his eyes that it's all very real and natural to him, despite the fact that what he's saying is completely insane.

"So if I understand, you make dolls for a living. Over there. Dolls that talk."

"Look, Detective, do you think I don't know how this sounds? Do I strike you as retarded, or delusional?" DelRoy started to answer, but Ned waved him off. "I mean aside from the story you're hearing now. You've known me for a week. I know how odd I may have seemed at times. I don't fit in here. I never have, and I know that. But truthfully, at any point this week have you thought to yourself, 'This guy is dangerously unstable?' Or have you been thinking more, 'This guy doesn't fit in?' Like maybe I was raised in a commune or something and don't know the social etiquette here?"

To tell the truth, that was pretty much exactly what he'd been thinking.

"Good," Ned said. "I can see I wasn't far wrong."

DelRoy grimaced. He was far from ready to accept the story. In fact, it was much more likely that Ned really was a master-class liar– one so talented that even a hardened city detective's refined truth senses could not pick it up. But even so, debating something this whacked out would only spin his wheels, so he opted to play along. Act convinced.

"Well," he began, letting a half-convinced smile pave the way. "This story of yours does fit the facts better than anything I've been able to come up with. Even I know it isn't some trick bottle you bought in Japan. I'm not sure what I believe yet, but I suppose it's possible that it isn't your story that's crazy, Ned. Maybe it's the facts that are crazy, and your story has just enough crazy to fit them. But does it have to be another planet?"

Ned shrugged and sat back in his chair. "I don't actually know what to call it. 'Planet' seems right, but I've never seen it from space or anything. I have no idea if it's a round ball that floats in blackness the way the Earth does, or what. Would it help to think of it more like the world on the other side of the wardrobe?"

DelRoy laughed nervously. "I guess that's better than the one down the rabbit hole." Ned smiled. "But you do realize nobody else is going to believe you, right?"

Ned rolled his eyes. "Of course I do. Why do you think I don't tell people?"

"But now you're telling. Just because I mentioned the feds?"

Ned nodded. "Yeah," he said. "But not because I'm going to stick out like a dancing corpse, as you so delicately put it. There's something else now. Maybe worse, and I don't know what it means. Although I have no idea how he found out about me."

"Who?"

"The hobo," Ned said. "The one who wrote Sue's note. He said, 'Follow Nafosh.'"

DelRoy cocked his head. "So?"

Ned leaned over to grab the gin and took a long pull. "My name is Ned Nackenfausch," he said. "But that name sticks out over there. It's too alien sounding, so nobody calls me that." Then he shrugged helplessly and pointed at the note.

And then it clicked. "'Follow Nafosh,' He meant you. You're Nafosh."

All Ned could do was nod.

That night, Detective DelRoy started making calls. Even after promising Sue he would do so, it had still not been an easy decision to keep that promise. The whole thing with Ned had come out of left field and now it just laid there, a time bomb, waiting to go off. If it did, DelRoy was going to lose some serious cred. Maybe even his job. But what choice did he have? Look the other way, like everyone else seemed to be doing? Let the nuns win, leave the vanished cases vanished, and let the kids just continue to rot in that hole?

And how would he ever face Sue again?

In the end, that was what made his mind up for him. The thought of Sue having to move on with her life, without ever knowing what had happened to her daughter. He pulled out his phone list and started dialing.

Not official calls, though. Only people higher up the command chain could make an official request to one of the national agencies, but with the number of familiar faces he'd seen at the nun's party, he couldn't be sure who to trust locally. So instead, he made some unofficial calls. To people he'd worked with over the years. People who were not based here in town. People who knew people.

With their help, and a little luck, he was finally able to reach somebody who seemed to give a damn. The Deputy Director of the newly formed National Children's Protection Agency. Unfortunately, being a new agency and eager to make its mark, the Deputy Director made an unexpected–and terrifying–decision.

He was going to raid the orphanage.

"There are children at risk," the D.D. said, when he called Del-Roy at home the next morning. "You've intercepted a serious threat made against them, and even if *you* don't think your vagrant was serious, I can't afford to take that chance. I had some of my boys take a look, and a lot of your facts check out. It's clear that these orphans are living in abusive conditions, abandoned by the system, left in the care of negligent guardians, and the surrounding infrastructure is not up to the task of correcting things. This is a textbook case of the state falling victim to its own internal issues and completely failing to fulfill its obligations to the people. Leaves me no choice but to intervene in the matter."

"But sir–"

"Don't worry, Detective Donnelly. You'll receive full credit for bringing this to our attention."

"But sir–"

"No, son. Don't thank me. I'm just doing my job. It's for the kids, after all. We'll be going in at fourteen hundred, and I'd really like for you to be there, if you can, son. It'll look so much better in the photos if we can spin the local-boy-does-good angle."

"But sir–"

"I'll see you on site at thirteen-thirty. We can coordinate the talking points then."

"But sir–"

"So long, Donnelly. You've done well here. Real well. We'll see you soon."

The line went dead.

DelRoy could only stare at the silent phone still gripped in his hand. The time was now eleven o'clock.

When he got to Sue's place, there was no answer at the door, although the newspaper lay at his feet, so she was probably still home. He pounded again on the heavy wooden door, and was just about to go around to the back, when a bleary-eyed Sue peered out at him through the window.

"Martin?"

She looked groggy. He must have waken her up. "Open the door, Sue. Things are happening quickly, and I need to talk to you."

Fifteen minutes later, they were ready to leave. As soon as he'd mentioned the impending raid, Sue had bolted to full alertness. "Somebody is actually doing something," she said, her voice edged with dreamy wonder.

"Yeah," he said. "But to these yahoos, 'doing something' probably means something that'll involve terrifying little kids with a bunch of storm troopers in riot gear."

Sue's shoulders sagged.

"If we leave now," he said, "we can get there before anything happens. Maybe we can get a chance to talk to the girls. Warn them or something." Then he looked around. "Where's Ned?"

"I don't know," she said.

"Here's Ned," Ned said, as he came into the kitchen. He was carrying a brown bag full of fresh bagels and two coffees. "Um, sorry, Detective. I didn't know you'd be here. I only–"

"Not now, Neddy. We're on our way out. The Old Shoe is about to be raided!"

"What?"

"We'll tell you in the car. Come on!"

When they got to the Old Shoe, everything was quiet. Rather than wait for the feds, as he had promised, DelRoy jumped out of the car and bolted up the front steps, with Sue and Ned right behind him. The front door was unlocked, and they went inside, pulling the heavy door shut behind them. Ned locked it.

"Better not," DelRoy said. "Could be considered obstruction." Ned's eyes widened, but he unlocked the door without complaint.

"Hello?" The detective's voice echoed throughout the old building, but there was no answer and the building reverberated in eerie, mid-day silence.

"That's odd," Sue said, stepping forward to peer into Sister Regalia's office, which was open, but empty. "There's always been somebody in the office before."

A loud thump from somewhere above them jerked everybody's eyes upward, but before they could react further, another thump knocked them all to the floor.

And with it, the entire building began to shake.

chapter 27

"Earthquake!" DelRoy yelled, as he pulled himself to his feet, clutching at the frame of the Sister Superior's office door. Ned and Sue helped each other crawl to the wall, and then clung there to ride out the quake. Outside, a car alarm squawked itself awake, alerting anyone who might not have noticed all the shaking.

That shaking went on for almost half a minute, but behind it, and behind the alarm... DelRoy cocked his head. There was another sound. Stranger. Quieter. Like a far-away whimper of a creature in pain, but he couldn't be sure. More likely just some sheet-metal twisting in the tremor.

When the shaking stopped, Ned looked up. "Did anybody else hear that moaning?" DelRoy nodded. So it hadn't just been his imagination. But whatever it had been, it was gone now. DelRoy reached into his pocket and clicked the key fob to silence the warble of his car alarm, leaving a very different kind of warble in the distance. The kind sirens made.

"Emergency response?" Sue asked.

He shrugged. "Or the feds, on their way here. Either way, we don't have much time." Then he turned and headed for the stairwell across the hall. "You try to find your helper-friends, Sue. Take them out to the car and get in the back. I'll find out what's going on upst—"

But Sue shook her head. "No deal," she said. "Something weird is going on. We stick together."

So that's what they did. They had checked the second and third floors—both empty—and were just reaching the fourth floor landing when the sirens were suddenly loud enough to be right in the stairwell with them. Then they stopped, to be replaced by the muffled thumps of car doors and shouts of command from outside.

"Damn! It *is* the feds, and they're here early," DelRoy said.

Somewhere above them, something crashed, like a stack of pots being dropped into a sink. A sink *inside* the building.

"Come on," he said. "Skip four. That came from the fifth floor!" His feet pounded like thunder on the stairs, echoed a moment later by Sue and Ned as they followed close behind.

As DelRoy charged out into the fifth floor hallway, he caught a strange odor. Tangy, like after a lightning storm, but fragrant too, like fresh-cut lumber or a greenhouse. It was a scent of living things, and it stood out brightly against the institutional smells of old dust and cheap floor wax. Below them, he heard the hollow booming of fists banging on the door. Not much time. DelRoy looked around quickly. There were half a dozen doors down the main hallway, and the first two were open. One on the left, one on the right. He waved Sue toward the right-hand door and took the left one for himself.

Inside was a large, squarish room with high ceilings. Bits of paper and cardboard littered the floor, and a low line of boxes ran along the far wall, underneath the windows. One section of the row had toppled over, and five or six bronze bowls lay scattered across the floor, having spilled out from a few of the boxes.

DelRoy looked around, but there was nowhere for anybody to hide. The commotion had probably been caused by the quake toppling a poorly stacked section of the box wall.

"Nothing here," Sue called, from the other room. "But I can see the police cars. They're getting out a ram."

He turned at the sound of her voice, and that's when he noticed the large red circle painted on the wall behind him. He stepped toward it and dabbed at the paint with one finger. It was sticky, and the detective stared curiously at the reddish fingerprint that now appeared on the tip of his finger. He rubbed at it with his thumb and the redness smeared into a streak.

"Still wet," he said.

"What's that?" Ned had stepped into the room, and a moment later Sue came in behind him. DelRoy held up his finger, red side out. "Paint," he said. "On the wall. It's still wet." Ned stepped further into the room to see what he was talking about, but Sue ignored it and came right over to where DelRoy was standing.

"The police are trying to get in," she said, "but the door is stuck." She turned a glare toward Ned as she said it, but her brother raised his hands in innocence.

"I *did* unlock it," he said. "Even opened and closed it to be sure I got it right."

Sue turned back to DelRoy. "Could the quake have jammed it?"

"Maybe," he said. "But even so, we haven't got much time before they break it down. Where do you suppose everybody went?"

There was a flicker of movement in the corner of his eye, and then suddenly, the room was filled with green light and the heavy scent of forest.

"Who the hell are you?" said a voice behind him.

Sue gasped and DelRoy spun around and. The wall inside the red circle had vanished, revealing a brilliantly lit forest in midsummer. In the middle of the circle, a nun was stepping over the threshold, out of the forest, and into the room. A wicked smile twitched at the corners of her lips.

"Sister Anthrax!" Sue said.

"Get them!" Sister Anthrax said.

And then DelRoy saw them, swarming from behind the nun. "Oh my god. You weren't lying," he said, as an army of monkey men boiled into the room. All of them armed with long, white clubs.

A dark haired man in a black rain jacket stood at the window of the upstairs dorm room, looking down at the scene on the sidewalk out front. The word "CAPTAIN" blazed from his back in bright, reflective lettering. Directly below him, the Deputy Director was striking a pose on the front steps, talking to reporters. Aside from that, all he could see was the assault van and the four dark, unmarked cars that were parked at various angles, blocking the street to traffic. Plus an extra unmarked. Probably DelRoy's, but no sign of DelRoy himself.

But that wasn't the only thing missing. Everything about this scene made him feel... wrong. Where were the gawkers surging up the sidewalk? The neighbors peering out of alleys, or from behind curtained windows on the other side of the street? Maybe it was that–the complete absence of any community around this place–that made him uneasy. Behind him, somebody coughed.

"Uh, Captain Fisher?"

"Any sign of DelRoy?" Fisher asked.

"No sir. Not inside."

Figures. The Captain turned away from the window to face his second. "Okay, Lambert. And what'd we get from surveillance?"

Lambert looked at his notes. "A man matching the description you gave did enter the building, sir. We're assuming it was DelRoy, but Mitch asked if you could ID the photo, just to be sure. The guy was in the company of a middle-aged couple, apparently civilians. No ID on them yet. That was at 12:40, about four minutes before we arrived on scene."

Fisher nodded. "Anything else?"

The lieutenant shrugged. "Just that whoever he was, he had no trouble with the doors, which apparently weren't even locked. They entered without incident, about a minute or so before the tremor. Looks like that's what jammed the doors up so bad for us. And of course, they logged the nun coming in."

Right. The nun. What had they been thinking? Head striking a nun making sandwiches.

"Anything more on her?"

"She went in at 12:25, carrying a bunch of shopping bags. Whatever happened, it'd probably already gone down before she got here."

He'd have words to say about the nun thing, but for now there were more pressing questions. Fisher took a pack of gum out of his pocket, selected a stick, and pushed it into his mouth, chewing thoughtfully. If DelRoy was on the level, there should be a dozen or more nuns in custody, and thirty or forty kids waiting to be processed by Children's Services. But all he had was that one semiconscious nun, and not even DelRoy around to yell at for answers.

"Where is she now?"

"We're holding her in the command car. I thought you'd probably want to talk to her."

"I do, Lieutenant. I do." Then he nodded across the hall to where the evidence team was doing their thing. "Have them double check each other, and make sure we get photos of everything. After coming in this heavy and nothing to show for it, we're going to want our asses covered a million ways from Sunday."

"Yes sir."

Fisher was half way through the door before he stopped and turned back. "Oh, and Lambert, if you do happen to come across Martin DelRoy around here somewhere, stuff him in a sack and bring him to me, will ya?" The lieutenant blinked back at him for a moment and then nodded. Nice guy, Lambert, but a little too stiff. The Captain winked at him and then stalked away down the hall.

Why did it have to be nuns?

———————

"Hello, Sister. My name is Fisher. Captain Benjamin Fisher. Can you tell me yours?"

Fisher was squatting on his haunches beside the open rear door of his car. The nun sat quietly inside. Her eyes kept darting around, but it didn't look like anything was actually registering. She moved one hand absently, and he could hear the sound of little chains rattling within the folds of her habit. Without breaking eye contact, he reached back to where he knew the custody officer was waiting, and he made a turning motion with his hands. A moment later, he felt a ring of keys press into his hand. Fisher reached out with them toward the nun.

"I'm sorry, Sister. I didn't realize they'd cuffed you. Here, let me get those off." He fiddled for a moment before he was able to get the cuffs clear of the black cloth, but then they unlocked easily and he handed the cuffs and key back behind him.

"Is that better?"

The woman rubbed at her wrists and then looked at him. There seemed to be a little more in her eyes this time.

"Sister? Your name?"

She opened her mouth. "Diaph...? Sister Di..." Then her eyes seemed to clear a little, as though she had just wakened from a long and troubling dream. "No..." she said, slowly. "Not Diaphana. French?" It was barely more than a whisper. As though she was feeling her way through a room she hadn't visited in decades. Then her eyes widened suddenly, and she turned to look at him with clear, intelligent eyes.

"Captain Fisher, my name is Regina Finch. And I'd like to report a felony."

chapter 28

Eliza raced through the trees and broke out into the clearing, then stopped fast in her tracks. The entire glade was a blackened mess, lit by the hundred tiny fires that smoldered everywhere, as remains of the Gnomes' watch fire still rained down on the dry grass. The guttering little fires illuminated tendrils of smoke that drifted above the grass, seeming to writhe in the flickering light. Of the original watch fire itself, nothing remained. It was completely gone. There didn't appear to be so much as a log or even a coal left on the island. There were no guards.

Nor any sign of Scraw and Mardu either.

Eliza reached out over their link. *Mardu! Scraw! Where are you?*

Silence.

Slowly, Eliza moved through the smoldering carnage in front of her, but her gaze remained firmly fixed on the ground as she peered into every shadow and clump for signs of the crow. Smoke stung the back of her throat and her eyes watered as a dreadful certainty grew within her. That she *would* eventually find her friends. In flaming pieces.

She wasn't sure whether to be scared or relieved when she reached the brook without any sign of them. The Gnomes, on the other hand, had not been so lucky. Eliza looked down into the water and had to fight to control her stomach as three blackened, smoldering bodies bobbed face down in the water. Like compass needles, each one pointing directly away from the blast zone.

But no crow.

Mardu? Scraw?

Mehklok came up beside her, his eyes as wide as her own, as he gaped around at the scene. Then he looked up at her. Eliza could only pantomime a bird-shape on her shoulder, and then she threw her arms wide at the devastation, asking the question with her expression. Where is my friend? Help me find my friend.

The little Gnome nodded and immediately began moving about the area, inspecting everything that looked big enough. Eliza watched him for a helpless moment, and then turned to continue her own search in the other direction. *Scraw?*

She found him at the base of a tree, on the outermost edge of the clearing. She wouldn't have found him at all, if it hadn't been for a pair of black feathers caught in the bark, halfway up the trunk. With an involuntary cry, Eliza darted forward, searching the scorched grass around the tree with her fingers. What little light she had was useless, obscured by tears. She knew what she was going to find, but still she patted gently at the grass, hoping against all odds to find him whole. A hand patted at her back, and Eliza whirled in a rage.

"Get away from me, you disgusting little creep! Get lost!"

Then she shoved the startled Gnome as hard as she could and spun back to her search, sobbing, and prodding at the grass frantically. Please, oh please, oh please. I didn't mean to hurt him. He's just a bird. He never hurt anyone...

Her hand squished into a damp mat of feathers.

Oh no! Eliza's head drooped down to chest and tears spilled down her cheeks. She eased her hand into the grass beneath him and gently scooped him up to where she could see. He was so light! But even in the scant glow of the fires that flickered behind her, she could see she was too late. One wing was bent backward and his head flopped to the side. *Mardu? Scraw? Are you in there?* But it was useless. The house was empty.

Both the Flame and the Voice of the Dragon were gone.

———

Mehklok trembled as he huddled himself down into the damp soil of the stream bank, seeking comfort from the dance of decay that played out among its tiny grains. But there was little to be found, and he deserved even less. The death godess had rejected him. Why shouldn't the soil as well?

The slowly dissolving remnants of death that were usually held in mud's holy matrix had been incinerated here into vapor and ash. By the flash fire. The melodious song of vim within was all but mute, and it left Mehklok feeling more isolated and disconnected than he could ever remember feeling. Even being lost in the forest had been better by comparison. And when the body of one of the guards bumped against his foot, not even that lucky omen could rouse Mehklok from his despair.

Death had rejected him utterly.

She had called out her grief song to him when she'd found the corpse of her familiar, summoning him, no doubt for his services as a chaplain of the Gnomileshi, and perhaps for his earlier experience as a harvester. This was only proper. She would want to free the vim still trapped within her little companion, that he might live on in some last charm of service to her. But when he had arrived, she had turned on him. Cursing him forever with a shriek uttered in some fearsome tongue of power. What had she done to him? Would his tongue turn to dust? Would his nose shrivel? Would his eyes begin to bleed? The longer he lay there in the wet dirt, the more vivid his fears became. Once again, he was alone in the forest. For a time, he had clung to the strength that flowed to him from his new-found goddess, but that strength had now been withdrawn, leaving Mehklok to sink once more into his deep and convulsing terror.

He should never have left Gash-Garnok. He should not have gone into Yechnarg to the market. He should have stayed out of that alley. He should have left the body where he'd found it. Every step in his last week of days had been a continuous march of mistakes, and now he had nothing to show for his troubles but troubles.

In the distance, he could hear her weeping. She had, of course, withheld the treasure of her emotions from him, spending them alone in the dark, rather than let even the most paltry flicker of it fall to him. Did she think him that callous? Did she not know that any gleam of sorrow she might share with him would be immediately offered up and given voice, so that it might echo with her own? He was no grief bandit. He was the Chaplain of Garnok's Rage, a church of the first rank. And one such as he knew better.

But still, why was she grieving? Even Mehklok had been able to see that life had still beat within the blackened little beast. So why cry now, before he had passed? Was she so soft that she needed him dead, but grieved over the waiting? Then why not end the wait and be done? It just didn't make any sense. And then his eyes widened.

Unless she did not know the bird yet lived. Was it possible? Mehklok had always thought the tears of sky-dwellers were a weakness. At just the time when their emotions spewed from them in fountains of wealth, tempting their fellows and blinding their reason, they chose to blind their eyes as well. It made them doubly vulnerable to those who would take advantage. Could it be that even the death queen was victim to this blinding deluge of eye-water?

And if she wept, then did this not mean she would prefer that the bird live?

Oh what to do, what to do? She had already shrieked her curse upon him. What might she do now if he guessed wrong? But on the other finger, how might she smile upon him if he guessed right?

Mehklok whimpered his fear quietly down into his throat and then stood up, squelching himself out of the dripping mud. It was his duty. And though it might get him killed, he at least had a chance now to redeem himself.

So with a quiver of hope trembling through him, Mehklok scuttled off to do what he hoped was right.

Ever since she'd opened her eyes in Mehklok's creepy lair, Eliza had been sure she was dead. It was the only explanation that made any sense. She'd made the mistake of trusting Sister Anthrax, following her up the stairs toward some last-minute change of plans... And then, nothing. Blackness and oblivion. Until she'd opened her eyes to see that terror leaning over her in the dim underground light.

So she'd fled. But the further she'd run, the more certain she'd become of her own demise. Statues made of bone and rotting meat... a cloud of flies thick enough to choke on... heat, humidity... and all of it set in some great, circular pit. She was dead. Fine. She could accept that, but there was one final thought she had been avoiding, as though by refusing to think it, she could make it not be true. But it was.

This was Hell.

One of the other Goodies, or maybe that Captain Angry One guy, must have snuck up behind her and caved in her skull or something. Although, waking up in Hell seemed kind of a harsh punishment for an orphan who had actually been dancing for joy at the time of her murder. Maybe Hell is for people who don't like nuns–even the evil kind.

Things had improved a bit once she'd climbed up out of that Throat place, but being lost in the Crayola Forest wasn't as much fun as it sounded. You can't eat colorful trees. In fact, when you don't know what can kill you, you have to assume everything can, even if it's pretty. Maybe *especially* when it's pretty. So although the scenery had improved, Eliza had been getting progressively more miserable.

Until Mardu had found her–or Scraw had–and that's when everything changed. Suddenly, she wasn't a lonely ghost missing her best friend anymore. She had someone to talk with. Someone to plot with. Someone to fill in some of the gaps. And it turned out that Mardu was in more or less the same boat, so helping each other out had seemed the thing to do. And Mardu already knew *she* was dead. She'd volunteered for it.

So all the getting to know you, becoming buddies stuff had turned out to just be more of the Welcome To Hell Committee's after-life torture program. Get the new girl to think she's really still alive, that she's got friends, and a purpose, then jerk the rug out from under her again. Ha, ha, ha! Look how scared she looks! Hasn't figured out that you never come back! Dead never goes away and it never gets better!

As she moped around inside her stupid, dead brain, Eliza had stopped paying attention to where she was going, and paid no attention when her feet carried her beyond the charred remains of the clearing, and began wandering among the trees, looking for something. Her mind was too busy wallowing itself in her misery. She looked down at her hands, at the tiny weight of feathers and stilled laughter in her hands. Scraw. That's right. She was still looking for somewhere less. . . bombed-out looking, to bury her friend.

Mardu?

Still silence. Make that, bury her *friends*.

Eliza was still staring down at the sad bundle in her hands, when the shrubs behind her burst apart and Mehklok came hurtling from them, arms outstretched. She turned slowly and could only watch in distant, sloth-like confusion as he snatched the dead crow from her hands and stuffed it into his mouth, and then turned and dashed back into the trees.

It was so unexpected, so totally beyond sanity, that all she could think to do was laugh. So with the last tatters of her mind threatening to flee into the Forest around her, Eliza sank to the ground, convulsing with great bellows and shrieks of laughter.

The kind of laughter that could break your heart.

chapter 29

"Hey, Whale Boy! Hold up!" Tayna stuck her foot out to the side, feeling carefully for the knob of rock that he'd told her was there, but there weren't any knobs she could find. A smooth hump or two, maybe. But actual knobs? Nope. Not a one, as far as she could tell. There was a mountain pressed against her face, and a little further down, just beyond her reach, there was a nice juicy crack. But with her left leg folded tightly beneath her and bearing most of her weight, there was no way she could extend her other leg far enough to reach it. Not without pulling her left foot from its secure real-estate and flinging herself down the mountain face in the process.

She looked across the exposed slope of rock, but Abeni had already moved past the jut and had vanished from sight. She called out to him again. "Um, little help?" But it was useless. He wouldn't hear her now unless she shouted, and they were still too close to the great Djin city to risk drawing attention.

Tayna sighed and then took a deep breath. He'd made this look so easy. Slowly, she edged the toe of her right boot over to the biggest wannabe-knob she could see, then she then shifted her weight carefully toward it. Her fingers were starting to sweat and she could feel them squelching and mashing against each other within the crack she'd found to jam them into, up above her head. But this wasn't about fingers. It was about toes. Trusting that her fingers would stay where she'd put them for a while, Tayna shifted a little more weight off her left leg and put it onto her boot-tip, testing its grip against the smooth stone.

It held.

Most of her weight was still on her left foot, which was cramped up below her, secure on a flat spur of stone, but there was real weight on that right toe now too. She wiggled her right ankle, and ground the toe into the face of the stone, testing to see if it would slip. It wasn't exactly a "confidence boosting" sort of grip, but it was a grip. Tayna could feel the tell-tale jitters starting to shake her left thigh. That leg had been bent for too long now, and it was beginning to shudder from the strain. Time to get moving.

Another quick glance across the rock. Still no Abeni. Oh well. Tayna held her breath and shifted still further right, letting that toe take more weight. She paused, waiting for the slip that would begin the end, but apparently the plunge to her death had been rescheduled. Her left leg began to jerk with fatigue, little sewing machine twitches, as the muscles got loopy from the lack of oxygen or something and began to giggle in distress.

Before she could panic, Tayna shifted all the way to the right, trusting the toe to hold, then she straightened her left leg out below her and shook it. Carefully. Her thigh tingled as blood raced back into forgotten neighborhoods of leg-meat, but this wasn't a good time for a block party. Now that her leg was no longer jammed below her, she was able to lower herself further down, and she did so, wedging her toes into that juicy lower crack that had been just out of reach earlier, then she quickly brought her right foot down to join it.

Great. It was over. One small step for a girl. Next up, one giant plummet for girlkind. When she'd had that leg jammed up under her and no knob to stand on, the flat expanse of stone stretching out before her had seemed a thousand miles wide. Maybe two thousand. But now, with both feet secure and the tingles starting to fade from her thigh, the road ahead seemed almost easy, with knobs and cracks for the whole family.

Once she got herself going again, her progress was swift, and soon enough she had crossed the entire face. When she pulled herself around the jut, Abeni was just sitting there. On a ledge. Waiting for her. And he was eating.

"Oh, thanks for waiting," she said, as she pulled herself up onto the ledge beside him. Abeni held out a small pouch and Tayna stuck her fingers in, pulling out a small, dense twist of the disgusting grimpi. It was sweet and tough, but oily too, and a bit floppy. And it smelled like wet monkey. Abeni assured her it was rich in all sorts of energy and nutrients, but of all the Djin foods she'd tried lately, this was the only one that actually made her gag.

"It's worse than those Gnome beak-putty snacks," she said, tearing off a piece and forcing herself to chew. Abeni smiled and pushed another piece past his big, white teeth.

"So where are we going?" she asked, after she'd managed to get the wad of grimpi unstuck from her teeth and down her throat. "Down to the Forest, of course, but where?"

Abeni shook his head. "That would be dangerous. Mabundi and Quishek will search there. The trails of the Anvil are too easily watched."

"So, what are we doing? Heading for the wild-water route? That's how you got down so quickly the last time, right?" But her big Djin friend just shook his head again.

"No canoe." He glanced significantly around them, as though challenging her to produce one from the pebbles and dust scattered on the ledge between them.

"Okay then, where are we supposed to meet up with the supplies you organized? Where are they going?"

"There was no time," he said, shaking his head sadly.

"What? You didn't send them? So now we're supposed to set up some kind of underground railroad to lead hundreds of Wasketchin refugees to safety, but we don't have any food? Or blankets? What about the ones who ran away without even boots on their feet? What are we supposed to do for them?"

Abeni hung his head and shrugged, miserably. "There was no time," he repeated, as though that made it all better. "We can do nothing now."

For a long moment, Tayna could only stare at him in disbelief. Then the disbelief twisted into irritation.

"Hello? What are you talking about? You swore an oath to Kijamon. And now you're just going to let this ring–" Tayna reached out to flick the iron bond ring on his arm that signified his newly-sworn duty, but couldn't seem to find it among the silver and gold bands. "Hey, where did your–?"

"We must climb," Abeni said.

Tayna looked up. "Excuse me? Climb? How does climbing help us? We have to get down, not up."

Abeni sucked another strand of grimpi from between his fingers and Tayna watched it waggle, like a stiffened worm. Her stomach flopped and she was beginning to regret having eaten any herself. She swallowed hard, trying to settle things back down.

"The Gnomes will search for you," Abeni said, quietly. "We must hide, for a time. When the search has ended, then we can go to help your people."

"Oh sure," she said. "Because the one thing they have plenty of is time to wait. That's seriously your plan? Climb higher? Up there somewhere?" She gestured upward with her chin. "And just *hide* until the Gnomes stop looking?"

Abeni shrugged, but would not meet her eye.

Tayna growled in frustration and looked around quickly for something to hit him with, but there was nothing. "I mean, what is *wrong* with you today, Abeni?" She gave him a shove on the arm, to emphasize her question. "What happened to all that Djinnish 'death before dishonor' stuff, huh?" But it was clear he had no answer for her.

Tayna stood up.

"Okay, there's no point in yammering about it more now. Don't we need to find somewhere to make camp for the night?" The sun was indeed beginning to sink toward the horizon. They still had at least an hour, but now that she knew how quickly light became dark on the Anvil, she did not want to risk getting stuck out in the open in mid-climb when that happened.

Abeni stood beside her. "Yes. Camp," he said, somewhat distractedly. Then he seemed to remember where they were, and he said it again, with more confidence. "Yes. We must find a camp. There is a place, only a short climb from here."

Tayna rolled her eyes. "A short climb? Meaning up?"

Abeni smiled sheepishly. "Yes, it is up. But from that place, Abeni can show you other places, where we can climb down, if that is what we decide to do." Tayna flicked another glance at the sun.

"Okay," she said. "We go up. But once we're there, we are so going to have a talk about tomorrow."

Rather than respond to that, Abeni turned to face the rock, and began to climb. Tayna watched him closely, paying attention to where he was placing his hands and feet. But while her eyes were focused on the business at hand, her mind was still trapped in its circular hamster wheel. What was wrong with him? Why was he being so un-Abeni-like? Then the way ahead was clear, and she pushed the hamster wheel into a mental closet and began to climb after him.

This was no time to be doubting her guide.

chapter 30

"Shaleen makes a poor joke," Abeni said. "The Little Fish would not leave without telling Abeni." The entire family—what remained of it—had jumped at Shaleen's call, and now stood pressed together outside the door, trying to peer past her into the tiny bedroom.

Shaleen shrugged. "It is no joke, my son. Her bed has been slept in, but she is not in it. I found only this." She held up the small black toy that had been in his room since before Abeni could remember, but now it crackled and spit with harmless arcs of light that danced around his mother's fingers. "I don't remember it doing this before," she said, her eyes flickering with the reflected display.

"Here wife. Let me see that," Kijamon said, pushing past Abeni and moving to take the stone from his wife's hand. But Abeni ignored the trinket, and looked closely at his mother's face. Among the family, she was the one most noted for her attempts to tease with wild stories. She would say, of course, that she did it only to teach her boys to question the world—to accept nothing without examination. But over the years, Abeni had reached a different conclusion.

Shaleen just liked to play jokes.

But there was no twinkle of delight in her eyes now as she handed the stone toy to his father, and that was wrong. Abeni had noticed that his mother always seemed a trifle more vibrant when she was in the midst of one of her teases. Yet at this moment, she seemed puzzled, more than anything. Confused, even.

Still unconvinced that this was not just an elaborate prank being played upon him, Abeni stepped past his parents to investigate the scene for himself. Could the Little Fish herself be playing a game?

The room was much unchanged from the way he remembered it. Mostly bare, with just a few very childish diversions set off to the sides. There was nowhere in the room for a girl of her size to be hiding, yet he swept every nook and corner with the keen eye of an experienced Way Finder. Clearly, the bed was still rumpled from having been slept in. *Actually* slept in. The blankets had not just been pushed around to give the seeming of it. Without question, the Little Fish had spent some goodly portion of the night rolling and turning within them. But the only other sign he could find of her was a small smudge of soil–Forest soil–on the ledge of the window. She had likely gone out that way, scraping her boot against the stone as she did. But that did not answer, why?

Abeni turned and left his long-ago bedroom, still confused, and not much wiser than when he had gone in. His parents had moved back to the forge, and when he rejoined them, Shaleen was pacing around it, her face pinched with concern. "She was safe here," his mother said. "She knew it. I could see it in her eyes. Why would she–?" Shaleen looked up anxiously as Abeni came in, but a quick shrug told her that he'd found nothing more, so she went back to her fretting.

Beyond her, Kijamon now held the black stone, turning it back and forth before his face, examining it closely. The crackle of energy that twitched around its surface lit his features with its flickering blue-white light.

"Abeni has never seen such a thing," he said, taking his place next to his father.

"Of course you have, Abeni," Shaleen snapped. "That toy has been in your room for years." It was a tone Abeni could rarely remember hearing from his mother, and his eyes sought hers.

"But never has it sparkled," Abeni countered. Shaleen sighed.

"I'm sorry, dear. I'm just worried for your friend. With Mabundi about to rule on the Ambassador's request, it does not look good that she has run away."

"It is no toy," Kijamon said. Shaleen looked at her husband in surprise, but just then the outside door opened.

"She is not with the Wagon," Zimu announced, as he came in and slumped into a chair. "Nor in the workshops, nor anywhere else within the Wind Forge. And she has not been seen upon the Trail of Sky either. It is as though she has fled the city itself."

"Where else can we look?" Shaleen asked. But nobody wanted to say what they were all thinking. Knowing nothing of this place, nor of the Djin ways, there was really only one place left to look. Running away in the middle of the night, with no guide, alone on the buttresses and ramparts of the mountain city, the Little Fish was not likely to have reached the road.

She was more likely to have reached her death. But none were ready to give that thought any time to breathe just yet.

"If not a toy, my husband, then what?"

Kijamon flicked a glance at his wife, and then leaned over, holding the rod up between them where she could see it. "See here? And here? These grooves are quite precise. Purpose built, or I'm a Gnomileshi muck sucker. It is a tool."

"A solid length of polished stone, with no moving parts, nor any features, save two small grooves?" Zimu asked. "To what purpose could such a tool be put?"

"Its intended one, to be sure, boy," Kijamon replied. "But I have a much better puzzle for you. After fists of years in this House, inert enough to have been mistaken for a common child's toy, why, after just one night in our strange girl's hand, has it suddenly revealed itself?"

All eyes around the forge looked at the old man, and his eyes twinkled as the sense of mysterious adventure swelled between them.

"Well? Don't you think we'd best find out?"

As one, the family's heads began to nod.

"So what is it?" Shaleen stood at her husband's work bench and poked at the crackling stone rod with a finger, rolling it across the rough stone surface. Arcs of blue fire danced as it rolled, flicking out to touch the tools and papers around it as it passed. Meanwhile, Kijamon rummaged about in a cupboard underneath. He'd called her into his studio moments ago–to tell her something, he'd said–but so far, he hadn't said much of anything.

"Hm? What's what?" Kijamon glanced up at her distractedly. "Oh, that. Well that's the question, isn't it. What is it?"

"Yes dear. I know. That's what I asked you. What is it?"

"Don't know. Don't know," he said. "I can only tell you some of the things it is not." But as he spoke, he turned back to his distracted searching and his voice wandered off with his attention.

In all the long years they had been together, Shaleen had learned many things about her eccentric husband, two of which were very important, yet entirely contradictory. On the outer side, she had learned that Kijamon did his best thinking when he chattered aloud about what he was thinking, but paradoxically, on the inner side, she had learned that the more deeply he thought about something, the more he tended toward silence, as he had done just now. So while it had always been his job to be the wise and brilliant Djin artisan, renowned throughout the Anvil and the Forest beyond, some days, she believed it was she who had the harder task: keeping the great man talking. But she would have it no other way, since it allowed them to spend so much time together. Hers was a job she loved, almost as deeply as she loved her husband. And she was good at it too.

"Okay then, Keej. Tell me, what is it not?" That earned her a quick smile, and her husband paused to glance at the cold polished rod on the bench, before returning to his search as he explained.

"Well, aside from a great many obvious things–a humming bird, an oak tree, and so forth–there are several very specific things it is not. It is not unliving. It is not dead. And it is not alive. Oho! Here it is!" Kijamon pulled an old scroll from the cupboard, then he closed the door with a hip as he straightened up.

"Really?" Shaleen said, as her husband unrolled his new prize. "I thought all things were in one of the three Natural Houses."

"So did I," Kijamon admitted. "Which makes it such a puzzle. Look here." He pointed to the silver tracings of old writing that skittered across the heavy paper. "Hakkar himself put it–"

Shaleen rolled her eyes. "Tell me that this is not the original Hakkar scroll," she said, shaking her head in disbelief. She already knew the answer.

Kijamon looked up from the words trailing under his fingertips and blinked at her in surprise. "What? Of course it is."

"And you've kept it here? Lost in your cupboard like a list of tasks for the cleaning boy?"

"Not lost, dear. Just... handy." Kijamon smiled mischievously at her. It was an old quibble. Yes, such documents were priceless treasures of Djin heritage, and as such should be carefully preserved and protected, she would say. But knowledge is meant to be used, he would reply. By doers. Not horded in disuse today so that its mouldering shell might one day settle a dispute between palsied old tongue waggers. Was the ink silvered or gilded? Was the paper woven or pressed? That was not knowledge worth knowing, but it is what the Keepers of History would have all knowledge reduced to. Yes. It was an old quibble, and one Shaleen knew better than to reopen now.

"So what does Bosuke have in his Hall, if you have the Hakkar here?"

"Um, a clever duplication," Kijamon said, but he could already see the rebuke rising in her eyes. "Stay your glare, my wife. It is a wondrous accommodation. I keep the Hakkar here, in its original form, where I can examine the faded scratchings, see the tremble of his hand—all as it should be, vibrant and alive. And old Bosuke has a much cleaner, tidier copy. Well, Wijen now. But all the better. What he has is much better suited to his failing eyes, and much more likely to survive the next eon than this old thing." He patted the scroll laid open in front of him with affection. "Joy for everyone."

Shaleen looked levelly at her husband, then she sighed. It was useless to argue, and worse, it might distract him from his progress. "You were saying about the Hakkar?" She nodded toward the scroll where his finger was still poised, waiting to make his point.

"Yes, here," he said, tapping the spider-scrawl of ink in a place where it had faded. "Here, where he talks of the nature of things... *And these shall be the Houses, each thing unto one House and each House unto itself: The House of Shezem, the House of Nazem, the House of Mern.*"

"What of it?" Shaleen said. "Every child learns the three Houses in the nursery."

"Well, that's just my point," Kijamon said, tapping the page in agitation. "He does not say 'three' and he does not say 'and.' "

Shaleen squinted at the page under her husband's tapping finger, but if there was any significance hiding in the traces of ink below, she couldn't see it. She looked at him curiously.

"Tell me the three Houses," he said.

"You just said them yourself," she replied. "The House of Shezem, the House of Nazem, and the House of Mern."

"Exactly!" Kijamon said, bouncing on his toes like an excited apprentice. "You said 'and,' – 'and the House of Mern' – but Hakkar does not. He most definitely does not! And look, see here?" He moved his finger and pointed at the period ending the line. "Look at the stop. I think it once had a tail, but it has fallen off, or been scratched away. And why leave such a long gap before continuing? There is room there easily for more words."

"More words? Keej, I don't understand. What are you talking about?"

Kijamon snatched up the black rod as it began to roll back across the scroll, and the dance of its light played around his fingers. "The Three Houses of Things are a lie," he said. "Hakkar did not give us three Houses–he gave us four–but the scroll has been altered! And this," he said, using the rod to point at the gap in the writing, "is of the fourth House."

"The fourth house? But what is left, my husband? What is there after Shezem, Nazem and Mern? There is unliving, there is living, and there is dead. What else remains?"

Kijamon's eyes glittered like a sweep of midnight stars. "Not what remains," he said. "Ask instead what came before."

Shaleen swatted at her husband's arm. "Don't play a drama for me, Keej. Tell me. What is it?"

"The House of Stegma," he said. "The House of Music."

"Music?" Shaleen stared at her husband in confusion. "How can it be made from music? Music is a sound. It is insubstantial, but your relic is not. I have held its weight in my own hand. It was cold and heavy. Solid. Surely it is some type of stone. Perhaps a type you do not know?"

Kijamon pushed himself back from the bench and began to pace around the room. "Even if there were such a rock–unknown to me or to any other Djin master–still that rock would be known to the test of Shezem. Hakkar doesn't just give us the Houses, you know. He also gives us a way to test each thing, to determine its affinity. They are in fact the last thing told upon the scroll, but curiously, the scroll ends after the test for House Mern, as if the stink of rot wasn't proof enough of death. Whatever followed has been torn away, and the spindle rebound to the raw end."

"The scroll has been altered in its length, as well?"

"It has," Kijamon said. Having crossed the room, he reached out to touch the comforting firmness of his forge and then turned to pace back the way he had come. It was an old habit, pacing from forge to wall and back again, touching each at every turn. "But whoever has removed this knowledge from us could not hide it completely. Even without a test for Music, it is but an exercise of logic to confirm it. There are four Houses and three tests. Since the relic does not answer any of them, it must be of the last remaining category. House Stegma."

"Unless there are five Houses," Shaleen said. Kijamon shook his head, reaching out to tap the bench with a finger and then turned back toward the wall.

"I have thought this as well," he said. "But the space in the scroll where mention of the Stegma has been removed... The gap is too short. There is no space for mention of yet another House. If there is a fifth, Hakkar did not know of it."

"But still, Kijamon, music? As a solid thing? A thing that can be held in the hand? How is that–" Kijamon turned to look his wife in the eye, and then he spoke the words that had ever preceded the greatest of his investigations.

"I do not know," he said. "But I mean to."

He's getting old. The thought struck her like an unexpected storm, buffeting her where she stood. The bowl trembled in her hand. Thankfully, Kijamon was too tired to have even noticed. Shaleen took only a moment to steady herself before she set the food on the table. Then, on a sudden whim, she moved to take a seat at his side. Not across from him, as was their habit, but beside him. Had those creases always been there, under his eyes and around his mouth? Or had they appeared only lately? The work was wearing on him. No, the work delighted him. It was the frustration that weighed so heavily on the flesh of his face. Her husband was lost somewhere, deep in the tangled path of his thoughts, so she took his hand in hers and simply held it.

"You'll figure it out, Keej. You always do." Tired, sunken eyes turned to her slowly, but for a time, she saw no recognition in them. After a long, quiet moment, gazing into the empty house of her husband's face, suddenly he returned home, and the smile that lit him was bright and genuine.

"Shaleen," he said, squeezing her hand. "What's that? Oh. Yes, yes, I'll unlock it. I'm sure of it. Any luck today?"

How like him to set his own troubles aside and ask after her own, but even there, she could not give him any peace. Every hour, it seemed, since that brief contact on the Leap, she had returned to that place of stillness within herself and quested outward, hoping each time to touch the mind of her distant son once more. But still there was nothing. She shook her head, and Kijamon nodded in silent understanding. They were both worried. Not just about Sarqi, but about all their children. And Tayna as well. They could see how her sudden disappearance drained the humor from their youngest, and even Zimu had seemed more somber lately. How had one young Wasketchin girl woven herself so deeply into the threads of the family, and so quickly?

"Well, worry cracks no rocks," Kijamon said. It was one of his favorite sayings—a defense against the brooding nature that sometimes threatened to consume him. Although, he'd been saying it far too often in recent days for Shaleen's liking.

The table they sat at was the small one she'd had brought down to the Wagon Hall. That was the rule between them. He was allowed to work anywhere he liked at all, so long as she was allowed to set a table near him. She'd told him it was so that they could still take their meals together, as husband and wife should. But in truth, she knew he resented having to take any time away from his work, and that if not for her bringing it to him, and then sitting with him while he ate, he would probably not eat at all. Especially now, when the lure of new knowings hung in the mist before his eyes.

Kijamon had insisted on moving his research out of their home level immediately after his discovery in the Hakkar. They knew so little of this Stegma magic, he'd said. It could easily prove to be wild when he finally figured out how to poke and twist at its tail. What if it proved to be a fearsome beast and he unleashed it in the great stone vessel that hung precariously above the entire community? The fact that he could imagine their great soaring home, with its massive arches and supports, carved from the solid flanks of the mountain in one continuous mass, as a danger to those below... Well, that thought alone spoke volumes about the forces he believed he might now be wrestling with. Or trying to.

"The bones yielded nothing?" she asked. At first, Kijamon had experimented with the usual Djin incantations, the magics of oath bonds, the words of metal and of rock, but found nothing. He had tested it with a variety of animals and plants, and even asked a Wasketchin artist to assist him for a time, attempting to tap into the rod with the magics of life and wonder, but all to no avail. Then he had tried a Gnome apprentice and their strange death magics—carcases, skins, horn, and even bone. Again to no result.

"I fear it may be triggered by the powers of the Other Dragon," he said. The Other Dragon. Grimorl. Few Djin would speak the actual name aloud, but even a replacement name had power if you spoke it too freely. Call him what you would, the being it signified was the same.

"Truly?" Shaleen said, her tone pitched with wonder. "Then that would mean..."

Kijamon nodded. "It would mean that we are stuck. And since we cannot afford to be stuck, it cannot be so."

Shaleen smiled. "So if it does not draw from our Houses, or from his, what remains?"

Kijamon shrugged. "The music, perhaps? Or perhaps nothing. I had hoped not to risk the music, but perhaps I must."

Shaleen showed him her best puzzled look. "I don't understand. Why have you not tried it already? You say it is of the House of Stegma, whatever that might mean, but you have not given it any vim of its House?"

Her husband shook his head. "The House of its Substance is not the same as the House of its Affinity. You know this. We Djin are *of* the House of Living Things. Nazem. Yet our *affinity* is for the House of Shezem, the Unliving. Even when the vim was rich in the world, no Djin could draw from any other House."

Shaleen nodded. "And the Wasketchin, and the Gnomes?"

"They too are of the Living, of course, but only the Wasketchin affine to that House, the Gnomes affine to Mern."

"And since you have sought affinity for this device of yours from all three of these Houses..."

"Without success. Yes. Then I must now test its affinity to its own House. And this is what worries me."

"How so?"

Instead of answering her, Kijamon asked an unexpected question. "Of all the stories from old, of the great heroes and the mighty magics, which of them would you deem the greatest? The most powerful?"

Her husband sometimes took these unexpected branchings in his speech, and Shaleen was quite practiced in following after him, although it had taken her many years to suppress the frustrations such darting had once embroiled in her, and to cultivate an air of acceptance instead.

"I suppose Xolile," she said, in answer to his question. "A mighty Queen who forged the first Houses from among the clans. She was always my favorite."

Kijamon smiled at her. "Yes, but I'm speaking of the vim now. Which of the hero tales speak of the mightiest magics?"

"Oh. Well that's easy. Notawhey, who is said to have flung the Judgment above the sky, with nothing but a sparrow for a helper."

"Do any others come to mind?"

"What are you striding toward, Keej?" But her husband just gazed at her, waiting. "Okay. Um, Perdine, perhaps? Wasn't she the one who made the rivers run backward for a span of three days? And, let me think... Oh yes. Ushua and his Vanishing Village. But what of them?"

"I agree," Kijamon said. "Those are the greatest of magics from all the tales we know. Do you not see the obvious? What do each of these three mightiest weavers of charm share with each other?"

"I do not know," she said. "They were all Wasketchin, but–"

"Exactly!" her husband said. "All of the greatest magics were uttered by beings *of* the Nazem, drawing *from* the Nazem."

"So?"

"And so, my wife, I had hoped to temper the magics of this device as I learn its uses. If it had taken from one of the other Houses, I thought its effects might be less potent, but now I have no choice. No paths remain but the only path there ever truly was. It seems I must give it what it craves, and I fear its craving may be great."

And then Shaleen understood. The rod would need music to release its full power and so her husband had been striving these long days to find anything else that could awaken a hint of its true purpose, because he feared that if he gave it a taste of what it wanted, that strange, eldritch device might not be satisfied with a mere taste. It might take more, gorging itself to its fill from the vessel that supplied its vim.

And she herself was the musician of the family.

chapter 31

A gust of wind woke her. It whipped down the narrow channel she lay in, swirling the space full of rock dust and sand that pelted her into consciousness. They had spent the night in the relative safety of this stone slot, far from any open chasms or sudden drops, but it was a bit too claustrophobic for Tayna's liking. Two tall rock walls faced each other, only an arms length apart. It was a crack in the mountain stone, and a short-cut from the front face to the back of the shoulder they had been climbing. Night had found them even more quickly than Tayna had expected, and by the time they'd reached its safe embrace, she had been too tried for anything but sleep, and had dropped to the ground in exhaustion. But now it was morning, and she stood up stiffly to begin stretching out the night's cramps.

"So, we still need to have that discu–" Tayna looked around.

Abeni was gone.

Tayna let her arms drop to her sides as she turned a slow circle, but there was no sign of him.

"Abeni!"

The answering silence was almost spooky. Tayna walked back to the front face of the defile and looked down. There were no Djin of any kind climbing below. She placed a hand on the rock to steady herself and then craned around to look up. But that face too was entirely Djin-free. Big Whale?

There was no camp to break, so when Tayna reached the spot where she'd slept, she just kept going, working her way further into the crack, toward the rear face. Maybe he'd gone in search of better food. But she found no sign of him anywhere along the zigs and zags of the narrow track, and finally she reached the other side. Still with no indication of where her guide had disappeared to.

"Oh," she said, as she emerged out of the dark defile to stand in the brilliant morning light. She was at the top of a spill of rocks and gravel that ran down a narrow V-shaped gully before spilling out into a wider notch. A wider hollow with a scrubby sort of vegetation scattered around the edges. Drab and gray, the low shrubs looked as though the rock itself had seeped into their leaves and branches and was in the process of turning them to stone. Not a lush mountain glade by any measure, but it was more life than she'd seen anywhere else on the mountain since leaving the Wind Forge, and it had a simple, rugged tenacity that made her feel kind of proud of it, actually. Just for managing to exist here at all.

Again she let her eyes roam the slopes, turning to peer carefully up the slope above her as well, but there wasn't so much as a shadow or a smudge of dirt to tell her where Abeni might have gone.

Below her, on the more level spill of gravel at the bottom of the notch, a pile of sticks and branches was nestled back against the mountain, where the slope of stone met the scattered rocks and pebbles. There was a dark hole at the front of the stick pile. Not quite a door, but possible an entrance to a hollow space inside.

"So it was a test," she muttered. "He wanted to see how long it would take me to find him." Tayna hated tests. Especially pointless ones. It made sense in a classroom, maybe. But here? This was stupid.

"I'm not playing, you big ape!" she called out, as she began to pick her way down the gravel slope. "Get out here and stop hiding. We have some serious–" But she was interrupted by a scream.

The scream of a terrified child.

The sound echoed around her, bouncing from notch wall to cliff face, from mountain slope to gravel slope. It was everywhere around her. But it was loudest from below. It seemed to be coming from the stick hut.

Without even thinking, Tayna jumped down the scree, and instead of stepping carefully, she was now sliding–surfing almost–on the clatter of gravel and stone that shimmered down the notch ahead of her.

"I'm coming!" she yelled. With arms pinwheeling for balance, Tayna managed to keep to her feet, but she had no idea what problem she was going to find when she got there. She needed backup.

"Abeni!" she hollered, hoping to get him to show himself, wherever he was hiding, now that there was a serious crisis unfolding. But a quick glance revealed no dark Djin smile emerging from the rocks around her.

Again the child cried. A girl, by the sound. Young. And absolutely petrified by something. It was a sound that tore through Tayna's defenses and reminded her of bad things. Bad memories. Old and long forgotten memories, and onward she plunged, trying to will gravity to hurry her along.

Her wave of rock reached the bottom of the little valley, and Tayna leaped clear. Then she turned and ran toward the stick hut. "Hold on!" she called. "I'm coming!"

But just then a figure emerged from the dark interior of the hut and Tayna's heart lurched into her mouth.

It was a smooth, black figure who stepped calmly from within and turned to look at her. His face was completely featureless, save for two small black horns on either side. The creature from her dream. The one who had held her on the mountain. With Angiron.

And in his arms, another child kicked and screamed against his vice-like grip.

Tayna felt all her fury drain from her, and in its place, terror flooded in. That same helpless terror that had once filled her, as it now filled this new girl in his arms. The smooth, black face twisted into a mocking grin, as though sensing her thoughts. Her paralysis. And then he turned and began to climb the rock face, while the little girl struggled and screamed over his shoulder.

"Abeni!" Tayna screamed, wrenching herself back into motion and wheeling around to search the rocks. This was no game or stupid Djin test. This was an emergency. "Abeni! Help!"

But there was no reply. And above her, the jet-black kiddy napper from her nightmares climbed smoothly away up the mountain face.

"Dammit, not again!" Tayna cursed. And with a sudden blast of fury driving her forward, she ran to the rock face and began to climb after him.

chapter 32

They sat on the ledge that, as boys, they had imagined gave them dominion over all of the city below. Situated a little ways above their family home, at the crest of the ridge into which it had been carved, this was the ledge that Kijamon had made for himself in that very first week of his labors. It had served as his kitchen, his workshop, and his sleeping pad for five years, until the very last cube of his great construction had been removed and his wonderwork polished to a high gleam, ready for a young man and his new wife to take up residence. Abeni had come here, at his brother's urging, so that they might talk in private. There was something bothering the Mizar of House Kijamon, and for some reason, he did not wish their parents to hear them speaking of it.

Below them now, the scurrying of people across the Trail of Sky, and even farther below, in the Mother's Garden, was no different than on any other day. But on this day, those movements seemed heavier. More ominous. As if every step and stride was filled with portent.

Or perhaps it was the day itself that hung heavy.

"He is no king," Zimu said. "No leader of Djin. He leads as a carrot might do, or this flake of stone." Abeni watched his brother pluck a splinter of the mountain from the ledge and squeeze it between his massive fingers, as though throttling the King in effigy.

"What does he do but sit still and listen?" Zimu muttered. "He hears all. But what does he say? Nothing. What does he do? Nothing. He leads nowhere. And that, even a rock could accomplish."

Abeni sat quietly through his brother's tirade. In all of his life, he could not remember a time when he had seen Zimu so angered. Perhaps when they had been boys, but certainly not since Zimu had come of age and taken the role of Mizar. Always, this had been the placid brother. Yet now, here he was, returned from only a brief sitting of the Court, and he could scarce contain his spit and temper over what had transpired.

"But surely Mabundi must listen and consider carefully," Abeni suggested. "Perhaps he will take action soon."

"Fah!" Zimu spat. "Today, the Gnome did not appear at Court, and what did Mabundi do? He did not pronounce any great decision. He did not continue to hear the complaints of those who stand outside his Hall waiting for the King's Wisdom. Instead, he Stilled the Court and sent all attendants out in search of the missing Gnome."

"Is it not proper for the King of All Djin to wish to know the thoughts of his neighbors?" If there was one aspect of Djin life that seemed foreign to Abeni, it was the undecipherable etiquettes and maneuverings of the Anvil Seat. Normally, he rejoiced that such concerns were rightly Zimu's, but today he felt only sympathy for his troubled brother.

"To hear? Yes," Zimu spat. "But to Still all talk until he can be found? That is not 'hearing.' That is 'toadying.' One can smell the rust stains gnawing upon the Seat already. And what of hearing *both* neighbors? Why does he bend himself to one while neglecting to even invite the other?"

"Perhaps Mabundi fears to offend the Gnome King," Abeni said, but Zimu shook him off.

"No. It is more. Tongues stretch out from the Throat to lick the Anvil Seat," Zimu grumbled, "and Mabundi King sees only these attentions. He has closed his eyes to his duty."

Even Abeni knew what that meant, and it filled him with cold shock. "Zimu would say this to him? Say to all Djin that Mabundi is oathblinded?"

Zimu nodded then and Abeni could feel the weight of his brother's gaze turn upon him. "It is why I have asked you to sit with me, Binto."

Abeni smiled. It was the name his brothers had called him when he was little. And for Zimu to remind him of it now meant that he was going to ask Abeni for a great favor. A favor that could only be asked between steadfast brothers.

Zimu lowered his voice. "I have learned of a way by which what must be done might be done," he said. "But it is best that Mother and Father be absent. So that they can rightly claim no foreknowledge of what I intend."

Abeni's eyes went wide. "But surely the Mizar would not bind the House without their knowledge!"

Zimu smiled. "What I intend will not bind our House, Binto. Nor bring disgrace to any, save myself, if I fail."

"But what then? What thing will Zimu do?"

"If I told you, you would not help me," Zimu said. "But it must be done. I ask you to trust that I will not endanger the House. But know also that if I am successful, a great many things will change. For the better."

Abeni could not remember Zimu having ever asked him for a favor. Not once. But if there was something that Warding the Wagon together had taught him, it was that Zimu always knew what he was doing. This was the brother who would never speak a word that he had not considered through a hundred different eyes. So different from Sarqi, who rarely even used his own before giving tongue to thought. In some ways, that bond between them–that of Warders– was even deeper than the blood they shared as brothers.

"Abeni will do as you ask," he said. "Now Zimu must say. What does the Way Maker wish Abeni to do?"

So Zimu told him.

———————

Zimu stood in the Hall of Honor, keeping himself near the back, and watched as Mabundi spoke the King's mind. The search for Quishek had been intense, but brief. And when the Gnome could not be found, the pressure of a hundred supplicants waiting outside the Hall of Wind to seek the King's Wisdom outweighed any preference Mabundi might have had for keeping the Court Stilled. So reluctantly, he had agreed to resume hearing grievances.

For as long as the Dragon's Peace had prevailed, most petitions brought forward would have been dealt with by the Wisetongues, representatives of the King, who knew the law and the King's mind, and could speak in his name on lesser matters. Such a one would investigate the facts of a grievance, interview any who might shed light upon it, and then render a wise and just solution.

But since the collapse of the Oath, the Wisetongues had been called upon to do more than simply ask questions and render judgments. They were now having to judge the truth of the words spoken by those in dispute, as well. This extra burden had created chaos and delays all across the Anvil. More and more Djin were learning that they could give accounts that were... fanciful, in an effort to sway the judgment. And they were doing so. This led to greater animosities between those in dispute, more devious attempts at obscuring the facts, and ultimately, more and more disagreements were now escalating, until they reached here, as an appeal brought before the King himself.

Unlike the Wasketchin and Gnomileshi courts, the Djin court had no fixed location. The Djin viewed their King as a servant of the people, and saw no reason why they should go to him for justice. So the King went to them. Every few days, the King would pick up and move his people and the great bronze Anvil Seat to another settlement, where he would set about renewing old acquaintances, strengthening ties, and dispensing whatever justice might be demanded of him while he was in residence. Or at least, that had been the practice before Mabundi had risen to the crown.

King Jallafa before him had presided over his honor court once each week, or sometimes twice, every time in a different enclave. This had been Jallafa's way of ensuring that he stayed in constant contact with his folk, and that they had constant reminder of the service he did them. It also kept his court constantly on the move, placing no strenuous burden of entertainment on any one holding.

Mabundi however, had no such ambitions, and since the collapse of the Dragon's Peace, the new King had been forced to hold his court with greater and greater frequency, to the point where he was now presiding almost every day, and the line of people waiting to lay their grievances in his lap never stood empty.

As was customary, Mabundi sat at the head of the room, trying hard to fill the mighty Anvil Seat while he listened patiently to yet another disagreement about who had said what to whom, and when. But Zimu had not come to hear the petty grievances.

He had come to make final judgment upon the King.

Not in hatred, nor even ill will. Mabundi had been a wise and patient teacher once. Before his ascension. He had even taught Zimu for a time, many years ago. Perhaps, in a more peaceful time, the teacher might have made a good king. Despite his many frustrations, Zimu could not help but be impressed by the compassion Mabundi brought to each case that came before him, no matter how trivial. Even as Mabundi rooted out a falsehood, or found conflict between the facts of some account, still he did so with a patient, knowing smile, like a favored uncle, treating each Djin who stood before him with honor. It was the mark of a good teacher.

But did it serve a king? Could the man not see that by submerging himself in the small disputes that rasped between every man, woman and child on the Anvil, he debased the very crown itself? Overseeing the minutiae of an entire People may have given him a sense of justice being done, but it also drained him of his capacity to engage in the larger matters before the Crown. Why did he not instruct the Wisetongues to deal with these petty complaints, as they had in the past? A king should not have to speak his mind on whether twenty bushels of corn was sufficient compensation for an overturned wagon load of pottery. Zimu sighed as the King pronounced that very decision.

"He coddles his people," Zimu said. He had not meant it as a compliment, but the old Djin woman beside him nodded.

"Such a patient man," she said. "He was always so good with the children. So understanding."

Zimu smiled back at her, but inside he seethed. Is that all we ask of our King? That he treat with us as though we were babes, still learning our letters? He might have said something too, but the King's aide called for the next case, and a frail Wasketchin man separated from a small group huddled against the side wall and shuffled forward.

"Dendril of the Wasketchin, and his folk, beg sanctuary from the King of the Djin," the aide read from the schedule of disputes etched on his tablet.

Zimu perked himself up. At last, a topic fit for the King's justice. Zimu watched as Dendril of the Wasketchin shuffled forward nervously. He kept looking back over his shoulder at the others of his group still clutching to each other behind him. They looked exhausted and frail, as though they had run all the way up the Anvil from the Forest below, and had set out on their journey with no warning, nor any time to prepare. Which very likely had been the case.

"You are Dendril?" Mabundi asked, when the man had come to a stop and looked up at the Djin throne.

"I am, sir."

"And this is your family?"

Dendril shook his head. "Just the one, sir. Johal there, that's my boy." A young boy of eight or nine years ducked further back out of sight behind one of the girls. "Then there's Di'reah and her brother,

Enger," he said, indicating two scared adults who clung closely to one another, "and the tall girl is Ve'ali. Those others found each other on the trail, before Johal and I met 'em. Then we all made the climb together."

"And you seek my protection?" The man nodded his head, as Queen Yoliq bent down from where she stood beside the throne, and whispered something to her husband. Mabundi listened for a moment, and then nodded before turning his attention back to the man standing before him. "From what?" Mabundi asked.

The man just gaped at him for a moment.

"Well, er, from the Gnomes, Mabundi King." The man's eyes flicked nervously toward a Gnome who stood there. Some functionary of the missing Ambassador.

The King looked at Dendril patiently, but Zimu noted that his gaze, too, flicked repeatedly to the Gnome, as though he was weighing out what even this lowly Gnome might think.

To one side, Zimu noticed a movement and looked toward the door. Abeni stood there facing him, and seeing that Zimu had noticed him, he bowed once, pressing the heels of his hands together and touching them to his forehead. So Binto had succeeded. Shaleen and Kijamon would be distracted for at least a day. Zimu nodded once to his younger brother and then watched as he slipped away, knowing that within moments, Abeni would be on the trail down from the city, leading his mission to the scattered Wasketchin below the Anvil. And with Sarqi away as well, that left Zimu completely free to do what must be done. He turned his attention back to the proceedings of the Court before him.

"You know that you are already free to stay upon the Anvil, do you not?" Mabundi asked the Wasketchin man. "The Djin are not at war. Any who wish to come here may do so. Why do you feel you need my protection above that? Do you not trust the Djin?"

Clearly, Dendril had not expected the question, and he looked back at his fellows several times. "B-beg your pardon, Mabundi King. We trust the Djin just fine. It's the Gnomes we don't. They've been taking folks off the trails and all, down by the Skirts. What's to stop—"

Mabundi's face darkened and he held up a hand to halt the man, then he twisted toward the Gnome aide. "Is this true? Have your Hordesmen been taking prisoners from Djin lands?"

The Gnome spent an oily smile and bowed in deference to the

King. "Not, uh, to my knowing, Mabundi King. Perhaps the man is mistaken." Dendril swallowed hard, but he shook his head firmly.

"We saw what we saw," he said, glancing again at his fellow travelers for support. They nodded timid confirmation, so he continued.

"Saw it twice," he said. "Once down below us, and the other time was across a gap, on the far slope. But both times we saw honest Wasketchin folks dragging themselves up the path, just as we were doing, only then they just sort of stopped still for bit, until a few Gnomes come crawling out from behind rocks and the like. Tied a rope around 'em and led 'em back down. Never did see either group again."

"Preposterous," the Gnome said. "The Horde has very precise instructions. No prisoners are to be taken from the mountain. He is either lying or the hardships of the trail have clouded his memory. It did not happen as he says. It could not have." The other Wasketchin along the side wall raised their voices in defiance, but Dendril just stood there, glaring flame at the Gnome.

This, at least, would be an easy decision, Zimu thought. And he was happy that he could allow Mabundi one last gracious decree before he himself did what he had come to do. But when the King spoke, Zimu felt it like a slap.

"Asylum is denied," Mabundi said, and the entire Court fell into a startled silence.

"I am presented with two conflicting reports," Mabundi said. "One says that the Gnomes have taken prisoners upon the Anvil, the other says they have not. There is no way to prove either tale, so I must hold both as unproven." Each word was another hammer blow in Zimu's heart. Such a simple decision. It would have cost nothing to be gracious, and gained everything. Everything except the pleasure of one Gnome. And perhaps of his various puppet masters. Even the King's compassion seemed now to have fled him.

Again the King's gaze flicked nervously to the Gnome, who stood preening with delight at the decision. And in that glance, in the timid dipping of the King's eyes before he could look once more at the Wasketchin man before him, Zimu saw truth.

Mabundi was not just weak. Or deluded. He was terrified of the Gnomes. But still the fool pressed on, trying to explain his faulty reasoning to a stunned and disbelieving crowd. As if a king must explain his decisions.

"So in the matter of asylum, I have no basis to believe that Dendril and his folk are in peril. And the Djin Crown will not take sides in a foreign dispute. We remain neutral in this contest, and I will not surrender that neutrality now, to offer unneeded aid to a man who is under no threat. Asylum denied. You may stay, if you wish, although I will grant you and your people sufficient food and supplies to return home if you would prefer."

Zimu fought to contain his shock. With every breath, Mabundi only shouted louder of his own inability to lead. To deny comfort to a friend in need? To insult him with empty solace? This was not the Djin way. This was the behavior of a craven gull! Zimu could feel rage blossoming within his chest, its petals smoking around his heart like paper among embers. Rage at a king who could not see the travesty of his reign. And rage at himself, for having seen the truth and having stayed his his hand so long. He could feel his hands shaking at his sides, as the muscles of his arms tried to clench the air within his fists to diamonds.

"Return home?" the Wasketchin said, his mouth hanging open in disbelief. "Where would that be, my Lord? My home has always been wherever my family could be found, but Johal is here and they have taken my wife from us. Do you bid me follow her into the Throat to make our new home? Shall I drag Johal there as well, to join us?"

Mabundi's brow wrinkled in irritation. "You must decide for yourself where to make your ho–"

"ENOUGH!"

That single word rang through the Hall like a clap of thunder, and the Court fell into utter silence. Zimu strode forward through them, oblivious to their gaping stares. Fury now blazed within him, fueling his every step. No one dared breathe and all eyes were fixed upon him as he crossed the floor to stand glaring down at the King. But the eyes looking back at him were glazed with fear and indecision. They were the eyes of a craven. Zimu raised his fist high above his head, watching in distaste as Mabundi flinched back, deeper into the Anvil Seat, the very image of cowardice upon the throne. With a bellow of fury, Zimu drove his fist down in a mighty blow, crumpling the left arm of the throne like tin, and driving it half way to the floor.

"I am Zimu!" he declared. "First son of Kijamon!" His voice was deep and dark and it crackled with a dangerous anger. "I am eldest son, Mizar of an acknowledged House of the Royal Court, and by the ancient laws, I claim the right of Challenge." Then he withdrew his hand, allowing all to see the silver spike that now jutted up from the wreckage of the royal arm rest.

"There is my tooth, Mabundi King! Placed there by my own hand. I give you the fullness of one day to pluck it by the power of *your* own hand, and then drive it into my chest." Zimu ripped his vest open to reveal the massive target which he now offered to the King. Then he leaned in close and lowered his voice to a rumble that vibrated the very metalwork of the throne itself, adding a shimmering echo to his final words.

"And if within this time you cannot defend your throne, then I will take back my tooth, and with it, I shall cut your reign from the memory of our people and claim your empty throne for the honor of all Djin."

Having issued his challenge, Zimu stepped past the throne, past its quaking King with his wide, staring eyes, and past the pale Queen who stood beside him. Then he placed his back against the wall and crossed his arms, wrist over wrist, against his chest to wait. With that, the oath was sealed, and a pair of iron bands appeared around each of Zimu's wrists, fused together where they touched, binding his arms tightly in an indefensible position. And so they would remain, until the day for Mabundi's reply had passed.

The Challenge of the Mizar's Tooth had begun.

chapter 33

"Are you sure this is the right way, Keej? Abeni said it was angled up off the bigger cavern. This is down." Kijamon glanced at her with his familiar twinkle.

"I am not even sure that cavern was the one he described. Shall we see if we can find it anyway?"

Shaleen sighed. Everything was an adventure to the men of House Kijamon. Especially to Kijamon himself. She waved her arm forward.

"I follow where you lead, my husband."

"As I lead where you direct, my wife."

This time Shaleen smiled. After all these years, the words of their binding ritual still had the power to delight her. And they were particularly apt words too, because they'd been walking and hunting for this blasted cavern of Abeni's for almost an entire night, and she was no longer certain whether *either* of them knew where they were going.

"If we haven't found it soon, we're just going to have to go back," Shaleen said. But her husband shook his head.

"No, Abeni was quite right," he said, waving the crackling rod of black stone in the air above his head. "We do not know its power, nor of the magics it might unleash, and my toes tell me it is important that we find out."

Kijamon and his silly toes. Why was it always his toes that told him? He'd never been able to explain that part. Why not his armpit? Or his lower teeth? Now there was a question for a master thinker–

"Ah, here it is."

The cavern was just as Abeni had said it would be, large enough to walk around in, but small enough to be strong and secure. But most of all, it was deep. Many hundredstrides below the city. Down where any calamities that might befall them would not shatter the stones of their neighbors' homes, or slice the great Wind Forge from its moorings and drop it on the city below.

It was also, most definitely, *down* from the larger cavern. Shaleen made a mental note to discuss that little error with her son when she saw him next. It had cost them almost half a day of wandering and searching through these dark, wet tunnels and chasms at the root of the Anvil.

"More light please, my dear." Kijamon was bustling about the small chamber, pushing the rod into corners and holding it up in the air, watching the walls with keen fascination as they responded to its light. Shaleen raised her own coverlight above her head and moved closer.

"Yes, this will do nicely," he said. "See here? The way the crystal of the wall turns milky in the brightness? It resists the light, as it will many other energies. Yes, Abeni has led us to *just* the spot." Shaleen wasn't so sure "led" was the correct word, but she held her tongue.

It took only a moment for Kijamon to complete his survey of the space and find everything to his satisfaction. Then he moved to the center of the room and turned to face her, holding the strange black rod out in front of him. She recognized the signs with a smile. Time to put on a show.

"When does a sound cease to be just a noise, and start to become music?" Kijamon asked.

Shaleen frowned. It was a question that lesser artists sometimes teased at, but to her, such questing had always been meaningless. Why not ask when darkness becomes light? Or when sickness becomes health? The point at which they became such would still be weak–poor light and poor health–so what matter? Would any person care to actually listen to a music so unmusical as to hover on the edge of noise? But this was Kijamon's way of organizing his thoughts when they were unfocused, so she did her best.

"I suppose when it becomes beautifu–" Shaleen paused. "No. When it presents a pattern," she said, this time with a greater measure of certainty.

"Hmm," Kijamon replied. "Will any pattern do?"

Shaleen shifted uncomfortably from one foot to the other. She didn't like these kinds of questions at all. They reduced her art to something... countable. And that robbed it of its essential spirit.

"Yes, I suppose any pattern... Keej, what are you–"

"Follow where I lead, dear. I mean to give this little curiosity only the slightest taste of what it wants. Just one taste, and nothing more. And to do so, I must know what 'smallest' is."

Shaleen knew exactly what he feared—what "something more" might mean. It was sweet to know that he still worried about her safety, no less today than on the day they'd first pledged.

"Alright," she said. "I suppose you're right."

They were standing together in the center of the little cave—as far from the living as they could be, deep in the embrace of protective stone. But not to protect *them*. Such a simple, innocent looking thing, but from all these precautions, one might think it held the very power of the sun. She hoped not, of course. Shaleen loved her husband fiercely, but this was too small an oven to be baked in with him. Still, she was the musician of the family, so this job was rightly hers, and it was fitting that if they should perish here, it would come from working together.

Shaleen straightened herself up and began to focus on her breathing. Even if she was to sing the song of their death, it would be sung properly.

At first she had thought she might bring her bells to play, but in the end, they had opted for the simplest instrument they could conceive. Her voice. When he was ready, she would sing for him. For it. And then they would see what they would see.

As they had descended the Trail of Sky, he had noticed a brightening of the sparks that played along its surface, and the purple-blue crackle had grown ever brighter as they'd continued their way down into the caverns. Now Kijamon was almost radiant in its purple-blue light. He looked so majestic, standing there, waiting. Shaleen shuddered. She suddenly realized that she didn't trust this little thing. This object that had lain dormant, sleeping, in the bed chamber of her children for so many years. The quiet crackle of its gleaming. The faint smell of burned metals. Despite its simple, visual beauty, was it actually an ugly thing? A wrong thing? Fear began to gnaw at the back of her mind.

Kijamon raised the rod a trifle, into what he judged to be the very center of the chamber. Then he took a deep breath and nodded to her.

"Simply now," he said. "A scale. Three notes should do. Nothing more for now. And slowly, if you would. Let's give ourselves time to stop if need be."

Shaleen looked at him. He was nervous. Shattered crystals, they were both nervous. She gave him what she hoped was a reassuring smile, and then drew in her air, letting the cavity of her lungs fill with the roundness of it.

"Shaaa-a-a-a-ah," she sang, letting the note rise slowly to fill the cavern. And then, while that note still reverberated, she offered another, higher tone to blend with it. "Draaa-a-a-a-ah," she sang, letting this note harmonize with her own echo. And then a third, completing the full clutch, "Zo-o-o-o-oh!"

The sound was haunting, beautiful, and it echoed throughout the chamber like a chorus of ancestors, filling the room with its power.

With the third tone added to the previous two, the rod had begun to shake, and Kijamon's eyes danced with the excitement of seeing a new thing. It shook so badly that it fell from his hands and dropped to the floor where it continued to rattle and shake.

And then it began to turn.

Slowly at first, and then faster, and faster again, until it spun itself up on end and began to whirl in a blinding blur of sparks and speed. The last tones of her song faded into silence, but still the rod spun faster and faster, and when at last it seemed it could accelerate no more, the spinning rod rose into the air between them. Sparks flared and danced, lighting the entire space with a blue and vengeful glow. The song was gone utterly now, but still the rod continued to spin.

Kijamon raised a finger and pointed. There, at the tip of the spinning rod, a blackness formed. And with it, a roar crashed around them, as though a great sea were rushing through the caverns toward them, or as if the mountain itself were bellowing in fury. Or pain.

The walls began to shake, and suddenly, Shaleen was aware of the wind. It had been rising all the while, but only now did she notice how the air rushed about the room, pulling at her hair and tugging at her shawl. Kijamon pushed her away, back toward the low entrance, and he moved to follow, but the shaking of the cavern was too great, and he could not seem to get a foothold against the floor.

Shaleen fell backward through the gap, into the tunnel beyond, and before her she could only watch in horror as a hole of air opened wide within the chamber. The mountain screamed and roared around her and the wind clawed like a desperate creature.

Again the floor threw her, and again she fell against the rocks. Kijamon was floating now, caught in the air that swirled around the chamber, and behind him, the hole of nothingness stretched wider. It was like a mouth of rushing air, and each time Kijamon's flailing form completed an orbit, he came closer and closer to its yawning maw.

Kijamon turned his face toward her, yelling something, trying to be heard above the screaming of the wind and the raging of the mountain. The cavern shook again, and a third time. Each time, Shaleen was flung farther back. With a desperate push, she regained her feet, pressing out against the stone with both hands to steady herself against the quaking of the world around her. She took one step. Then a second. Straining against the banshee of wind and bouncing stone. Trying to reach for her husband.

In the air in front of her, Kijamon had given up trying to make himself heard. He was tired. And when his eyes fell on hers, she knew.

"NOooo!" she cried, her voice tearing a hole through the noise and echoing from the very stones, but it was not enough. Kijamon touched his heart briefly with one hand, and smiled at her, and then his eyes twinkled in delight at the unknown.

And the vortex claimed him.

Kijamon, Master of Beauty, Architect of the Wind Forge, thrice declined king of the Djin–her husband–was gone.

The world crawled past her in streaks and smears of color. Sounds reached her only as distant throbs, dim pulses of life that pressed against her shattered senses, trying to get in.

But Shaleen had not yet seen or heard them.

How she had found her way out of the caverns she did not know, nor how long she had been gone. The sky above her was bright. Daylight. In some abstract sense, she knew she had found her way back to the city, but she wandered through it now as though a child. Bewildered. Confused. Desperate. Some nodded greetings as she passed, others showed frowns of concern, but none approached. None pressed. None forced her to scream her news in a public place and then collapse upon the stones once its weight had escaped her lips.

Because her news was the only thing holding her together. She must tell someone. Someone in charge. Someone in authority. But who? Echoes of names rose to suggest themselves in her mind. Zimu. Abeni. But she did not know where her sons would be. And the Trail of Sky was so tall, and the Wind Forge so high above her. She could not climb so much higher today.

The people she passed were huddled in small groups, talking urgently and quietly among themselves, but they stilled themselves when she approached. They watched her, many with sadness in their eyes. Had they heard? How could they know already? But she saw none she knew well, and her words must not be wasted on strangers.

A turn, and then another. A small rise. And then she knew where she was, only now realizing that she had been coming here all along.

The private apartments of Mabundi King. He would know what to do.

With her grief powering every swing of her fist, she pounded on the King's door. It was not Mabundi who answered, of course. But nor was it a servant.

It was Yoliq.

The Queen stood before Shaleen, eyes red from weeping and her hair frazzled from its normally tight-wrapped bindings. How could she too have heard? It did not matter. Shaleen lurched forward two final steps and fell to her knees.

"Oh! My Queen!" she cried, gasping for enough air to deliver her message. "All is lost! Kijamon is lost! And more! We've killed the Dragon!" And then she collapsed upon the cold, bare floor. "My husband is dead!" It is well that she did not see the expression her news brought to the Queen's face.

It was a smile of unexpected delight.

chapter 34

Sarqi was the first to emerge into the light, and he stood there, blinking in the welcome brilliance. Beyond the tip of the Spine, where he now stood, the vast open bowl of the Gnomileshi Throat lay spread out below him. A smudge of gray-brown blurred the air, making it hard for him to discern any actual towns or villages. The great flying crop was thick and plump today, centered lower down in the middle of Gnomileshi territory. It did not reach all the way up to the Lip, leaving that portion of Gnome land plainly visible below him. So plainly that he could easily see the lack of pursuit. No Horde scampering up the slopes. No trackers climbing the flanks of the Spine to recapture the missing Wasketchin Queen. It appeared that they had gotten away.

The wide and distant view felt like new breath in his lungs after such a long, cramped climb up through caverns and tunnels in near-total darkness. But at last, Sarqi turned to where Qhirmaghen's face poked from the ground, still framed by the crowding gloom of the tunnel mouth.

"We are clear," Sarqi announced. Glancing around nervously, Qhirmaghen clambered up out of the tunnel into the light, drawing the Queen along in his wake, still vacant and unresisting.

Though some disputed the fact, this place where they now stood was properly Wasketchin territory, and Lord Malkior would not likely be pleased to learn that his Gnome neighbors had dug a secret tunnel into his lands. But Sarqi could only hope that he would receive the news with more grace when he learned that it was also the route by which his Lady Wife had been brought to freedom.

Qhirmaghen ducked back down into the tunnel to retrieve their packs, and for a moment, M'Ateliana seemed to stand alone, in solitary vigil, unconsciously mimicking the great Mourning Dove statue that had been erected in her late daughter's honor, and which, until recently, had stood upon this very spot.

But that statue had been seen as an affront by the Gnome people, and by destroying it, Qhirmaghen had taken a bold stand in his recent bid to become King of the Gnomileshi Horde.

Happily, neither the Wasketchin nor Gnomileshi Kings knew of this tunnel's existence. Angiron did not know that it might be used as a means of escape from the Throat, and Malkior did not know that it might be used by Gnomes as a hidden path into his territories. So neither King had set a watch here. By all portents, it would seem their escape had succeeded.

With two packs in hand, the Gnome climbed up out of the tunnel and came forward. Sarqi took the burden from him with a nod of thanks.

"The Horde will be looking for you down along the rim of the Throat," Qhirmaghen said. "They won't be on your trail. You should have no trouble reaching safety from here."

"So you've made your decision then?"

Qhirmaghen nodded. "King Angiron tells me little of his plans," he said. "My value as an informant to Lord Malkior would be empty. I'm just an administrator. I keep things running while Angiron plays his games of war and conquest. I can be of much better help working from within his Court. If I have not been discovered."

Sarqi nodded. "And you have remembered nothing more that might assist me in undoing this wickedness?" He raised his hand, and the Queen's with it. When Sarqi had finally caught up to them, just as they were disappearing into Ishig's Book, he had taken her hand then and sworn a new oath upon that spot. At the time, he thought he had felt a slight squeeze of thanks from his absent Lady, but since then, there had been nothing. Only the empty staring eyes and this infernal shambling listlessness, but he knew she was still in there, and he was determined not to present her back to her Lord husband still in this... distant condition.

Qhirmaghen shrugged. "Only what I have said. The vim Angiron uses is not of this world. It is carried in a water that arises in some other place. Some say it comes from the River of Death itself. I know only that this is what each of his Hordelets carries with them into battle. But I do not know the charms of its magic, nor how to break them. You will have to discover that for yourself."

Sarqi's face twisted in a grimace of annoyance. "And you are certain I will recognize the craft of these death chalices that you speak of? The ones that carry the vim water?"

"You will," Qhirmaghen said, nodding rapidly. "Brilliant gold in color. They were made by your father."

The Djin's sour expression deepened. He had no reason to disbelieve the claim, which he had heard several times already, but he still resisted the possibility of any association between House Kijamon and the vile magic of King Angiron's war. Had his father known? Sarqi shook his head in annoyance. Of course not.

Sarqi reached his free hand out and placed it in firm thanks upon the Gnome's shoulder, squeezing only a little. A grip of camaraderie. "Well, safe journey to you then, my friend. Go back to your darkness and work whatever mischiefs you can to disrupt the coming battle. I will see her Ladyship to safety." Then he let his face beam with the brightest smile he could muster, filling it with all the warmth he felt for his absent brothers and letting it wash over the little Gnome. "Spend that wisely," he said.

Qhirmaghen nodded his thanks, and then turned away, scuttling back into the blackness of his dark road home.

"I hope they do not lie in wait for you," Sarqi mumbled, then he too turned from the spot and lead the Queen away along the crest of the Spine.

They still had a long journey ahead of them.

Water was everywhere on the Spine, though little of it was usable. It seeped directly from the stone itself, beginning as a thin sheen of surface dampness near the central ridge, and then flowing outward from there, but it seldom collected deeply enough to be useful–not before it had plunged down the sides to collect at the base of the Spine, anyway. It was a trifle deeper out on the sloped flanks, but anyone who ventured out that far to collect it risked slipping on the water-polished stone and a quick plunge to their death, several hundred paces below. The waters shimmering down the flanks of the Spine gave rise to the rivers and streams that sustained all life throughout the Forest. Ironically though, all that water was of precious little aid to those who walked upon the Spinetop itself. Only a very few places on the upper surface were cracked or scalloped enough to allow the flow to collect to a useful depth.

So as they made their way northward, Sarqi kept his eyes open for a suitable place to make camp, and it wasn't until night was nearly upon them that he found what he was looking for. A shallow pool of water glinted only a few dozen strides from a large thrust of rock that jutted from the Spine, a break against the winds that constantly shrilled and swirled around them. Upon finding it, Sarqi ushered the Queen forward quickly, pleased that he was able to offer her shelter from the constant buffeting. Perhaps he would be able to get her to take some tea.

There were no trees to speak of growing on the barren ridge, but there were a great many mosses at hand, and some few tiny shrubs, all fed by the constant sheen of moisture. Sarqi was able to gather enough of this humble fuel to make a small fire. If he could keep it burning, the warmth of the blaze would keep the worst of the night's chill from M'Ateliana's bones.

While he worked to establish their simple camp, Sarqi worried. The Wasketchin Queen still had not awakened from the Gnome spell that robbed her of her awareness, and he was beginning to fear that the charm might never be broken. Certainly not by him. He was neither a loremaster, nor was he especially talented in any uses of vim that did not relate to the shaping of stone or the Warding of the Wagon. Those thoughts teased at him as he worked, ducking in and out around his own logic, until finally, with an effort of self-mastery, he banished these unproductive worries to the back recesses of his mind, and focused on establishing camp. The job of healing the Queen's condition must be left to the actual loremasters and vim experts. Sarqi's job was merely to deliver her to them.

Darkness had fallen swiftly on the exposed ridge, and with it, the winds had slackened somewhat. Sarqi was pleased that, for the first time since leaving the tunnel, he could hear the simpler sounds. Once again, he could hear the rustling of his clothes as he moved his arms, the gentle "duff" when he tossed a handful of moss onto the flames. He heard it sizzle and pop as the green bits heated rapidly and burst from within. When the dry clump at the center of the moss caught, it did so with a satisfying whoosh, and threw a brighter light onto the rocky slab that hung over them. But M'Ateliana seemed to take no satisfaction from any of it. She just sat there, with her back against the stone, her features flickering and dancing in the shifting light. It was the closest thing to a lively expression he'd seen on her face since he'd first spotted her in the Gnome prisoner march. But rather than take heart, this only worried him more. Would her face ever dance with a light of its own again?

Sarqi sighed. Worrying about such questions solved nothing. There was still work to be done.

Now that the fire was crackling, he rooted about in the pack and found the small supply of dried meat that Qhirmaghen had given him. It had obviously come from some Wasketchin supplier, since the Gnomes themselves did not like their meat in solid form, but even so, he had not been able to get the Queen to eat any. He'd tried earlier, hoping that its familiarity might ignite her interest in other foods, but even though she hadn't shown any interest then, he dug out another small piece now and set it in her hand. Perhaps the day's continued exertions might have awakened a more demanding hunger within her.

His next task was water. After watching M'Ateliana for a moment to see if she might eat, or move, Sarqi sighed in disappointment. She'd be safe enough for a moment, it seemed, so he left her huddled there beneath the stone sentinel and walked back to the shallow pool to fill his water skin. It was a bladder of some kind, fashioned from the hollowed out organ leathers of some unknown creature and provided by Qhirmaghen, but Sarqi didn't really want to know more. Those with empty hands did not shrug their shoulders at any gifts placed in them.

He unrolled the stiffened bladder and plunged its neck into the chill water, then waited for it to fill. While M'Ateliana may not eat, at least she would take water readily enough, by some vacant reflex. All he had to do was spill it into her mouth, and her body would do the rest, as though it knew enough to keep itself alive, even when its owner did not.

A burp of air bubbled up out of the skin and then it began to fill in earnest. When it had bubbled its last bubble, Sarqi hefted it over his shoulders and carried it back to the fire.

"Any thought for where I shall take you, my Lady?" The Djin Ambassador settled himself at the fire once more and pulled a small metal cup from the sack. "The time of our deciding is almost upon us," he said, making simple conversation to mask the sorrow that the Queen's silence fostered within him.

"For the moment, our route is known–to the Cleft, by way of the Stair. But beyond that, where shall we go?" Seeing that she still hadn't eaten the meat, Sarqi plucked it gently from her open hand and dropped it in with a few other ingredients that he placed in his cup, along with some water from the bladder, and then he set his thin soup into the low flames to simmer.

Since leaving the Gnome tunnel the previous day, they had been proceeding northward along the relatively barren top of the Spine, making for the enormous V-shaped notch of the Cleft, up ahead, that served as the only pass between the forested lands on the east and west sides of the Spine. All day he'd been wondering how he would lead M'Ateliana down the Jalmin Stair and into the pass itself. So now, with the evening camp established, his thoughts returned to this devious puzzle.

Once at the Cleft, where some great and ancient cataclysm had fractured the Spine, cleaving it almost down to the level of the Forest below, Sarqi and M'Ateliana would face the twin stairs. The Jalmin Stair descended into the notch from this side of the Spinetop, and the Zalmin Stair ascended back up on the other side.

Named after the twin Djin brothers who had been commissioned by an ancient Wasketchin King to cut a trail into the unyielding stone, the result might more properly be called "ladders" than "stairs." The stone of the Spine–dragonstone–was the hardest known in all of Methilien, and even given twenty years to complete the task, Jalmin and Zalmin had been forced to limit their ambitions. No great soaring verandas. No sweeping curves of tread upon tread, ascending with stately grace. All they had been able to achieve was a simple series of notches, wide enough for a man to place two boots into, side by side and toes deep. Nothing more. Fearing that their Wasketchin friends might slip and fall on such scanty stairs, the brothers had cut them in a zig-zag course, leading first left and then right again, alternating back and forth as they ascended the steep, stony face. This way, if any should fall during a climb, at least they would not be likely to plunge straight down the path of the ladder, dragging any who followed them down to join them in death.

And many times in the centuries since, that foresight had proven to be wise.

So this now was the puzzle Sarqi pondered. How to take a near-comatose Wasketchin, who had to be led by the hand even to walk a straight line, and get her safely down the Jalmin Stair? She would not even close her hand around food. How was he supposed to get her to hold herself tightly to the rungs? The Stairs were as treacherous a journey as any Wasketchin could ask for in any of the stony places at the top of the world–even for those who were fully conscious. It was the chief reason that so few Verge-folk had ever visited this bare and treeless strip of land, even though the terms of the Dragon's Peace had ceded it to them eons ago.

"Must I carry you, my Lady?" Sarqi knew he could manage it–if she behaved. But that was a risky assumption. What if she moved suddenly? What if she awoke from her dreaming prison at just the wrong time, and startled in fright when she opened her eyes to see the world yawning so far below them? It would only take one small shift of weight to topple them both from the Stair.

But treacherous as it might be, it was the only route open to them. The east and west faces of the Spine were slick with the constant runoff, and speckled with nearly-invisible patches of stone-dark lichens that clung weakly to the damp rock and were so slippery that not even the toughened skin of a Djin could grip it. Only an experienced climber, in good health and fully alert, could hope to make such a climb.

Which only left the Stair. And Sarqi, with the silent Queen slung over his back.

Having reached the same conclusion a dozen different ways, Sarqi snarled his irritation to himself and pushed his fears to the back of his mind, then he pulled the cup from the fire and set it aside to cool. He'd given the Queen a helping of water earlier, which she had swallowed mechanically, but he worried that she had taken no other nourishment–not for several days at least–so he had prepared this tea soup. With any luck, some little spill of it would reach her stomach, where it might do some good. But for the moment, the brew was still too hot.

"So yes, down into the Cleft," he said. "But then where?"

Beside him, the vacant Queen said nothing.

"Shall I take you down into the Verge and east, to your Court at Bethil Glen?" Not likely, he thought, answering his own question while waiting to see if she might respond. Take her through a Forest now brimming with Gnomes? They would be captured within a day, and he didn't think it likely there would be a second Ambassador waiting in the Throat to free her.

"Perhaps west is better, into the wilder reaches." Better to avoid the Gnome raiders probably, but also harder to find the Wasketchin Court, or to find anyone else who might be able to help her. Sarqi sighed. "Does Shaleen not say that difficulty is brother to merit?"

He jabbed a finger into the soup, as though testing mash for an infant. "Cool enough," he said to the slack-willed queen at his side.

Her unseeing eyes stared past him as he brought the cup up and held it to her lips.

"Please, my Lady. Take some. Do not be yet another light going out of the world."

She answered him with silence.

chapter 35

They had been walking for half a day since they'd broken camp and the sun was high in the sky above them when the Gnomes came.

M'Ateliana had indeed taken a dribble of the soup he had prepared for her, and today he thought she showed signs of improvement. They'd been making good time since breaking camp, and the Queen seemed a trifle less sluggish, though she still showed no signs of awareness about anything–not the howling of the wind that tugged at her hair and clothes, nor the slickness of the stones she stumbled and slipped over. She just followed along, oblivious to it all, wherever Sarqi led, holding to his hand with the faith of a blind woman. As they crested a small hump on the uneven ridge, Sarqi was pleased to see the dark gap of the Cleft ahead in the middle distance, visible as a deeper darkness set into the dark stone of the Spine. They had nearly reached it when the Gnome Hordelet boiled up at them from its closer lip, climbing up from the very Stair that Sarqi had been making for.

At first, he thought the squad's presence was mere coincidence, and he hurried to move M'Ateliana into what scant shelter he could find. A slight crevice in the ground. Little more than a crack really, running along the ground, behind a low flat stone, but it was all there was. He could do no more than lay her lengthwise along the gap and hope that between the slight depth of the crack and the slight height of the flat stone, she would not be too obvious from a distance. It was barely even shelter from the swirling winds, which had shrilled awake with the rising sun, let alone safe from prying eyes. And of course, her kirfa would be damp before long too, but that could not be helped.

Sarqi crouched himself as low as he could and positioned himself to watch the Gnomes, but having gained the ridge, they did not hesitate, and hurried swiftly forward. Sarqi's heart sank. This was no chance encounter. Despite his efforts to keep hidden, the

Gnomes must have known they were there. Had they been spotted from below? That seemed unlikely. Had Qhirmaghen betrayed them? Probably captured and forced to talk. But it mattered little now.

"Stay hidden here, my Lady," Sarqi said, patting her on the shoulder. Then he moved forward, still in his crouch. The wind was cold and fierce, and Sarqi marked how erratically it buffeted the Gnomes as they approached, forcing them to hunker lower down and seek more carefully for their footing on the damp stone.

There were three of them, and behind them, a tall, pale figure loomed almost twice their height. A strange, fur-covered creature, the likes of which Sarqi had never seen before. The group was close enough that he could see their mouths moving as they communicated their plan of attack, but the wind did not chance to carry their words to him. The two in front separated and spread out wide, cutting off any chance that Sarqi might have of flanking them. And then the entire group advanced.

Growing up in the shelter of the Dragon's Peace, Sarqi had never fought a battle before, but times had changed, becoming more perilous of late, and he judged that this gap in his education was about to be filled. The nearest he had ever come was in boyhood. He'd been adventuring out on the back shoulders of the Anvil, alone, hoping to prove to his brothers that he was just as daring as they were, just as capable.

And then he'd been cornered by a mountain cat.

Had it truly been the lean and hungry beast he had thought it to be, an adolescent Djin like himself would not have been much of an opponent. But at the time, Sarqi had not known this. Quaking with fear, certain that he was about to be devoured by the ferocious beast, Sarqi had turned to the only defenses available to him–the stones scattered about him on the mountain slope. With a scream born more of fear than aggression, the young Djin had picked up a dozen or a hundred stones and hurled them as quickly as he could. Too frightened to take careful aim, Sarqi's missiles had rained down upon the startled predator in a pitiful squall of clattering stone. But it had been enough, and the cat had elected to sleep off its recent meal somewhere less troublesome.

But today was different. These were no well-fed cats creeping toward him on sleepy legs. They would not startle at the first clatter of stone, and they would offer more than a simple hiss of irritation in reply. Their every step and the determined set of their shoulders told their story plainly. They meant to kill him.

Sarqi quickly gathered five or six hefty rocks from the meager choices around him and then straightened up into the wind to face those who would come between him and the oath he had sworn to this silent Queen.

He stood there, silent himself, eying the Gnomes as they advanced. They were some seventy or eighty paces distant. Still too far for a sure throw, so Sarqi held his ground and waited. Let them think him cowed, afraid. So far they had made no aggressions toward him, but he knew that he could not wait for them to make their intentions plain. As with the cat, Sarqi knew in the pit of his being that a timid Djin would be a dead Djin. He knew nothing of fighting. He was a worker of stone and a sometime Way Chanter for the Wagon of Tears—skills of little use in a fight for one's life, surely. But the woman behind him had even less, and he intended to do right in her service.

The Gnomes had closed to sixty paces now, but still he could not hear their chatter over the fluttering winds that filled his ears. Which of them would be the most trouble? The tall pale one? Sarqi knew from his boyhood tussles with Zimu that the creature's longer arms would put him at a grave disadvantage if it came to grappling. But the two closer Gnomes held themselves in what looked to be a practiced fighting stance, while the tall creature at the back seemed almost disinterested, its matted fur twitching and flapping in the wind as it shuffled along vacantly behind them. No, the Gnomes were the greater threat.

The two in front each carried a dragon's leg, the vim-imbued staffs that the Gnomileshi had always favored. He knew that they would each be charged with death vim, giving the Hordesmen a slight advantage in the strength of the charms they might command, but they were scarcely a match for him in physical size and power.

Sarqi had no illusions about his fighting skills. Unarmed Djin to unarmed Gnome, his size alone would ensure him victory, but he doubted he could best three at once. And with the shambling giant added to their number, he was unlikely to even give them pause. Clearly, he could not allow them to get close.

Shifting his feet slightly on the damp rock, Sarqi dug in, making sure his footing was secure. The Gnomes continued to sidle and creep forward, never taking their eyes from him. Sarqi remained still, his head bowed, glaring at his opponents from beneath his furrowed brow as they advanced. The wind whistled in his ears and flapped at the leather of his vest, while his arms hung at his sides, each hand wrapped around a heavy stone the size of his foot. They had closed to perhaps fifty paces, but still Sarqi waited.

The giant in the back was a puzzle, but beside it, the third Gnome was less so. This one advanced with his comrades, and though he did not shamble like the giant, he too stayed well to the rear. Nor did he carry a dragon's leg. Instead, he held something close to his chest. Something small, and round. He also appeared to be talking, constantly. But to whom? To the other Gnomes? Or maybe he was chanting? If only Sarqi could hear him. Perhaps it would give him some clue about how to fight them, but the swirling chorus of winds shredded the Gnome's words into the sky.

The closest was perhaps forty paces distant now, and closing with increasing confidence, as Sarqi just stood there, waiting. He knew that he could throw that far, but he had chosen heavy missiles. Could he be accurate at such range? If not, he did not think he would get many chances before his attackers came too close for throwing, and that would leave the grappling. One Djin against two dragon's legs, a sorcerer, and a giant. Sarqi took a breath. He would give them just five more steps.

The wind shifted around him then, sighing down, and Sarqi saw the third Gnome puff himself up, making to shout his song higher into the subsiding winds. For a moment, Sarqi thought he could hear the Way Chanter's Song. He cocked an ear and turned his mind to follow it, his presence melting off into the gap that hovered between worlds. Floating.

Drifting.

A shriek of wind tore through Sarqi's mind like a dragon's call and he opened his eyes. Suddenly, the Gnomes were less than twenty paces away, and almost running in their exuberant lurching gait. How had they closed so suddenly?

And then he knew.

Uncoiling like a snapped spring of fear, Sarqi whirled his arm. His first throw arced out across the stony terrain and took the rearmost Gnome in the throat, crushing the song from his lungs in mid-warble. The sorcerer spun with the force of the blow and collapsed unmoving upon the ground, but Sarqi did not linger to watch.

The Gnome to his left was the more distant of the two, but he'd raised his dragon's leg high over his head and was preparing to cast some vile mischief with it. Sarqi tossed his second missile into the air from his left hand, grabbing it with his stronger right, which was already moving into its arc. Again he whirled and released. At first, Sarqi thought his throw would go wide, but the Gnome, who had been rearing back to wield his staff, chose a bad time to unleash his attack, lunging forward to hurl his words with greater effect. Instead of delivering the deadly charm he had prepared though, he leaned into Sarqi's incoming package, catching it square in the temple. The rock clattered to the ground at his feet. The dragon leg fell beside it. And then the Gnome joined them.

Sarqi stooped to snatch up another missile, but there was no time left to let fly, and he felt a hot fire rake across his ribs, as the fore-edge of his third attacker's staff scored a touch, enhanced by some charm of burning. Pain lanced through Sarqi's chest and he spun away from the thrust, pulling sharply on the staff and jerking the little Gnome toward him. The Hordesman's eyes widened as he lunged unexpectedly forward, arms extended. He seemed too surprised to let go of his spear, but it was already too late and Sarqi brought his fist down, landing a furious blow on the hairy shoulder that now loomed unguarded in front of him.

A terrible crunch ripped the air as the rock-wielding fist tore through sinews and scraped past shattered bone. Sarqi ignored the sounds and wrenched the stone free, raising it again above his head for another blow. But the Gnome was already down, writhing upon the wet stones. His shoulder had been completely shattered and the arm now hung uselessly from tatters of exposed muscle and bone. Sarqi could only stare at the wreckage in horror. A simple fist cannot do such damage, he thought, watching dumbfounded as the little creature thrashed on the stones before him. Sarqi's arm spasmed, and his hand jerked open, releasing the mass of granite, which tumbled to the ground beside his victim. It was almost as big as the Gnome's own head, he saw. The Gnome gave a last twitch and then, with a gurgling sigh, stopped thrashing.

Sarqi stared in horror, his chest heaving from the exertion of battle. Within his chest, an egg-like bubble of power had swelled as he fought, and now it cracked, releasing a wave of heat that washed through him. A feeling he had never felt before, both euphoric and devastating. And in that moment, he recognized it. From the stories of old. It was battle fury, fleeing his sickened heart. The fury of war.

A rage that stole a Djin's mind, making him a demon to behold. Like the quaking of mountain.

And as the fury fled him, Sarqi was left shattered by its legendary cost: the Gahrama. The knowledge that he was safe, that no enemies remained. And the full tragedy of the lives he had taken.

Three Gnomes, killed in the space of as many heartbeats.

Sarqi fell to his knees and wept.

After a long while, Sarqi gathered himself to his feet and took stock of his situation. It was an eerie landscape that greeted him. Filled with people, yet none of them moving. Three Gnomes, dead at his own hands, lay scattered on the rocks in front of him, a white furred creature stood vacant beside the body of its fallen master, and the Wasketchin Queen lay wedged into a crevice behind him—living, but showing no greater awareness than the dead. It was a chilling scene.

When the Gnomes had first appeared, Sarqi had taken the white beast's dull-eyed shamble as a sign that it was no more than a pack animal of some kind. But as he circled it now, with its long, muscled arms hanging motionless at its sides and its eyes fixed firmly on the horizon, Sarqi recognized the same spell-wrought listlessness that he had begun to loathe in his own lady Queen. This creature was more than a bearer, despite the heavy pack that hung from its back. He felt sure that this had once been a sensate creature. A person, of sorts, now ensorcelled by vile Gnomish magics. One simply did not bother to bewitch a cow.

Judging the White One harmless, and knowing the Gnomes to be beyond aid, Sarqi returned to M'Ateliana. A shudder ran through him as he looked down upon her motionless form, still tucked into the shallow ditch, her kirfa stained and damp. She would stay that way until she starved to death or froze, and never make a sound. He knew it as an ugly truth. A certainty. It was an abomination that made his skin tremble and his blood rage. He had tasted the emptiness for himself, if only briefly. The Gnome Mind-Chanter's song had held him for only a few short moments, but even that had been too much. He had felt his mind being drawn into the abyss, sliding down a thin, oily trail of thought into nothingness. Maybe it had been the wind, rising up to shred the music of the song, or maybe the singer had stumbled, but Sarqi knew that he had only narrowly avoided the same fate as the Queen, who now lay uncomplaining in the dampness at his feet. It had almost taken everything from him, almost robbed him of his... selfness. The realization left him shaking and unnerved. Almost as much as the battle-fury had done. The Gnomes had fashioned a song of utter undoing. The unmaking of minds.

And with it they unmade everyone who stood in their way.

"I will help you," he said, as he reached down to take her by the hand and draw her up to her feet.

M'Ateliana was soaked wet on one side, and the wind that snapped and snarled around them no doubt chilled her, but there was nothing Sarqi could do about that. They had no other clothes for her to wear and there was no shelter. Now that she was on her feet, they would have to rely on the sun and the wind to dry her. At least the air was warm. Soon she would be as comfortable as any could expect her to be. Even if she would not be aware of it.

With the Queen seen to, Sarqi returned to examine the White One more closely. He had never seen its like before. It was tall and slender. Taller than most Djin, with a dense coat of white-gray fur over strange, lavender skin. Thick muscles corded across its chest and shoulders, and ran down into long, tapering arms. The legs too were thick and powerful. Sarqi was glad he had not had to fight such a foe, yet he could not imagine why the Gnomes might have brought him along if not to fight. What other purpose could such a companion have served? The creature still stood next to the body of the Gnomileshi Mind Chanter. A small strand of rope bound them together, with one end tied tightly to the creature's wrist and the other ending in a tight coil wrapped around the hand of the fallen Gnome.

The White One offered no resistance as Sarqi untied the rope around his wrist and then lifted the large sack down from between his shoulders and looked inside. There were a few small blankets, and some Gnome food, which although unpleasant, might prove useful, so Sarqi left it all in the bag. But there was nothing else. No portable shelters. No cooking gear. These Gnomes had not come far, and they had not expected to be long upon their errand, which meant that there were probably more of them somewhere nearby.

As he worked, his movements pulled at the muscles of his chest, and reminded him of the fire that still burned there where the Gnome had speared him, but he did not think it was putrefied or poisoned. It burned only in the way that a rock scrape might burn, and it felt clean when he paused to probe at it with a finger. Not as deep as he had feared, but the only cloth he could find to bandage it with was the blanket inside the White One's pack, and there was no way Sarqi was going to press any part of a putrid Gnome blanket against an open wound. He would just have to be careful to keep it clean and let it heal naturally.

Turning his attention to the bodies, he was surprised by how little they revealed. The Gnomes themselves had carried no bags, nor did they seem to have any belts or pockets that he could find. The dragon's legs were vile, of course. Gnome magic, and Sarqi had no use for them. He paused only long enough to snap them into pieces before turning his back on them completely. The stories about how such things were made was something that even he could not believe, but he would risk no further contact with such depravity either.

It wasn't until he had finished dealing with the dragon legs that Sarqi remembered the chalice. He had to search for some time before he found it, underneath the body of the Mind Chanter. Sarqi rolled the body to one side and snatched up the metal urn. It was made of bronze and had seen rough usage. The bowl was badly scuffed and scratched, but even that layer of scars could not disguise its origin. It was clearly a product of Kijamon's forge.

Despite his best effort however, Sarqi could not get it open. The upper rim of the bowl had been dented in the fight, perhaps when the Gnome had fallen on it, and the lid would no longer turn freely. Sarqi did not know what might be inside, but from the way its weight sloshed and lurched in his hand as he examined it, it held some kind of liquid.

Tucking the chalice under one arm, Sarqi led the White One back to where the Queen was standing, and managed to press the tall creature down into a sitting position on the low rock that had been the Queen's only shield. Next he urged the Queen to sit as well, and after a moment's hesitation, he took out one of the Gnome blankets and wrapped it around her shoulders. Better that she be warm than proud.

Then he picked up the chalice to examine it more closely.

Before the attack, he had planned to descend into the Cleft as soon as they reached it, but he had not expected to find Gnomes this far from the Throat. Given recent events, and the likelihood of a Gnome camp down below, he now felt it would be best to wait here, out of sight, and to make their descent by starlight, when the chance of being seen would be least. A risky plan, to be sure, but his choice was among a slim collection of ill-advised options. There was nothing to be done about it.

Sarqi shook his head as he prodded at the dented metal, testing its resilience with his fingers while his mind wandered. Too much had happened in the world while he had been down in the Throat. He could no longer trust his knowledge of circumstances. To think that the Gnomes had such free run of the Wasketchin lands... It did not bode well. He must get the Queen to safety, as far from the Gnomes as he could manage. As soon as darkness fell, they would descend to the Cleft and go west. Any other path would be foolhardy.

He would have to risk carrying her down the Stair, hoisted over his shoulder after all, but that could not be helped. Once they were down into the pass, they would need to hurry to the western apron and down into the wilder parts of the Forest. Hopefully that territory had not yet been overrun by the Gnomes. There he would have to find Wasketchin who knew where Malkior had gone, and with their help, he would see the Queen safely back to her King.

Unfortunately, that meant he would have to leave the White One here. The creature could not even stand or sit without physical coercion, so he was unlikely to be able to climb down a mountain by himself, and there was no time for Sarqi to make two trips down the Stair with piggies on his back. Not if he intended to reach the protective cover of the trees before first light. Perhaps he could find help to send back for the creature. Deep inside, he knew the truth of that. He was very likely condemning the beast to death. But the final decision was still hours away. Maybe he'd think of something later. So with that puzzle set aside for the time, he turned his mind back to the one in his hands.

The urn felt heavy in his hand as he held it up to the light, turning it slowly to inspect the lid from the sides. The light revealed a slight dimple on the rim. A subtle flattening of the vessel's roundness. This was probably what had jammed the lid tight. Fortunately, it did not appear to be a difficult repair. The dimple was not deep, and there was just the one. Still, Sarqi did not want to risk damaging the vessel either, so he worked at it slowly, pushing the dent back out by small degrees, turning it slowly in his hands, inch by inch, as he pressed the metal rim back into shape with the tip of a smooth, triangular stone. He worked diligently as the sun lowered over the trees in the west and their shadow skeletons marched their daily assault across the field toward the Spine. Normally, the colors of the forest soothed him, but today, all Sarqi could see were the reds and deep oranges of blood and fire, so he kept his eyes on the chalice and worked at freeing its mysteries instead.

Finally, as the sun touched the distant horizon, Sarqi hefted his prize and turned it slowly, eying the sheen along the upper rim. There was now scarcely any wobble at all when the light played across the once-crimped corner. So, with more than just a little curiosity, Sarqi placed his big Djin hand over the lid and twisted.

There was a gritting resistance, but it turned. Slowly. After twisting it through one quarter circle, the lid flopped, dipping down into the chalice on one side as the other side came up. Only a quarter turn? That seemed odd, as though it had been designed for quick access instead of a tight seal. Sarqi set the lid down carefully on the stone beside him and turned his attention to the cup itself.

It was faint, and by day he might not even have noticed, but in the growing twilight, there seemed to be a pale orange glow to the liquid that swirled happily around the bottom of the container. There was no smell that he could discern, nor was it either hot or cold. With some trepidation, Sarqi extended the tip of his finger into the cup and poked the surface of the fluid. It felt... wet. Withdrawing his hand, Sarqi touched his fingertip to the outside of the chalice, but saw nothing unusual. Several times he wetted his finger and then repeated his test, touching a slight droplet of moisture to the rocks around him, to the leather of his vest, to a patch of moss. Nothing shriveled up. Nothing died. Nothing broke into tendrils of acrid smoke, or changed colors, or melted. It seemed to be exactly what it appeared to be. Water. Glowing water, granted, but water, just the same.

On a whim, Sarqi reached his finger to his mouth and let a little taste of the fluid moisten the tip of his tongue. It was flat, and almost sweet. Like rain water that had been left standing in the sun, but with the barest echo of melon juice.

For several long minutes, Sarqi stared down into the chalice, trying to imagine how stupid he was about to be, but it couldn't be a coincidence, could it? The tall creature had been tied to one Gnome. That Gnome had sung the Mind Chant that misted over

Sarqi's self, nearly emptying him into the same hollow vacancy of the tall creature, and of the Queen, who now slumbered quietly at his side. That Gnome had carried only one thing, foregoing even the traditional weapon of his people–their cherished dragon's leg– in order to hold onto that single object. The chalice. It could not be a coincidence. It simply could not.

Sarqi tipped his head back and drank from the great cup.

When the water flooded his mouth, Sarqi knew that he'd been wrong. It was not water. But he was not afraid either. The taste of melon seemed to ebb into the flesh of his tongue and lips, seeping outward through bone and muscle and skin. He held the liquid there in his mouth, wondering if his face now glowed with that same pale orange shimmer. He swallowed. It had only been enough for the one swallow, but even that much felt like he'd devoured a hurricane. He hadn't swallowed the liquid–it had swallowed him. And its glow radiated into the air around him as he was filled with a sense of power. And of strangeness. Strange words and images rippled through his mind. Towering structures of stone and glass, vast machineries of metal. Great, pounding fires, and brilliant screaming lights.

There were sounds too. Thundering, towering storms of noise, and explosions, violent concussions, and music. All jumbled together, with no edge between them. The music was a screaming thunder. The explosions had melody. The storms held rhythm. Without knowing how he possibly could, Sarqi *knew* this place. It was the world of the Dragon Grimorl. Astounding. Terrifying. And everything he sensed seemed to have but one purpose, to convey one jubilant, trumpeting message.

The Dragon Grimorl was coming home.

When the water that was not water finally reached his stomach, the visions subsided, and Sarqi was left shaking and uncertain. He set the chalice down on the stone beside him and then carefully placed the lid back on top, turning it the one quarter turn to seal its contents away once more. What it was, he could not say. Some essence harvested from another world. Some elixir of all things not of here, but of there. Not of Methilien, but of Grimorl.

Not of our Dragon, but of theirs.

And into his body, this elixir of another world now released its vim. But this was not the weak and paltry vim of his fathers. He knew that in an instant. This was raw, and angry. This was power beyond telling, and ability beyond the sun and the stars.

Sarqi stood up and felt his eyes brush the tops of the atmosphere. He felt his toes stretching down into the bowels of the mountain and the soil even deeper below. He felt his lungs draw in air like a great bellows, firing the furnace of the world, and he felt the blood of his veins circling through the land about him, carrying his ebbing power to the shattered remnants of the world that had been. Some little trickle of what once he had commanded. Reaching out with his thoughts, he touched everywhere and nowhere. He felt the racing of a stag's heart, and the fear of Wasketchin children. He even touched the mind of his own mother, for a moment, sharing his joy and feeling her own echoed back.

And then the expansion of his senses collapsed into a focus and he was back. No longer weeping over shattered oaths. No longer yearning for a world that had ceased to be. He was powerful again. Creaking at the seams with the need to reach out, and to change.

So he did.

With a cool breath, Sarqi threw back his head and began to sing. It was a familiar, low, sorrowful lament, but deeper now. Despair had edged its way into his song. A despair born of violence done. Not the violence that had been shown to him in his vision of music, but the violence he remembered, still burning in the bones of his hands. Hands that had flung the rocks. Hands that had killed.

But he knew what to do now. He recognized how the Mind Chant was akin to the Chant of the Wagon, and he of all people understood that song. It had been the core of his identity, the one thing that he had clung to, that he did better than either of his brothers. Among the Djin of the Anvil, there were none better suited to the Wagon than the sons of Kijamon, and among those three sons, there was none so well-versed in the currents of its Song as Sarqi himself. His brothers had never even guessed that the soul of the Wagon was a plurality. Only Sarqi had ever touched the aching that lay within it. The eternal longing of those drifting souls. In them, Sarqi recognized the same empty draw, the same lure of confusion and timelessness that he had felt during that moment when he had been clouded by the Gnome Chant.

With a confident vibrato, Sarqi sang the Way Chanter's song, but he turned it anew. Instead of lifting up the great mass of the Wagon with the vim flowing through him, he reached forward instead, into the crawling grayness of their realm. The Fields of Forever. He called out, gathering them to him, like a lantern in their night. He could see them then, so many souls, wandering, drifting, alone. A great many. But as he sang, calling to them all, only two curls of being broke away and came floating toward him. Two pulses of existence, of thought, of mind. And when they pressed their wispy selves against him, Sarqi gathered them together in arms as long as the years and huddled eternity around them.

Then he opened his eyes.

For a long time, he could only sit there, uncertain what had happened. Frightened that it had been just a dream. Terrified that it had not. And then, in the darkness, a voice broke the stillness of the air.

"They're coming."

The Wasketchin Queen had returned.

chapter 36

They came to him in the trembling hour, when the sun still threatened to take to the sky, but had not yet found the courage. The first to enter was Wijen, who, as Master of Histories, would act as official witness to record the event. Zimu watched the old man approach across the floor of the Hall. The old Djin's eyes flicked up once to meet Zimu's own briefly, but quickly fled, and the man hastily busied himself in organizing the stylus and scroll with which he would record his official observations.

The King and Queen arrived together, some few moments later, Yoliq striding imperiously over the cold morning floor to take her place beside the throne, while Mabundi did his best to keep pace. As he stepped up to the Anvil Seat, the King stumbled, and had to raise a hand to keep the crown from slipping from his brow. Zimu smiled at the portent.

The Queen too, noticed her husband's slip, and it burned her face into a rigid glare. "You intend to continue in this outrage?" she barked, glaring at Zimu with all the fury she could muster.

"I do," Zimu said, bowing slightly, with his hands still crossed neatly over his chest, fused together by the iron bands on his wrists.

"Then let us have it done," she declared. "Mabundi! Take up that chisel and kill this fool. A King has better things to do than to parade around his court for the amusement of some trifling oaf and his delusions of honor."

Mabundi glanced quickly at Zimu, as though noting for the first time just how large the son of Kijamon was, and then he quickly looked away, turning his attention to the ruined arm of his throne. The silver handled chisel still gleamed from its place, rising up out of the fist-shaped crater Zimu had pounded into it.

"I do this, not with joy, but with sorrow," Mabundi intoned, with the even, uninflected pace of a well-practiced speech. "For the good of the Djin and for the security of the Crown, I hereby accept the

Challenge of the Tooth." And then, with a single jerk of his hand, Mabundi snatched the chisel from the arm of the throne and raised it triumphantly above his head.

Or rather, he raised his hand in triumph. The chisel was still firmly rooted in the wreckage.

Wijen looked up from where he had been scratching down the King's majestic speech and then hastily wrote an additional note. The Queen just rolled her eyes.

Mabundi smiled at her weakly, and then returned his attentions to his task, grabbing the chisel firmly in his hand. Then he pulled again. But again the silver shaft did not budge, and the King could only strain there for a long moment before giving up with an abrupt release of breath. The veins on his neck throbbed and his face was flushed from the effort. Mabundi's eye came up to meet Zimu's then, and the King seemed to appraise his challenger with newfound respect.

Yoliq however, was growing frantic. "Hurry, you fool! The sun has almost risen!" Suddenly, she whipped around to Wijen. "And you! Don't write that. I was... You misheard me. I said, 'Hurry, my King.' Mark it so." Wijen nodded and bent himself to further scratchings.

Back at the throne, Mabundi now had both hands wrapped around the silver grip and one foot up on the throne, heaving and tugging like a young boy trying to move his father from the circle in his first play-grapple. But no matter how he twisted or turned, and no matter how he cursed or grunted, the chisel would not so much as wiggle. At last, exhausted and fuming, Mabundi kicked at the massive throne and managed to nudge it back a full fingerwidth. Yoliq stomped over to stand in front of Zimu. Her eyes shone with anger.

"You have bespelled the tooth!" she spat. Then she turned and called out to Wijen. "Make it known that I name Zimu of House Kijamon a cheat! He has used a cement of some kind, and the chisel cannot now be pulled from its place. Not by any man, nor any five Djin acting together!"

Zimu's blood began to boil, and his hearing began to wash out with his rising anger. He strained at the bond rings that still held his hands bound together before him. Mabundi's time was not yet up, and so he remained in his place and struggled to maintain his composure, breathing slowly, as his mother had often advised Sarqi to do.

But the Queen barked another ill-spirited laugh. "Where is your righteous anger now, upstart? Even could you win this challenge, still you would not be King. The crown cannot be won through trickery and deceit. It will not bond to you for your honorless frauds."

In the silent pause of suppressed rage that followed, all four in attendance heard the metallic click, and suddenly, Zimu's hands fell free at his sides. The sun had risen. The King had failed to protect his throne.

And now it was Zimu's turn.

"Watch him!" Yoliq shouted, laughing, and pointing at the throne even as Zimu advanced toward it. "Watch as he now feigns surprise at his own strength that planted it there. I tell you now, mark these words upon your scroll, Historian! The tooth will not come out, and the son of Kijamon will deny malfeasance, saying only that it has been sunk more deeply than even he can withdraw. The great Craven Zimu will now give us a show!"

Anger burned white-hot in his flesh as Zimu took the chisel between his hands. Mabundi stepped back. Zimu pulled.

"See how the tooth remains fixed—" Yoliq crowed.

The silver handle cried out in anguished protest, and then slid from the ruined throne, silencing the Queen. Zimu raised it aloft, breathing heavily from his effort and the rage that still burned within him. The world hung in a heartbeat. Mabundi looked up at him with awe, at Zimu's silver-handled chisel gleaming in his fist, poised in the light.

And for a moment, Zimu hesitated. This was the Honor Hall. The Anvil Seat. This was the very heartstone of the Djin people. The nexus of all they were and all they believed. It was bigger than any man. Bigger than any king. It was the bond ring of their entire world.

Mabundi continued to stare up into Zimu's eyes. But it was not fear Zimu saw there, or cowardice, or rage. It was hope. And in that moment, Zimu knew that Mabundi was trapped in this moment, just as surely as he was himself. Trapped by the forces of history. Trapped by the powers that wrestled throughout the land. And trapped by his wife's ambitions. Yet both knew that those forces would not let either of them back away from this brink. The Djin needed a king. A strong king. And they needed him now, today, without any dissembling or delay.

Behind them, the Queen sprang to her feet. "Cravenheart!" she shouted. "You have spoken the words but your own tongue will not swallow them! Zimu of House Kijamon, I name you cowar–"

A look passed from the one-time teacher to his younger student. A look of pride. Of forgiveness. And Zimu raged that such a good man, whose only failing had been in being too kind for his crown, must become the pawn of history in this way. There was no escape. And with a bellow of rage and despair, Zimu brought his hand down, driving Mabundi back onto the throne and plunging the chisel point deep into his chest, and through it, pinning the man to the great bronze chair.

"My King!" Wijen shouted, jumping forward, scattering his tools around him.

"Thank you," someone whispered.

"My crown!" Yoliq shrieked, leaping forward to grab at the band of gold still girding her husband's brow, where it would remain for as long as the King drew breath.

Zimu glanced at her in disgust.

"I did not make a very good king, did I?" Mabundi whispered. His words cut into Zimu like a knife. Like a chisel.

"You only played the fool," Zimu said, as understanding began to unfold within him.

Mabundi nodded tightly. "I was the wrong king for this time," he said. A weak cough shattered his face in pain, but he continued. "I hoped it would be you. But even you were blinded by tradition. These are new days... We need, new traditions..." The smell of blood filled Zimu's nose, and around them, the shrieking of a vanquished Queen echoed from the walls like the cry of bats returning at dawn.

"You provoked me."

"Had to... make you see," Mabundi said. A grimace twisted his face. Life was draining quickly from him. "To awaken... something."

"Awaken arrogance," Zimu said.

The dying King shook his head and opened his mouth in the shape of a reply, but he was wracked by a painful cough, and though he fought to say what was in his mind – "Awaken a kuh! Kuh!" – he could not master breath enough to shape the word. Zimu felt another spasm tighten the body in his grip, and then it slackened. The cough had finally passed. And with it, Mabundi King as well, the whisper of his final word, escaping his lips on the wind of his final breath. "King," Mabundi whispered. As that word resonated in Zimu's heart, the band of gold that circled the King's brow faded, and dulled into the quiet dignity of stone.

The King of the Djin was dead.

With tears in his eyes, Zimu sagged against the body of his former teacher, in grief. And shame.

Then the floor began to quake.

———————

The shaking of the floor seemed right to Zimu. It was appropriate that the mountain should tremble with sorrow at the passing of Mabundi. He had not been a good king, but he had been a good man, and in the end, he had found a way to let the one out-matter the other. Around them, columns of stone wobbled on their bases in woe, and the air was rent with the ancient shriek of a being in agony. Decorations and the oddments of state clattered and fell like grieving attendants. Wijen too had collapsed at Zimu's side, his old joints made liquid by grief at the falling of his King.

Zimu squeezed his eyes tight, but he knew he must get up. The time for proper grieving would come. For now, he had new duties to see to. The duties of the new King. Slowly, he pushed himself back from Mabundi's lifeless form and made to stand up, but an unexpected blow caught him on the back of the head, and Zimu pitched forward to sprawl over the throne as blackness swirled around him.

Dimly, he could hear shouting. "Help!" someone cried. There was terror in the voice. And glee? "The challenger has broken his vow! He did not wait the full time! He has killed the King before the challenge had expired!"

"Wha... ?" Zimu muttered as he struggled to stand. "Not correct... Must tell... "

But then a second blow crashed into the back of his skull, and as lightning jags of pain lit up his mind and then flickered out, they dragged Zimu down with them.

Down into oblivion.

chapter 37

Sarqi lowered his legs over the edge of the precipice, questing for the first rung in the darkness with his toes. He could hear the urgent shuffle and scrape of skin and fabric sliding over stone below him. The moment the Queen's eyes had opened, she had bolted away into the night, leaving Sarqi unsure whether she was even truly awake, or whether she was in some new madness of the Gnome spell. Happily, she had not marched blindly off the edge, but she hadn't stopped either. She'd just called out to him, and then begun her descent, with no guide to assist her.

"Hurry!" she'd cried. "We must cross before they close the pass!"

"My Lady, wait! The Stairs are dangerous. I–"

"There's no time for caution, Friend Sarqi. If I fall, I die. But if I delay, we all die. So I will hurry, and hope that Death is too busy elsewhere to pay us a visit now."

Left with no alternative, Sarqi had followed, and he was onto the rungs above her now, moving surely down the Stair, despite the darkness that shrouded everything. The Yeren had not followed, but Sarqi could spare no time to worry after him. The Queen below was his only concern.

Darkness forced him to move by feel as much as by sight, which was fine enough for a Djin. They were at home on the bare stony slopes of the higher places. But M'Ateliana was not Djin. How was she moving so quickly? How had she not already fallen to her death in the dark? But that was not a question he wanted to ask aloud just now. Calling the night's attention to an impossibility that had escaped its notice seemed unwise.

"Why do we climb with such haste, my Lady?" Sarqi called down to her, as his hands moved in alternating rhythm with his feet. "Who comes? And where do we go that we must get there first?" By keeping her talking, he would be better able to judge how far below him she was, and maybe he could keep himself from kicking her off the Stair with a misplaced foot.

"We must cross to the northern Spine," she called. "My Lord Husband rallies our people there. It is a place we can defend."

"So, you *do* resist. That is good. But why the mad rush? Can we not arrive tomorrow more safely than tonight?"

"The Horde has learned of our plan," she replied. "And they converge on the Cleft even now." The stone and the cold night air between them muffled the Queen's voice, making it sound as though she were far away. "They have nearly reached the approaches to the Cleft from the Forest below, both to the east and to the west. They will fill the pass in little more than an hour. And I intend to be on the northern ridge when they do."

Sarqi paused. How could she know this? She'd been ensnared in vacant dreams for days, and had only awaken ten minutes earlier. Were some tendrils of dream still with her, leading her to her death, chasing half-remembered fears?

"Are you sure you–?" he started to ask, but she cut him off.

"The Yeren. Halar. He spoke to me, as he speaks to his kin. His folk are among the Gnome Hordelets and they sent warning. The Horde is coming. Now. They converge on the Cleft."

Sarqi could sense the tension rising in her voice at the mention of Gnomes. The other topic seemed... safer. But Yeren? The creatures of fable? Sarqi forced himself to keep moving, climbing steadily down and edging left with each step, following the angled path of the rungs. "Yeren, my Lady?"

"The white-haired ones," M'Ateliana replied. "Those Who Wait. They speak together in their minds. Halar was able to speak to me as well, when we were... quieted. Angiron thinks he's so devious, placing one of them with each of his Hordelets. By linking to the Yeren, his captains can report to him from wherever they are, or receive instructions from him, but he is an idiot. He does not understand even the least bit of the magics he employs."

"How so, my Lady?" A flutter of sound, a scraping, sliding sound came to him from below, along with a quiet gasp of air. Sarqi froze. "My Lady?"

"I'm okay," she said, after a moment. "My hand slipped."

Sarqi breathed out slowly. What could he do? If he were below her, he could perhaps set the pace, hold her back from the furthest extremes of recklessness. But instead, he was above her, where all he could do was follow along and listen for the final slip that would come before the shriek of her plunging demise. If it were day, he might be able to leave the Stair and climb down the stone itself to get below her, but not on damp stone at night. All he could do was keep her talking and try to keep her calm.

"So the Yeren spoke to you?" he asked. A moment later he heard her move her feet and continue her descent.

"Yes," she said. "His people live deep within the mountain, caring for the Dragon, tending to his needs. But they have been taken from that duty and they fear for his safety. They want only to return to their home and resume their duties."

Sarqi nodded to himself as he climbed, remembering the stories of his childhood. Among the Djin, there was talk of the darkwalkers, monstrous beings who moved through the unlit tunnels and deep chambers. It was said they could walk through the stone itself, and that they served some ancient power. But they were just stories, told to children, to keep them from exploring too deeply on their–"

"Oh no!"

Sarqi froze. "What is wrong, my Lady?" But she made no reply. Sarqi strained his ears, listening for the slightest sounds, but he could hear nothing above the wind. Heartbeat piled upon heartbeat and slowly his panic grew. Had she fallen? Had he failed her already? But then she spoke.

"The stairs have ended! I cannot find the next foothold!" Sarqi was so relieved to hear her voice that he almost laughed aloud. He was about to tell her happily that she had simply reached the first switchback, and that she would find the next step waiting below her on her right side, but then he realized that this was the opportunity he had been waiting for.

"Do not fear, my Lady. Hold your place for a moment and I will investigate." As he spoke, Sarqi slipped his toes from the secure notches of the Stair carved into the rock, and quested down lower, seeking the natural knobs and cracks that would let him descend straight down. With M'Ateliana safely halted at the end of the first zig, he should have no trouble descending a few feet of open rock to reach the zag that doubled back below her. Then he would be in the lead, and would be better positioned to keep her safe. Or as safe as anyone could be while descending the Jalmin Stair in the dark.

A few moments later, Sarqi's toes found the next set of rungs on the lower span and he called out. "As I thought, you need not

345

worry, my Lady. You have only reached the first switchback. You will find your next step below and to your right." Sarqi listened as the Queen's foot scraped at the rocks to the left of his own face, seeking her next step, and he sighed in relief. Now he felt like a guide.

"Found it," she called out, and Sarqi waited, listening to her next movements as she shifted her weight and reached out with her hand, and then adjusted her other foot. Satisfied that she was once again on track, he moved to his own next step, staying far enough ahead of the Wasketchin Queen that she would not accidentally strike him and startle herself off the Stair, but close enough that he could reach out and grab her if it became necessary.

"It seems a crooked Stair is more dangerous," M'Ateliana said, as she reached for her next foothold. "More likely for a climber to miss her grip. Especially in the dark."

"Indeed, my Lady, each climber is perhaps a trifle less safe, but the increased danger buys much greater safety for the group." While he spoke, Sarqi brushed chips of rock and dust from the notch next to his face before moving on.

"How so?" she asked, as her toes probed and then settled into the notch he had just cleared.

"On a reversing stair," the Djin replied, "when a climber falls, he will not strike all those who climb below him."

The regular sounds of M'Ateliana's movements stopped. "Oh," she said. A moment later, she resumed her climb, but from that point on there was no further talking.

"Don't be ridiculous," Arin said. "You are needed up above. I am not, and I would just slow you down."

Lan'ia Sha looked at the old woman, and then beyond at the narrow handholds cut into the damp rock of the wall behind her. She let her gaze follow their angled path up the rock face to where they vanished behind a twisting jut of stone. The rest of their little group stood huddled against the wind, near the foot of the Stair. As leader of their party, they waited for her to decide how they would proceed. Her pride told her that she herself should be the last one up–that she had brought her people this far, and that it was her duty to see that every one of them made it to the end of the trail up above.

Especially now that they were so close.

But in her stomach, she knew that plan was silly. Arin was right, of course. The old woman had surprised everyone by keeping up over the last five days, but with the Gnomes pressing close behind them, they could not afford to dally on this last leg of their journey. And climbing the Zalmin Stair was not an easy thing–no simple trudge through the Forest. The ascent was going to be difficult, dangerous and slow–troublesome even for the fittest among them. She had held them here as long as she could after their night-time ascent from the Forest below, up here to Cleft. She'd been waiting, hoping for just a little more light, but they could not afford the luxury of waiting any longer. As spry as Arin might be for her age, she would hold them all up if she went first. And if she fell. . . Well, on top of dying herself, she'd be a danger to every single person who climbed behind her.

"Alright," Lan'ia said, nodding her head. "You're right, of course. The King awaits me, and I must not delay." Then she turned to look at young Winry, who was crouching in the rubble behind her grandmother's kirfa, apparently playing some kind of game, stacking little handfuls of stones into vaguely human shapes. It was a shame to have to seperate them. The four-year-old had been so good for Arin on the hike, keeping the old woman's spirits up, and helping her in a dozen little ways. Arin was a proud woman, and the child seemed to have the knack for helping without tweaking the old woman's nose with the fact of it. Lan'ia had watched with pride as the bond between grandmother and granddaughter had strengthened during the march, each providing what the other needed, without asking. But there was no way a child of Winry's age could handle the Stair. Even if her temperament was more mature, the girl simply wasn't tall enough to reach the hand-holds. Someone would have to carry her. Someone younger, with more energy. Story Uncle Keshlin, perhaps. He had taken a bit of a liking to the girl.

Lan'ia glanced significantly at the child, catching Arin's eye as she did. There followed an exchange of meaningful gestures and nods, as they expressed their mutual understanding and agreement. Winry must be taken separately, so that Arin could concentrate on her own climbing, without having to worry about the child. With a final nod, Lan'ia turned to survey the rest of their party.

"Keshlin! A word, please?" Then she wandered away from Arin, drawing the story uncle aside with her, where they could work out a plan without the child overhearing. Keshlin was happy to assist and between them, they determined that a slumber charm would be best, keeping Winry's fanciful imagination from creating ill-timed chaos on the climb, and it would also allow them to secure her tightly to his back, leaving his hands free for the climb. When they returned to share the plan with Arin, they were surprised to find the girl already asleep in her grandmother's arms.

"Figured you'd not want her wavin' her arms and talkin' in your ear the whole time," Arin said.

Lan'ia nodded her thanks to the old woman and then stepped in to assist with the bindings as Arin hoisted the girl up into position on Keshlin's back. When the Wayitam saw that it was done, and that this part of their group was ready, she took her leave. It was time to get their party moving again.

"Arkenol!" A gust of wind whipped her words away and flung them around the notch of the Cleft, but the clothier must have heard her anyway, because he turned at her summons.

"I'm going up now. You follow with the rest, quick as you can. Mother Arin will come last." Arkenol nodded his understanding and turned away to get the others organized.

Then, when it appeared that she had done everything she could do to see to the safety of her people, Lan'ia Sha pushed all other thoughts of them aside, reached up to her first handhold, and started to climb.

The first stray glimmers of dawn were teasing at the eastern horizon, framed by the dark walls of the Cleft, when Sarqi finally stepped onto the floor of the pass and reached up to help the M'Ateliana down to the uneven stone beside him. Around them, the winds were picking up again, driven by the coming of the light. As he watched, several small shapes bobbed up into view, silhouetted in the east against the dawn sky.

"Oh fracture!" Sarqi spat, as he pulled back against the Cleft wall, leaning close to the Queen. "The Gnomes have arrived," he said, raising his voice just enough to be heard over the swirling wind. "They approach even now." He pointed his long, muscled arm, indicating the silhouettes to the Queen.

The two watched for a moment as a group of Gnomes climbed up from the Apron Trail to stand upon the stony pass. For now, there were just the three, a single Hordelet, like the one that had attacked them above, but this group had no Yeren. If Halar's information could be trusted, this was just the first of many more to come. Soon enough, the entire pass would be choked with Gnomes.

Sarqi turned to look the other way. The western end of the Cleft still brooded in the pre-dawn gloom and he could see nothing. But he knew they were there, already climbing the western Apron, no doubt. They may not have reached the pass yet, but the way was as good as blocked, just the same. The only way open to them was the Zalmin Stair that climbed the far wall. The morning light had not yet penetrated deeply enough to reveal its sinuous trail of handholds rising up the rock face, but Sarqi knew it was there, waiting for them, scarcely thirty paces away.

But the Gnomes were no more than fifty paces.

"It will be a close thing," he said.

M'Ateliana nodded. "And the longer we wait, the closer it will be," she replied, and she was right. Any moment could bring more Gnomes up to join their fellows, or the ones already here could decide to explore further into the pass. And with every passing heartbeat, more light filled the Cleft, making it harder for anyone to cross unnoticed from one Stair to the other. "How well do they climb?"

"Gnomes?" Sarqi shrugged. "In tunnels of filth, where no fall awaits them, they are the demon kings of scurrying, but out here, in the bright and open air? Away from the damp embrace of their soils? Here their terrors rule them."

"Then they'll be slow. We have to hurry." Sarqi shook his head.

"We sneak until we are seen," he said.

"And *then* we run," the Queen replied. Sarqi smiled his agreement and led the way out into the pass, crouching low and keeping himself between M'Ateliana and the Gnomes, so that they would present as little to see as possible.

They were half way across the gap when it happened.

Sarqi placed his foot a little too firmly, a little too quickly, and the tiny vibration of his step caused a small pile of stones to collapse. They clattered like glass shattering on the floor. All three silhouetted Gnome-heads jerked at the sound.

"Run!" Sarqi hissed.

And so they ran.

———⌄——— ——

They hit the base of the Zalmin Stair at a dead run, with Gnomes scrambling toward them across the stony ground almost as quickly. Reaching the wall first, Sarqi placed his back to the stone and laced his hands together in front, making a quick lift-ladder for the Wasketchin Queen, who stepped into it without any hesitation. Sarqi had to restrain himself from throwing the woman up the wall, and simply raised her up as high as he could reach. Once she had found her footing and stepped up off of his palms, the tall Djin stooped to scoop up several piles of stones that were lying about the base of the Stair. He stuffed these quickly into his travel sack and began to climb.

The winds of morning had strengthened to a shriek and they tugged at Sarqi as he climbed, trying to pry him from the Stair, but he was a Djin upon the stone and he laughed his joy at their frustration. Below him, the Gnomes were just now beginning their ascent. Sarqi was ten full paces above them. It had been a close thing, but it appeared that he and the Queen had won the race. She was climbing well, and even though her hand grips were not as sure as they could be and she fumbled more with her toes than he would have liked, still they had gotten to the wall first. And even a tired Wasketchin could climb faster than a Gnome.

Looking down again, Sarqi could see that the last Gnome–the captain–had one of Kijamon's urns strapped to his back and he appeared to be singing his song of befuddlement, but the winds whipped his melody from his throat and dashed it against the wall. Sarqi heard none of it. For a moment, he considered taking the captured urn from his own travel sack and returning it to the Gnome captain. Violently. Or maybe he would present his little neighbors with a stone or two, to make them cautious, but there was no need. With M'Ateliana climbing two rungs for every one the Gnomes managed, their hairy pursuers fell further and further behind.

Sarqi was still beaming his delight down upon the heads of the Gnome squad when his own head bumped against something softer than stone. He looked up, startled to see that he had dislodged the Queen's foot from its rung. She scrambled against his forehead with her boot for a moment before she regained her stance, but why had she stopped? He looked up at M'Ateliana, letting his expression ask the question that the wind would not allow his voice to ask. Horror shone from her eyes as she looked down at him, and then turned to look up, drawing his own gaze up with her. There above them, an old woman struggled her way up the Stair.

And she was climbing much, much slower than the Gnomes.

All witness the great Ambassador Sarqi. See how he severs diplomatic ties with the Gnomes on one day, and then gets the Wasketchin Queen killed on the next. Inciting war with two neighbors in a matter of days. Did this not make him truly a master of diplomacy? For a time, it had appeared that things might actually work out for Sarqi, but no. The appearance of the old woman upon the Stair above them was a return to a familiar universe, with death and destruction looming, and nobody to blame but himself. Still, he must try.

Sarqi waved his arm at the Queen, indicating that she should climb on. She would not reach the old woman for a few minutes yet, and in that time, perhaps he would think of something. He looked down again at the hunched shoulders and large noses that climbed the wall below. Small hands. Big feet. Being squat of build, the rungs were placed too far apart for a Gnome's comfort, which is what made them so slow upon the Stair, but those tiny hands produced a powerful grip, and even though Gnomes did not climb quickly, their stance was solid. They would be hard to prise from the wall. Sarqi considered climbing down to kick them from the Stair, but that would only bring him close enough to hear their spell song, and he didn't have to be a brilliant warrior to know that if that happened, he would never get to the kicking part of his plan.

The closest Gnome was two zig-zags below him, and Sarqi watched as the Gnome reached out, straining up on his toes to reach for the next rung. Each "step" of the Stair consisted of three horizontal notches cut into the stone: one notch for the toes, and then two more notches at chest height, one just above the other, creating a bar of rock between them that could be gripped by fingers and thumb. This was how Djin and Wasketchin climbers used the Stair. Once secure on a step, the toe notch of the next step was knee-high, to the left or right of the current step, and was not a difficult height for most people to step up to, and from there, they could then reach up for the next hand hold quite easily.

But Gnomes were not tall enough to reach the hand holds above the toe wells, so instead, they crab-climbed, standing with their toes in one well and then reaching back to use the hand grips of the lower step beside them. It meant that they had to lean themselves over at an angle as they worked their way up the Stair, but with the phenomenal Gnome grip, it was not as taxing as it looked. Just slow. The real trouble, from what Sarqi could see as he watched, was that their large powerful feet, designed for digging tunnels, were almost too thick to fit into the toe wells.

And that gave Sarqi an idea.

After making sure that M'Ateliana was progressing well, he backed himself down to the middle of the span of steps behind him, then he reached into the sack that hung from his shoulder and pulled out a stone. Smaller than his fist, it wasn't large enough to do much damage if he threw it, but it was just the right size to jam into a toe notch. And if anybody knew the ways of working stone, it was Sarqi. Aside from his command of the Way Chanter's song, stonework was his greatest skill. Working feverishly, before the Gnomes could get close enough to serenade him over the howl of wind, Sarqi jammed his stones into the toe wells of three successive steps in the middle of the run. It might not be enough to stop the Gnomes altogether, but it would certainly slow them down. Maybe even long enough for the old woman to reach the top of the Stair. The Gnome captain glared up at him, and Sarqi watched with satisfaction as understanding illuminated the captain's eyes.

Satisfied that he had bought them some time, Sarqi nodded a caustic greeting to the angry Gnome and then climbed quickly up to see what else he could do.

When he reached M'Ateliana, he found her in a loud conversation with the old woman, each straining to be heard by the other over the swirling wind. The woman's name was Arin and apparently, she had been traveling with the Wasketchin Wayitam. The Queen was excited to to be reunited with the group, and seemed pleased that learn that the wise woman had survived as well and was even now waiting for them at the top of the Stair. But she was also disappointed when Arin was unable to say whether the King had arrived upon the Spine as well.

With Sarqi's arrival, the conversation turned from travelers' news to the more immediate problem of getting everybody to the top before the Gnomes overtook them. With the full winds of mid-morning already blowing through the Cleft and tugging at their bodies as well as their words, Sarqi was not confident that he could leave the Stair and climb the bare rock without falling. He would risk it, of course, if no other solution could be found, and he was fairly certain that he could catch himself if he did lose his grip, but who might he hit and sweep from the wall before he regained control?

The old woman assured them she could reach the top, provided she had time to do it at her own pace, but the Hordelet below now made that seem unlikely. Perhaps Sarqi's trick would slow them for long enough, but none of them wanted to hang their futures on that thin hook.

Nor was there any way for Sarqi or M'Ateliana to climb past the old woman. Stories were sometimes told of two travelers meeting upon the Stair, in the middle of their climbs, with one going down and the other going up. And while some few had managed to pass one another with acrobatic feats of daring, most commonly, one traveler would reverse course and climb back the way they had come, allowing their chance-met friend to leave the Stair and clear the way before resuming their own journey.

They were still debating their options when Sarqi saw the Queen's eyes go wide and she pointed back down the Stair. Sarqi turned to follow the line of her pointing finger and his heart sank.

Below them, the Gnomes had reached his blockade, but instead of being slowed by it, they had simply abandoned the toe wells altogether, swinging their bodies from hand-hold to hand-hold and relying on their powerful grip to keep them safe.

As a result, they were now moving much, much faster. And they had Sarqi to thank.

"Hey, Granna! Want me to make you fly?" Arin craned her neck upward to see young Winry's face peering back down at her from the safety of the Spinetop above. She was surprised to see how close she was–close enough to actually hear the little imp over the wind–but she knew she was still not close enough. The Gnomes were almost dancing up the Stair below them, and she could tell that they would be close enough to use their vile song of mind fog before she could pull herself up the last row of steps.

"Be quiet, child!" she called out, putting more venom in her tone than she actually felt. It wasn't Winry's fault that they were all about to die. It was her own. Just a slow and clumsy old woman who hadn't been able to do anything right for years. A constant drain on good folk.

Reaching sideways for the next handhold, Arin grabbed at it and then used it to pull her sorry old bones over to the next step. Plod, plod, plod. Her knees screamed their torment at her, her back ached, and the fire of ill-used muscles flamed up both arms. So close, but not close enough. Behind her, the Queen urged her on. The Queen! Another fine person who was going to die because of some stubborn old mare who clung greedily to the last few heartbeats of a useless life.

Movement above caught her eye and she glanced up into the deep scowl of her granddaughter's face. What in the Dragon's name...? But before she could complete her question, Winry's face exploded in a comic impression of adult rage. "Bydalovada hopless hairy dragon!" she shouted, flicking her hand with an imperious wave. Arin recognized the invocation, and a sudden smile twisted her lips. It was one of her own favorite curses. Or close enough. The child was trying to repeat the charm Arin had uttered in her sleep a week or so back. The one that had flung that Tayna girl into the sky and flown her off to a cliff top. Winry was trying to help her grandmother fly to the top of the Stair. Arin paused with one hand half-way to the next handhold. Could the child possibly...?

But of course, nothing happened.

Up at the cliff's edge, Winry held her dramatic pose for a moment, but when she saw that the charm wasn't going to kick in after all, she lowered her hand. "How come it worked for you, Granna?" she called, inspecting her hand intently. "That's the charm you done to get *her* to fly."

Arin sucked a "tsk" under her breath and turned a glare up toward her granddaughter, as she pulled herself to the next step. "It most certainly is not," she said. "Besides, you're too young for charms. You haven't flowered yet. Now get back from that ledge before I come up there and—"

Suddenly, the cliff itself began to shake. Arin grabbed tightly to the handholds and pulled herself in close to the rock. A frightened

scream ripped the air above her head and she looked up...
...into the terror-filled eyes of young Winry, who had toppled from the ledge and was now hurtling toward her.

———————

Sarqi surveyed the scene, trying to judge the situation. He did not like what he saw. Beside him, M'Ateliana was half way across a run of steps, climbing upward to the right. They were holding back a ways, leaving the old Wasketchin woman room to struggle her way up the switchback, which she insisted on doing by herself, lest she fall and drag them all with her. Arin had only one more course of steps up to her left and then a half run up beyond that to the right and she would be at the top. But she moved so slowly!

If all they had to worry about was Gnomes grabbing at their ankles, there would be plenty of time to reach the safety of the Spinetop. Once there, they could threaten their pursuers with heavy rocks and the chase would be over. But the danger was not in the grasping Gnome hands. It was the voice of their captain that held the peril. So long as the Gnomes were three courses below them, the rush and flutter of the wind seemed enough to obscure his song and pull its teeth, but Sarqi did not think the wind would protect them at any closer distance than that. Already he had felt a tug or two of oblivion, when all the winds had chanced to pause together for an inhale.

No, at their current rate of climb, the Gnomes were going to reach effective charm distance well before the old woman could complete her journey. Even something to stuff in their ears might be enough to protect them for what little time they needed, but sadly, there was nothing to be found in any of their pockets that might do the trick. Nor could anyone above throw anything, for fear of striking Arin, who was between them and the Gnomes below.

Sarqi looked down again, trying to judge the speed of the rapidly climbing Gnomes. They were too fast. For the moment, they had bunched together at the right-hand switchback, only three courses below them. The Gnomes seemed clumsier on the switchbacks, slowing down and bunching together, getting in each others' way, but soon they would be free of the snarl and swinging quickly again, like monkeys dancing along a branch. Sarqi judged that they had only minutes remaining. Three? Two? He was frantically trying to think of another stalling tactic when the very world itself began to shake.

Sarqi reached out instinctively to be sure the Queen was secure on her own stair, but a shriek from above jerked his attention up the steeply sloping rock face, just in time to see the child come over the edge.

Time slowed down as he took it all in. The girl was on her chest, sliding down the rocks and picking up speed. The old woman and the Queen both reached out a hand, trying to grab her as she shot between them.

"No!" M'Ateliana screamed, as the girl's kirfa brushed the Queen's fingertips. Neither woman had been close enough.

Without thinking, Sarqi leaped.

The tall Djin stretched out, reaching, as he sailed through the air, oblivious to the scraping of the rock against his knees and feet. One long arm trailed behind him, dragging across the stone, and the other reached out toward the girl. Time slowed even more as he felt the fabric of her clothing slip between his fingers before he could close them, but in the very last instant, he felt one fingertip brush warm skin and he snapped his hand closed with crushing strength. Instinctively, his trailing hand grabbed at a passing hand-hold, and a moment later, he hung there from it. In the other hand, he clutched a screaming child, caught by the toes of one foot.

And then a croaking song raked at his ears from below and he knew no more.

Arin's heart broke as the terrified face of her young granddaughter shot past, and her own fingers closed on empty wind. Please, no. Not again. It had been hard enough to outlive her own daughter, Siani P'leth, taken earlier this year. But now, to have to watch, help-less, as Winry too was taken... Two generations of her own kin lost to the pits of Grimorl, while she herself still clawed greedily to life. Beside her, the Queen cried out in grief and loss, but Arin could not make a sound. There was too much sadness lodged in her throat. It threatened to choke her, and for the briefest instant, she considered throwing herself after the child, wondering if her own heavier body might reach the ground first and at least allow her to precede the child into the next world.

Then, wonder of wonders! The scowling Djin threw himself like an eagle across the sky. Arin felt her heart leap, pounding with disbelief, as she watched him snatch her precious girl from the air. Oh, how she had wronged him! All of his squint-eyed glares and surly mutterings of the last half day were gone in an instant–erased from her memory, as she watched him grab calmly onto the Stair with one hand, Winry dangling from other. Safe. Somehow, miraculously, heroically safe! Dragon protect him. If ever there was anything she could do–

But before she could finish that thought of praise, the wind brought a snatch of Gnomish moaning and revealed the cruel truth. The Djin's valiant flight had taken him within range of the Gnomes who were clustered together below her. Singing. Even as she watched, still flushed from the joy of Winry's reprieve, she saw everything change. She saw the light fade from the Djin's upturned face, as he swung there from that one mighty arm. She saw the puff of the captain's chest as he filled his lungs to continue his chant. She saw the look of hope that had spread upon the Queen's face turn sour, as she too caught ear of the song. And in all those seeings, Arin Sha'eh made her choice. As calmly as though she were walking to the river, the old forest auntie reached out her arms to make herself as wide as possible.

And stepped off the Stair.

chapter 38

When Qhirmaghen returned from the Spinetop to Angiron's Court, he had expected to be thrown into a cell. Beaten, for certain. Perhaps even tortured. He wasn't sure how, but he knew he would be punished for his crime. Treason.

It turned out however, that in order to be punished, your crimes first had to be discovered. And if they weren't, well then, apparently you got invited to parties instead. Because that's exactly what happened.

To Qhirmaghen's complete and utter surprise, none of his deeds of the last few days had come to anybody's attention. Nobody had noticed his absence, and nobody had reported any of the Wasketchin prisoners missing. And wonder upon wonder, he was surprised to learn that while everybody did indeed know that the Djin Ambassador was missing, nobody much cared about that either.

Because they thought he was dead.

Ishnee had reported the collapse of Sarqi's new embassy building, when he had found it lying in ruins on the morning of the escape. But the building had been erected right at the edge of the river, and with one entire wall and several sections of roof missing from the rubble completely, everyone has assumed that the missing stone had simply slid into the river and dragged the Ambassador's body in with it. A brief message of condolence had been sent to the Djin King, but there had been no inquiries or complaints, except from one old thumb harvester, who had been hoping to add a specimen from House Kijamon to a collection he was amassing: Thumb Bones of the Great Houses. Nobody else had even commented on the Djin's death.

As for Qhirmaghen, with so much else going on to conduct the war, and King Angiron so busy with his "special projects," even the Fallen Contender's three-day absence had escaped notice. Whether that was a comment upon how little he was needed, or on just how

358

much chaos had descended upon the Horde of late was anybody's guess, but Qhirmaghen decided that he didn't care. He was too busy feeling relieved.

No shackles, no beatings. Instead, the King's Master of Tasks and Schedules–a spineless eel named Geck–had simply arrived at Qhirmaghen's lair that morning and handed him an invitation. To a fancy ball. Rather than being beheaded, he would be expected to sample dainties, chat with the King's guests, and maybe to cavort a little, if anybody asked him to.

It was in that moment that Qhirmaghen realized that the Resistance might have a chance. They had begun as a few disenchanted Gnomes, hiding in corners and whispering about how terrible things were. But real resistance required more than simple grumbling. In Qhirmaghen's eyes, it required more than merely striking a useful blow for the cause too. Even a blind fool can find the sniff-pot on the first try sometimes. Doing so didn't make him a scent artist. The real test–the thing that made the Resistance real to him now–was simply this: they had gotten away with it. That was what made a successful rebellion–the ability to not only win battles, but to also survive long enough to win more. And realizing that he would get the chance to do just that left Qhirmaghen feeling so eager that if he wasn't careful, he might accidentally spend a grin.

Geck could not tell him what the party was about, of course. Useless skite. Some dignitary or other that the King had invited. A new alliance of some kind. That's all he would say. The Master of Tasks either did not know any more than that, or would not say any more, but it seemed a grand idea to Qhirmaghen. What better way to celebrate a successful raid than to eat and drink to excess from the table of your enemy? And maybe, if Urlech or one of the others was in attendance as well, there might be some time for further plotting too. Right under Angiron's nose.

The party was held in the Squabbling Warren, a large chamber attached to the royal court, that was normally used for settling grievances between private citizens. Located in the caverns below the harvest tables, the Squabbling Warren had a ready and steady supply of offal, charnel and decomposing bits and bobs–all the necessary ingredients for a good squabble. Adversaries would gather in that chamber before the King's Adjudicator, and then snarl their grievances while rolling in the more vimful tailings and flinging the weaker mucks at each other. They would then perform some test of power set for them by the Adjudicator, using the vim they had managed to accumulate in the snarling round. Whoever won the joust was judged to be victorious, favored in the dispute by the Dragon himself.

For the party however, most of the tailings had been cleared from the room, although some choice gobbets and smears were still visible in the corners and higher up on the walls, giving the function an air of extravagance and sophistication. Qhirmaghen was fortunate not to have any other duties or errands for the day–who made plans for the day *after* they expected to be executed?–so he was one of the first to arrive, and managed to secure a particularly slick corner for himself, wriggling with delight at the texture and fragrance of his surroundings as he settled into his corner to watch the other guests arrive.

Most of them Qhirmaghen recognized from court. The Warden of the Table Yard, The Keeper of Tales, the Crop Master and his three Seeders. Qhirmaghen locked eyes briefly with Seeder Chuffich before the Crop Master dragged them all off to find a wallow they could dominate, but it was just as well, this was neither the time nor place for them to be seen chatting.

After the Seeders came a variety of Hordesmen. Middle ranks mostly, but a few of the more senior staffers were still on hand to attend. Qhirmaghen knew very few of Angiron's military stick wavers, but Barker Shleth was a hard Gnome to miss. Taller than most, but scarcely half Qhirmaghen's mass, composed entirely of gristle and tendon, Barker Shleth was a wiry old root who had commanded the Gnomileshi Horde under both of the previous two Kings. But Angiron had set the old Gnome aside and taken command of the Horde himself, turning them from a labor force into an army, and what did a Master Tunnel Digger know about fighting battles? Shleth was Barker now in name only, but having served at court for so long, he was still very well connected, and he used those connections well. King Angiron could not openly slight him. Not if he wanted the Horde to continue following orders, anyway. Most Hordesmen were blindly devoted to the old man, as were many of the other more seasoned courtiers. An open quarrel with Shleth might have unsettled the newly won crown on Angiron's head.

Qhirmaghen would have loved to bring the old man into their Resistance, but he'd never been heard to say even a single word against the King, nor to grumble or gripe about having been cast aside. The risks of approaching him were simply too great. That was a tunnel they could not dig until they knew what kind of soil the old man lay in.

Following Shleth, there were few new arrivals of note, and Qhirmaghen shifted his attention from watching the entrance hole to watching the ebb and flow of power about the room. People power, that is. Not vim. When it came to vimstench, Qhirmaghen himself was the current king of that odor, owing to his choice location.

Inevitably however, there was little to learn. Most of the attendees were experienced party-goers, and knew better than to say anything of importance where unintended ears might be listening, and the less experienced guests were also less powerful, so they had little of interest to say.

Everyone was still awaiting the arrival of King Angiron and his mysterious guest when Qhirmaghen was startled to find Barker Shleth at his elbow, which was quite a feat in itself, given how hard it is to sneak up on somebody who has wedged himself tightly into a corner.

"Quite the lofty perch you have there, Contender. You must have arrived early." Shleth was holding a cup of effluent and had slurred a few of his words, but Qhirmaghen was not fooled. The old man would never allow himself to be compromised at such a gathering. But he would certainly stoop to letting others believe he was.

"It's Fallen Contender, as you well know, Barker," Qhirmaghen replied. "The Contest is over."

"Is it now?" the old man grumbled. "You're sure about that, are you? So you haven't gone and lost any dead things lately, then? Something that by rights belonged to the King?"

Qhirmaghen froze. If he'd had any terror left to his name, it would have leaked out all over his face, but as it was, all he had to put there was blinking puzzlement.

Shleth ignored the denial, and waved his drink companionably around the room. "Oh, I'm not saying it was you yourself, understand. But a body goes missing–a valuable one like that–and somebody high up has got to know, don't you think?"

Qhirmaghen lowered his voice. "Barker? I– I don't exactly know what you're suggesting. You th– think I've done something... inappropriate?"

Shleth shot him a quick, squint-eyed glare and lowered his own voice for just a moment. "Keep your voice up, you skite. Nobody pays attention to a loud conversation at one of these things, but a whisper's an invitation to snoop." Then he patted Qhirmaghen on the shoulder, like a concerned uncle. "That's right," he said. "Vanished like a puff and nobody even knows it's gone. Quite the feat, wouldn't you say? Almost as great as bringing the Fury's Finger to the Arch. Has the look to me of a Contender who's still Contending, that's all. Not that I'd blame him. No sir. Not one bit."

Shleth slapped him on the nose in a too-chummy way, playing up the inebriated oldster, then he turned and wandered away again, leaving Qhirmaghen short of breath. His eyes darted around the room, trying to see who might have overheard their conversation, but it seemed the old man had been right. Despite the loud, almost treasonous talk in the open, nobody was looking his way. There weren't even any mysteriously quiet folk standing around, staring at their own hands or feet. Not a single soul seemed to have heard them.

And had Qhirmaghen heard him correctly? Had Barker Shleth, commander of the Gnomileshi Horde, just declared his sympathies for the Resistance? And what was that veiled jab about a body? Qhirmaghen hadn't trafficked in any bodies. He'd taken a prisoner. A very important, and very much *alive* prisoner. What body could the old man be referring to?

The Fallen Contender would have spent more thought on the question, but Angiron chose that moment to arrive, scurrying down the entrance tunnel and emerging into the room with a flourish of the cape that he had taken to wearing at social functions, instead of the traditional crown. When all eyes were on him, he gestured back toward the entrance and waited, and all eyes turned with him. The outer door had been left open and the brighter light of the world above flickered and dipped as someone stepped into the tunnel and strode down it. The light continued to dim in spastic twitches as the figure reached the bottom, a silhouette wreathed in the yellow-white light of day, and then stepped into the gloom.

"Give greetings to the Battle Mistress, Princess of the Miseratu," Angiron announced. "Newly returned from exile upon the Cold Shoulder, by way of the very fires of Grimorl." He bowed low as the hairy woman stepped further into the room, still overlit from behind and hard to see. Those in attendance craned their necks forward, peering against the strong light. "I give you my new Lady Wife and Consort." The woman stepped forward where all could see her and nodded her head as though acknowledging their gasps of surprise. She was as ugly as a tree–a hairy tree–with long blue ear lobes.

"Please, make welcome your new Queen. Queen Regalia."

chapter 39

"I'm getting too fat for this," Qhirmaghen muttered, then he remembered where he was and cursed himself for speaking aloud. Sure, he was burrowed in under the floor, but that didn't mean he was safe from prying ears. It would be just like Angiron to have a personal snoop inspect each room before he entered it. And how would that be, to be dug up by some Undergrunter and executed for treason? Qhirmaghen hunkered down in his hastily dug tunnel beneath the King's lounging chambers and resigned himself to a long–and silent–wait.

After the reception, he'd rushed away as quickly as he'd been able, to Ishig's Book, in search of Urlech. After all, Urlech was the one who'd told them that the King's new wife was a Wasketchin girl, and now here was Angiron, flaunting some other... creature, as his new Queen. Qhirmaghen wasn't sure what she was, but she was certainly not Wasketchin, and she most definitely was not a girl, no matter what manner of beast she turned out to be. Every inch of her had radiated a single notion: ancient evil.

Urlech's response had been to consult the bones.

"The Wasketchin girl is still bound to him," Urlech had reported, after the clicking and dripping had ceased echoing throughout the cavern.

"As wife?"

Urlech shrugged. "Bound. That is all I can say. The bones speak without such subtleties."

"Then who is the crone?"

"A replacement?" Urlech suggested. "Let us judge by the events upon the Arch during the Contest. The girl defied him openly, and stole his Pledge. Does it seem that our King enjoys the faithful obedience of his young wife? Perhaps she is more trouble than he had hoped."

"Could he have annulled the marriage and chosen another?"

Qhirmaghen asked, but Urlech shook his head.

"No. An annulment would have broken the bond. More probably, he has secreted her away somewhere, out of public sight, so
that she cannot interfere further. This new Queen may be a decoy.
Someone to present to the Horde for now. Someone more agreeable
to his aims."

Now it was Qhirmaghen's turn to disagree. "No, the crone may
be a decoy, but he does not have the girl. He doesn't even know
where she is. He's been running around ever since the coronation
trying to find her, but still she eludes him."

"Indeed?" Urlech said, widening his eyes in surprise. "A mere
girl outfoxes our Trickster Prince?"

"So it would seem," Qhirmaghen said, nodding in agreement.
"Or perhaps he simply wishes us to believe so. But where does that
leave us?"

Urlech paced around the dark cavern for a moment, rubbing his
nose in thought. Then he stopped. "There are two routes to be
taken," he said. "First, we must find the girl, and give her any aid
we can."

"Agreed. And the second tunnel?"

"Curious for you to use that word," Urlech had replied. "We
need more information about the crone..."

And so here he was now, Qhirmaghen, Fallen Contender and
Overcaptain of Minor Works, cramped into the end of a tunnel like
a common Grunter, lying in wait under the King's private chambers,
hoping to overhear something of consequence.

All he needed now was the King.

For almost an hour, Qhirmaghen sat quietly, his ear pressed up
against the thin dirt cap that stood between him and the King's
chambers. He had chosen his route carefully, and knew that he
was below the corner of the room–a location none would ever stand
upon–so he had been able to scratch his tunnel to within a very slender breadth of breaking through the hard-packed ground without
fear of being discovered by a misplaced foot.

After a lengthy wait, he heard shuffling from above. The King?
Qhirmaghen tensed up in anticipation, but the voices spoke in quiet
tones and he relaxed. Servants of some description. Qhirmaghen
suspected they were talking about their Overcaptain, given how
poorly they spoke of him. But what they said was of little concern. It was just the idle grousing of minor folk. What did matter

was how hard it was for him to make out their snide whispers as they moved around the room. What if Angiron were to reveal some crucial piece of information in just such a quiet tone?

When the attendants had completed their tasks and departed, Qhirmaghen pulled a small pouch of tools from inside his jerkin and withdrew a slender length of bone from the collection inside. It was longer than his longest finger, but only a fraction of a finger wide, and pointed at the tip. A pin bone from a large fish, stiff, but with some flex to it. When he was certain that the servants were gone, Qhirmaghen worked the slender bone carefully up into the soil above his ear, until he felt it poke out into the room above him. Crumbs of dirt rained down on his face and nose as he worked the bone around a little, creating an open air channel that connected him more fully to the King's chamber.

A sound hole.

Qhirmaghen placed his ear against the dirt once more and confirmed. Yes. He could hear the hush of the room now. As he listened to this more voluminous silence, several more crumbs and pellets of soil bounced from his cheek. Had he weakened the floor too much? He didn't think so, but still, he would have to take care. No more poking and prodding. He would make do with what he now had.

It was perhaps another twenty minutes before the King and his "Queen" entered the chamber, followed by another pair of servants, but Angiron ordered them to leave. Qhirmaghen held his breath and listened.

"You overstep yourself," Angiron said, as soon as he and his bride were alone.

"Do I? I thought you wanted a queen. That's what queens do."

"Wrong!" Angiron barked. "Queens do exactly what their kings tell them to do, and this king is telling you to mind your place." Then his tone softened into an oily purr. "Or I'm sure one of your sisters can be convinced to play the role more to my liking."

There was a slight pause as Qhirmaghen imagined the two of them glaring at each other.

Then, "Yes, my Lord."

"That's better," Angiron replied. Somebody moved and more grains of grit sprinkled into Qhirmaghen's ear and tickled at the side of his nose. He flicked it away.

"Speaking of your sisters, where are they?"

"They're vacating the last of the children," the fake Queen said.

"They'll join us once it's done."

"You're sure you've got them under control this time? I'm tired of having to chase after your little sprats whenever I need one. They're not even close to broken."

"If we'd broken them, they'd have been useless to us. Can't wring much misery from a simpleton. But now that we're home..." The woman's voice trailed off dreamily. "So much prey here," she said. "So rich. We had forgotten what it was like."

"Feed all you want. The miserable Ketch are yours. Just leave those children for me."

"Gladly!" the Regalia woman replied. "And you should have no trouble with them now, my Lord. Your magic has left them as docile as rag dolls. Do with them as you like."

Children? Being dragged into the Angiron's war? Qhirmaghen did not like the sounds of this. Were even the weakest of beings mere tools to this mad king?

The Overcaptain of Minor Works risked a quick breath and prepared himself to hear the worst.

"Your magic has left them as docile as rag dolls," Regalia said. "Do with them as you like." She stood in the center of a small, underground room. The King's private receiving room, richly appointed in the Gnome fashion, with soft benches of muck along one wall for seating, as well as a trove of bones, sinews, fleshes and the like. Anything a King might want.

Angiron whirled away from the door where he'd been pacing, and faced his "wife." "Of course I'll do as I like, you stupid brain-parasite! Have you found either of your other girls yet? My real wife? Or her ridiculous friend?"

"Not yet, my Lord, but we will. Their scent is quite—"

But the room lurched and cut off her reply. Without warning, the floor and walls rumbled and shook and a great cry rose up from the very soil around them. It was a cry of agony and despair, as though the world itself were lamenting its own impending demise.

The Gnome King threw himself to a low, earthen bench and clutched at it for support, as Regalia staggered into the corner of the room, fleeing the open center where the ceiling above them bounced and rattled, raining clumps of moist dirt onto the floor.

"Oh... What is *that*?" she cooed, as the sorrow behind the wailing of infinity washed through her. It was enormous. Limitless misery. As though she fed upon the despair of a god. The Miseratu Princess felt herself fill, restored and rejuvenated, as though her long exile from the world and the Prey had never been. "Oh sisters, do you feel it?"

Regalia spread her arms in ecstasy and took a step out from the corner, her eyes closed and her head thrown back, as the pain of the world filled a space within her that she had forgotten. It was more than misery. More than pain, or fear. It was all of these, and more. A feeling that perhaps only the gods felt, and not being such a one, she had no word to describe it.

Other than "delicious."

"Yes!" she cried. "Fill me! Power beyond all power! For the first time, I am alive!"

And then the floor beneath her collapsed. As she fell, a squeak of terror caught at her expanded senses, and in a flash, her hands shot down into the soil, questing. She groped through the filth and dirt until she snagged a squirming bundle of fear.

"It would seem your underlings are truly beneath you, my 'King.'" Scorn dripped from Regalia's tone as she flung the creature into the room and stepped easily up out of the hole to follow him.

"You!" Angiron shouted, his eyes bulging with rage. Qhirmaghen lay in the center of the room as the shaking subsided. The Gnome King advanced, one hand already raised, ready to beat his traitorous Aide into pulp.

"Leave him!" Regalia snarled. "I want to play."

Angiron flung her a glance of purest disdain. "He's mine, you ignorant fear-cow!" Then he reached out and to grab the Fallen Contender by the throat.

Behind him, Regalia threw back her head in delight. "Oh, but you mistake me, little worm. It is not your contemptible wretch that I mean to play with." Then she cuffed Angiron in the side of the head with a casual swing of her arm, hurtling the King across the room, where he hit the wall with a wet thud and slid slowly down toward the floor.

"I want *you*. And I have quite a lot to teach you. About pain."

Then she pushed up the sleeves of her robes and moved in to begin the lesson.

chapter 40

With the wracking sobs finally under control, Eliza rolled over. It may have sounded like laughter, but there had been no hint of merriment about it, and the feeling that remained in her gut had the somber aftertaste of despair. Slowly, she opened her eyes, and was not entirely surprised to find herself lying on the ground. Sometimes, the little things could completely undo you.

Like the time five or six years ago, when Sister Manipula had rushed Rhonda to see a doctor. Eliza could easily remember how furious she'd been about the whole thing. Not because the girl had received prompt medical attention, or because Rhonda had escaped from Goody chores for three whole days in the hospital. Eliza had been furious with jealousy, because when Rhonda came back, she'd had a souvenir of her adventure, visible as Sister Manipula had marched her back into the Old Shoe. A little slip of paper sticking out of her fist. A bus ticket. Having never been on a bus before, that ticket could only have meant one thing to Eliza's child mind: a chariot ride to adventure.

She could remember the rage that had stampeded through her then. She'd wanted to hit Rhonda with something heavy, to jump up and down, and scream. To break things. But her body had rebelled then, just as it had now, and she'd sat down. Laughing. Suddenly and uncontrollably. Right in the middle of the hallway, forcing all the other kids to walk around her as they made their way to the basement for lunch.

Faced with such overwhelmingly conflicted emotions, laughing on the floor had just seemed to be the most appropriate response. What else do you do when nothing makes sense? It was unfair how the Goodies treated everyone, how they picked favorites. And un-favorites. It was unfair how some girls got to be sick and have adventures while other girls did not. But most of all, Eliza had been angry with herself–angry at how badly she'd wanted to hit Rhonda, for doing nothing more than getting sick and being miserable. Overwhelmed by her own inability to make sense of those conflicting angers, Eliza had just plopped herself down on the floor. Her emotions had gone on strike, and laughter had been put temporarily in charge.

Like now.

Seeing Mehklok pop Scraw into his mouth, Eliza's first instinct had been to punch him, and she might have done it too, if she'd been able to move. But she'd seen his face in that moment before he'd turned away. She'd seen his sudden realization that, once again, he had done something wrong. He had no idea what, but she had seen that betrayal clearly registered. He'd been doing something that seemed totally natural to him, and had then been brought up short by her unexpected judgment.

It was in that moment that Eliza first saw herself through his eyes, his alien, Gnomileshi eyes. And what she saw there was more horrifying to her than anything she had ever seen before. Because the look that had scampered across his face had been uncomfortably familiar. She had seen it before. On the faces of her friends.

When their souls were being crushed by one of the Goodies.

One of the good things about gut-wrenching laughter–no matter why you're doing it–is that, when you're done, you feel clean. You feel as though the entire world has been reset, and you could handle anything again.

Eliza got slowly to her feet. Her knees were a bit rubbery, as though even they had taken an active part in the laughing fit. Was it a bad sign when even your knees were laughing at you? But as she stood, she heard a sound, coming from a little ways off through the trees. Opposite from the direction Mehklok had run.

At first it had sounded like an echo of her own laughter, but when it rose again, it was more of a warbling trill, like a dove in a trap. She really ought to go find her strange little companion– the only companion she had left now, she reminded herself–but the cooing sound called through the trees once more.

And it sounded a little more frantic. A little more desperate.

Deciding that she would just have to trust Mehklok for a few minutes longer, Eliza turned toward the strange animal cry and set off to investigate.

Eventually, Eliza tracked the sound. It was coming from a dense cluster of trees. They formed a ring at their base, and looked like a traveler's dehn that had been allowed to grow wild. The trill was coming from inside the ring.

"Hello?" Eliza called as she approached. The trunks were pressed tightly together, all the way around the circle, and as high up as several yards above her head before they thinned enough to show gaps between them.

The trilling continued, although the pitch had lowered some in response to Eliza's call. It was now more of a whimper of unhappiness than a cry for help.

If Scraw was here, he'd be able to– Eliza felt a pang of sadness then, as she realized that Scraw was not going to come suddenly bursting out of the trees to help her. She would have to solve this problem herself.

Walking around the column of trees, Eliza found a small chink in the armored palisade. A twist in one of the trunks that left a gap between it and its neighbor. Not a gap that went all the way through, but one that was deep enough that she could get her toes jammed into it, and after a bit of grunting and pulling, she had climbed high enough to see in through the gaps above.

It was the Gnome squad's Yeren. The creature was tied up inside the tree ring, obviously in distress. The rope they'd tied her with wasn't even long enough to let the poor creature stand, and she was hunkered down, pressed back against the tree wall, trembling. And still trilling her fear. How long she had been there was anybody's guess, but that didn't really matter. At least this gave Eliza something to think about. Another distraction to help her while away the eternity of death.

At her first approach, the creature had flinched back even further, as though trying to press herself into the tiny crevices between the tree trunks that were her cage. Her enormous eyes glittered in fear. But when Eliza dropped lightly to the ground, clearly not a Gnome, the wideness of those eyes relaxed, and the tension in her bearing seemed to melt a little.

Eliza couldn't be sure, but she'd already decided this was a she-Yeren. There was something about the soft roundness of her face, and the slenderness of her arms that suggested girlishness. Gorilla girlishness maybe, but there was a definite femininity there.

Eliza quickly squatted down, to make herself look less threatening. "Are you okay?" she said, in English, holding out a hand as though she was approaching an unfamiliar dog. "I'm not going to hurt you."

The poor thing didn't likely understand her words, but she seemed to respond to Eliza's tone. Her hands were bound together with a silvery cord, and the other end was tied to a thin branch overhead. Too high for the Yeren to reach, and with her hands tied, too high for her to climb, too.

Eliza stared up at the end of the rope for a moment, trying to figure out how she could climb up there to untie it, when she suddenly realized that she didn't have to. She reached out slowly and gave a gentle tug on the middle of the rope. The Yeren reached out with her bound hands and Eliza moved cautiously forward. More scared of frightening the creature than of any danger to herself.

When she got close enough, she could see that the knot wasn't particularly complicated, and she began working at it with her fingers. The Yeren seemed to relax a little more, and the pitch of her trilling dropped even lower. Almost to a purr, but not quite low enough for that. Nor calm enough either.

The rope was thin and the knot had been tied tightly, making it hard for Eliza to get at it without pulling. Beneath the circle of rope, the creature's skin was exposed in an angry ring of redness. The fur there had been rubbed away by her struggles, and the fur immediately surrounding the area was matted into sticky clumps of dirt and dried blood.

As she worked, Eliza made shushing noises at the poor thing and stroked the fur of her arms, trying to appear friendly and helpful, and saying nonthreatening things. "I'm trying to help. I won't hurt you. Stay calm."

It took several long minutes of working at it before the knot finally began to unravel, but eventually it did, and as she unwrapped the rope from around the creature's wounded wrists, Eliza tensed herself a little, fully expecting a violent shove as the freed captive made her escape and bolted away into the forest. But the shove never came.

Instead, with her hands at last freed from those painful bonds, the creature gestured for Eliza to move back and then stood, slowly unfolding her cramped limbs and standing, and unfolding, and then standing some more, until she was fully upright. Eliza's eyes widened.

"You don't play basketball by any chance, do you?"

The creature was at least seven feet tall. Maybe eight. But instead of fleeing, this gentle giantess moved into a slow, sinuous dance, stretching herself in a fluid kind of yoga ballet. Utterly calm, she exuded a profound grace, an elegance that seemed to mark her in Eliza's eyes as a sort of Zen Buddhist priestess of dance, if there was such a thing. There was little sign of recently freed slave creature about her. Even the full-body fur coat she had going seemed part of her magic, and Eliza was entranced. It was like watching a private moment of some famous Russian ballerina maybe, after she'd first climbed out of bed. The kind of dancer who performed for kings and queens and only ever ate oranges and salads. Eliza could easily imagine that between performances, she spent her days working as a professional artist's muse, and that by night she appeared in the dreams of little girls, teaching them to be princesses.

When the stretching was over, the white-furred dancer bowed gracefully before Eliza, bringing her forehead down to touch delicately against Eliza's. She held herself there for a moment, and then looked up, meeting Eliza's curious gaze with her great, brown eyes. There was a question there, Eliza thought, and then a sadness, a disappointment perhaps. And intelligence. Definitely intelligence. This was not some dull-witted she-beast, but a wise and thoughtful creature.

When the little ritual of thanks was over, the wise and thoughtful fur woman stood up once more. And then she walked away, reaching up with her long arms and lifting herself gracefully up to the gap between the trees. Then a moment later, she lowered herself beyond them and was gone.

"Wow," Eliza said. "That was intense."

She had a moment of panic, wondering how she was going to get out of the tree-ring, but then she noticed the rope, now just laying there. A few grumbles and scrambles later, she had untied the other end and used it to climb up high enough to squeeze through the gap, and she too was free once more. But of the graceful Yeren woman, she could find no trace. Eliza sighed.

Hell was easily the strangest place she had ever been.

Oath Keeper

———⌐— ——⌐

Since the Forging of the Oath, she had slumbered, waiting, a vouchsafe against the day when the Dragon's Peace might fall and she
would be awakened– Wait a moment. We've done that already. The
Peace already *has* fallen. And then I awoke... Memories flooded
back into the Flame of the Dragon, Keeper of the Oath. Recent ones.
Brilliant pebbles of recollection set against the quieter smear of long
ago. A girl. A bird. A fire. Then, with a sudden shift of thought,
she remembered herself.

Mardu.

Mardu looked out at the world. She was in a box. A shell. A
thin disk of entrapment. The Flame of the Dragon That Was, Keeper
of the Oath, looked out at the sky beyond her barrier and smiled. At
least it was still now. There was still time.

Her prison tasted like dragon.

———⌐— ——⌐

The greatest challenge about being dead, it seemed, was figuring
out what to do with all the me-time. Now, for the first time since
Scraw and Mardu had been killed by the blast, Eliza came face-to-
face with where that left her. What was she supposed to do now?
Meeting Mardu had seemed to solve the problem of how to spend
her blissful ever-after. The strange ghost-girl had provided her with
a purpose and a direction, which had taken her mind off her own
troubles for a time and held the unfairness tantrum at bay. But that
had only lasted three days. Now she had no Mardu, no mission,
and still no idea what the rules were in this strange land of death
and crow-eating midgets.

Feeling lost and more alone than she had felt since first waking
up here, Eliza wandered through the trees until she came to the
edge of a stream and sat at its edge to pull off her borrowed boots.
It was the same stream that flowed on into the clearing, she figured,
but she didn't want to think about what lay downstream just now.
She just wanted to stand in the river and let it drag the sadness out
of her through her toes. It seemed like as good a plan as any.

Lifting up the trailing bits of her dress-toga thing in one hand,
Eliza stepped out into the current, and closed her eyes as it tugged

gently at her skin. Her toes sank into the cool, sandy bottom. And in that quiet moment, the tears came. She didn't know for whom, but they came anyway. For Scraw? For Mardu? Maybe. A little. But if she was willing to be totally honest, no, not even for them. There was something bigger, of course. The humongous thing. The thing she had been pushing away every time it had demanded her attention. Eliza wept for the one death she had not been able to let herself think about.

Her own.

It wasn't fair. Why did God have to jerk things away from little kids? Had she been evil? Was there something she'd done that deserved a nonstop suck-hole life of constant punishment? Only to be followed by a suck-hole *afterlife* of punishment? What could she possibly have done to deserve that? Or did God just get his jollies kicking little kids, like a grade school bully pulling the legs off spiders?

She couldn't remember her parents, and she'd gotten over losing them eventually, but that's when it had all started. The first of all the badness. To be followed quickly by some judge throwing her to the Goodies, and then the years of drudging slavery on the fifth floor. Her friendship with Tayna had been the only good thing that had happened in all the years she'd been there, tortured and abused by those... ghouls. But even Tayna had turned out to be just one more thing to let her love and then take away. In all those years, she had dreamed a million dreams of getting out, of finding new parents and a new place.

And she had come so close, too! Less than an hour. Minutes really. Just another handful of seconds and she'd have become Eliza Nackenfausch. For real. Daughter of Ned and Sue Nackenfausch, and part-time intern at the Barbington Clinic for Toyfolk, providing full service health care to puppets, manikins, stuffies and dolls of all descriptions. That's what Sue had told her, and she should know, because Sue was owner and chief surgeon of the place. To live with cool parents in a doll hospital wasn't the life she'd always dreamed of, but that was only because her imagination had never been able to make up something that totally amazing. If it had been, then Eliza knew without a doubt that the Barbington Clinic would definitely have become her go-to happy place from the very moment she'd first conceived it.

But that life was gone.

All she had left was this stupid robe-dress and the water rushing past her. It felt good, flowing over her calves and ankles. Loose grains of sand suspended in the current tickled as they bumped over the tops of her feet. But as nice as it felt, standing in the stream wasn't solving anything. It didn't bring her life back. It didn't bring her friends back. It just took. Rivers were like life, she realized. All they ever did was tear things away from you.

And with that sad thought rolling around in her head, her enjoyment of the current's gentle tug flowed out of her, just one more thing to be snatched up and swept away by the water. She turned around and lifted a dripping foot up to climb out onto the bank. And then a movement caught her eye.

Eliza looked up and was surprised to see the Yeren watching her from the forest. She wasn't spying or trying to hide. She just stood there, her big eyes open and filled with curiosity. Somehow she even made standing still seem an act of grace and elegance.

"Hello," Eliza said. "I didn't think you'd be coming back." When the creature did not respond, Eliza shrugged and stepped up onto the mossy bank and began to negotiate with her boots.

Her feet had puffed up a bit in the water, and the scratches and cuts she'd accumulated during her barefoot phase still hadn't healed, so even though the boots were a bit big, it was difficult to convince her feet to go back in. The scent of moss and then a quiet cooing sound told Eliza that the creature had come closer, but it wasn't until a pair of white-furred hands reached out to probe gently at her sore feet that Eliza realized how much closer. She glanced over her shoulder, but saw only curious compassion in the creature's eyes. No. Not creature. Woman? Eliza wasn't sure, but she was definitely more intelligent than something you would call a "creature." Although "woman" didn't seem right either.

"Guess I'll just have to call you Lucinda," she said, as "Lucinda" continued to probe delicately at all the scabs and scratches that Eliza's feet had been busy collecting over the last few days. And speaking of injuries, she noticed that Lucinda's wrists were now each completely wrapped in a tight-fitting clay bracelet of some kind that hid the angry red sores that had been chafed into her skin. Eliza reached out and touched one of the bracelets, gently, and Lucinda paused to let her examine it. The material was dry, and rough like paper, but heavier to the touch, although it seemed to flex readily whenever Lucinda's hands moved beneath it. A sort of bandage.

Actually, an almost perfect bandage.

"Do you have one big enough for an entire foot?" Eliza said. "Probably not."

She went back to trying to coax her feet into the boots when Lucinda suddenly looked downstream and cocked her head. A moment later, she stood up and hurried off down the bank toward the river's bend and whatever sound it was that had drawn her attention. Just before she vanished, Lucinda turned back and gestured to Eliza in an unmistakable sign. Aren't you coming? Then she rounded the bend and was gone.

Ignoring the aches and twinges, Eliza jammed her feet into the boots as quickly as she could and then hobbled off to see what the hubbub was all about.

Immediately after the bend, the stream flowed straight into the blackened clearing. Lucinda stood at the center of it all, on the island. Well, *in* the island, actually. A good bit of its soil had been flung away by the blast, leaving behind a cone-shaped depression, which is where the tall willowy creature now stood, visible from the waist up. She was peering curiously at something in the crater, near her feet.

"At least, I hope she still has feet," Eliza muttered as she trudged across the charred landscape, sending up puffs of black flakes in her wake that smelled like barbecued hay.

She had to take a running jump to get across the river, onto the island, and she stumbled on the uneven ground of the crater, but Lucinda reached out one long white arm to steady her.

The crater was deeper than Eliza had expected. Maybe three feet at the center. But it was the shape huddled at the center that had captured Lucinda's attention.

Mehklok. With the bodies of all three dead Gnomes arranged around him in a circle. And in his hands, the feathers of the crow were twitching and shuddering in the breeze. Then Eliza's breath caught in her throat.

There was no breeze. Scraw was alive!

Eliza flung herself to the bottom of the crater and threw her arms happily around the Gnome's furry head and neck.

"How did you do that?" she cried, but she knew he did not

understand her words, and hoped only that he was picking up on her happiness. He held up his hands, offering the crow to her, and she couldn't help but be embarrassed by the uncertainty in his eyes. Was he really that afraid of her? Moving slowly, to show him she meant no harm, she ruffled the fur between his ears. "Relax. I won't hurt you. You did good." Then she gathered Scraw up delicately in her hands.

"Are you okay, Little Buddy?"

But Mehklok had already turned away with a curious look in his eye. As soon as his hands were free, he dug down into the soil, feeling around below the surface. Then he pulled, hard. After a moment of straining, something let go, and Mehklok was at last able to drag his prize up out of the dirt.

Eliza hadn't been paying close attention. Instead she'd stroked Scraw's feathers softly, just glad to have the little guy back. He wasn't flapping or scrawing yet, but he looked a lot better than the last time she'd seen him. A gleam of metal caught her eye, and she looked back to Mehklok as he held his hands out to her with a round, silvery disk. A dinner plate? Maybe. But strange. It shimmered like water and there wasn't even a speck of dirt on it, despite having just been pulled from the ground. Mehklok seemed to want Eliza to take it, so she handed Scraw into Lucinda's large gentle hands, and then reached to take the plate. But it was heavier than it looked, and she had trouble lifting it. Everyone crowded around to get a look, and they were all peering down at the strange disk of metal, when the earth beneath their feet began to moan.

And the world around them shuddered in agony.

———⌇——————

With the great shudder of pain that shook the world, Mardu's confinement exploded, like a doorway opening into a hurricane. In an instant, forces of magic tore through the portal, swirling her in a vortex of power that threatened to strip her unanchored self away and fling it to the edges of oblivion, as the magic of there, of Grimorl, thundered back through the wedge he had left in the doorway to here, his original home, and to where his magic had now been summoned. She was a leaf, caught in its tornado, and any moment she would be torn from her tree. She needed shelter. An anchor.

But through the maelstrom there could be no vision. She could see no faces, hear no thought-voices. There was only a barely pal-pable tug of firmness. Three firmnesses, any of which could anchor her to the world while everything else shredded away into the mad-ness. The scream of forces grabbed at her being, pushing, pulling and tearing, all in the same instant, straining to fling her toward the wherever. It was so strong! Too strong.

Mardu gripped her mind furiously to the edge of the doorway, trying to make a plan, but the vortex shrieked in her mind, drown-ing out all thought. Find an anchor! But she could not tell who was who in the upside-down tumbling scream of other-vim. She could feel her grip weakening, instant by instant. No time! It had to be now, while she still had strength. She drew a mental breath and then—quickly!—released the focus of her nexus, forcing it to ex-pand, then she let go of her entrapment, just as her nexus gave itself to the riptide and shot away. Mardu flicked desperately with her thoughts, flinging a last tendril of her nexus toward the closest anchor as it flashed by, willing herself to its center, dragging and clawing against the cyclone, heaving to get a second grip on it, and then diving within, yanking the nexus closed behind her.

Had she made it? Mardu shrugged the shoulders, and bristled as the host body resisted her control. She wiggled her existence and felt herself settle more deeply into the oneness. It had all happened so quickly! She expanded the chest and thrilled as the lungs drew breath. No resistance. That was better. She was centered. But where? Who?

Slowly, Mardu blinked the eyes open and peered out, trying to see in the brilliant stillness of reality. Two startled faces peered back. The *wrong* two faces.

"Oh no," she said aloud. "Not this one."

But it was done, and there was no going back.

chapter 41

For a while, the climbing was not difficult. The rock face was almost vertical, but being near the peak, the stone was exposed and weathered. There were long cracks, and plenty of knobs and handholds, and Tayna took full advantage. But even so, she could not seem to make headway against the creature of darkness above her. And she didn't have a screaming child over her shoulder to contend with.

On the other hand, he wasn't exactly getting away. And he wouldn't either. Not so long as Tayna had any strength left for the chase. The frightened little girl's cries echoed down the mountain slope, like an avalanche of fear sweeping towad her, and they sent a chill through Tayna's blood. They haunted her. Though she could not remember being taken from her parents, she knew now that she had been. She had not been orphaned. She had not lost her parents in a tragic accident, or to some crippling plague.

She had been kidnapped.

Even without a specific memory of the event, Tayna could remember the feeling of it. A feeling now brought back to her by the terrified shrieks of the little girl above. A little girl being carried away by the very same creature who had taken a young Tayna, and delivered her to this lifetime of misery and isolation that she was now living.

No, if Tayna could do anything about it, that little girl was not going to suffer the same fate.

She dug in her toes and continued climbing.

The rock beneath her hands was reddish in color now. She was on the Bloodcap—the famed location on which the kings of old had sworn their great pact, and to which every king crowned in the days since had returned to renew that vow. She smiled thinly as she climbed, remembering how Elicand had told her that some believed the Bloodcap to be the place where the Dragon Methilien's blood still flowed through the stone of the mountain. Sorry. No dragon blood here. Just red rock. But thanks for playing. Better luck next time.

Tayna pulled herself up onto another ledge and paused to look up, dragging an arm across her sweaty brow and swiping again at the wet clumps of hair that kept slapping against her face. Mountain climbers must shave their heads. Above her, another shriek dragged her gaze upward. Blackness boy had stopped on the next ledge and was shifting the girl to his other shoulder, but he seemed to be tormenting her too, letting her think that he was tossing the girl off the edge, and then pulling her back. Tayna felt a growl escape her throat and she dug in with new determination. How sick was this guy?

Whether it had been two hours or three, Tayna couldn't be sure. And there were several times when the slope got steep and the hand-holds melted away like frost in the sun, and she wondered what the hell she was doing climbing a freaking mountain in the freezing air, without any ropes, or, like, experience. But then the swirling winds would shift, and she'd hear a sob, or she'd catch sight of a power-less little fist beating against that smooth, black back, and it would be enough to keep her moving. Just one more reach. Just another wedged toe, one more scraped finger. And Tayna would climb on. Inch by inch. Yard by yard. Always going up, and always forcing the creature to climb higher again.

Towards the end, as he was rapidly running out of mountain, the dark figure slipped behind a raised thrust of ridge, and Tayna lost sight of him. She didn't lose sound, though. The little girl's terror had now fallen to a steady, almost rhythmic whimper, punctuated by the occasional sob. Eventually, even sheer terror gets monotonous, and Tayna could only rage at the unfairness of subjecting an innocent child to such... monstery... badness. The ferocity of her anger had robbed her of even words, and her thoughts of rescue and revenge took more pictorial form in her head now, rather than sentences. Images of crushing and bludgeoning and black, pudgy person-messes being splashed into sticky puddles. Still she climbed.

And then suddenly, there was nothing left to climb. Tayna sidled around a column of rock, and there he was. Standing on the flat plane at the base of one last towering wedge of stone, with the girl slung over his shoulder, limp and unmoving. But it wasn't the creature from her nightmares at all.

It was Abeni.

———⌄——————

"No! You can't be!" Tayna yelled.

In front of her, Abeni just smiled, but it was a smile full of sharpened teeth and murderous intent. The girl on his shoulder did not move.

"What have you done to her?" Tayna hissed, edging herself closer, one eye on the motionless child, but the other stayed fixed on Whoever-he-was.

He answered by lowering his arm, letting the girl flop backward. Her dark, curly mop of hair slumped over, and she stared up at Tayna with dull, lifeless eyes.

"NO! What have you done? She was just a kid!" Tayna reached out to shake the child, but Abeni's arm flashed, and his massive Djin fist clamped around Tayna's wrist.

"You will finish this," he said, clearly. On his arm, the dead girl spoke too, echoing him in her high-pitched voice. ". . . finish this."

Tayna's eyes widened as she watched the pink little mouth speak the same words in perfect sync.

"It has been an age of ages," they said, their voices blending in a disturbing harmony. Tayna took a step back, but she could not break his grip. In her head, she began to see pictures. Of this place, but another time. Of a small group, climbing the path long ago. A Wasketchin man and girl. An elder Gnome and boy. A Djin and his son. Three Kings, each with a member of his House in tow. But they were not the three races as she knew them now. These were tougher, more hard-lived versions, marked by scars and other signs, that spoke of a life of warfare. These were the First Kings.

And they had come to make the Oath.

But Tayna saw no celebration on their faces. The impending moment of their liberation brought no smiles to their lips or laughter to their souls. They had been dragged here. Coerced. She could not see what forces might have compelled them, but they were no more pleased to be together at the top of this mountain than she herself was.

"We came because the Dragon willed that we should come," Abeni and the girl said.

"What?" Tayna said in confusion. "What do you mean, 'we'

came? You're not there, creepy boy. Just some old guys and their kids."

"Watch!" the creature and the girl hissed together. Then his grip tightened on Tayna's arm, and she felt the images return. "The Dragon Grimorl had been expelled. The land was at the mercy of the last Colossus. Armored in stone a mile thick, he settled himself into our midst and demanded tribute. One child from each House. With his magic, he ensnared us, and so we came."

One by one, Tayna watched in her mind as each of the Kings of Old shoved the child he had brought with him up against the cold, black wedge of the stone peak. The Dragon's Ear. One by one, she watched as each King, with terror in his eyes, and shame, jerked a knife from his belt. She watched as those eyes pleaded with the world, with his fellows, with anyone, to make it stop. But the hand with the knife raised itself up into the air. One, two, three, times she watched as the knives flashed down, and blood flowed upon the stone. Only the Wasketchin King had deviated from the grisly ballet, struggling his free hand out before him, fighting all the while against some great, unseen compulsion, so that he might cover his daughter's eyes before his blade fell.

"No," Tayna said. "This can't be true! That's not what happened." She twisted around to look at the stony peak behind her, overlaid with the images in her head. She watched as the crimson hue of the children's blood seeped slowly into the dark stone, staining it, and spreading outward.

She watched as the body of the young Gnome rose and hovered for a moment, then saw it rocket up high into the sky where it exploded, more brilliant than a starburst in the night. "Yarmagh!" screamed the Gnomileshi King, as his hand clawed upward, grasping feebly toward the point of light that had once been flesh of his House. As the shimmering sparks of the boy's remains arced out across the sky, they quivered the air behind them, leaving a vast dome to stand high above the Forest. And when it had sparked its way down to the ground, enclosing a vast territory, the dome vanished, and became clear blue cloudless sky.

"The land was closed against those who would not swear," Not-Abeni and the girl said. "The Judge of Changes. Wrought from a life taken, not given freely."

"Yama," Tayna said, startled by the realization.

"But it was not enough that those outside never be allowed to return. All hope inside must also be stilled. The hope of escape. The hope of freedom."

And so, a second body arose from the stone. The young woman. After hanging for a beat in front of her weeping father's eyes, the body thinned and dissolved, fading into a ghostly nothing, and then it sank deep down into the rock.

"The Flame of his Might," Tayna heard the voices say. "Keeper of the Oath. She who will come, should the Dragon's Will ever be unmade. She who will enslave the People anew."

But then there was a commotion in the vision. Unnoticed by the Dragon, the three Kings had managed to reach out their hands, trembling, toward one another. And when their fingers linked, it was as though a great chain had snapped, and they stood taller, their dark eyes flashing with anger.

"It was my father who wrought the hope of victory from their defeat," he said. "Their forces combined, it was great Ixheef who pooled their vim and struck back."

The third and last body rose from the stones. The Djin boy. With a gesture from the Kings, each moving as one, the boy's eyes flew open, and a great roar split the air of that mountain top image. The Dragon's wrath.

The Kings gestured as one and fire streamed from their fingers, transfixing the boy where he floated in the air before them. The crackle of their magic burned and twisted, and their light shone from his fingers, and toes, and from his ears and from the topknot of hair that now stood tall upon his head. And as Tayna watched, he darkened. And melted. The surface of his form flowed like oil, until the moment was done, and a dark form hovered in the air before the three Kings.

"Oathbane, they named me," the Abeni-shape said, and the little girl's voice trilled along in tune. "The Spear of Vengeance. Last hope of the conquered kings. To me was given the task of tearing down the Dragon's evil. To that end I have fought for an age of ages." Then in her mind, the black figure that had once been a Djin boy named Suriken, shivered and flowed. In his place, a great eagle beat his wings against the sky. After a brief, piercing look at the Djin King, the bird flipped, beat its wings once, and was gone, plunging down the mountain side, soaring along the winds of freedom. Away from the brutal stain of the Dragon's crimes.

The images in her head receded after that, and Tayna stood once more on the Bloodcap, staring at a twisted Abeni, or Suriken, or whatever, holding a little girl in his arms.

"But, the girl . . . ?"

The creature grinned. "I needed for you to come," he said. "But she is done." Then the girl gave a little wave.

And melted back into Abeni's body.

"What? No!" Tayna lunged forward, reaching for the girl, but it was too late. The creature had absorbed her, or something. Eww! But his display was not over.

As Tayna watched, his skin began to ripple, and then he was the girl. "What the . . ." But even as Tayna formed the question, the girl's form shifted, melting again, and flowing. This time, when it stopped, he was Quishek, the Gnome Ambassador.

"It is the power given to me by the last Free Kings," he said. "The power to take form. To mimic." Again his skin flowed, and Tayna watched as other faces flowed through his shape. The Wasketchin man she and Abeni had tried to catch in the Forest. A Gnome, who didn't look familiar, but then she had it.

"The mug thief!" The little Gnome Tayna had seen on near the Braggart's Arch. The one who had led her to Angiron.

Oathbane settled back into what Tayna assumed was his natural form–the rippling black creature of muscle and grace that she had seen earlier. Two small rounded horns, also black, protruded from the sides of his head, and his eyes, if he had any, were as black as the rest of him. Like a super-hero carved from black wax and left out in the sun too long. He stood there now, holding a boh-cho mug and grinning.

"You've been manipulating me," she said. "All this time, and it's all been you." In front of her, his black form nodded, and Tayna slumped herself against the base of the Dragon's Ear that towered above them. "And you've been working with Angiron."

He nodded again. "The Gnome King thinks to use me," he said. "But it is he who carries out my plan. Angiron thinks to restore the Dragon Grimorl, and win power from the Brother Dragon, but he is a fool."

Tayna nodded, beginning to understand. "Grimorl comes home and bye-bye Oath, am I right?"

Oathbane nodded. "It was a simple matter to convince the princeling that the Brother held power far greater, and that he would be grateful to any who could return him from exile."

"And all that, just to get me here." She waved a hand at the cast of characters he had just shown her. "Why?"

"Surely you've guessed," he said. "Born in this world, raised in that. A girl steeped in the vims of both worlds. Only you can open the gate."

And then it clicked. The magics that she'd been drawing on. Not just the magic of here. There had always been something else, some other factor. How stupid! It had been staring her in the face all along. "Grimorl magic."

"The magic of exploitation," he said. "It powers your world, even as doe-eyed wonder reigns in this one."

"And I have them both." To that, he nodded again, and a slow grin rippled across his molten skin.

But there was something wrong with this picture. Something didn't make sense. His story was about being a victim, but that's not what Yama had told her. Yama had claimed that the Kings had come willingly to join with Methilien. Freely. To ensure a peace for all the races. She said as much.

"Enough," Oathbane said. "It matters not the how, or the why. It stands now but to do. To complete the goal that has eluded me these many long millennia. Let it be done!" Then he grabbed Tayna's wrist again, and dragged her to her feet, pressing the palm of her open hand against the red stone.

"Call to him," he hissed in her ear. "Open the way and summon Grimorl. Bring him home that I might at last be free."

He was trying to rush her, trying to cut her off without time to think. But why? If his story was true, wouldn't she want to help him?

"Open it!" he urged. "Open it and be done!"

Tayna quested outward, from within herself, as she had done before. Pulling from Oathbane as well as from herself, she felt the connection form, but she wasn't prepared for what she tapped this time.

Power. Vast and unyielding power.

"Yes," he hissed in her ear. "Feel it flowing through you. I was right! I can see it in your eyes. I can feel it burning through your flesh."

But Tayna could scarcely hear him. The power coursing through her was different now. Bigger. So much bigger. And hotter. It seemed to scream through her, scalding her, like steam in her veins. And along with the steam, there was darkness, oozing along with it. Another power shaping and directing her own. Bending it to his will.

Oathbane's power. Oathbane's will.

And then she smiled. Because in the knowing of all that, she knew something else too. Something that even Suriken had not yet guessed. Something that just might change the balance of everything that was going on. Something that made a difference. And she laughed.

Suriken's face quirked then, and he pulled back, looking into her eyes with sudden suspicion. Quickly, he released her hands, cutting her off from his portion of the power. The Djin portion. But still the power sizzled through her being. It was too late. The revelation had shown her the certainty of her purpose. She had never needed him in the first place. Or Angiron either. They wanted to use her power? Lock her up for ten years and torture her? Fine. Because she knew now that she was more powerful than they had yet imagined. Way more.

And now she was going to show them what that meant.

Tayna pushed hard with both hands, forcing her fingers deep down into the stone of the Dragon's Ear. Even as Oathbane grabbed at her shoulder, trying to pull her away, she kept pushing, deeper and deeper into the torrent of power that lay there. Waiting for her. She pulled it out to show him, and somewhere, she heard a roar, a scream. Then, with the power burning through her, she simply reached out...

And quaked the worlds.

Books by Jefferson Smith

Finding Tayna series

Strange Places

Oath Keeper

Inverted Worlds Short Stories

The Old Soft Sell

Bodies of Evidence

Famine, With Fries

(Shorts available free at creativityhacker.ca)

We should talk

Really, I'd love to hear from you. Feel free to make contact at any of these coordinates. Tell me what you loved, what you hated. Send me a picture you drew of Tayna, or a poem you wrote about evil nuns. That stuff really energizes me.

Google+ (+JeffersonSmithAuthor)

CreativityHacker.ca (my blog)

Twitter (@Jefficus)

Facebook (Jefferson.Smith.585)

Can I ask a favor?

Would you consider rating this book at one of the online sites? Just go to GoodReads or Amazon and then click on the star ratings to tell people what you thought. Even that little bit would be very helpful.

And if you happen to go further and write an actual review, don't keep it to yourself–let me know about it. Contact me through one of the above coordinates and shoot me a link to what you posted. Reviews really do help, so as my way of saying thanks when you post one, I'll send you a free ebook. And then we can do the dance all over again.

So that's it from me. Thanks for spending your time in Methilien, and I hope you'll come back for the exciting conclusion in *Book Three*.

27064589R00224

Made in the USA
Charleston, SC
01 March 2014